ANGEL ON A HARLEY

Do you believe in ang⸺⸺⸺ Lord of the Land of Shadows asked.

Thorn answered h⸺

The Lord turned ⸺⸺⸺⸺⸺⸺s face for the first tim⸺⸺⸺⸺⸺⸺d not frighten him; instead ⸺⸺

You should believe in angels, now, the ⸺⸺⸺⸺ed. You have become one.

Thorn looked at his arms, checking for telltale wings that might have sprouted when he wasn't looking. "So what did I do to earn this honor?"

You died, the Lord replied. *Most spectacularly, I might add.*

Thorn held his arms up, flapping them like a bird. "So do I get a harp? Where are my wings?"

You get something much better to fly upon than wings, the Lord said.

In the distance Thorn heard a familiar growl of internal combustion. His heart leaped. "Valerie?" he said. Riderless, and in pristine condition, Thorn's motorcycle rode up to him and stopped; Valerie had become a living, thinking being.

You loved your motorbike. You created a soul. The Lord of the Land of Shadows began walking away. *You will become familiar with my land, and travel it with ease.*

"As an angel?" Thorn asked, still unable to comprehend it.

As a Rider Guardian, the Lord replied. *A guardian angel, for living souls who very much need a guardian.*

"Whose souls?" Thorn asked.

The riders of motorcycles will need protection, said the Lord and disappeared.

SPIRITRIDE

Mark Shepherd

BAEN

SPIRITRIDE

A Baen Books Original

Baen Publishing Enterprises
P.O. Box 1403
Riverdale, NY 10471

ISBN: 0-671-87775-5

Cover art by Larry Elmore

First printing, April 1997

Distributed by Simon & Schuster
1230 Avenue of the Americas
New York, NY 10020

Printed in the United States of America

To Pony and D

Prologue

I'm going to go in, keep my mouth shut, do my four years, and maybe the law will leave me alone, Wolf remembered thinking, a full year and a half earlier. Back then he was running with a biker gang in Texas, engaged in activities which had not pleased the judicial system. When the time came in court for them to hang something on him, he had a choice: prison or the army.

Now he was standing in an ocean of sand, far from home, twenty-five miles south of Baghdad, fighting in a war that officially hadn't started yet.

A massive buildup of multinational forces lay just on the other side of the Saudi Arabia-Iraq border. Operation Desert Shield had been in place for months, the troops biding time while fighting little more than crabs and sand mites. But Wolf had been seeing action, plenty of action. As a sergeant in the Rangers, he had taken part in a number of missions, all deep in Iraqi territory, all very hush hush. Blackhawk helicopters dropped them in, then picked them up when their job was done. This was one such mission, and their target was a small town, not far away.

He marched in a squad of five, toting an M60A2, a 9mm Beretta and a full field pack. Their objective was a suspected amphetamine factory Saddam was operating to keep his troops razor-sharp and wide awake. This was supposed to be just another mission, but Wolf knew something was going to go bad on this one.

The M60 was not a small gun, and not a particularly good patrol weapon, but a good tool to have in an all-out gunfight. Wolf had the honor of carrying the monster because he could consistently hit a half dollar-sized target with it at four hundred yards, but he had mixed thoughts about making himself such a prime target. But then, he wasn't there to think, he was there to listen and obey orders, and maybe even get out of Iraq alive.

The squad of Rangers met up with a platoon of 81st Airborne, twenty-five foot soldiers armed with M16s who had dropped in the day before. Among them was a kid Wolf remembered from basic, who might have been older than he looked, seventeen. Wolf was a year older and was a sergeant, so the kid looked up to him.

"Mister, are we going to make it out of this?" the kid kept asking, and Wolf told him they were, if he stayed with him and his M60.

He's scared, Wolf thought. *Hell, I am too.*

They were ordered to march through a town, but before proceeding they double-checked the orders, as something like this was not approached lightly. The place was a typical village, which meant a deserted village. There were a few jeeps on their right, but other than that there were no signs that anyone had been there for some time. Wolf counted twelve stucco buildings, not much else.

They reached the first of these structures when the Iraqis sprang their ambush. The 81st platoon dropped to the ground where they were, with Wolf in front. He lay down with the M60 and went to work.

He still couldn't see where the fire was coming from, but men were dropping all around him, and rounds were hitting the ground and buildings. With men screaming behind him, he lay down suppressive fire, targeting windows at random, still not knowing where the hell the snipers were. He loaded belt after belt, five hundred rounds each, spraying the buildings with bullets. In no time at all he melted his barrel.

He saw the kid, lying on the ground, not far from him. Bleeding. Wolf thought about the deaths he'd seen, and the deaths in the movies.

Death takes a while, he reminded himself, watching the kid die. By the time he decided to get the hell out of there, the kid was hit twice more.

I'm dead, he thought, contemplating the glowing tip of his weapon.

He was getting ready to shake himself free of the paralysis when he saw the waves of blue emanating from his hands.

With the blue, his vision sharpened. His fingers felt warm, and he instinctively ran them across the barrel, cooling it, healing it. With his new vision he saw the Iraqis, on the second floor of a building, their auras yellow and brilliant red, stick figures crouched over their weapons. He reloaded his own, aimed, and picked off the Iraqis, one by one.

He didn't question his new powers. Instead he put them to use, laying down more fire so the rest could get away.

Wherever this is coming from I'm going to save our butts with it.

At a lull in the fire, Wolf scrambled behind a building, where the other survivors of their doomed mission were; two rangers, three airborne. A radio, but no radio man. Someone called in the situation.

If anyone thought Wolf's healed M60 was peculiar, they didn't say anything about it. A disembodied voice on the radio ordered them to a location ten miles away, where they would be picked up by Blackhawks.

They had to leave, the sooner the better, because they were never there.

Chapter One

Petrus led his elvensteed toward a shallow stream, its trickling sound muted by fog. Thick, white blankets chilled the air with a wet coldness the young elf felt in his bones, despite the mantle of bearskin that covered his doublet. He allowed his 'steed, Moonremere, to drink only a little. They had hard riding to do that day and he didn't want her to overindulge.

The 'steed finished drinking, and looked up. Petrus urged her toward what had been the great Palace of Avalon, foregoing the rotted, smashed drawbridge and leading her across a dry moat. Through the gloom, fragments of wall stabbed the sky. He led Moonremere on, making a wide path around the ruins; he felt the wards as if they were branded into the deep green moss covering the ground. Double layered, and tied directly to the power nodes, the protections discouraged all but Avalon elves from exploring this place.

Petrus had been a child when Zeldan Dhu's forces attacked Avalon. He remembered the war, the panic and then finally the futility, but most of all he recalled the terror when the bombardment began. He was the only one of his family to survive. The others, his mother and father, two sisters, and older brother, a guard in the King's army, had not been as fortunate. He didn't want to remember their ghosts, but they came anyway, and he allowed the painful memory to descend over him like a veil.

It had happened so quickly, Petrus remembered, glancing up at the remaining walls. His father was a nobleman, who had recently been awarded quarters in the palace. They had been packing the last of their belongings when they had seen the sudden movement of King Traigthren's troops. Thirty or so of the elven soldiers had marched past their cottage. The troops' actions had seemed more urgent than usual, but he had made no connection with an attack.

"Wonder what they're doing out there?" Father had said absently as he packed a wooden crate with stoneware from Outremer. *Mother was in the back room, Jenel and Maron were playing in the front room, and Sameal was on duty, guarding the palace.* He had often wondered if Sameal had died in that first attack, or if he was among the troops that fell afterwards; things had been so confusing that none of the survivors, King Aedham included, had known for certain. Father had looked up, confused, as node power crackled in the air.

"Petrus, get *down,*" Father had said sharply, and the desperation in his voice had made Petrus obey immediately. The levin bolt had struck with a sharp, deafening explosion. The impact had blown the roof off and taken with it three of the four outer walls, but all Petrus knew when he came to was that he could not hear, and something big and heavy was on top of him.

He had squirmed out from underneath whatever it was, coughing on the cloud of dust that was everywhere, and had cried out when he saw that Father, or what remained, had fallen on him. After that were vague recollections of looking for his brother. The palace grounds had become a sea of chaos, with nobles and commoners alike running hither and yon. Bodies had lain everywhere, amid fallen rock and mortar. An entire section of outer wall had been destroyed, and beyond that a vast army had gathered on hilltops some distance away. Petrus had never seen their like; monsters, some of them, all wearing dark armor, with black banners.

Someone had grabbed him from behind and pulled him toward the palace. He was too stunned, and too weak, to object. A small part of him had known that he would be safer deep inside the palace. Yet another part of him had known it would make no difference where he went, that Avalon was doomed.

Petrus pushed away the memory, annoyed that he was shaking. *That was so long ago. I was a child then,* he thought, climbing down from his 'steed. He stood at the wreckage of the old cottages. Aedham had seen to it that all the bodies were collected and given a proper burial. Even so, blood still stained the ground. The King had ordered the old palace to remain as it was, while he built a new one in a more secure location. He had wanted Traigthren's Palace to be a reminder, so that Avalon would never again be lulled into a false sense of security.

He saw the remains of a weathered crate, and when he pulled at it the wood crumbled in his hand. But he saw what it contained: stoneware, in the distinctive style of Outremer. He knew then this had to be his home, the very place where his family was killed, and the blood he saw staining the ground was theirs.

This was not what he had come to see, he realized as his knees gave out, and he fell kneeling on the ground. The grief rose from his chest with a ferocity he wasn't ready for. *I have never really grieved for them,* he thought, as tears filled his eyes. *I had been caught up in the chase in the humans' world, and had put out of my mind what had happened here. But now I am here. I cannot deny . . .*

He sat sobbing, grateful no one saw him here. Then

he knew someone *was* watching him, feeling for him like a true friend would. Moonremere nuzzled the back of his neck gently, the wet coldness shaking him from his grief. The 'steed looked over his shoulder, nuzzled the side of his face. He reached up and held her, the 'steed's huge jowls warm against his forehead, until the grief was a gray shadow, far away, beyond reach for now.

They are gone, and there's nothing I can do about it, he thought, wondering why he didn't feel any hate, or even anger. He felt only a helplessness, and deep surrender. *I can do nothing now. I was only a child, and I could do nothing then, either. I did what I could, and that was to survive, and defeat Zeldan Dhu.*

And defeat him he had, or at least helped in the endeavor, as much as any child could have. He smirked when he remembered when Zeldan had cornered him in a garage, and Petrus had attacked him with a staple gun. Tiny flames had shot from the cold steel of the staples as they stuck in the Unseleighe's flesh, and Zeldan had turned loose a satisfying scream. It had only delayed the inevitable abduction of himself and Wenlann, another young elf of noble blood, but it had proved a gratifying diversion. In time King Aedham had come to save them, and had destroyed Zeldan Dhu in the process. Even then, it was tempting to think that the Unseleighe threat had been dealt with once and for all.

But he knew such was not the case. Some of Zeldan's minions had escaped to Underhill, while others had been here all along, ruled by Zeldan's second in command.

Japhet Dhu. His son.

Years had passed, with no sign of Japhet, his minions, or the clan of demons ruled by Morrigan, one of Zeldan's allies. The defeat of Zeldan had evidently demoralized the remnants of the Unseleighe band, since they had not so much as made themselves visible after Avalon's victory. The elfhame had collectively assumed that the

Unseleighe had fled to other areas of Underhill. Searches had turned up nothing, and the elfhame turned to other, more immediate endeavors, such as restoring Avalon to its former glory.

Aedham had also protected the nodes with elaborate wards, encrypted with keys only the elves of Avalon understood, as it was the loss of these nodes which had preceded the fall of Avalon in the first place. Yet Petrus knew Japhet was loose, somewhere in Underhill. It would be the Unseleighe way to retreat, rebuild, and attack Avalon again.

Petrus shrugged off his morbid mood as much as he could, turned his attention to the task at hand. *I'm here to serve my King, not stand around feeling sorry for myself.*

King Aedham and Niamh, another mage whose abilities tended toward human technology, had for days been detecting some disturbing energies coming from this direction. Something new lurked here. He had risen early to get a lead on the others, perhaps impress Wenlann with his thoroughness. Wenlann and Odras were still asleep when he'd led Moonremere out of camp.

This other thing, this new, possibly dangerous thing, left him wondering if perhaps he'd made a bad move.

He pushed the thought away. *Of course not! There's nothing here that can hurt me. It is just bad memories, nothing more.*

Petrus was not going to let the shadows startle him, as if he were some little child. *Wenlann's feigned maturity notwithstanding . . . she is not going to best me!*

He proceeded through the ruins, carefully guiding Moonremere through the boulders. Then he saw the form standing, not far away, and he drew his sword smoothly without a second thought.

"Who are you?" he shouted at the still form. "How dare you violate this sacred space!"

The figure didn't respond, or move. It wore a black cloak, or was that a dress? Moving closer still, Petrus began to sense something inanimate about the intruder.

Within paces of the black cloak, Petrus laughed out in relief.

It was not a being, but a banner hanging from a tall staff. The laughter was short lived, though, as it occurred to him who this banner might belong to, and what it might mean.

Zeldan's banner. Therefore, Japhet's banner.

The banner itself was emblazoned with the black eagle crest, with black silk ribbons hanging on either side. This was no leftover from the battle; this banner was new, and recently planted, right in the middle of the old palace grounds. It could only mean one thing.

A challenge.

With his sword still drawn, he looked around for the fight the banner seemed to be asking for. But no one was present to back up the challenge. Once he was confident it had not been tainted with traps, magical or otherwise, he seized the banner's staff, a thin, spindly section of a black wood that resembled a vine more than a branch, and set off for camp.

Petrus tied his 'steed with the others, then approached the fire, readying himself for another blast of Wenlann's wrath.

"Of *course* it's a challenge," she said petulantly, regarding the banner Petrus had flung to the ground as if it were a slain rodent. "Why else would they leave it in the middle of the old palace?"

Petrus tossed on a new log and held his hands to the resultant heat. Their companion, Odras, seemed determined to stay out of their argument; the old mage gazed at a handful of *topolomite* stones, which he'd found in a ravine during their short journey. Silently, as if scrying for some hidden meaning in the stones, the mage refused to be distracted from his find. There was something significantly magical about the stones, but whatever it was Odras wasn't saying.

"Then why was no one there to accept the challenge?" Petrus said evenly, pulling his thick mantle off and laying it near the fire. The problem with a wet cold, which had been their fate this entire trip, was that it was next to impossible to get warm without removing the wet garments. "Why did they just leave?"

Wenlann was putting her riding gear on, piece by piece, making a point of checking the edge of her sword before putting it on her belt. Though she had grown much in recent times, she still had about her the air of a spoiled noble brat. Even on trips like these, she insisted on wearing her silver pendant. The ornate, heart-shaped Celtic knot clung to a deceptively delicate-looking chain. One of Niamh's constructions, the chain was anything but fragile, constructed in a matrix of carbon crystal and given the look and feel of silver. But despite its immense strength it was the kind of jewelry one wore for formal gatherings, *not* chasing Unseleighe.

Granted, he and Wenlann had a similar upbringing, but since the fall of Avalon he had set his past aside and concentrated on being a soldier, one of many assets Avalon was in short supply of. To his dismay Wenlann had taken a similar path and, while he hated to admit it, she had become a formidable opponent in the practice ring. It was during times like these she liked to emphasize that she was every bit his equal, if not superior, even if Petrus was in charge of this particular campaign.

"If indeed they were Unseleighe," Odras said cryptically. He spoke toward the fire, poking it with a branch. "There are pranksters throughout Underhill who would find such a 'challenge' amusing." Elves from other domains had volunteered their assistance in rebuilding Avalon, and had then petitioned for citizenship. Odras had been such a volunteer, and not only had shown loyalties but also exceptional magical abilities.

"This is no joke," Petrus insisted, then realized Odras was simply making conversation. *Or does he know something about this banner that I don't?*

Odras stood from his crouched position, unfolding his strong, wiry frame to its full height, seven hands above Petrus. His long, brown suede tunic draped loosely over him. A thick belt with an unadorned gold buckle held the garment in at the waist. With a flourish he threw a black cloak around him. The long mane of silvered brown hair reached to his belt. He had never revealed his age, but from the length of his ears and the rasp in his voice, he was old indeed. Nonetheless, he retained the strength and agility of youth.

Odras regarded the banner with visible distaste; Petrus thought he was going to spit on it.

"It *is* Unseleighe," he said softly, after a moment's deliberation. "And recently made," he added. "That staff, the vine it's made from. It was cut down only yesterday."

"From around here?" Wenlann asked, reaching down to pick up the banner. Flag and ribbons hung limply from it as she studied the wood closer. "Swords made these cuts," she announced. "I don't recognize the vine." She held it aloft, swung it in the air. One of the ribbons fluttered off. "This is not something they would take into battle."

"Of course not," Petrus said. "It's poorly made. *Anyone* can see that," he added, casting a heated glanced at Wenlann.

"It was not made to be taken into battle, or anywhere else. It was made to *provoke,*" Odras announced. "Which, it seems, it has." He stopped short of saying something else, but Petrus had a pretty good idea what it would have been. He and Wenlann had been arguing over any number of small issues since their departure from Avalon, and he suspected it was getting rather tiring for Odras.

"No good can come from this," Odras said. "So blatant a gesture. On the sacred ground of Old Avalon, no less." His eyes veered from the banner, and gazed over the low hills of the area. With only the occasional bush and tree, the area was ideal for staging an attack.

"We might do well to consider this a warning," Odras said to the younger elves. "We are, after all, only three."

"But if this *is* a challenge, Petrus said, not liking the way the discussion was going, "I cannot turn it down."

"Understood," Odras said. "But unless I'm mistaken, you are not required to take on an entire army by yourself."

"If we are evenly matched or not, it won't matter," Wenlann said bitterly, and began gathering the sparse gear they'd brought. "Zeldan never considered himself bound by such rules. And I doubt his son would even *know* of such rules, much less operate by them. He was, after all, planning to overthrow his own father."

Petrus admitted that she had a point. "Perhaps we should . . ." he began, but stopped when he glanced up at the horizon.

At the top of one of the hills stood a mounted horse, its rider a dark figure, partially concealed in the mist. In the rider's right hand was a sword, and in his left was the outline of what was probably a shield. He made no move to approach, or take flight, and seemed content to stay where he was, regarding the three patiently while the 'steed nibbled at the grass.

"I take this challenge," Petrus said suddenly, before Wenlann could say anything. It would have been just like her to try to take this opportunity from him, to prove once again she was capable of holding her own among the males of the Elfhame. Now the challenge was Petrus', by the rules.

"Suit yourself," Odras said, sounding strangely unalarmed. Instead of preparing for a potential battle he tossed another log on the fire, looking completely detached. "I think you will be disappointed in this . . . confrontation," he said as he sat down again.

Petrus wanted to ask him more, but he knew from experience that to do so would be futile. *He would only answer in riddles*, he thought before mounting Moonremere. He checked his sword, made certain the sheath wasn't bound, grateful he had put a good sharp edge on the blade the evening before. He had a small shield that under most circumstances would be inadequate; they had packed lightly. *It will have to do*, he thought without regret, remembering he had considered omitting it altogether.

"Is there only one?" Wenlann asked as she brought the remaining two elvensteeds closer to the camp. Odras didn't answer, and Petrus didn't wait to see if he would. *If there were more he would warn us*, he reasoned as he sized up his opponent, who seemed to perk up at the prospect of battle.

Petrus maneuvered Moonremere to one end of the field, as the other took up a position on a higher end, which might give him some advantage of momentum. He frowned at that, wondering if this was going to be a fair fight after all, and shook the doubt off as soon as it had occurred. *This is the beast that left that banner on our grave site. And he has picked this particular fight.*

Memory of the banner, and of his family, fueled him with anger which he tried to defuse with calm. Angry thoughts tended to cloud judgment, and he pushed them away.

The other called, across the field, in a deep baritone voice that had no trouble reaching his ears. "Are you the Seleighe vermin that has infested this part of Underhill? The pathetic rats we killed ages ago, at yon ruin?" He pointed his sword in the direction of the palace. "And you have dared remove my rightful claim to this moor?"

How dare the bastard! Petrus thought as the hatred surged through him despite his best efforts to divert it elsewhere. Blood boiling, he glanced over at Wenlann, who simply shrugged. He expected, and wanted, no more; this was his fight. Odras, however, did not deign to even look in his direction, and had started sharpening his own sword with no apparent urgency.

"You have no claim here!" Petrus shouted. "This is the land of my father, my father's father, and our ancestors before him! What right have you to trespass on the Kingdom of Avalon!"

The opponent laughed uproariously. "O, Avalon, is it! My father destroyed Avalon long ago!"

Careful, now, Petrus thought, now seeing red. *If this is the Japhet Dhu, he is a tricky one, and cannot be trusted.*

"As my King destroyed your father, Japhet the Pathetic!" Petrus shouted back.

"So you know who I am," the opponent replied, sounding not the slightest bit humbled. "And you know why I'm here."

Enough talk. "You are here to *die!*" Petrus shouted, and kicked Moonremere into action.

The opponent followed suit, shrieking a cry that brought back vivid images of the long-ago war. Petrus charged ahead, tensing his left arm with the shield, and beginning the delicate balancing needed to inflict sword damage while remaining perched atop a 'steed. But as he drew nearer he saw to his extreme displeasure that Japhet was much larger than he had first estimated, as was his 'steed. A war 'steed, in fact, bred for height and muscle, which his own 'steed in its present form was lacking. Too late to make adjustments now, he knew, then realized Japhet's sword was not the bronze or silver their folk used in battle, but the death metal, iron. *How can an elf wield such a weapon?* he thought fleetingly. *If I don't strike him down the first time, I have no chance . . .*

Petrus screamed something unintelligible as he leaped from his 'steed's back, choosing a fighting tactic one can use only once in such a battle. He intended to deflect the death metal with his shield, and strike Japhet somewhere vulnerable, with any luck knocking him off his horse and thus evening the battle some. Instead, he squawked as something completely unpredictable happened instead.

Where his shield would meet sword, it met space, dismal nothingness, as did his weapon. Japhet and 'steed, flesh and bone moments before, suddenly, inexplicably vanished. In the brief moment of flight that followed, his mouth opened, but had no time to release the scream he was preparing to turn loose. As he landed in the marshy, soggy grass he felt his sword sink in the mud up to the hilt, his body connect savagely with the turf, and his face find all manner of grief as grass and marsh flailed at it. Then, silence.

Except for a cackle, some distance away, that was female laughter. A familiar sound, from someone he knew well.

Petrus struggled from the mud, which had turned out to be a relatively soft landing medium, and reached for his sword while looking around to see where, if anywhere, Japhet Dhu had fled. He pulled on the sword, which was inelegantly stuck firmly in the mud.

"*Shit,*" Petrus said, remembering vocabulary from his days living among the humans. He pulled and yanked ineffectually on the sword's hilt. Finally it yielded, making a sound that reminded him of a disgusting biological function as it abruptly withdrew from the ground. He fell backwards with the sudden release, landing arse first on the ground. Though coated with mud, the sword was at least *something* he could use for a weapon.

He scrambled to his feet, ready for combat, looking around wildly. But opponent, and horse, had simply vanished.

This cannot be, Petrus thought frantically, even though he knew it had to be, because it was. With Wenlann's laughter echoing across the moor, piercing his ego, he knew that he had been fooled by something magical. Moonremere returned, snorting something that might have been amusement, and with as much dignity as was possible Petrus led her back to camp. Covered with mud, he didn't want to ride her; he'd just cleaned her saddle before the trip, and didn't much care for doing it all over again. He was still unwilling to believe Japhet Dhu had simply vanished, and remained wary as he trod back to the others.

Odras patiently sharpened his blade, with a determination that looked unshakable. Wenlann stood with her hands on her hips, appearing rather pleased with the situation. Petrus avoided her look.

"What was that you were saying earlier about disappointment?" Petrus asked.

Odrás looked up, looking vaguely annoyed that Petrus had interrupted his blade sharpening.

"Did the Unseleighe strike you as being brave enough for a fair confrontation?" Odras asked calmly. "Though without mage sight I suppose it would be difficult to see the opponent for what it was."

"Being?" Petrus asked.

"A projection, of course," Odras replied, testing his sword's edge with the fat of his thumb. "A well executed one, granted, even if I've seen better."

Petrus cast a long look over the surrounding countryside. They had intentionally set camp in the hollow between two hills, limiting their view while making them less visible from a distance. It also gave them the disadvantage of being downhill from any attack, but when they'd settled in for the night, attack was not a consideration.

"If you are still thirsting for battle," Odras said softly, "you may have your opportunity yet. The source of that projection is nearby."

Petrus quickly wiped the mud off the blade, the complexion of the situation having changed suddenly. *Blood, perhaps,* he whispered to his blade. He listened, but heard only the winds caressing the hills around them.

"Where are they?" Petrus asked urgently. *He must have been probing the area for them while I was out swimming in the mud, making a fool of myself.*

"Beyond that rise," Odras said, getting to his feet. "There are four of them. One is a *mage.*" Odras smiled nastily. "The mage is *mine.* The others are yours to deal with."

No argument with that, he thought. Petrus had never seen Odras in full magical form, in combat with another mage. He both anticipated and feared the prospect, knowing the results would not likely be gentle.

"Let's ride," Petrus said, mounting his 'steed, the cleanliness of his saddle no longer an issue.

Odras stood very still, and closed his eyes as he fell into trance. Petrus felt the familiar tingling of a glamorie falling into place around them, a shroud of magic that would not only make them invisible to normal sight, but to mage sight as well—assuming they found no countering spells that were stronger than Odras could handle. The mage opened his eyes. "If we are to attack, we must go now."

They left the gear behind and rode immediately, with the intention of surprising the group with their sudden appearance. A shallow valley branched off to the right. A thick grove of trees surrounded it, and Petrus saw that it was a clever place from which to send a projection.

"We should come up behind them," Petrus said, remembering a narrow trail they had passed the day before. "We may even trap them."

The trail narrowed as it wound through massive boulders; not liking their vulnerability, Petrus looked about for an alternate route, but saw none. The trail opened suddenly on a clearing at the hill's summit.

"Damn them *all*," Petrus sputtered as he saw a black banner, identical to the first, planted in the center of the clearing. "Where did . . ."

Then he saw where they must have gone. Another trail led sharply down the south end of the hill, directly to the moor. And at the base of the hill he saw the small black forms, atop 'steeds that were too large for them. *Youths,* Petrus thought acidly, conveniently forgetting that he himself had only seventeen summers. *Mere Unseleighe children. Playing games with those much their superior.*

As they approached the banner, Petrus felt their glamorie shatter around them, reminding him that at least one of the wretched Unseleighe was the mage Odras had sensed. Whatever they had bespelled the banner with was enough to counter Odras' work. The mage frowned when Petrus met his eyes, then turned his attention to the four Unseleighe, who even at that distance looked collectively uncertain of their next move.

"After them!" Petrus shouted, as the four Unseleighe turned tail and ran. Odras and Wenlann pulled their swords as he unsheathed his, and Moonremere sprinted after them. Seeing the enemy renewed old hatreds, stirred up old memories. *They killed my family. They killed so many of us, without provocation.*

He knew he was angry, and that the anger might hurt his fight, or add to it; no choice but to let it run its course. The Unseleighe didn't seem to be much of a threat, particularly when in retreat, but that didn't make the sight of their blood, preferably all of it spilled on the ground, an unworthy goal.

At the base of the hill they found an open plain. Unseleighe tore away at a fast gallop, their taunting whoops and shouts echoing across the hills. The mist had cleared some, but still lingered in a soupy blanket across their path. They pursued the band to the edge of a dense forest, where Petrus paused. He heard their horses and laughter drifting through the trees, and he very nearly followed them into the dim interior of the woods.

"Don't be a fool," Odras said and pulled his 'steed up beside Petrus. "There are ten more where they have gone. This entire ruse was a trap."

"But . . ." Petrus began, wanting desperately to ignore Odras' warnings and chase after them. But the mage made sense. It was the perfect setup, drawing them into an unfamiliar, closed environment, perhaps so tight a space as to make their swords useless. The young elf stared at the forest, listening for clues that might tell him more, but all he heard were retreating hoofbeats, fading to silence.

"The *odds*, Petrus," the mage said. "We are only three."

Wenlann joined them at the forest edge, her ears turned to the woods. "He's right," she said, turning to Petrus. "There are more in the forest. I smell a trap."

"I suggest we return with reinforcements," Petrus said. "So that we can dismember them *properly*."

"To the palace, then," Odras said.

"*We'll be bahk*," Petrus murmured, in an exaggerated Austrian accent.

Chapter Two

By the summer of 1922, Randolf "Thorn" Wilson had only been racing for two years, but had quickly made a name for himself in the small but enthusiastic world of motorcycle racing. In his first race he had acquired his nickname by riding his Harley into a thicket of brambles, finishing the race covered head to toe in thorns. A dubious distinction, though it was a name people tended to remember.

Thorn had slept fitfully in a barn's loft, which had been donated by a farmer for use by riders without the wherewithal for a motel room. At the first hint of daylight Thorn rose with a light, energetic feeling, despite his lack of sleep. Out of his duffel bag came his race gear: the leather flying helmet, complete with goggles, a well worn pair of work gloves and, finally, the leather aviation suit he'd modified for motorcycle riding. It buttoned down the right side, and was lined with camel's hair, with a tight-fitting collar around the neck to keep the air out. It only made sense to wear something designed for flying high when flying low. Wind was wind, wherever it was. It was also Thorn's answer to safety, having dumped another bike and lost a goodly amount of skin from shoulder to butt. He liked the idea of sliding on someone else's skin.

Off came the well-worn knickers, replaced by the breeches. Then he pulled on a pair of old riding boots. They worked better than shoes when you had to slow a bike down, and helped keep you from spraining an ankle. He put on the gear with all the methodical care of the aviator he'd been too young to be during the war.

Outside the spectators were already gathering for the start, and it looked like half the bikes had already lined up, including the four of the Harley-Davidson team. Thorn checked in at the registration table, affixed his number 13 on his front fork, and strolled over to the line of bikes.

A few more bikes lined up, another Harley, a Sport single that had seen better days, and a few Indians with their bright red frames and ridiculously white tires, with their riders dressed as if they were going to a reception, not a motorbike race. Wearing *bowlers*, of all things, not even the silly caps that tended to blow off unless they were turned around. There was a four-horse Yale, an Excelsior with too much shiny nickel plate, a Pierce with a rider who didn't look like he was old enough to shave.

The race coordinator gave the usual speech, asking everyone to play fair, take turns at the gas stations, and stick to the course. The latter point was made for humor; besides the course, a stretch of muddy highway winding through Kansas, there *were* no other roads. It was an unwritten rule to stop and help an injured cyclist, but it was repeated here anyway.

His motorcycle, Valerie, turned over laboriously, pop-popping until she was up to operating speed. He let her idle, took a deep breath, and took one long look at his competition before the race started. The coordinator dropped his flag, and the bikes all lurched forward. He knew it wasn't all too important to get ahead right away in a cross-country, but you did have to keep the leader in sight. Already Walter Davidson had the lead, with two of his teammates following. They would be easy to spot, with big white letters spelling *Harley Davidson*.

Let the rest fight it out, he thought, shifting to second, keeping his eyes on the bikes closest to him. *Only two hundred ninety-nine miles to go . . .*

By midday Thorn estimated he was number five or six, having lost the edge by letting Walter slip way out of sight. He eased her up to fourth, hugged low to her frame, and gave her gas. Soon he was hitting around eighty miles per hour. He pulled back a bit on the speed to negotiate some bumps and, on passing a farmhouse, found himself on straight, open road.

Up ahead was the dust cloud of another rider. Thorn pulled a scarf over his mouth, leaned low and wrapped himself around Valerie, his face directly behind the handlebars.

If I'm gonna take this guy, it's gonna be now, he whispered to his bike, feeling the wind whip by.

Wind gave way to dust and pebbles, bouncing off his goggles and helmet like hail, as the distance between himself and the other rider closed. It was none other than Walter Davidson himself. Thorn hazarded a glance at his speedometer: 95 mph. On rough dirt road like this, it was next to suicide, but he had conditioned his body into a springy, wire framed shock absorber.

Despite Davidson's best efforts, Thorn blasted past by a good ten miles per hour. Now past Davidson's dust cloud, Thorn had a clear view of the road . . . which turned left, sharply, a few yards ahead of him.

By the time he realized he was in trouble he'd already run into a barbed wire fence, feeling nothing besides the sudden absence of gravity, which turned to black. The envelope of darkness wrapped its fragile wings around him, shielding him from an intense, white light that now sought to claim him. Then he felt a presence, an entity, a voice.

Your future is not on the other side. Not yet. Words appeared as thoughts, images. Whatever it was, it spoke directly to him.

Who are you? Thorn asked. He had never been religious but was now having second thoughts. *Are you God?*

I am the Lord of the Land of Shadows, the voice replied. *I am a god.* From the darkness came a candle flame, lighting a vast plain of desolation. A single bare tree stood in the distance. *This is the Land of Shadows. It is always winter, here.* Thorn saw himself, a transparent ghost, still wearing the aviator's suit, the helmet, the goggles. He felt naked without his motorcycle. Remembering Valerie, and the way in which she must have died, sent a pang of guilt through him.

The Lord was a tall wiry figure, standing next to the dead tree, his back turned to the cold wind that blew in from the north. The wind whipped at the edges of a robe of thin, black fur, wrapped tightly around him.

"I'm not sure I follow." Thorn looked down at himself, taking in his ghostly image with a critical eye, wondering what if anything he had to barter with. *With what? With who?* he thought, now wishing he had gone with the white light that had abandoned him.

Do you believe in angels, Thorn? the Lord asked.

Thorn's first reaction was to laugh. But when considering recent events, the humor drained out of the question. He answered honestly. "Not much."

The Lord of the Land of Shadows turned to him slowly, and Thorn saw his face for the first time. What he first took as the pallor of snow white skin was revealed as a grinning skull. The sight did not frighten him; instead it filled him with warmth.

You should believe in angels, now, the Lord continued. *You have become one.*

Thorn looked at his arms, checking for telltale wings

that might have sprouted when he wasn't looking, really wanting to laugh now. "So what did I do to earn this honor?"

You died, the Lord replied. *Most spectacularly, I might add.*

Thorn held his arms up, flapping them like a bird. "So do I get a harp? Where are my wings?"

You get something much better to fly upon than wings, the Lord said.

In the distance he heard a familiar growl of internal combustion. His heart leaped. "Valerie?" Thorn said, looking toward the sound. Riderless, and in pristine condition, Thorn's motorcycle rode up to him and stopped; Valerie had become a living, thinking being.

You loved your motorbike. You created a soul.

Love flowed from the bike, a pinkish, red haze. When he touched it, it flowed through him.

Become familiar with my land, the Lord said, and began walking away. *You will learn where it goes, and travel it with ease.*

"As an angel?" Thorn asked, still unable to comprehend it. However, he could think of worse fates than riding Valerie for an eternity.

As a Rider Guardian, the Lord replied. *A guardian angel, for living souls who very much need a guardian.*

"Whose souls?" Thorn asked, though he already had an idea.

The riders of motorcycles will need protection.

The Lord was gone, and Thorn tested Valerie, revving her motor with a delicate twist of the throttle.

"Let's see what's out there," he said to her, and they were off.

Chapter Three

They reached Castle Tuiereann after a long day of travel, and no small amount of bickering between Wenlann and Petrus. Odras rode in silence, as if lost in his own thoughts, but out of the corner of his eye Petrus had seen him looking rather amused.

King Aedham had built the new castle at the fork of the massive Arannan and Gruac Rivers. Aedham made the river deeper, wider, and swifter, then established his new home between the two river branches. There had already been a sizable hill here, and with the five stories of castle it seemed even taller.

Petrus' own chambers were on the third floor, and commanded a striking view of the surrounding landscape. The sight of the castle was a welcome relief! He hadn't realized how much he'd enjoyed living in cushy comfort until trying to sleep on a blanket on a soggy moor.

They paused at the gatehouse before crossing a drawbridge. The house was an elaborate affair with a tall, pointed arch and a thick, bronze gate. A second gate of cold iron lay concealed behind wood panels, against the walls of the house, ready to be closed over the bronze gate should they again be attacked by the Unseleighe. Despite the concealing planks of oak, Petrus flinched at the death metal's heat every time he passed.

"Aie, Scoriath." Petrus called the guard on duty. The guard stepped forward with the reverence due Petrus as one of the highest ranking elves of Avalon. "Another good day for hunting. There's Unseleighe vermin on our lands to the north, in the thick forests. Care to join us when we return in force?"

Scoriath's eyes lit brightly at the mention of a hunt. The Seleighe was an expert with horses, and an excellent warrior. He and thirty others had emigrated from Outremer to join Avalon in their rebuilding. Scoriath and his brother, Rochad, had grown up with Petrus, and had taught each other a thing or two about swordplay.

"*Unseleighe?*" Scoriath said, sounding more intrigued than surprised. He had stepped closer to Moonremere and had started scratching her jowls, his bright, blond hair cascading past his shoulders. "How many?"

"Twenty, perhaps."

Odras yawned expressively. "I didn't think their mage was very good."

"Good enough to fool Petrus with a projection," Wenlann countered. "One that vanished the moment our hero here decided to leap on it. Instead, he leaped on some rather treacherous mud. Didn't he, Odras?"

Odras said nothing, and Petrus glared at Wenlann, remembering a nugget of advice the mage had once offered. *Never get involved in a boy and girl fight. Odras seems to be taking his own advice.*

"I suppose the King would want to speak with you directly," Scoriath said diplomatically, stepping back to allow them entry. "If there are Unseleighe to contend with he will wish to know immediately," the guard added.

"Aie," Petrus replied, making a point of looking *away* from Wenlann. "And I'm tired as well."

"There may be leftover supper," Scoriath said as they passed. "We dined only a candlemark ago."

Petrus nodded, hoping the rumble in his stomach wasn't loud enough to be heard. He felt the magical shields snap into place behind him as they took the drawbridge across a moat, a wide channel guarding the northern side of the castle. As they approached the stables a page came for their 'steeds.

I'll gather our gear later, he thought, as he started for the castle, not caring if Wenlann accompanied him or not.

He found the Great Hall empty. The thick ceiling timbers matched the stoutness of the entire castle, which had an ornamental rock exterior laid over a dense, granite frame. This castle would, according to the mages who had assisted, withstand levin bolts twice as strong as the ones that had leveled their previous home.

Petrus decided on a quick change in his quarters; casting a glamorie to hide his mud-soaked clothes would be tricky, and impolite. Etiquette required all business with the King be done without disguise, magical or otherwise. Besides, Aedham would see right through it, and would likely find it all the more amusing. *It will only take a moment to make myself presentable,* Petrus thought as he ascended the main stairwell at the end of the hall. But as he passed by the King's solar, Aedham called out as he tried to sneak past.

"Petrus? Is that you?" Aedham inquired, and reluctantly Petrus turned and entered the solar, mud and all.

"Yes, Aedham," he replied. "As you can see, I am less than presentable."

"Since when have I cared about a little dirt?" Aedham said cheerfully. Today he looked more like Adam McDaris, teenager, than King Aedham Tuiereann, Ruler of Elfhame Avalon. As he often did, he had forsaken his royal robe, crown and scepter for more casual clothes. The slogan on the simple red T-shirt was certainly appropriate, reflecting Petrus' mood as well: *When It*

Absolutely, Positively Has To Be Destroyed Overnight. U.S. Marines. He sat at a long narrow table salvaged from the ruins of the former castle. This was the same table King Traig had used in his final minutes while holed up in the bowels of the castle, and Aedham had grown attached to it. On it sat a pink Lava Lite, a halogen desk lamp, and a hundred or so compact disk holders spread around him in a semicircle. Depeche Mode's *Songs of Faith and Devotion* played through four deceptively small Bose speakers hanging from the ceiling's rock.

Aedham was barefoot, wearing a pair of well worn and faded jeans, with holes for knees, his face illuminated by the dim glow of a computer screen. The pc sat upright on the floor, wires spilling out its back, with the big crystal port sitting on a shelf behind him. It was one of the Unseleighe technologies Niamh had learned to convert to peaceful use, and was the means with which Aedham was able to dial into the human array of computer systems called the Internet. Other elves questioned this link to the humans' world, fearful it might be traced back to Underhill by unfriendly humans. But Niamh had assured all that such a thing was not possible. The King had used it from time to time when he was feeling nostalgic, and wanted to converse with unknowing humans.

A long wooden torch burned on the wall in eerie contrast to the technology spread out on the ancient table. Petrus might have mistaken the King for a young human man, if not for the pointed ears protruding from his curly mop of shoulder-length hair.

Aedham took in Petrus' muddied condition, visibly suppressing a smirk. "I take it your trip was eventful?"

Petrus nodded, meeting the King's eyes. "It was. We encountered Japhet Dhu, my King. They are here, and they are looking for trouble."

Darkness fell across the King's face like a portcullis. He calmly tapped a few keys, turned off the monitor, then the computer. Its falling whine sounded like a dying animal.

"Are you certain?" Aedham said, his demeanor now completely different. He stood slowly, rising to his full height.

The look Petrus saw in his face was frightening, and one he had not seen for a long time. "Yes, I am certain." Petrus told him about the first encounter that turned into solo mud wrestling, and about finding the banners.

"The son of Zeldan," Aedham said, pacing the floor. Sparks of energy flared around him, a sure sign the King was very, very pissed. "How dare they defile what they have already destroyed."

"We pursued them to the edge of the Black Forest," Petrus said. "I wanted to go after them, but Odras urged caution."

"How many?" Aedham said. His human clothing had changed to more elven attire. Gone were the jeans and T-shirt, replaced by a gold fur-lined robe with large cuffs, hose and short boots. The ring with the large letter A had also appeared on his hand. The transformation to his elven self was sudden, and startling, and a certain sign the King wanted blood.

"Twenty, perhaps, according to Odras. I only saw three. A mage is among them."

Aedham frowned, and continued his pacing. "Dammit all, I knew things had gotten too sedate around here."

The King's anger made Petrus nervous, and he began stammering an apology. "Forgive me, if I have failed you. I—"

"You've done no such thing," Aedham said acidly. "You were right not to go after them." He stopped pacing and walked over to Petrus, putting a hand on his shoulder. "If there were as many as Odras says, it would have been suicide to follow them into the forest. We need our heroes alive, thank you. I need to speak with Odras."

As if on cue there was a knock on the solar's entrance. "Sire?" Odras said hesitantly.

"You have met some of my old enemies, Petrus tells me," Aedham said. "A mage was involved?"

"Aie," Odras replied. Petrus repressed a surge of his own annoyance. Didn't the King believe him? "One capable of projections." Odras didn't elaborate, and Petrus was grateful. "They tried to lure us into a vulnerable place."

"No forces to be concerned with this evening?" the King asked.

Odras shrugged. "They are hardly a force worthy of attacking us here."

King Aedham turned and walked to a narrow window, which overlooked the Arannan River.

"We must launch an attack," the King said. "And rid ourselves finally of the vermin."

Petrus slept fitfully, and when he did fall into a deep sleep it was already morning; he must have looked as exhausted as he felt, since the King argued against his joining the raid on Japhet Dhu. Time was of the essence; the King wanted to attack right away, before the Unseleighe had time to move. Yet he found the energy to convince the King, and himself, that he was fit to go.

Wenlann opted not to go with the troops, to Petrus' relief. She was exhausted, and not afraid to admit she would make an unfit warrior in her present state. The King had ordered forty soldiers to take part in the campaign. If he had needed more he might have been tempted to appeal to the other Elfhames, but twenty Unseleighe opponents seemed a small lot. He voiced his doubts to the troops, as they assembled quickly on the castle grounds, that this scruffy band of Unseleighe would be any sort of a threat.

King Aedham also announced to the troops that a mage

was among the Unseleighe, and in the same breath reminded them that their King was a mage as well, as was Odras.

"Our magic has beaten theirs before, and it will do so today. The nodes are better protected than they ever have been, and energy from one of them would be sufficient to counter any magical attack," Aedham announced. Fion, Captain of the Guard, stood at the head of his mounted ranks. His second in command and younger cousin, Liadin, was busy in the castle armory collecting weapons. A dozen new crossbows had yet to cure completely, and Fion had made a last minute decision to replace the new crossbows with older weapons.

The troops were divided into cavalry and foot soldiers. The latter would ride to the Black Forest on two long wagons. Each mounted warrior bore a sword, shield, helmet and lance; each wore a long coat of chain mail. Bronze was the elven metal of choice, strong enough for armor and weapons, without the lethal side effects of iron.

Petrus, eager for battle, had donned his mail. A surge of adrenalin revived him somewhat, but he still had to feign energy when movement was required. Hatred for the Unseleighe joined the different groups from the other Seleighe courts, and despite their slight differences in speech they had formed a formidable, cohesive fighting unit.

During his brief stay in the humans' world, Petrus had seen weapons that could do far more damage than their swords and lances. Images of Rambo, toting the enormous M50 and Schwarzenegger in *Predator* flashed through his head.

If we had one of those Gatling machine guns, he thought, remembering how it cut down a jungle in the time it took to draw a sword, *there would be no contest*.

The Seleighe adhered to the traditional weapons, as the Unseleighe would never use anything but the sword, arrow and spear. To defeat the Unseleighe by using modern human weapons would be a hollow victory indeed.

With a nod from the King the forces set forth across the drawbridge, and began the journey to the Black Forest.

Petrus led them to the campsite on the moor. The black banner lay where they had left it. After one glance King Aedham said, "It is indeed. The same as Zeldan. You were right, this must be his son." He led his horse over the banner, trampling it with disdain.

From the moor's crest they saw the edge of the Black Forest, a dense area of oak and ash that stretched over several hills; to the north was a bare hill which would make an excellent staging area for any direct attack on the forest.

But where did they enter? he thought, gazing across the homogeneous line of trees. *It all looks the same.*

"There," Aedham said, pointing to a thin spiral of smoke drifting from the forest interior. "A campfire."

"Would they be so stupid?" Odras asked, riding up alongside the King. "What better way to give away their position?"

"They're not stupid," the King said warily. "They simply don't care. Or it is a false fire, burning far away from where they actually are. That would make the most sense."

A rumble of surprise rippled through Aedham's forces. Petrus looked toward the bare hill. To his horror a vast army had appeared, filling the horizon with black silk ribbon banners and the eagle crest flag. The opposing forces must have numbered in the hundreds. They all seemed to be cavalry; horses as black as the uniforms, elvensteeds that seemed to be as well trained as their own. Fatigue forgotten now, a new surge of energy swept through Petrus, accompanied by a queasy feeling in the pit of his stomach.

Aedham turned, slowly, to Petrus, and said with the utmost calm, "I thought you said there were only twenty."

Petrus shrugged. "Give or take."

Odras leaned over and whispered to the King. Petrus overheard him say, "Sire, as I am only half the mage that you are, surely you must see this spectacle for what it is."

The King looked at Odras, at Petrus, then the enemy. His eyes seemed to unfocus a little, and glaze fell over them. *Mage sight,* Petrus thought, and turned his sight to the foe. But after a long moment Petrus still couldn't quite see what Odras saw.

"It's a projection," King Aedham said. "A good one, too." He regarded his forces anxiously. "We must tell them . . ."

"It would be more efficient," Odras interrupted most diplomatically, "to simply rid our landscape of this abominable sight." Odras bowed, most humbly. "With your assistance of course, Sire."

The King frowned. "In many ways your mage powers are superior to mine, dear Odras. Now is not the time for humility. What do you need from me?"

The old mage's eyes narrowed as he scrutinized the army. "Power, Sire. Node power."

"Consider it done," the King said, and closed his eyes. Petrus felt a familiar buzzing that vibrated up from the ground to his inner ear. It was, he knew, only an echo of what was happening between the King and Odras.

"Aye," Odras said, breathlessly. "That is . . . more than sufficient."

"Sire, look," the captain said. "They are sending someone to parley."

Four horses advanced from a brief opening in the

army's line. The fourth rider seemed to be the leader, and from the finery that adorned uniform and tack, Petrus guessed this to be Japhet Dhu.

"Now," the King whispered, and Odras dismounted and took a few steps forward, his arms spread. Then he waved his arms, as if casting a net. A crescent of energy leaped from Odras' hands and sailed through the air, gaining speed and size as it flew. The group of four Unseleighe slowed, then stopped in their tracks as the wave of power passed over them, spreading wider as it approached the enemy's line. When the crescent connected with the projection, an ear-splitting whine sliced through the air. The Unseleighe army froze, then shattered and vanished.

Standing atop the hill was a lone figure in a long, black robe. *This can only be their mage,* Petrus thought. He seemed disoriented, even from this distance; Odras' gift must have stunned him.

"I know that mage," Odras muttered as he gazed at the lone figure on the hill. "That is *Nargach.* A powerful one, indeed."

The four horsemen glanced back, uncertain of their next move.

"These odds look a little better, don't you think?" the King said, turning his attention back to Fion. "Captain, sound the charge please. One unit of cavalry should be enough."

"*Aie!*" Fion shouted, raised his hand toward the army, and rattled off orders to the nearest soldiers. In tight formation seven cavalrymen charged down the hill toward Japhet Dhu and his men. They hadn't gone too far when Japhet and the other three turned and ran.

"Captain, we must follow them. Have the foot soldiers follow up in the rear . . ." the King shouted.

"Sire, I must urge caution," said Fion. "They may have prepared an ambush in the forest."

"So they may," acknowledged Aedham. "Be prepared, then, but we *must* follow."

Fion gave the orders and the remaining cavalry poured down the hill, followed by the foot soldiers. Aedham's cavalry disappeared over the crest of the hill, and the moment Petrus had cleared it he saw a broad, well-trodden path leading into the forest.

The path narrowed, and forest thickened around them. Petrus heard the clash of swords and the scream of wounded elves.

Rounding a bend in the path, they came upon a battle. Two Unseleighe had already fallen, and a third was fighting desperately with a broken sword. The single Seleighe cavalryman overcame a parry, and his blade met the Unseleighe's throat. Blood poured as the elf fell from his horse.

The King rode past, leading his remaining soldiers down the path. The trees closed in from each side and above, forcing the riders to crouch over their steeds' necks. Sounds of battle drifted through the dense wood, and Petrus fought back frustration. He wanted to be in the middle of the fray, wanted to feel his blade connect with soft Unseleighe flesh, to spill Unseleighe blood. But as a senior member of the Elfhame, his duty was to remain at his King's side.

"There," Odras said, pointing ahead. "That clearing . . ."

The King and Odras were a few horse lengths ahead when an Unseleighe warrior leapt from a tree, knocking Petrus from his 'steed. A rock connected with his hip and pain shot down his right leg. Gritting his teeth, Petrus scrambled to his feet, drew his blade and confronted a young Unseleighe holding a broad sword with both hands.

"*Argan greched sargann . . .*" the Unseleighe muttered in ancient Elvish, a tongue Petrus had never had the patience to learn. As the Unseleighe swung at him, Petrus saw that the sword was too heavy for the youth's slight frame. He dodged the attack, not wanting to parry with his lighter blade. As the youth lunged past him, Petrus planted a foot on the foe's rear, sending him tumbling to the ground. The broad sword was lost in the brush and the Unseleighe youth drew a long dagger as he regained his feet.

Petrus took a fighting stance and met the Unseleighe's eyes. *This was the little bastard I chased yesterday*, he realized, and his blood heated further. Petrus attacked, and the youth parried. Off balance, and feeling his bruised hip, Petrus stumbled.

"Mergach . . . Avalon!" the Unseleighe shrieked as he lunged forward. Petrus leaned sharply to his left, bringing his blade up. The Unseleighe youth ran headlong into the blade, driving it into his neck to the hilt. Ascertaining that the youth was no longer a threat, Petrus moved along the path, searching for Aedham.

Seeing the King's back, Petrus called out, "Sire!" Aedham was pulling his blade from another Unseleighe.

"This way," the King said. Odras rejoined them at the edge of a clearing, where six Avalon warriors lay dead or wounded.

Captain Fion, one arm bleeding, studied a luminescent disk hovering in the center of the clearing. "A Gate, Sire," he said dejectedly. "Already up when we got here."

"How many made it through?" the King asked grimly. *"Who* made it through?" Aedham turned to Odras. "Can you find where that Gate took them?"

The mage nodded and stepped forward, the light of the Gate reflecting brightly off his dark features.

"Should we follow them, Sire?" Petrus asked. He was no stranger to gating, and would gladly step through to continue the hunt. He did not care to see the Unseleighe escape.

The King hesitated, considering. "That would be foolish," he said. "Tempting as it is, it would be too simple for them to kill anyone coming through. And we don't know yet *where* it went."

Ah, but we will soon, Petrus thought, regarding the mage hopefully.

Odras lowered his hand and strode over to the King. "They have fled to the humans' world, sire," the mage said, looking frail and tired. Extracting information from the construct must have been more difficult than it appeared. "I know precisely where they have gone, and when. However, this Gate—" Movement to his right distracted him. The Gate dimmed, shrank to the size of a shield, and popped out of existence altogether.

Odras continued in the silence that followed, ". . . will not exist much longer."

The King stared at the empty space for a long time, and Petrus stepped back, leaving him to his thoughts. Aedham didn't look beaten, only temporarily set back.

"We will follow them," the King whispered. "We will follow, and destroy them."

Chapter Four

A month after Lucas turned fifteen, he was absolutely convinced that he was going insane. Not just going crazy insane, or having a bad day insane, or lust for the opposite sex insane, but literally insane, clinically insane, hopelessly, irreversibly psychotic.

Lucas was fairly certain about his diagnosis. A year ago his best friend, Mike Vaughan, had awakened one morning believing he was a werewolf. The night before, Lucas and Mike had taken an impromptu trip to Santa Fe on Mike's new Suzuki Katana. The 750cc sport bike was too big, but Mike managed to keep it on the road, somehow, and in the warm summer night they went off riding. The experience was exhilarating. Lucas' hair was hopelessly matted from the wind, and it took a good hour to comb through it, but he was hooked. He wanted a motorcycle too.

Soon, though, the urge cooled. The day after the ride, Mike told his parents, in complete sincerity, that he had shapeshifted into a wolf while riding the motorcycle. His insistence led his parents to send him to a private mental institution in Colorado.

Within six months, Mike had been released, but he didn't return to school. Lucas tried to call him once, but Doctor Vaughan, Mike's father, said Mike wasn't taking calls. Three days later Lucas read in the paper that Mike had committed suicide by taking a hundred over-the-counter sleeping pills, an undisclosed amount of Valium, and a half pint of bourbon. His parents had thought he was just sleeping in.

Now Lucas was the one who was screwed up. Would he end up like Mike? He tried to talk to his stepdad about how he felt, but it didn't seem like he was getting through. Alvin Tatum had a constant *upness* about him, which may or may not have been genuine. When Lucas tried to talk about his friend's suicide, Alvin had looked at him blankly. He might as well have been talking to a mannequin. His mother referred him back to stepdad. Lucas gave up, and buried the pain and the loss as far down as he could.

He spent a month trying to find himself in psychology books. Soon he knew about the many forms of schizophrenia, as well as other psychoses, neuroses, paranoias, and an entire alphabet of phobias. He checked out a huge book entitled *Schizophrenia* and carried it around with him. His grades fluctuated between C's and B's, and his fascination with mental illness continued. Once he screwed up the courage to make an appointment with the school counselor, Mr. Burden. Lucas carefully explained that he was insane, and needed psychiatric help, if not antipsychotic drugs. At first the counselor seemed genuinely concerned, but after a few questions about his family and sleeping habits, Lucas realized that Mr. Burden was suppressing a smirk.

"There's really nothing wrong with you," the counselor said, looking out the window. "You're an adolescent. These changes in your body are normal, your feelings are normal. This is the way it is." Lucas returned *Schizophrenia* to the library, feeling empty, like a hole had been bored through him.

The hole widened, threatening to consume him. Other

students avoided him, and he didn't know why. He took to wearing a pentagram, an ankh and a Star of David, sometimes all three on the same day, but that seemed to make matters worse. He heard about the Axe, a juice bar that occasionally got raided for serving alcohol, while in his freshman year. The kids who frequented the Axe looked like they had just walked off the set of a horror movie. They wore black clothes, probably black underwear too, and favored pale makeup that made them look ill. Their attitude spooked him right away, and he didn't see how he could adapt to their mold even if he wanted to.

It became a chore to get up in the morning, and an even greater chore to go to sleep at night. His mother made him chamomile tea with spearmint, but was otherwise unconcerned. Instead of being awake and anxious, he was awake and relaxed. He became an avid reader, favoring Anne Rice, Poppy Z. Brite and William S. Burroughs novels.

In the second semester of his sophomore year his grades began to dip, the C's becoming more frequent as the B's became less so. He walked the halls feeling like an alien sent to study earth with only rudimentary knowledge of how things worked.

Then on a rainy, stormy night in April, Lucas had a dream that changed his life forever. They had told him about wet dreams in sex ed, and that they would be normal and a regular part of growing up. The teacher didn't go into too much detail, and Lucas had the impression there was something vaguely naughty about having one.

On this particular night Lucas had finally managed to fall asleep sometime around two or three in the morning. In the dream, he was in a dark, dank castle, with a raging storm outside, walking through the keep wearing a long, black robe with nothing underneath. He was being followed by something, perhaps an animal, but definitely not a human. In a corridor where tall mirrors filled the walls, a gust of wind poured in through one of the wind holes, whistling a sad, eerie note. Something had joined him in the hallway, something which didn't walk, but flew.

It landed behind him, wrapping long pallid arms around his chest. As it breathed in his ear, he saw it in the mirror; neither male nor female, it had long, scraggly hair, wings like a bat and two long fangs, which had disappeared into the flesh of his bare shoulder.

Lucas woke with a start, shivering. He was damp with sweat and . . . something else. Light headed, he sat up on the edge of his bed, realizing what that something else was. Sex ed had been very specific about that. He felt unclean.

He bathed himself thoroughly and meticulously, as if he were covered with hazardous, radioactive material. The dream had already faded, but he retained a brief image of the vampire in the mirror. *Male or female?* He wanted to believe the vampire was female, but he couldn't be sure. Something told him the sex of the vampire was the least of his concerns.

My first orgasm is about vampires. What is wrong with me?

After the vampire dream it became difficult to look people in the eye, for any reason. He felt that if he did anyone could look into his soul, and see the dark secret he kept there. He started wearing only dark clothes, and sunglasses regardless of the weather. He welcomed cloudy, rainy days and hated the sun.

He started going to the Axe. There, listening to Bauhaus and smoking clove cigarettes, he felt less alone than before. But he spoke to no one, and no one spoke to him.

Some of the kids rode motorcycles; Suzukis, Yamahas, Kawasakis, a Triumph or two, a Beemer. He yearned to ride on one. Lucas thought that some time soon he would be able to open up, and attempt contact with these strange beings. He wasn't quite ready, and was content to simply stand in their presence, listening to the music, and watching them ride their motorcycles. But one night, when he wasn't there, the police raided the Axe and closed it, shutting the door on any hope that he might find someone he could talk to.

Meanwhile, his grades had turned to shit. *Straight D's, as in Dogturd,* he thought dismally, as he tore up his grade card. School had no meaning, and when the Axe closed, nothing else did, either.

He woke up one morning, wet from another vampire dream, uncertain what day it was.

What does it all matter? he thought, staring at his face in the mirror. Not knowing when it had happened, he saw that he had quit living. That day he pretended to go to school, but came back after his parents had left for work. On the way back he bought two bottles of Nytol, the quick working kind, only vaguely aware of what he was about to do.

I don't belong on this planet. The logical thing to do, the only thing to do, is to get the hell off it, he thought, going through his parents' medicine cabinet. *Here it is . . . only a few left.* Lucas dumped the bottle of Valium out on his hand. *Fifteen . . . sixteen . . . twenty. That will have to do.*

It would be six or seven hours before anyone came home, possibly more if they went somewhere else, the store or something.

Off. This. Planet. He stared at his bedroom wall for a good hour, thinking absolutely nothing. Then he went to the kitchen and poured a glass of 7-Up and white wine over ice. With his cocktail he chased both bottles of Nytol and the twenty Valium, wondering how long it would be before Scotty beamed him up.

✧   ✧   ✧

"There's probably a lot you won't remember," the nurse said as she checked his IV. She reminded him of Praga Kahn of the *Lords of Acid*, tall and lanky with long black hair. He could have sworn he saw her wearing white stiletto heels with her nurse's uniform.

He felt pretty shitty. His throat felt like it had been scraped out with a potato peeler.

I remember, he thought. *I wish I didn't.*

The nurse came back in with a doctor who looked frazzled, but attentive.

"I'm Doctor Vaughan." The doctor fixed him with an unnerving stare.

That name sounds really familiar. And I've seen this man, somewhere, before. He looks so surprised to see me awake, Lucas thought. *That bugs me.*

"So, how do you feel?" the doctor asked, sounding genuinely concerned.

"Terrible," Lucas said. "Sleepy. What time is it?"

"Four," the doctor replied. "In the afternoon. This is Wednesday."

At least two days had passed. *Just as well,* he thought, *those were two days I didn't have to deal with. Or will I?*

Doctor Vaughan took a seat next to the bed. He looked tired, truly tired. "What happened?" he asked.

At first the question seemed ridiculous. *I swallowed a bunch of drugs, that's what happened,* Lucas thought. "It sounds stupid, but I don't know what happened. I remember what I did. I don't remember why."

Doctor Vaughan nodded, as if he understood the explanation. "You're lucky. The combination of diphenhydramine and Valium caused you to go into a deep sleep. It wasn't quite enough to kill you, but you could have been a vegetable. Brain dead, but alive. Your parents would have had to decide whether to turn off the life support."

Lucas didn't know how to reply to that. Failure wasn't one of the things he'd planned on. For Mike, it had been so easy, he'd thought.

"How close did I come?" he asked.

"Closer than you think. You were in a coma for over a week."

"Oh," Lucas said. *This is the second Wednesday. Nine days. Not two.*

"Another week, and we would have thought about whether or not to keep you as an expensive plant."

"I'm not a plant," Lucas seethed. *This is not what's supposed to happen . . .*

"You almost were," the doctor said, but now he looked more tired than anything. The nurse had left again, and now returned to whisper something in the doctor's ear.

"I'll be back in a few minutes," the doctor said, getting to his feet with extreme effort.

Lucas lay staring at the ceiling. *A goddamned vegetable. That's what I would have been . . . no, was.* Then he remembered the dreams, the nightmares, of darkness, disembodied voices. *Dreaming. I would have been a vegetable, dreaming nightmares. Forever. Or until Dad decided to pull the plug.*

I want the hell out of here, he thought with steel plated conviction.

He heard voices in the hallway: the doctor's and his father's. He'd know that casual disinterest anywhere. His ears perked when their discussion mutated to an argument.

". . . he is *not* okay," Vaughan said emphatically. "Physically it looks like he's going to be fine, but I'm not so sure he's not going to just turn around and try it again."

He has a point, Lucas thought. How to convince them he wasn't going to try to do himself in when he wasn't certain himself?

"Don't be silly," Alvin Tatum said. "These things . . . happen. Lucas was just goofing off, like teenagers do. He's already been here a week. I think he should go home today."

"Your son tried to commit *suicide*," the doctor replied, his anger rising. "If you think this is normal, that nothing is wrong, you are sadly mistaken. It is the tip of an iceberg. It's a symptom of a greater problem."

Got that right, thought Lucas. But he had no idea what the problem was. He didn't know why he didn't care about living. An image of his comatose body hung before him. He imagined being one of those fuzzy ball things from *Invasion of the Body Snatchers,* the version with Leonard Nimoy and Donald Sutherland. Growing, pulsating like an exposed heart, he saw himself bursting forth from the gelatinous shell, standing, then walking. His mind would be dull and uncomprehending, following signals blindly from some unseen force. Not a nice existence.

The reality would be much worse; he would be dreaming, big black nightmares with no end. Perhaps in these dreams, which would become more lucid as he got better at having them, he would realize that he would never wake. He would scream futilely at the walls of the dream, knowing his real mouth was frozen, unmoving. He would scream, but nothing would happen, no one would hear him except himself.

Despite the argument in the hall, Lucas drifted off to sleep. This time it was a real sleep, and he knew he'd wake up.

Evidently Doctor Vaughan had won the argument, because it was Thursday morning before Lucas' stepfather returned for him.

"Up and at 'em, boy." Tatum's greeting was infused with his usual good cheer. "Time to go home."

Vaughan arrived as Tatum was helping Lucas dress. "I must reiterate," he said, "that this is *not* a good idea. Lucas should be kept for observation for at least another day."

But Tatum would not be moved. "We'll observe him at home." He smiled at Lucas. "He'll be fine. A couple of days off from school and he'll be good as new."

Doctor Vaughan stopped by the house on Friday while Lucas' folks were out.

"I want to show you something," he said.

For a while Lucas thought Vaughan was taking him to school, but instead they turned into Sunset Memorial Park Cemetery, which was right across the street from his high school.

"I've never been in a graveyard before," Lucas said.

"This won't take long. I don't spend much time here, when I do come," the doctor said, sounding sad. He stopped the car on the narrow road that wound through the cemetery.

"This way," Vaughan said, leading him through the grave markers. Lucas remembered reading somewhere that one shouldn't step directly on the grave, so he did his best to stay between them. Somewhere down there, six feet under, were boxes of dead people, he realized.

They stopped in front of a tombstone, small and new.

MIKE VAUGHAN
MARCH 13, 1980 — NOVEMBER 20, 1994

Lucas stared at the marker, the name sinking in, like a thin veil dropping over his head.

"He was my son," Doctor Vaughan said. "Did you know him?"

He looked up at the doctor, feeling weak all over again. "I need to sit down."

"Then sit," the doctor said, helping him down. Vaughan joined him on the grass, right at the foot of the grave.

"Yes, I knew him," Lucas said. "Why wouldn't you let me talk to him?"

Vaughan stared at him. Then understanding softened his features. "I thought your name was familiar."

They both looked at the grass between them, which had recently been mowed. The smell was refreshing, reminding Lucas that it was spring.

"He was on medication. Anti-depressants," said Vaughan. "He didn't want to talk to anyone, not even you." His eyes wandered to the grave, and his lips pressed together. "Not even me."

Lucas felt numb, inside and out.

"We were trying a different drug, something we hoped would make him snap out of it. It didn't. It made his depression much worse."

Lucas shifted position on the grass. Looking at Mike's grave, Lucas started to feel grateful that his own attempt had failed. "I was depressed, I saw no way out," he said, more to Mike than to his father. "I was so certain I was doing the right thing."

"If you're depressed, you are not thinking clearly," Vaughan pointed out. "You can't do your best thinking because you're impaired."

They sat quietly. The doctor looked down again, his half hidden face unreadable. *Is he blaming himself for what happened to Mike?* he wondered. *Does he really think he had something do to with it?*

A gentle breeze caressed the graveyard in the bright afternoon sun, spinning the pinwheels people had placed on graves. Flowers were everywhere, it seemed.

A hawk called overhead, and he glanced up to see the great bird kiting gently in the wind. The greens of the grass, the trees, and the vivid colors of some of the fresher flowers stood out as if highlighted with a special marker, one which underscored the beauty of everything in nature. Lucas took a long deep breath.

As he exhaled he felt an enormous load slide off his shoulders.

I don't have to die, he thought. *Whatever it is . . . I can deal with it.* He thought about the vampire dreams, the Gothic elements of his life, and the dazzling brilliance of all the living things around him. Suddenly it all meshed, as if a key had been dropped in his lap. Something between all these things connected, and the result would, somehow, bring him closer to whatever it was he was looking for.

But how to get there . . .

In that moment, something *changed* in Lucas.

He sensed Mike's body, cold dead, and lifeless, somewhere beneath the earth he sat on. Mike's face came back to him with startling clarity, a young kid his own age, full of life and lusty dreams, full of promise. Lucas realized that he had never grieved for his friend, had never shed a single tear.

"I'm going back to the car," Lucas said, but his voice cracked, betraying the tears he was fighting so hard to hold back.

Mike's dead. It felt like news.

Doctor Vaughan stood with him but neither started for the car. Lucas wouldn't remember who reached for who, but in the end it didn't really matter. Lucas found himself hugging Doctor Vaughan and sobbing into his chest. The doctor held him as if he held his own son.

"I'm sorry . . . I'm so sorry," Lucas managed to blurt out, as the grief subsided. "I didn't think what it would do to anyone else . . ."

"It's all right," the doctor said, stroking his head.

During the ride home he learned that there was a suicide prevention hotline in the phone book. *They'll talk about anything,* the doctor had said, driving the Beemer through Albuquerque rush hour. *You won't shock them.*

Lucas had his doubts, but already he was feeling better.

Chapter Five

From the glaring whiteness of the Gate's interior, Japhet Dhu drove his elvensteed into the uncertain darkness of the humans' world. The 'steed landed unsteadily, then regained her footing. Japhet heard the familiar sound of loose gravel and the scuffing of hooves against dirt.

He and his 'steed stood atop a mesa looking down on a brightly lit city, in the blackest of nights he had ever seen. It seemed like a lake of light at the bottom of a canyon, but as his vision adjusted he discerned streets, and moving lights following these streets.

He turned to face the Gate. He had thought the others were right behind him. Where were they now?

The Gate glowed a dull orange, still active but diminishing in power. He pulled his sword in case Avalon elves charged through it instead of his own soldiers. The escape had been close, but it had looked like most of his elite forces would make it through.

Where are they? Japhet seethed.

The Gate flickered, then blazed white as a mounted 'steed, followed by another, leapt through. He immediately saw they were his men, and drew back to give them room. Japhet counted four, followed by a smaller shadow he recognized as Mort, a demon who was eager to serve any Unseleighe who happened to be in charge.

A fifth shadow, a robed mage Japhet recognized immediately, crossed the Gate's threshold. His eyes glowed white, and bore directly on Japhet as his 'steed trotted toward him.

"There are no more, Sire," Nargach told the Unseleighe leader. "At least, none of our elite group."

"Then dismiss the Gate," Japhet said, "I have the forces I need to rebuild." He spoke with faked confidence. If he showed any weakness in this new world he would lose his command quickly. Nargach would see to that.

"As you wish," Nargach said, turning toward his magical construction. Japhet saw that the Mage was rattled. His escape must have been made at the last possible moment, as the Avalon forces closed in.

Nargach raised both arms, murmured something in ancient Elvish; the Gate shrank to the size of a coin, then *blipped* from existence. They were left with the darkness, the desert, and Japhet's uncertainty as to what to do next.

He needed time to think, alone and without interruption, and he knew he had to disguise his indecisiveness. Japhet dismounted and stormed off to the edge of the mesa, which gave way to a steep slope. Beneath him, spread majestically, was the human city.

What manner of power causes these lights? he wondered, sensing no elven magics that might account for the display.

This he would learn later. Now, he needed to concentrate on inventorying his assets, and determine what he could do with the small group he had.

The mage. At the very least, I have Nargach, he groused, knowing his presence was a threat as well as an asset. Japhet's succession to ruler of this Unseleighe court had taken place without debate; he was, after all, Zeldan's son. Though it didn't hurt that he had cultivated his own power base while father was away, this particular clan of elves held blood ties, particularly *noble* blood ties, sacred.

His remaining three were all seasoned soldiers, skilled in all the tools of warfare, though each with their own special talents. Youthful Rochad was an expert at bow and arrow, while Semion was a champion swordsman. Domnu, the eldest of the warriors, had trained the others to fight in battle with whatever happened to be handy. If he'd had the chance to hand pick his best three warriors, he would have likely chosen these.

Then there was the oddity, Mort, a demon who had found a place among the Unseleighe, although a tenuous one. Mort had been allied with Morrigan, with whom Zeldan had formed a partnership, and the demon had been included as some kind of bonus. The details were vague; Japhet had been too busy pulling together his own people to pay much attention to their arrangement. What he did know was that as soon as Zeldan fell, Mort had been more than happy to throw in with Japhet.

With whoever was in charge, with whoever was winning, Japhet thought wryly. Mort had also been with Zeldan while he was among the humans. *Mort knows this place!* he realized with relief. *He was here before and operated in it, manipulated the humans, took advantage of their weaknesses.* Mort had also been one of the few to escape to Underhill when Aedham defeated Zeldan, which in itself was either suspicious behavior, or a redeeming quality. It would be a matter of time before he determined which it was. This explained the little demon's smugness when they had been discussing possible flight to the humans' world.

Japhet rejoined the others, who were still mounted on their 'steeds, barely visible in the darkness. The leader's own 'steed had remained where she was, though she looked like she might be nosing around the ground for grass to eat. None was to be found on this patch of earth, a rocky, dusty land.

"Sire, look!" Rochad said, pointing to something behind him. Japhet reached for his sword as he turned around. On the horizon, creeping up from behind a range of mountains, was a deep orange sphere, spotted with pockmarks.

"Is it the sun?" Domnu inquired. Japhet's eyes remained fixed on the disk, a fascinating sight. Its size and apparent distance revealed more of the land's vastness. Though this world was chaotic, and absent of the magic Japhet was accustomed to, its size was staggering.

"It is not the sun," Mort said. "It's the moon, and it will rise and make more light for us."

Japhet returned his attention to the little demon, who was standing casually off to the side. Indeed, the moon was already making it easier to see. The demon was a small creature, with thin arms and legs. Dark and green of skin, and bearing a close resemblance to the gargoyles of Underhill, Mort had the long, pointed ears of elves. Perhaps this was why he chose this particular form, if choice were involved. He wore no armor, as he did not fight, instead assuming the court dress of a high ranking servant.

"The moon is not as bright as the sun," Mort continued, sounding confident, knowledgeable. He folded his arms with the ease and grace of an insect folding its wings, cupping his elbows in either palm. "The sun's arrival will be slow enough. It won't blind us."

"You've been to the humans' world before," Nargach observed.

"Once or twice," Mort said, casting a sly, knowing look toward Japhet, then looking away. "The humans can be . . . great sport, as it were."

"What he means to say," Japhet interjected, "is that

the humans are easily manipulated. I learned as much from my father."

Mort looked ready to reply, when something else distracted him.

Two beams of light appeared at the far end of the black path, grew in size, and started growling like an animal.

"It's only a car," Mort said, moving to Japhet's side. "Probably some pathetic *young* humans, by the sound of their carriage and the hour of the evening. Carousing." The demon sniffed at the air as the car came closer, slowing as it seemed to find the end of the path. "Hmmm, and a very nice carriage, at that," Mort exclaimed as the car passed them and came to a stop. "A *Camaro* unless I'm mistaken."

Japhet saw his men dampening their steeds' fear with spells of calming, and did the same to his own mount as this strange carriage pulled to a stop, belching foul-smelling smoke.

"This might be fun," Mort said. "Allow me to indulge myself, Sire?"

Japhet cautiously nodded his permission.

A door on one side of the Camaro swung open. A light from within revealed a young male human in black leather. The youth leaned out and began retching his guts out on the pavement. Mort was careful to stay clear of what the human had been drinking that night; it made a sizable puddle.

"My my *my*, what a *mess*," Mort said amiably as he walked over and stood on the *other* side of the open door, leaned his elbows on it and peered down with a feral, gargoyle expression. Japhet noted with amusement that his minion had made his eyes fiery red. "Tsk tsk. You boys haven't been drinking the devil's brew this evening, have you?"

Indeed, there were two inside. The other didn't seem

to be that coherent, but then again neither did the first, who appeared to be the one driving the vehicle. He stared at Mort, unblinking, uncomprehending.

"What the *hell*?" the boy mumbled, apparently recovering from his illness.

"What the fuck *is* that?" said the other, stirring a bit on his side, leaning over to get a better look at Mort. He looked like he regretted the move.

Mort, however, appeared to be enjoying himself. If the two humans saw the other elves in the darkness, they made no comment on them; transfixed by the demon, they looked completely confused. They were not yet afraid.

Mort meant to change that.

"You ever hear of Satan?" Mort asked jovially, breaking into a low rumble of laughter. Flame appeared in a halo around his head, and two long horns grew suddenly from the demon's forehead. Behind him, flicking back and forth was a long forked tail Mort had summoned. The illusion was convincing, and Japhet had to admit admiration for the demon's ability to invoke illusions. And this was clearly the proper illusion for the "fun" he'd had in mind. The humans were terrified.

"I don't know, maaan," one of the humans said. "I'm freakin' out, man. It's the Underwood Deviled Ham dude or something. What was *in* that joint, anyway?"

"That's not the Underwood dude," the driver said, pulling his door shut. The halo of flame turned to burning snakes, writhing toward the driver's face. "That's Satan! That's the devil! Our shit's gone, man!"

Amid the brouhaha Japhet sensed a black power from these humans, a force associated with their fear. *The same force my father harnessed!* he realized gleefully, remembering the system of energy transmission Zeldan and Morrigan had set up. *Fear, terror. The very force the Unseleighe thrive on.* Using a drug synthesized by

Morrigan, Zeldan had induced horrible images for the unwitting humans, tapping the resultant power for his own use, and trading the rest to Morrigan for more of the drug. *Mort's raising the same power with his antics, or very nearly so. . . . But does he really know what he's doing, short of scaring the life out of some human kids?*

"Rise! And be healed! And *feeel* the presence of God!" Mort's halo became less fiery, and the court dress shifted to black, with a thick, white collar around his neck. But the horns and gargoyle face remained intact. "I shall cast the demons from your soul!" Mort continued, walking after the Camaro as it sped away in a shower of gravel. It moved away from them at such speed that Japhet thought they might have an elvensteed; but no, this was just human technology, which had its limits.

Mort was clearly pleased with himself, laughing heartily at the results of his work. They both stared after the twin red dots, until they were gone.

"I'd almost forgot what fun humans can be," Mort said. "It has been so long. *Far* too long."

Japhet's thoughts were on other things. "Tell me, Mort. What is this *Satan* that invokes such terror?"

"Just one of their myths," Mort said casually, but already he was considering ways *Satan* might aid them. "Many things scare these primitives. Many, *many* things."

Mort was pleased to see this fear of Satan had remained intact over the centuries; but the demon knew this was only one of many methods with which he might harvest terror, the nectar of the Unseleighe.

The fear is the same, Mort thought as he watched the Camaro's taillights fade from view. *Hallelujah!*

"We must see where we are," Japhet announced, sounding as if he were simply trying to assert his authority. Mort knew Japhet probably felt lost in this place. Even so, the demon knew it would be a challenge to stay ahead of the elves, in spite of his head start in assimilating the human's strange world.

Japhet remounted and led the rest down the road. The uneasiness seemed to have left the Unseleighe, Mort sensed. Riding behind Japhet was something they were accustomed to doing, and they fell into its familiarity.

Mort walked alongside, easily keeping up, as he was not truly walking; as a demon he was more spirit than matter, and ghosted alongside them as a matter of respect, staying a few paces behind Japhet's 'steed.

They must think I am still their pawn, the demon thought giddily, sending his thoughts ahead, to see what might await them. Reaching through this atmosphere was like wading through a churning river, with currents and eddies shooting off in all directions. The magic here was powerful, but disorganized, no surprise given the lack of magical abilities of most humans. In a place like Underhill, where most of its inhabitants wielded magical power to some degree, the force was carefully parceled out and guarded in natural and manufactured pools the elves called nodes. Here the power was wild and untapped and, alas, mostly useless, at least for their party. The white noise of the free-flowing power drowned out whatever vibrations natural nodes might have emitted here.

The Seleighe would thrive on this sort of power, Mort thought forlornly. *No wonder they have developed a liking for these useless humans, and their primitive world!*

Once his mental probe cut through the noise of raw magic, Mort fixed on one location, a place where many humans had gathered. From this distance it appeared only as a flickering neon light accompanied by faint music of unknown type, but Mort knew there was amusement to be had here. It was a place called a bar, and inside there were many drunken humans. No doubt this was where their welcoming party in the Camaro had originated. Had they returned, and warned the others? Somehow Mort believed such an account would be met with ridicule.

"Sire," Semion ventured. "Tavern ahead."

"I can see that, you fool," Japhet hissed. The music was louder now, and the demon made out the distinctive pounding of rock 'n' roll.

"But our appearance . . ." said Domnu.

"It matters not what we look like to these vermin," Japhet spat. "When needed, we can change our appearance."

If we know what to change our appearance to, Mort thought, not knowing where and when they had arrived. The brief glance at the Camaro and its occupants gave important clues, along with the bar's music, but it was not enough to fabricate convincing disguises for them all, if it came to that.

Once they drew closer to the bar, Mort made out the vague outlines of something in the dark, just outside the building. Too small to be automobiles. The Camaro was nowhere in sight.

"What manner of beast . . ." Japhet began, as he took in the strange sight before them.

A row of about twenty of the vehicles, lined up as if they were 'steeds, stood at the edge of a gravel parking lot. A variety of smells came from the beasts: gasoline, motor oil, warm and burning rubber, a lingering human sweat. It was a strong smell, but not one that would come from anything living.

"They call them *motorcycles*," Mort informed Japhet, who got down from his 'steed and walked over for a closer look.

Mort knew the make of bike would lend important clues to the rider, and whether or not they should be worried about the occupants of this bar. He scanned the line of bikes briefly, noting the elements they had in common: High handlebars, low seats, bars to lean back against, foot rests. Some looked new, some looked ancient, with everything from spoked to cast wheels, fat tires, flat tires, thin tires. Some looked to be pieced together from several different bikes, the pieces not quite fitting perfectly, but enough to make the thing go. But most of them were Harley Davidson motorbikes, or tried to be. Then Mort had an idea.

A sound from behind them distracted his planning, at least for the moment. A low drone at first, the sound bloomed into the full blown roar of a Harley Hog, a loud, rude two cylinder steed, *blam blam blamming* in the dark. Its headlight pinned them as it turned toward them.

"Easy, now," Japhet muttered to his men, who had all reached for, but hadn't yet drawn, their weapons. "Let's see what this human has to say. *Then* we shall do as we please."

Mort watched Japhet and Nargach's reaction to the newcomer; they weren't as confused as most Unseleighe would have been when confronted with human technology. The mage's probes reached forward, thin yellow wisps invisible to humans, and studied the motorcycle and its rider in intimate detail. It was the sort of scrutiny necessary for *kenning,* or recreating objects magically from some sort of original. It looked as if Nargach were preparing to ken a motorcycle, a singularly surprising notion given the technophobic reaction most Unseleighes had to any and all man-made machines. The bike rolled to a stop several paces away. Headlight and engine ceased together, and its human rider dismounted.

"So what are you assholes doing around those bikes?" the rider shouted. He was big, even by human standards, and wore leather from head to toe. Steel studs in the jacket twinkled in the light of the neon, as did the blade he held in his right hand. As he took in the horses, his brisk stride slowed. He didn't look like he knew quite what he was getting into.

Nargach continued to study the human, his energies swirling around the biker like a whirlpool, taking special note of the cold iron knife he wielded, along with the full face of hair that made him look vaguely doglike. Even the man's scent did not escape scrutiny. Mort was impressed with the mage's thoroughness. *He's better at this than I thought*.

"Who the hell are you guys?" the biker said, now suspicious. "SCA or some shit?"

Japhet didn't reply. Instead he nodded subtly toward the rest, the signal to prepare for battle. Semion and Domnu drew their swords, long polished bronze weapons that reflected the neon light. Rochad remained mounted, and nocked an arrow in his bow. Nargach also remained on his 'steed. If the mage were preparing any magical defense Mort didn't sense it. The biker saw the bow, the arrow and the swords, and stepped back a pace, his knife hand falling to his side.

Three men came out of the bar, walking unsteadily, one taking an occasional swig from a large brown bottle.

"Hey, Rat," the first biker said. "These guys are messin' with the bikes. *Your* bike. Ain't that softail yours?"

Rat was a round man, bigger than the first biker. He did not look pleased. He smashed the bottle against the side of the building and took a step toward Japhet.

Mort stood nearby, keeping an ear turned to the bar. He wondered what kind of fight this would be. A straightforward, physical fight had its advantages, since only the elves had swords. But the biker's blade was made of cold iron, and even a nick from such a weapon might be fatal.

The breaking glass must have been a signal. Seven or eight more bikers came out of the bar, in varying degrees of intoxication, most of them wielding cold iron of one sort or another.

Now what, Japhet? Mort thought, not liking the odds.

But the leader seemed unperturbed. He looked back at Nargach and said, "Our presence has been graced by new friends. Alas, the light from this dim lamp is not enough to see by. Nargach, I think we should shed more light on this area." His voice lowered, "*Much* more light."

A grin spread across Mort's face. The demon knew what was coming, and could not resist: a good simulacrum of mirrored Ray Bans blipped into place over his face.

"Of course, Sire," Nargach said regally, before he dismounted. Ignoring the crowd of pissed humans assembled before him, the mage stepped forward, holding his hand out, palm up. A sphere of light the size of a clenched fist appeared, floating just over it. It had a brassy, yellowish hue, but was bright enough to cast shadows. Murmurs of alarm rippled among the humans. Mort tried not to giggle.

"What the hail is that thang?" someone said. The sphere had everyone entranced.

"Look deep into it," Nargach said, in his deep, magical voice. "You will see treasures beyond your wildest imaginings. . . . Just look, look into the light. . . ."

And indeed, it appeared everyone was doing just that.

The next second the sphere exploded silently, its yellow igniting to a white hot light that swept the entire parking lot, and a good deal of the territory beyond. It was a tool Japhet used when dealing with lesser creatures of Underhill. The light blinded the humans instantly, scorching their corneas like a branding iron. Some screamed and stepped back, holding their hands to their face.

"Wha'd you do!" one of them screamed helplessly. "I can't see, I can't—"

"Well done, Sire," Mort said, careful to compliment Japhet as well as their mage. "I might suggest a hasty retreat, however. That bright light will not go unnoticed in this city."

"Indeed," Japhet said, glancing about him. His eyes settled on the mage. "Nargach, I have a plan."

One of the bikers stumbled against one of the Harleys, knocking it over. A chain reaction sent three to the ground, and the other bikers moved around a little more urgently now, their hands in front of them, feeling for obstructions they could no longer see.

Japhet and Nargach conferred privately, but Mort had an idea of what they talked about. To blend with the humans it might be a good idea to masquerade as outsiders, violent ones at that, so as to discourage humans from contacting them. Zeldan had done a similar thing among the street people, living among them with their shopping carts and aluminum cans, before putting together his final plan.

At any rate, they didn't have much time to decide. And as the first humans for the mages to have a clear impression of, they would have to do.

The transformation required a great deal of power, more than the two mages were capable of producing at that moment, so the other elves and Mort contributed to raising the magic. It seemed to take a dreadfully long time to the demon, but soon they tapped wild energy feeds lurking in the area, in the desert, in the mountains beyond. They were brief fountains of nodal energy which ran dry as soon as they were accessed, but it was enough, just enough, to accomplish their task.

The 'steeds took well to being motorbikes, images of the ones they saw around them; Mort knew they would have to make changes in their final appearance later, lest they be misidentified by one of these goons as their *own* bike. Mort grinned wryly at the prospect of one of these humans mounting one of their elvensteeds, and trying to kick start it. Japhet's 'steed became a later model Fat Boy Harley, with chrome wheels and a sidecar. The other 'steeds became other patched-together jobs; a

Yamaha with a variety of different parts, a Harley, another Harley.

The nameless substance that mimicked steel in the motorcycles was inert and harmless to Elves; on command, the new bikes even flashed headlights, and sounded like motorbikes. On closer inspection, however, Mort discovered that each had the same sound; the roar of the bike that first approached them. It was the one and only sound of a motorcycle the mages had ever heard. The issue would have to be addressed later. A rice burner sounding like a hog would not go unnoticed and unquestioned in this world.

The transformation of 'steed to bike required the most power, and by the time they got around to their own appearance their pool was nearly depleted. The glamories Nargach implemented did little more than smooth out the rough edges; the elves looked less elvish, their ears became rounded, a little more human looking. Their attire was the easiest to change, as the former livery and court dress became the raw material for the ragged jeans, leather and denim jackets, the black boots. Mort didn't bother to mention helmets, since not a one was in sight. This crowd didn't seem to find them necessary.

Most of the bikers had wandered off, some still screaming, some looking, apparently, for the bar. No newcomers had arrived on the scene, but Mort knew that wouldn't be the case for long.

"We should go now," Japhet said, pointing away from the city lights, to the expanse of moonlit desert. "Out there, somewhere. Away from the city."

Mort hopped into the sidecar. As a unit, they eased onto the road and took off as a pack, five different bikes having the same, ringing roar.

Chapter Six

Wolf came awake with a start, reaching for the Beretta that wasn't there.

There are Iraqis out there in the desert, and they're coming, he thought as he struggled to get up. But something *else* was wrong: this was not a sleeping bag, and he was inside somewhere, away from the desert sun. He didn't taste or feel sand grit anywhere. Still looking for his gun, he rolled over on his side, but nothing was there to hold him up. His fall to the floor was brief but painful, and sent a shooting pain through his still-healing ankle. His panic ebbed and he focused on his surroundings.

Dangling from the ceiling was a Chaniwa dream catcher, a five-pointed pentagram in its center, woven of wool and sinew, rocking gently in the breeze that wheezed through the trailer's postage stamp windows. He groaned, realizing he was thousands of miles and six months removed from Desert Storm. Wolf gazed at the dream catcher, remembering the dream, the Iraqi Guard.

Thought you were supposed to bring good dreams! he thought, now aware of a pain in his back. As he lay on the floor of Grampa's tiny trailer, he knew this was the only spot on the floor long enough for him to stretch out. The trailer wasn't a mobile home, it was a temporary, weekend shelter for hunters, campers and fishermen, and was never meant to be a permanent residence for anyone.

From the trailer's only other room, Wolf heard his grandfather, Fast Horse, cackling softly to himself. No doubt the old Indian had heard Wolf's noisy waking, again. He had heard the dry laugh nearly every morning since his return from the war, a response to some amusing way Wolf had decided to greet the day. Fast Horse had wisely moved the double barreled shotgun from its place on the wall to his bedroom, lest Wolf's vivid dreams prompt him to take up arms. Somewhere in there was also a Ruger Security Six, though he was uncertain where; which was probably a good thing, given the nature of his dreams.

As he stood to his full height his head knocked the edge of the dreamcatcher. Then he remembered *her*. He took two steps to the kitchen, which was a sink, two propane burners and a counter, and smiled.

The dreamcatcher worked after all. The dream opened up in his mind like a flower, and within the petals he saw the girl who had been haunting his sleep. It was as if setting foot in New Mexico had bespelled Wolf with this vision, a consistently beautiful and unexplainable vision, of the most beautiful female he had ever seen or imagined.

He spooned three scoops of coffee into the open maw of the paper filter, yawned, and added another scoop. The drip coffee maker, fondly referred to as the "Mr. Wake the Hell Up," was amber with use, the color of whiskey. He filled the glass pot with tepid water. The pleated, environmentally incorrect bleached filter looked like an open moonflower, reminding him of the girl.

Even though she stirred him up and made his stomach flutter, she was not human. She was *chi-en*, of the Chaniwa mythos, human in all aspects except for her long pointed ears and slitted cat's eyes. Her alien appearance made her all the more inviting, with long blond hair and blue eyes that could bore holes in steel. The *chi-en* were said to be the distant relatives of the Chaniwa tribe, but this was all fable, bedtime stories which Grampa kept alive.

Once the coffee was started, Wolf turned to a pack of Marlboros on the floor next to the door. It was a morning ritual, fall out of bed, hide from Iraqis, make coffee, sit on the front step with the oval door propped open with a cinder block and have his first cigarette. After putting on a well ventilated pair of cutoff jeans he sat on the step and looked out over their tract of desert, the dusty dirt road winding toward Highway 60, about a quarter mile away. A match flared to life. In the distance were the Manzano mountains, and beyond them the Sandia mountains, which shadowed Albuquerque. This was not quite the desert Iraq was, as there were things growing on the hills, and rain occasionally fell here. In Iraq there were dunes, rolling, shifting, turning layers of hot dry sand, no rocks, no brush, no trees. Here you had scrub, pinyon, and one-seed juniper, clumps of small green Christmas trees. The juniper dotted the land thoroughly and consistently with splotches of green. It was a dry, mostly dormant land clinging to life, awaiting the brief but often torrential downpour of the winter rains.

A single strand of electrical wire traveled the horizon on leaning power poles, detouring to an ancient meter affixed to the trailer's far side. Out here there were no neighbors, not even other buildings, just wind and sand and lots of sun. Just the trailer, a flimsy shack for storage, and the fragile umbilical cord that gave them power. The equally ancient water tap on the line that ran to Mountainaire, several miles down the road, was a blessing.

Water and electricity. The staff of life. No telephone, no cable, no hassle.

The coffee pot blurted loudly one last time, announcing the end of the brew cycle. He drew on his cigarette and regarded the isolated landscape, realizing when he glanced at his watch that he had been here six months, to the day.

I'm getting restless, Wolf thought, remembering the first few weeks here with Grampa. It was as if his life had come to a screeching halt after the war; once the army discharged him, with honors, he didn't really know what to do. His parents had died when he was young, and he was independent and unrestrained at an early age. He had known he had a grandfather somewhere in New Mexico, but he hadn't known where, or if he was even still alive. Running with the biker gang in Texas had taken up most of three years, starting when he was fourteen and ending when he was busted for marijuana. But the judge knew who he was, who he was running with, and what he would become if drastic measures weren't taken. Those drastic measures turned out to be enlistment in the Army, at a time when Kuwait was furthest from President Bush's mind.

During boot camp he watched with growing alarm as Iraq brazenly invaded its tiny but oil-rich neighbor, claiming it for its own. He knew, then, that the Army would be more than a job, that he might even see battle. Certain commanding officers came to talk to him shortly after boot camp, officers involved with the Rangers. Was he interested?

He was, and within a week he was on his way to his new assignment, a special kind of boot camp in a place that had no name. In two months he was on a plane, bound for Italy, where he would be based. His commanding officer had made no secret of the fact that they were all hand picked, and groomed specifically for missions in and around

Baghdad. At their last stop in Turkey, they boarded Blackhawk helicopters and took off, destined to be dropped in Iraq by parachute, in squads of five. Wolf had done three such drops before the one in which his psychic powers came rampaging to the surface. The experience still had him spooked, even though he had been unable to invoke the powers a second time. On the following mission, while they were drifting on chutes, a squad of Iraqi snipers opened fire on them. To avoid being hit he dropped in faster than was safe, and broke an ankle when he landed. The mission was a washout, but when they evacuated he had a distinct feeling this was the last time he would see Iraq.

From a hospital bed in Germany, Wolf watched the UN forces invade Iraq and Kuwait. This was the real battle, the one that mattered, the one that everyone knew about. In two days, it was over. Saddam Hussein was still in power, but that didn't matter much; Wolf was tired of playing soldier boy, and he was going home.

He had located his Grandfather's address in some old papers that had belonged to his mother. During boot camp Wolf had sent a letter to Grandfather, and even though he had never written back the old man was waiting for him at the airport. In the following weeks Wolf spilled out the story of his experiences, including the incident of the healing power. Fast Horse nodded in understanding. He knew about battle, having served in the Pacific during the Second World War. As Wolf told his tale, he realized why he had wanted to come here to live with his grandfather. He had to know what these powers were, if they were real or some sort of hallucination.

Grampa understood because he was a shaman, the last Chaniwa medicine man, and he knew how to reach the spirits. For the first time in his life Wolf took the powers seriously. Fast Horse assured him that the powers were real, and a vital part of him. The power ran in their family, and existed in his grandfather, and in his grandfather's father and grandfather before that. But his were undeveloped, Fast Horse admonished. Wolf was the only Chaniwa with the gift who had undergone no training whatsoever.

So Wolf agreed to stay with him, and learn the ways of the shaman and of the Chaniwa. Wolf plunged headlong into the training, into the fasting, the hours of meditation, the songs, the dances. Fast Horse made him build his own sweat lodge, which he had done by digging a pit and covering it with a dome of branches and canvas scraps.

Then after a physical exam at the Veteran's Hospital in Albuquerque, Wolf learned he had brought back a little gift from the Gulf.

Some soldiers who had fought in Desert Storm— including a large number who had, like himself, fought behind enemy lines beforehand—were coming down with an unknown illness, tentatively dubbed the Gulf War Sickness. Wolf reported a numbness in his hands when waking, which had only gotten worse as the days went by. It was a progressive and sometimes fatal illness, something the doctors knew nothing about, except that it affected the central nervous system. Army Intelligence had speculated that it was a nerve agent released by the Iraqi army, as it was also well known they had used bacterial and chemical weapons during the war. But what precisely had been released, and where, and who it had affected, was still "under investigation." Wolf knew enough to read between the lines. Likely, they would never know what this was.

The news landed on him like a ton of bricks. *To survive the Gulf, and be nailed by this . . . something you cannot even see.* For a time the condition improved, and now he hardly ever felt any numbness when he woke. The doctor had suggested he try an unproven treatment, a course in coenzyme Q_{10}. Either this or the healing herbs Grandfather had given him was having some effect, or the disease had gone into remission on its own. The doctors at the VA didn't know what to tell him, except that he might have a milder form of the disease. Only time would let them know one way or another. Keep using the Q_{10}, they'd said.

That was some weeks ago, and his training had gone on as before. Only now he didn't feel the same urgency he did when he began, and he often found himself questioning the importance of his shamanistic learning. If Fast Horse noticed, he didn't say.

Before they turned in the night before, Grandfather had dropped some strong hints that today's training would be important. Wolf suspected he was only responding to his apparent ambivalence toward the Chaniwa way of life. If so, he was right, he was questioning the whole thing. Especially in view of the fact that his life might be cut short in the next few years by a disease that didn't even have a name.

He poured his first cup, and a second for Grampa, who had emerged from his tiny bedroom. He was a thin, old man, but far from frail, wearing a thin *konsainta*, a garment resembling a nightshirt. He had about ten or twelve of them, one of them a ritual robe that was over a hundred years old. This was also part of the ritual; Grampa didn't get up until his cup was poured. Coffee was the only white man vice he permitted himself.

"*Po-kwa-te*," Grampa said in Chaniwa. It was not a "good morning" but a generic greeting used on waking, whenever that happened to be. "Sleep well?" Grampa added with a smirk.

"Could have been better," Wolf replied, pushing the bed up, making it a couch again. "Same dreams, same girl."

"Mmmm," Grampa said, taking a sip of the brew. The

old man preferred it stronger than this, but they were running low on coffee. They took chairs at what passed for a small kitchen table, their place to drink coffee, talk, and wake up.

Fast Horse was probably around seventy-five years old, but no one really knew for sure. He had the hard brown, leathery skin of someone who lived in the sun; Wolf had become considerably darker himself, having sat in the sun for hours in meditation, several times during the week. Horse knew the Chaniwa language fluently, and was teaching it piecemeal as the studies progressed. The old man had long, white hair, double braided down both sides, and when he smiled his whole face contorted in a riot of creases and wrinkles, each one a tiny smile.

"Morning energies," Horse said, and Wolf was surprised he had them already. Perhaps he had been lying awake for some time already. "Your ailment. Let me see."

Wolf presented his hands, palms up, on the kitchen table. "They're fine this morning," he said. "No numbness."

Horse wasn't paying any attention to what he was saying. His eyes were closed as he took his wrists in his old, callused fingers. This was a part of the training that hadn't yet been covered, the healing with the use of earth energies. Wolf had often wondered if this, instead of the herbs, was responsible for his recovery. Relaxing his hands into his grandfather's, he thought of them as being apart from himself, giving them over completely, surrendering his ownership of his hands to the medicine man.

He felt a sudden heat, as if he'd stuck them over a stove, and when Grampa turned them loose the backs itched.

"Well?" Wolf asked, scratching them.

"You play with yourself too much," the old man said. "You need to find you a woman. Get married."

Wolf blushed, but knew better than to argue. "Tell me about it!" he said, flicking his ash angrily into a mangled pop can. "I dream of the perfect one every night, but she's only a dream."

"Why only a dream?"

"She's *chi-en*. I'll never meet her." He looked away, knowing his grandfather was scrutinizing him.

"Why never? The *chi-en* were our ancestors."

"Yeah, right," Wolf said. "We're descended from elves."

Fast Horse laughed loudly and heartily, his usual response whenever Wolf distrusted the legends. "So much you don't know, Wolf."

He drank his coffee in response. "What are we going to do today?" he asked, feeling the urge to get up and do *something*. The caffeine was doing its job nicely this morning. "I'm thinking about taking the Harley into town. We're low on coffee."

"You can take the truck," Grampa said, but Wolf knew he was baiting him. He knew how he felt about the bike, how he sought every opportunity to ride it, in spite of their lack of funds to buy gasoline. Wolf received a small sum from the VA but it wasn't much. They usually waited until they had a long list of things to purchase, making the bike impractical. If he went now, while the list consisted only of a can of coffee, he had a chance of getting out of there on two wheels.

"Are you ever going to get that old Indian motorcycle working?" Wolf asked, knowing that parts for the thing were probably next to impossible to find. It was a classic '46 Chief, but had fallen into disrepair. The rubber on the tires was old and cracked, and something was wrong with the electrical system. When Wolf drained the gas he found a lot of water in it, a bad sign for the bike. Under the dust, the old red Indian was beautiful.

But Wolf's mechanical time had been spent on his own Harley, which ran fine, even if it did leak oil. *Marking its territory*, he'd told Grampa. *All Harleys leak*. The Indian had never leaked.

"Well, then let me give you this," the old man said, pulling a scrap of paper out of nowhere. "There are some other things we could use as well."

Wolf took the list, biting back anger. There was no way he could get all this stuff back on the bike. *This shouldn't surprise me. This really shouldn't.* He was still going to go riding today. Suddenly he was anxious and restless, more so than he had been in a long time. *Living with Grampa in a tiny little trailer in the middle of the desert for six months would have that effect on anyone,* he reasoned.

"Maybe later on," Wolf said. Whatever was planned for "class" today, he wished it would go ahead and be over with. As hot as it promised to be, he didn't much look forward to another day meditating in the sun. The thought had even occurred to him to refuse, and he seldom entertained such rebellious thinking.

If Grampa sensed his impatience, he didn't indicate it overtly. But then, everything about Grampa was subtle, particularly when it came to shaman training. Grampa put a sheathed knife on the table, a hunting blade that was around a hundred years old, with a bone handle and a pitted, irregular surface. The blade always remained razor sharp, though Wolf had never seen him sharpen it. From under the table he produced a chunk of gnarled pinyon the size of a large orange, and began carving away.

"What are we going to do today?" Wolf asked.

Grampa didn't answer right away, but Wolf knew he was just taking his time. The old man knew when he woke what they would be doing, and likely had planned it the previous night.

"Today I tell you about your powers," the old man said. "The ones you saw when you were fighting in the desert, over in Africa."

"Iraq," Wolf corrected, knowing that it wouldn't make

any difference to him. Anything overseas was more or less jumbled into the same geographic lump. Such details weren't all that relevant, as his ears had pricked at the mention of *his powers*. He had waited months for his mentor to tell him about them. The incident in Iraq had more or less been the reason for the training. Fast Horse had refused to tell him anything about them, as he "wasn't yet ready," and Wolf had accepted this explanation respectfully. But that was six months ago. He was ready to know, now. Today.

"The Chaniwa have had many enemies, some physical, some of spirit. Our physical enemies have already conquered us. We are a conquered people, but we are a proud people. Our lands have been taken, and we can no longer fight the white devils and the other tribes, but our souls are still free."

With his bare arm, Grampa swept a layer of wood shavings from the table and resumed whittling. The shape was too vague to tell much about what he was carving. Perhaps it was a turtle, or a bear; he had often carved fetishes from wood, as it was easier to work with his arthritic hands than stone.

"Before there were Chaniwa, there were the wandering tribes who hunted the buffalo and followed them with the seasons. One season, a small group split off and went south, following the trail of a small herd. Their medicine man told them they should go south, that their destiny was with this small herd of buffalo. He was a powerful medicine man, and much respected. But the other tribes thought them foolish, and returned north.

"They followed the buffalo to a large river, so vast they first thought it was a lake. The hunt was plentiful, and they spent many days drying the skins and the meat. There was a long rest, but they grew anxious in the heat. They yearned for home. Even the women complained."

This was not entirely new information for Wolf, who

had been told the history of the Chaniwa already. He sensed that this time the history would include more of the secrets Grampa had been holding back all this time.

Grampa continued, "Then they saw the canoe with wings, pushing up the great river, against the flow. They thought these creatures were gods, as strange as they looked."

Wolf ventured a question. "Is this canoe with wings the sailing ship you talked about?"

"That is the one. It was a ship, but still looked more like a canoe. It's on the coin. Now, I will show you the coin."

Wolf watched, fascinated, as Grampa unwound a strip of leather at the knife's handle. He had heard of the coin before, some ancient artifact that had been passed down, but he didn't know what it looked like, or where he kept it. Until now.

In the exposed bone handle was a slot, out of which fell a small, metal circle, a little larger than a quarter. "It is not currency," Grampa explained. "It is a written record, passed down. There is magic connected to the coin, that is why I keep it hidden."

Wolf knew it would be futile to ask for a date, or even a number of years. He examined the relic, on which was the unmistakable rendering of a Viking ship. On the other side was a design of the four directions, the elemental points of the Chaniwa religion. Finding a blending of European and Native American cultures on such an ancient piece was spooky, particularly when that culture was one's own.

"The wandering tribe followed this ship as it took a branch of a smaller river, which flowed less swiftly, keeping a respectful distance. The medicine man remained silent when asked about these gods. He either didn't know, or was not allowed to speak of them. The tribe knew something important was about to happen.

They should follow the gods to see where they led them.

"Weeks passed as they made their slow progress up the river. The tribe observed things about them that questioned their position as gods. They argued among themselves, in a language no one understood. On some days they tried travel and gave up, because of rain, or because there was no wind. The tribe learned the wings were only big skins, and the wind was blowing them upstream. If they were gods, why didn't they control the rain and the wind? And why did they argue among themselves? Such things were considered weaknesses when it happened among the tribes. And most suspiciously, if they were gods, why didn't they know they were being followed?"

Wolf fought back an urge to yawn, and got up for another cup of joe. He refilled Grampa's cup, who took a long drink before he continued.

"Then the elders realized they had wasted valuable time following these strangers. They should have been traveling north, to catch up with the buffalo herds. They were already far south, and the course they had taken had led them into areas they had never been before. They saw mountains to the north. For a tribe that depended on the buffalo, they were in quite a bind, and the leaders didn't know what to do.

"They blamed the medicine man for failing them, but he told them they had made the decision to follow the strangers, not he. The tribe began to split. One wanted to return to their familiar path to the east, and another wanted to strike out across the mountains. Either way there would be famine, if they didn't adapt their hunting skills for game smaller than the buffalo.

"On the day there was to be a confrontation between the two groups, something amazing happened among the strangers and their winged canoe.

"A scout came running into camp, telling of a division

among the strangers. It appeared some of the strangers had killed the others, and had destroyed the canoe, sending it burning down the river. There was something strange about the victors. Perhaps they were gods, or children of gods, after all.

"The 'Go East' faction wanted nothing of this, and set off before they wasted any more time. The 'Go Over the Mountains' group wanted to approach the strangers, to see if they were gods, and then maybe see if they could aid the tribe in their journey over the mountains.

"This made sense to the medicine man, who wanted to see the strangers himself. They set off to talk to the gods."

A gust of wind swept in off the desert, shaking the tiny trailer and pushing a bit of cool wind through it, reminding Wolf how hot it had been lately. *I could sit in here all day listening to Grampa talk. Even if he never gets around to explaining how I fixed an assault rifle by looking at it.*

"The first god they encountered was a *chi-en*, but right away the medicine man sensed evil in this one. The tribe blocked his passage in a narrow valley and drew weapons because he looked evil and wicked. Speaking to the wind, he said his name was Nargat, and demanded he be allowed to pass, making the mistake of being discourteous to the medicine man, angering the warriors. But they permitted Nargat passage at the medicine man's urging. This one was trouble."

Speaking to the wind was a form of telepathy. This was something he had wanted to know about right away, but again, Fast Horse had told him he wasn't ready.

Grampa continued, "Soon they saw that others pursued this Nargat. They observed the chase from a respectable distance, as three *chi-en* and a white woman hunted him. In a valley they watched a fire of strange colors appear, and into this Nargat ran. Then the fire disappeared, and there was nothing left of the evil one, not even ashes. The others gave up their chase and set up camp with what little they had. No teepees, not even skins, at least not the kind this tribe was accustomed to seeing.

"Again, the tribe was having second thoughts about the strangers. Perhaps they were gods after all. The medicine man went to speak to the three *chi-en* and the white woman alone. Right away he knew these people were good, and they welcomed him and the tribe to their camp.

"At first they spoke with the wind to be heard, then before long the strangers knew enough *Akaniwa* to be able to speak without the wind. The Indians never did learn much of their language, except for a few words like *wikka*, which meant medicine.

"They spoke all night, learning about each other, until the sun rose the next day. There were two women *chi-en* and one man *chi-en*, a brave who was younger than you, Wolf. He was the son of one of the women, but the women were young and beautiful, with long blond hair and blue eyes. They had pointed ears which made them look wise. There was a human woman among them, the white woman, who was also young and beautiful, with red hair and pale skin. She was a medicine woman too, and it was from her that we received the Hand of the Chaniwa, as it was a symbol of her medicine, *wikka*."

Fast Horse pointed to the "Hand," the five-pointed star woven into the dreamcatcher. Wolf wondered if there was some influence of the old Celtic religions, but didn't see how this could happen. A ship sailing from Europe to the New World, down its eastern coast and around the Gulf of Mexico, and entering the mighty Mississippi river, then branching off on probably the Arkansas river, was a little farfetched. But the Vikings had been known as explorers, he remembered reading once. And the Chaniwa had a different past, and a different gene pool, from the rest of the North American tribes. European blood introduced to the tribe nine hundred years ago would explain the differences in their appearance, as well as certain points of their religion, but again there was no solid evidence to point to, just the long tales passed down through the ages.

There I go again, Wolf thought as Grampa rambled on. *Thinking like a white man. Maybe there is something to what Grampa is saying, even if it's not written down in black and white.*

"The three *chi-en* and the human had been Nargat's slaves. They came from across a great ocean, from a place called *Islen.* Nargat was a wealthy landowner who wanted to start his own kingdom in the New World, but his armada of ten ships encountered a violent storm, and he lost all but the one ship. They were blown off course and discovered a warm land. Since they had lost their provisions, Nargat decided to explore. They followed the coast all the way to the rivers. Once they were inland, the slaves were able to tap the natural reserves of power on the land itself, and secretly build it until the right moment, when they unleashed it and broke their magical bindings. They rebelled while their masters slept, set the ship ablaze and cast it adrift down the river. Burning the ship was necessary to complete the breaking of Nargat's spell over them. Nargat escaped, however.

"The medicine man asked about the fire Nargat had disappeared into. That was a doorway to the spirit world, they told him. And only the most powerful of their medicine men could construct such a thing. Nargat had escaped, but it was unlikely he would come back. His plans were a failure.

" 'And what of you?' the tribe asked. 'What is to become of you?'

"They told the tribe they were far from their homeland, and had no way of returning. They had nowhere to go, and knew nothing of this lush, wild land. So the tribe struck a deal with the *chi-en* and the white medicine woman, to share their knowledge, and help each other to survive. They became part of the tribe, and from that time on the tribe was known as the *Akaniwa*, which means 'three peoples.' The white, the *chi-en*, and the rest of the tribe. All looked different. All became the same tribe. *Akaniwa* became *Chaniwa*, but it all means the same thing."

Wolf squirmed in his seat as he fished another cigarette out of the pack. "So what about the buffalo? Did they go back to their old lands?"

"No, the Chaniwa never did return to their buffalo herds. In their new land they found abundant game, deer, birds, wild turkeys. The *chi-en* taught them how to build houses out of logs, and established a community near where Nargat had been defeated. The women married with braves in the tribe, and the son took a wife. Those are our ancestors. That is how the Chaniwa began."

Yes, but what does this have to do with seeing through concrete?

By now the heat was becoming oppressive, working its way into the trailer gradually. Granted, drinking hot coffee didn't help matters; Wolf knew he would soon need to start consuming the water they kept in the refrigerator to keep from getting dehydrated. Sweat had beaded on his forehead, and he wiped it as surreptitiously as possible. If Grampa saw he was having trouble with the heat he might suggest a day in the sun, something he wanted to avoid. Unless, of course, he was on his Harley.

"That was not the last of Nargat, however. He did not return, but he sent a demon spirit in his place to haunt and harass the Chaniwa. This didn't happen right after Nargat's defeat, instead showing itself to the Chaniwa a generation later. Those of mixed blood, *chi-en* and human, were more vulnerable to attack. They had the sight to be able to see this spirit, but not the power of a full blooded *chi-en* to ward it off. This is what the following generations of medicine men were trained to do, to keep the spirit away. The spirit's one way to affect us is to block our powers, so we cannot use them to banish him to the spirit world.

"You are descended from the medicine men of the Chaniwa, Wolf, whether you like it or not. That your powers arose when you were far away tells me something else, something important."

Fast Horse whittled away at the carving, its form coming free from the wood. It was not a fetish; the limbs were too defined. Wolf knew this was going to be one of those one-sitting jobs, which also meant this conversation might take even longer.

"Our medicine men descended from the offspring of these first Chaniwa, their blood mixing with the white woman and the *chi-en*. This is why other tribes thought us the enemy, this is why the Chaniwa lived in isolation. Since the beginning, the medicine men have made prophecies, and passed them down from mother to daughter, father to son.

"The most fearsome prophecy has to do with the death of the Chaniwa, and the ashes from which it rises. Its new birth. *This prophecy is at hand.*"

The urgency with which Grampa had made this last statement drew him back into the lesson.

"When there is one Chaniwa left, there will be a new cycle. A cat spirit will try to kill the very last one of our tribe," he said as he glanced over Wolf's head, "and the *chi-en* will rise from their underworld, the good and the bad. Nargat will return to seek his vengeance, as will others who are his enemy. There will be a white brave, adept at *wikka,* but he will not know his true path until he goes on a great journey to the underworld."

"So who wins?" Wolf asked, trying to sound interested, but the heat was beginning to distract him again.

"That we don't know," Fast Horse said. "The battle has yet to be fought." Grampa was getting excited, in a way Wolf found disturbing. The old man was starting to sound irrational. Wolf considered ways to appease him. "The Chaniwa have a power, which sometimes skips generations. Your father didn't have it. But you, Wolf, you have something he didn't. You *are* something he wasn't."

"Which is?" Wolf asked, trying to sound polite. "What am I?"

"You are . . ." Grampa began reverently, "you are *chakka*. Shapeshifter."

Wolf's heart sank. The *chakka* were bogeymen of bedtime stories. *Chakka* were the Chaniwa equivalent of werewolves. *Unacceptable.* He was willing to accept his powers having to do with his own natural abilities, which obeyed only himself. Now Grampa was bringing in spirits and ghosts and shit, things he didn't accept, didn't believe in. At least not yet; if Grampa presented some convincing evidence he might accept the notion of spirits, and make the knowledge his own. That he was a true *chakka* was beyond belief.

Grampa is starting to unravel.

"The evil cat spirit, the one Nargat summoned, her name is Ha-Sowa," Fast Horse said, looking above Wolf at the trailer's ceiling. "Never speak it unless you are gazing into the Hand. The Hand will keep the spirit away. Otherwise you may invoke the spirit. As a *chakka*, you may discover your other self."

"Okay, sure," Wolf said, half listening. He wasn't convinced.

Grampa gazed at him with an intense, hostile look that chilled his blood. "You can believe me now, or you can believe me later. Either way, you will believe! When the spirit challenges you, you will become what you do not believe. You will find that the spirits are not as kind as I am!"

Fear turned to anger, once Wolf realized Grampa was doing something he had agreed not to do, and that was to force his beliefs on him. Wolf should have known the old man would have trouble knowing the difference between religion and facts. Perhaps in Fast Horse's world there was no difference. In the hot, steamy trailer in the middle of the desert, Wolf's patience ran short.

"Kind or not, I've never seen the spirits," Wolf blurted. Fast Horse's eyes narrowed. "All I have seen and felt is some weird energy that came from inside myself. I came here to learn about *that*, not the entire mythology of the Chaniwa tribe."

"Because of the spirit, your powers are restrained. When you were overseas in the war, you were far from the spirit and its influence on your powers. The powers emerged when you needed them the most, and you put them to use. You haven't seen them since you've returned home, have you?"

Wolf shook his head stubbornly. "That doesn't prove anything," he replied.

Grampa shook his head, disappointed. "So many white man ways you must unlearn."

"Why unlearn them?" he asked, his patience snapping like a dry twig. "So I can become a Chaniwa and live in a shitty little trailer in the middle of nowhere? There's something I don't think you understand, and that's we're the last two of this damned tribe! I'm sitting out in the desert, getting sunstroke staring at the rocks, when I should be out looking for work, or better yet go back to school. I've got VA benefits for that."

"Money will not protect you," Grampa said evenly. "You must be ready for the spirit, to know what you are—"

"You mean a damned *chakka*? I think I can see the advantages. Hell, we could buy one of those twenty-five pound bags of dog chow, that would last me at least a week. But the shots and the vet bills and all that . . . I mean, have you really thought this through? And out here in the desert will I need a flea collar?"

"Why do you think your parents named you Wolf?" Grampa said softly.

The comment stopped him short. "What do you mean, they named me? Wolf is a nickname."

"No, grandson. It is not. Wolf *is* your real name. Your white foster parents named you Paul, but they changed it from *Wolf.*"

Interesting, he thought, wondering why he had never been told this before. "So it's my Chaniwa name. Big deal. What does that have to do with silver bullets and my occasional wild urges to chase cats up trees? *If* there were any trees around?"

"You still don't see," Grampa said sadly. "Go on. Go into town. I don't have the strength to talk sense into a child."

The old man got up suddenly, leaving the woodcarving and his knife on the table. While they were arguing he had finished the carving, and Wolf hadn't even noticed. It appeared to be a mountain lion or cougar; the lines of the cat followed the swirls of the pinyon grain. But it was too manlike to be a cat, and it was standing upright.

"What's this?" Wolf asked, picking the carving up.

Fast Horse glanced at the carving, and while looking into the Hand of the dreamcatcher, said, "Ha-Sowa."

Wolf set it down as if it were poisoned. Grampa looked tired, and tottered over to a chair in front of an ancient black and white TV. "Oprah Winfrey," he said, as he turned the set on.

The comment about being a child still stung, try as

he might to let it go. Suddenly the Harley seemed the ideal solution to the conflicting feelings he was juggling.

Get the hog up to a hundred. Everything in the world goes away. Instant Zen.

Yeah, that was the ticket. Go riding. Screw the shopping list.

As he got up to look for his motorcycle garb, he glanced down at the carving again, and did a double take. *Had it changed positions?* he wondered. It was in more of a crouch than standing up. But now the light was hitting it directly. *That was it. Play of the shadows. Where are my damned leathers?*

Behind the trailer was a small shed built with scrap lumber and about a hundred odd pieces of rusted sheet metal. Inside this Grampa kept miscellaneous junk—an oily transmission that had come out of the truck, an old trunk with Chaniwa relics, a box of battered tools, a few dried up cans of paint. But the important items were Wolf's Harley and Grampa's Indian. The Harley ran perfectly, but the other hadn't turned over in ten years. The front fender of the Indian had been removed for some reason, and put in the corner, where it lay like a wilted, dusty rose. The rest of the old 1946 Indian Chief lurked under a piece of canvas, but Wolf remembered what it had looked like when he went over it months ago. He didn't even try to start it, knowing it would need a thorough restoration, from the engine out, before it would go anywhere. Right away he had found something wrong with the ignition, or possibly the battery. Finding all the necessary rubber parts would be a real trick even if there were any Indian clubs around, and probably impossible if there were not. To do it right one would need to sink five or six grand into it, and six months of uninterrupted time. It was the perfect project for an idle, wealthy man, and Wolf wasn't wealthy.

The Harley, though, that was another matter. His baby was a legendary 1957 Harley-Davidson XL Sportster, in decent but not cherry condition. It needed a paint job pretty bad, the muffler was toast, and the forward handlebar bearings had to be replaced, but the bike ran like a champ. His friends in Texas had disassembled it and shipped it to his grandfather when Wolf had enlisted in the army, and it was still in the crates when Wolf returned after the war. It needed new tires and an oil change, but everything else was still in pretty good shape. After a week of scrounging for a used muffler, he had gotten it tagged, inspected and insured, gave it a poor man's tuneup, and fired that muther up.

Which is precisely what he had in mind now. Wolf had thrown on a pair of old black Honcho cowboy boots and a pair of jeans, waiting until he was on the bike before zipping on the leather jacket. She started on the second kick. Her throaty roar filled the shed with life. He eased the sunglasses on his face and eased her cautiously onto the dirt drive. By the time he reached the highway she was warmed up enough to back the choke off, and he turned her loose.

It happened whenever he rode the machine, no matter how bad the weather was, or how angry he might be, or if he was having a nicotine fit, or just plain in a bad mood. Once he had the bike on a highway, unimpeded by traffic, he felt freed of his emotions. The anger went away, as if blown off his body by the winds. Seventy-five, eighty miles per hour . . . the jacket ballooned around him, the wind stinging his bare chest. Ninety, ninety-five . . . and he was no longer mortal. Nothing in the universe mattered except the bike, the pavement, and the two rubber tires keeping them separate.

Instant Zen . . .

No traffic whatsoever. His mirrors were tilted too far

down, giving him a good view of the highway passing beneath him, but he didn't want to fiddle with them now.

Nothing in front of me, nothing in back of me. Freedom . . . Ninety-five, one hundred. He quit looking at the speedometer. Nothing mattered except the road directly in front of him.

One-ten . . .

He had the sudden feeling that something was behind him. Backing the speed off to about ninety, he pulled the rear view up into position, where it should have been. Behind him was a cop car, lights flashing and eager to pull him over.

Oh shit . . . he thought, knowing in that split second that he had probably been pacing him since he got on the road. *He's paced me at one-ten, at least* . . . *I'm in deep shit.*

The cop was so unexpected that for a moment he'd forgotten what to do. This was his first encounter with the law since his return from the Gulf, and he was substantially rattled.

Shit shit SHIT! he thought, taking the handlebars firmly. He was slowing down drastically now, as was the cop car. Still going at a good clip, he pulled over on the shoulder. *Can't let him think I'm trying to outrun him* . . . Such tactics would only land him in jail, a place he never wanted to see again.

But the shoulder was gravel . . .

Too late to pull back on the highway, he felt the bike going sideways, the rear wheel slipping out and away from him. His last act of control was to put the bike into a slide, lest he begin flipping end over end. The bike screamed its pain as it connected with the ground, and Wolf reluctantly pushed himself away from it, hoping it wouldn't end up on top of him.

For an eternity he slid alongside the bike, the jacket

taking the brunt of the impact. Nevertheless he knew he was hurt, and hurt bad, before he came to a stop in some hot, spongy sand.

Then the darkness seized him, and Wolf knew what it was like to die.

Chapter Seven

His first thought was of his bike, of whether or not he should turn the engine off.

But he couldn't find the bike anywhere, which was the first indication that something out of the ordinary had happened to him. The second sign was that he felt no pain. *I must be in shock,* he concluded. *And unconscious. But if I'm unconscious, then why am I thinking?*

The desert came into sharp focus around him. As he viewed it from a slightly elevated position, he noted something terribly wrong; he had either grown twelve feet in height, or he was flying. The latter became apparent when he looked down at himself, and saw only sand and a sparse scattering of juniper.

I must have died, he thought, feeling strangely unalarmed. During his rigorous meditation in the desert, in which he concentrated on a single tiny object, he had learned to tune out his body, surrendering his being to the object of meditation. This was a similar sensation, he thought, now knowing the purpose of the meditation. He had some clue as to what was going on, whereas a year before he would have been utterly lost, floating above the desert like a balloon, not knowing what had happened. Grampa claimed to be able to leave his body for extended periods, and that Wolf would also learn this trick. But he doubted Grampa meant for him to accomplish this with the quick and dirty method of dumping his bike while doing a hundred.

Then he saw the twisted remnants of his Sportster, and felt that pang of death all over again. Its frame had contorted into an impossible angle, and the front tire had flown off somewhere. *She's dead,* he thought, shuddering with grief; then, *I'm dead?*

Wolf saw his body lying some distance away, face up on the sand, looking as if he'd just decided to take a nap alongside the road. Rather peaceful, he looked. Only his sunglasses were missing, no surprise given the magnitude of the crash. Wolf idly wondered if he'd suffered any broken bones.

The Sheriff's car had pulled up in front of Wolf's sleeping body, idling with the lights still flashing. The deputy was talking into a mike. He had turned pale, and didn't look well at all.

Wolf felt detached from the whole scene, feeling like an observer. Then he became aware of another observer, someone or something that had only now made its presence known.

He appeared as a lone motorcycle rider, off in the distance. The sound was a thin, constant drone that sounded like a cross between a diesel engine and a chain saw. But the bike's tires didn't connect with the sand; it, like himself now, was some feet off the ground, riding an ether Wolf could not yet see.

The rider drew nearer, pulling up to a stop near Wolf, who stood entranced by his bike. It was not an old but an *ancient* Harley, circa 1920s or '30s, with the famous Harley-Davidson name on the thin, tubular gas tank. No lights, signals, or windshield . . . the only accessory appeared to be a crude speedometer affixed to the front wheel fork. The rider was relaxed, almost bored as he dismounted and pulled the bike up on a rear kickstand;

which seemed rather silly, since they were both in some other world where gravity and matter didn't, well, *matter.* Both rider and bike were transparent, the juniper and pinyon being vaguely distorted when viewed through him, as if his body were a lens.

Somewhere between ghost and god. Where the hell am I?

The rider was a kid about his own age, wearing a leather helmet, goggles, and one of those old aviator's jackets that buttoned down the side. And with the black riding boots, he looked like he'd just climbed out of an old rag-wing Sopwith Camel.

"Went down kind of hard back there, didn't you?" the kid asked, not in a snide way, but in understanding, as if he'd done the same thing himself once. Given his ghostly appearance, Wolf realized this was highly likely. "I'm Thorn," said the young rider, moving closer to Wolf and pulling a well worn work glove off his right hand, then extending it. Wolf took the hand reflexively. Warmth flowed through the touching palms. Nothing solid, but not imaginary, either. Thorn was just a country kid who obviously had the same obsession for Harleys as he did, though in a different time and place.

"Went down, and out," Wolf said, glancing back at his prone body on the sand. "The bike's probably totaled, too."

"You can get another bike," Thorn said softly, his feet shifting nervously in place, as if he were standing on something solid. "Another life, well, that's a little trickier." A boyish grin spread across his young features, making his freckles leap out like a connect-the-dots puzzle.

Fear and uncertainty tugged at Wolf, and blood would have drained from his face, if he'd had blood or even a solid face.

"So did I die down there, or what?" Wolf asked, trying to keep the impatience out of his voice.

"No," Thorn said simply. "Or you wouldn't be talking to me. You would have gone on, to the other side, through the great light. This conversation wouldn't be taking place. At least, not here. And not with me."

In the distance Wolf saw another set of red flashing lights, rolling toward them on Highway 60 from the east. The deputy had gotten out of his car and was touching Wolf's neck. He looked surprised.

"Other side of *what*?" Wolf asked, feeling control, if indeed he'd ever had any, slipping away.

"If you haven't been there, you won't know. If you've been there, you wouldn't ask. When you go back after this, then you *will* know," Thorn said, looking like he suddenly needed to be somewhere besides here.

This didn't make a bit of sense, but then neither did anything else, right then.

"I can't go back," Thorn said suddenly, but he didn't sound regretful. Indeed, he made the announcement proudly. "My purpose is to protect you, and other riders. Like a guardian angel."

Wolf looked back at the mangled mess of his Sportster.

"I think it's a little late for that."

"Normally, I wouldn't have encouraged a slide like the one you just pulled off, going down. But I needed to take drastic measures." He gestured down the highway, to a cluster of five or more boulders several yards away, each the size of a VW bug. "Or you would have gone directly into them. Then we *wouldn't* be talking now. You would know what you don't, now. You would be on the Great Ride."

This kid was starting to sound cosmic, like Grampa, and it was giving Wolf the creeps. But he believed everything the kid was saying.

"I . . . did things, to cushion your fall. You're going to survive this one," Thorn said, taking his old bike by the handlebars and pushing it off the rear kickstand. "I'll be watching over you, but you're gonna have to be a little more careful next time. I might not be able to intervene. It might be too late."

The old Harley roared to life, started by means Wolf did not perceive.

"Thorn?" Wolf called as the rider took off, but his only reply was a brief wave over his shoulder. Then the antique bike shot away at an incredible speed, far faster than he would have imagined of *any* bike, and was gone.

With Thorn's departure, Wolf knew that his time was up. His body called to him, pulling him down, the sensation something like landing feet first in a pool of water. Then the pain, slamming down like a hammer, as his damaged cage of flesh closed around him.

He knew he was home, and already he didn't much care for it.

With the screams of the blinded bikers still echoing pleasantly in his head, Japhet Dhu led his band away from the city to the open desert beyond. He considered their group lucky, having encountered no human resistance as they rode their adapted elvensteeds into the comforting darkness, roaring like a pack of wolves. Perhaps, Japhet speculated, it was for the best that they withdraw to this human domain. Perhaps their fortune lay in preying on these human imbeciles, instead of on the Avalon elves.

They made camp in a narrow ravine, some distance from the main road. Drawing on the untapped energies just below the surface of the ground, Nargach and Japhet cloaked their camp in a shroud of concealing glamorie. The shell they constructed rendered them invisible to the casual observer, and cooled the air to the chill and damp of Underhill. Japhet granted his men permission to rest, while he and Nargach stood guard.

"These energies are all but unused," Japhet said, noting

the strength of their sheltering spell, and the ease with which he made their environment comfortable. "I see why my father was so fond of this crude land."

Nargach shook his head slowly in disagreement. Japhet's anger rose, but he hid it from the other mage. "It is abundant energy, but it is weak energy. We can cast glamories and ken garments with it, but beyond that its usefulness is limited." He turned to their leader, his eyes narrowed. "Certainly *you* already knew this. He who is the son of the mighty *Zeldan*."

Japhet ignored the jibe. He was about to change the subject by mentioning Mort's understanding of these humans and their Devil, when something else caught his attention.

"Aie, and what might this be," Japhet said as he watched the lone motorcycle rider flying down the highway. Within the concealing spell the elves dwelt in a plane that intersected both the physical and spiritual realm, and from this vantage he had seen, blazing through the spiritual darkness like a beacon, an aura so powerful he thought at first he had seen yet another elf, and an Avalon one at that. On further examination he saw that this was only a human.

His power is surprising, Japhet thought, aware that Nargach was silently observing this newcomer with equal interest. *I had thought only creatures of Underhill could claim such brilliance.*

The highway wound through a shallow valley, with a sparse green forest, more shrubs than trees, dotting the landscape. The Harley burned a hasty trail for the horizon, as if something pursued it, but this was not so. The rider seemed to be making speed for the sake of speed alone. The blatant disregard this human had for the law interested Japhet.

He may be useful.

Then another vehicle came into the picture. It had

apparently been in pursuit of the bike for some time, but the rider appeared to be oblivious to it. Lights flashing, siren wailing, the black and white car left no doubt in the elf's mind that this was indeed the cops, out for blood.

"The human runs from the law," Nargach observed. "We may have some things in common with this creature besides the steed he rides."

"Perhaps," Japhet said absently, itching to mount his elvensteed and check out this situation, from a discreet distance.

Nargach evidently sensed his thoughts. "I'll accompany you," he said, as they both mounted their bikes and took off after the humans.

Their concealing spell remained active as the distance between them and the police car closed. The human evidently saw what was behind him, and began to slow. Japhet and Nargach kept a respectable distance.

Apparently the human had tried to stop safely beside the road, but something went horribly wrong. The rear tire suddenly slipped out from under him, and the bike started sliding sideways. The human threw himself clear of the machine, slid a good distance on the ground, and stopped. The cop hit the brakes, swerved, and just avoided striking the bike, coming to a stop beyond the rider. The bike's front tire flew off and rolled down the highway, over a rise and out of sight.

"Then again, perhaps he won't be much use to us," Nargach said. Japhet paid him no attention, instead scrutinizing the motionless rider.

Dead?

Perhaps. The rider had sustained injuries, as told by the dark, sickly color of the aura. The elf quickly fortified his own spell, rendering themselves invisible on this plane, so as not to be seen by this new spirit.

"We are not alone, here," Nargach said suspiciously.

Another entity came into the picture. He rode a motorbike as well, but it seemed to be of a much older make, perhaps of a different time. Japhet could not hear the conversation, but it looked as if the human's spirit straddled both worlds, committed to neither. Whatever he was hearing from the other seemed to be convincing him to return to his body.

"We must investigate this," Japhet said. "Immediately, before this being returns from whence it came."

The rider had already begun to incorporate into its body, returning reluctantly to the damaged flesh. Before the rider had entirely left this plane, Japhet managed to pick out a name from the conflicting mass of data of its soul: Wolf. The Unseleighe also saw with startling clarity the power of this human, his mage potential.

I must possess this human, Japhet thought as he commanded his elvensteed to pursue the other entity. *And I must know what this spirit is. . . .*

As a Rider Guardian, Thorn watched over many a motorcyclist, and followed the evolution of two-wheeled technology. Thorn found himself drawn to the Harleys. He had watched over the U.S. Army recon units as they scouted for armor. He had watched over the 200-mile Championship at Daytona Beach in 1953, the Hell's Angels on their choppers and the officers on their 74 OHV Police Models. Thorn had presided over a thousand deaths, and as many near-deaths. There were sometimes long periods between the deaths, during which he explored the edges of his domain, where he discovered other populated realms. His favorite was Underhill and the elves who dwelled there. But soon duty would call, and another situation would summon him. He did not know how long he had been a Rider Guardian. He didn't care; he still got to ride Valerie. And he knew these were the only terms under which he could do so.

The contact with Wolf had been typical. A young rider, angry about something, riding fast, riding wild, mind distracted by other things, mind on everything but the road before him and the two wheels beneath him. But unlike others, Wolf's soul had burned brightly, as if it belonged to something other than a human. Thorn did not know what this might mean, however, and simply accounted for it by Wolf's Chaniwa heritage. These things he gleaned off the surface of the confused soul before contacting it; best to know what one is intervening in.

Even while speaking with Wolf, Thorn knew they were being watched by something else out there. Thorn had only rarely encountered such spirits, lost souls Thorn could do nothing about. On occasion he had even found powerful spirits, demons, who would do him harm. Early on he learned he had one powerful defense, the ability to flee danger at a high rate of speed. Nothing in this realm had harmed him, but then he had never stood up to anything of real strength.

He steered Valerie into the darkness, away from the edge where it met the physical. The ride was slow and leisurely. He wanted these mysterious beings to overtake him; he wanted to know who they were.

We are watched, Valerie said, with a hint of anxiety. *Take flight? Flee?*

"No, not yet," Thorn said casually, shifting to second. "First let's see who these critters are."

They're not Guardians, Valerie said, but Thorn already knew that.

"They will not hurt us," Thorn said. "Rest easy. Didn't you complain just the other day how dull things had gotten?"

Valerie's only reply was the purr of her eight valve motor.

Thorn rode a piece, not glancing back to see if they were following. They were, he had no doubt. Two of them. And they were riding motorcycles . . . or at least something meant to look like bikes. The desert had all but disappeared, replaced by an endless darkness, the Land of Shadows. But he rode the edge of this land, not wanting to retreat to the power of the Lord, who lurked deep within the shadows. He wanted these two to follow, but not be frightened away by his ruler.

Suddenly they overtook him, riding past him on either side and cutting him off. Bad motorcycle manners in any world. Thorn frowned, slowed, then stopped Valerie. The two critters did the same, blocking his way.

With Valerie idling beneath him, Thorn regarded the two inquisitively, with an expression of mild annoyance. *Let them think I can't get away. Then we shall surprise them, if the need arises.*

Thorn had felt their hatred for absolutely *everything* ooze off them like sweat. He pretended to be bored as he turned Valerie off, and surreptitiously probed them for clues of their origins. *They are not demons,* he discovered with some alarm. *They are elves, Unseleighe elves, from Underhill. This might be a real problem.*

"That was a most interesting exchange back there, with the foolish human thrown from his steed," one said, and from the demeanor and body language of the other, Thorn guessed him to be the superior of the two. "Why would you *bother* with such insects?"

"They have souls," Thorn pointed out. "And I used to be one of those insects." He wondered if it might have been an error to tell them this, but it was too late to recall the words. "You are not of this realm," he continued. "Are you visiting, or are you planning to take up permanent residence here?"

"And what if we *were*?" the leader said, his hostility radiating from him in thick, black waves. "What would you have to say about that?"

"I would say 'welcome'," Thorn said, faking a pleasant

expression. "There's plenty of room for all of us. But it is such a dismal place for most beings. Why would you be interested in hiding here?"

The leader's face darkened. *"Who said we were hiding?"* the elf hissed.

"Poor choice of words. I don't speak very much out here, and my language is rusty. I'm rather isolated."

"You didn't seem to have that problem with the human," the other said. He moved around behind Thorn, making it impossible for him to watch them both.

"The human was one of my charges," Thorn said. "I help those in need, those who ride motorcycles. That is my purpose. That is what I do."

The two exchanged looks, turning from confusion, to amusement. "That is your purpose?" the leader said. "Whatever did you do in your past life to receive such a sentence?"

"I'm just lucky, I guess," Thorn said. "I get to ride even after I'm dead."

They roared with laughter, which further convinced Thorn these two were impostors. *If they don't understand the importance of riding for the sake of it, they don't belong on those machines, whatever they are made of!*

"So who was that human you helped?" the leader said, pushing his amusement aside. "He was very powerful for a human, one I might have mistaken for elven if I knew no better."

So they sensed it too, Thorn thought, and wondered if they were pursuing this boy, Wolf, for some dark reason. "He was just a soul in need of help," he replied. "No other reason."

They stared at him hatefully. *Did they see through the lie?* His own thinking startled him. *Was it a lie, that this was just another motorcyclist?* He thought back to the exchange with Wolf. *Typical young male human, thinking little, angry over nothing. But underneath all*

*that there was something special, a spark that I don't
see in most people. These creatures must have seen the
same thing.*

"I don't think he's telling us the truth," the other said.
"He even doubts his own words."

Drat! Thorn swore. *They are more than I can handle.
I must escape, right now.*

"We want that human," the leader said. "We want you
to help us capture him. We can use his power. Nargach,
what might we be able to offer him in return for his
services?"

"Gold," the Unseleighe said casually. "We can *make
anything.*"

Thorn pretended to be interested in the offer. "Let's
talk," he said. "But I must include Valerie in this
discussion."

"Valerie?"

"My steed," Thorn said, touching the engine with a
tiny bit of magic, enough to turn the engine over. *That
is one advantage of being an angel on a motorcycle,* he
thought wryly. *You don't have to roll start your bike!*
The move startled them, as if they were afraid he might
flee. *Well, that's exactly what I have in mind. Time to
bluff.*

"I have to turn her over so she can speak with us,"
Thorn said conversationally. This too was not entirely
true; she had been patiently taking in the entire exchange,
despite her urge to bolt. She was idling smoothly, feeling
like a graceful cat, ready to leap. *Well, she's going to
get that chance.*

"So tell me, which of the Seleighe families chased
you out of Underhill? Outremer? Avalon? They must
have really whipped your ass."

Rage stifled any immediate reply the leader might
have made. His face turned a hideous purple.

"You'll *pay* for that insult!" the Unseleighe managed

to spit out. Thorn sensed them drawing power from the desert, raw, natural power few beings could manipulate. But the problem was at his back, as Valerie shot between the two; a moment later, the elves were barely visible dots on the horizon of the Land of Shadows.

His relief at escaping them soon turned to consternation. *They are going to find Wolf eventually, and they probably don't have his best interests in mind. It is my duty to aid him. He is injured and vulnerable. I can't take these two on by myself. I need help.*

I need to contact the Seleighe, find out what's going on. Avalon is nearest. Perhaps they know who these abominable creatures are. . . .

Chapter Eight

Lucas' hope that there might be an end to his personal hell had evaporated the very day he left the hospital. He had even begun to wonder if he'd imagined the whole suicide thing.

It was a few weeks into summer vacation. He had discovered one night that The Axe was still closed. The long walk had taken him along Central Avenue, a fairly active party strip bisecting Albuquerque. On his way back he stopped at a motorcycle dealership, gazing through the plate glass at the godlike machines within. A shiny new Katana which looked identical to Mike's caught his eye. When he saw the word USED on the paper tag hanging off the handlebar, he saw that it could well be the very same bike. The price was outrageous. You could still get a new Geo for that amount of money.

So if I get a bike, it would have to be used, and something else, he thought, but the other prices he saw were as daunting as the first. Then he saw a price in his range. His hopes sank like the *Titanic* when he saw what the tag was attached to: a little beat-up scooter, with tires the size of bagels, the kind of thing that might be appropriate in Rome, but would be humiliating in the open spaces of New Mexico. *And it would sound like a weedeater! Forget it.* He walked away in disgust. So much for getting a bike.

A Ford Escort pulled up and stopped a few feet ahead of him. Lucas noticed right away the muffler was about to fall off, and on the back of the car were a variety of bumper stickers: "Satan Lives" and "Christ Lied" dominated the noisy mobile billboard, accompanied by skulls, inverted crosses and a goat head.

"You wanna ride?" the kid inside asked. He was about the same age as Lucas, with long blond hair and some sort of black tattoo on his right arm, but he didn't recognize him from school. Something was burning in the ashtray, and it wasn't a cigarette.

But Lucas was bored stiff, and not a little bit tired from his long walk.

"Sure." He shrugged and got in.

The Escort pulled away faster than was necessary. Lucas noticed an expensive looking Nikon camera sliding around on the dash, its cyclopean eye staring at him accusingly.

"I'm Satanic Panic. My group calls me Panic, for short."

Lucas wondered if he'd made a mistake. The kid turned to him and said, with a crooked smile, "Speakers are all fucked up. Can't play the radio. Here, have some of this."

He passed Lucas the burning joint. "Just came over the border. It's the best," he said as Lucas took it.

Lucas had never had any real interest in pot, or anything else the other kids were indulging in, but tonight something was different. Nothing really mattered, so what the hell?

He thought he was going to cough his lungs out after the first drag, but Panic didn't even comment.

"It's dusted," Panic said, pulling the Escort back into the lane it had wavered from. "Come on, let's have some fun. I've got spray paint in the back seat."

Lucas wasn't about to start huffing paint, but apparently

that wasn't what Panic had meant. Lights had begun to cascade before him, and a mesmerizing fist tried to close his eyes. The word "dusted" took on new significance. One minute he was staring out the windshield, and the next they were laughing like hyenas, over nothing. Lucas decided he liked Panic.

Panic pulled off Central to some lesser, unlit streets, and stopped in front of a tall iron gate. A chain and padlock secured it from night visitors, but this didn't deter Panic. The engine idled roughly, rocking the car as one or more cylinders misfired, as Panic got out with a pair of bolt cutters. Lucas watched in fascination as he clipped the chain apart and opened the gate with a noisy *creak*.

"No problemo," Panic said, driving into the cemetery.

Lucas was a little confused as to what they were doing there, until Panic tossed him a can of spray paint and grabbed one of his own. "Graffiti time," he said, with a giggle.

Lucas followed the crazed Panic who, in the bright light of the full moon, found a row of headstones and began painting. Inverted pentagrams, "Satan Lives," "Satan Rules" and just plain "Satan" went over the granite and marble, the names, the dates.

What the hell, Lucas thought, remembering something someone had told him, but not recalling precisely who. *Funerals are for the living.* Looking for another marker to paint, he stopped in front of one tombstone, blinking at the name.

MIKE VAUGHAN

MARCH 13, 1980 — NOVEMBER 20, 1994

Panic painted a swastika over his name. Then he looked up and said, "Oh shit. Time to get out of here."

On the other side of the graveyard, patrolling the street

beyond, was a cop car with a spotlight. The beam swept the cemetery with jerky, sudden motions. Lucas followed Panic to the car and, with the lights off, they eased out of the graveyard. Once on the street Panic turned on the lights on and floored the gas. The Escort's speed increased a little.

"That was close," Panic said, looking in the rearview mirror.

Painting over Mike's tombstone really bothered him, now that the drugs were wearing off. He was about to tell Panic what a jerk he was for doing it when Panic pulled another joint out from somewhere and lit it with a Bic torch. A moment later he was trying to remember what he was all steamed up about.

Panic took him home. "I'll pick you up tomorrow night at nine and we'll have some *real* fun."

"Okay," Lucas said.

His parents had long since gone to bed, for which he was grateful. He found his way through the darkened house to his bathroom, closed the door and turned on the light.

His eyes were red and puffy, and in the mirror he saw he was having trouble standing up straight. The fist of sleep was descending on him, but the evening's activities nagged like a splinter under his skin.

"I can't believe I did that shit," he said, to the mirror, looking at himself with some difficulty. Then, *I painted over Mike's tombstone. . . .*

The grief and remorse began to well up behind his eyes. He turned the light off before he saw the tears. In his bedroom he turned on the dim desk lamp, and looked for Doctor Vaughan's card. He had left it on the big gray blotter, but it was nowhere to be seen. He looked in his thin phone book for the number. The "V" page had been ripped out.

Lucas was convinced that he had to call Mike's father. He was the only one who might, *might* understand . . . or care.

He looked in the Albuquerque phone book for M. Vaughan, Physician, and dialed it from his black rotary phone.

"Yes?" a man's sleepy voice said. "Doctor Vaughan here."

"Yes, Doc, this is . . . uh . . . Lucas."

"Who?"

"Mike's friend."

A long silence followed. Lucas was about to hang up when Doctor Vaughan said, "Are you okay, Lucas?"

"Yeah, I'm . . . at home." *How in Hell's name can I tell him I vandalized his son's grave marker?*

"Well, Lucas. I can't . . . talk to you. Your father called and said that I was to have no further contact with you."

Lucas stared at the phone, then at the wall that divided his bedroom from his parents. *You bastard.*

"Please do this for me," the doctor said. "Are you with me?"

"Yeah," Lucas said. "I'm with you." But he had already given up hope.

"No matter what happened tonight, call the suicide hotline."

"No, you don't . . ." Lucas stammered.

"No buts. Whatever you were going to tell me, tell them. Please."

"Okay," Lucas said. "I miss Mike," he managed to get out.

"I do, too," the doctor replied. "Please do it. Goodbye, Lucas."

The line went dead, and Lucas replaced the receiver on the hook.

Damn him, he thought, wishing his father dead. The prospect chilled him. *Is this what Panic would want me to wish?* He turned out the light and lay down on his bed. As he stared at the dark ceiling, Mutant, his black and white Manx, hopped up on the bed. The cat curled up between his arm and body, resting its head on his elbow and purring like a chainsaw. Mutant seemed to always know when he was upset, and slept as close as possible to him.

At least Mutant gives a shit, he thought as he gently curled around the cat. Then the tears came with a vengeance, and he cried himself to sleep in the cat's fur, an ordeal Mutant endured without complaint.

True to his word, Panic showed up the next evening promptly at nine. Panic was dressed in all black, even to black gloves with the fingers cut off. Around his neck hung a huge silver pentagram, point down.

"You really are into this," Lucas said, recalling the bumper stickers.

"You bet," Panic replied. "You still want to be initiated?"

Lucas looked at Panic blindly.

"You remember, don't you?" Panic persisted, and the edge of disapproval in his voice made Lucas nervous.

"Well, yeah," Lucas lied. "I guess I was a little stoned. I'm not so sure now."

This was the wrong thing to say. Panic's silence filled the car like thick fog; wordlessly he reached under his seat and pulled out a large manila envelope, then flipped on the dome light. "Here," Panic said abruptly. "Have a look."

Curious as well as a bit intimidated, Lucas withdrew the contents of the envelope, a thin stack of glossy photos. His heart skipped a beat when he saw they were photos of himself spraypainting grave markers.

"Thousand speed film," Panic said cheerfully. "Full moon gives excellent light. Now, what were you saying about the initiation?"

Fear leaped into Lucas' throat, temporarily stifling a

reply. "Okay, what do we do?" he asked, without emotion. "Initiation into what?"

"The Temple," Panic said solemnly, touching his pentagram lovingly. "The Temple of Satan."

Lucas knew he should have guessed it, though he had never heard of this group. *I'll pretend to go along,* he decided, *then get the hell out, with those pictures and the negatives, and forget this ever happened!*

"You have an appointment with Damien," Panic said, putting the car in drive. "We will not be late."

Howard Hull had belonged to a Satanic organization in Burbank. His parents had passed away, leaving him a tidy fortune in real estate and oil and gas royalties, allowing him to retire from his profession as a "Sanitation Engineer." Though he had dabbled in the occult as a teenager, and had studied Anton La Vey's *The Satanic Bible,* his beliefs in the black arts hadn't really taken flight until much later.

Howard learned about the Church of Baphomet and wheedled an invitation to a meeting. To his delight, they quoted from *The Satanic Bible* chapter and verse. From the very beginning Howard was able to convince them of his sincerity by reciting from memory LaVey's Nine Satanic Statements.

Howard joined the Church, changed his name to "Damien Szandor," and started a goatee. A few months later the group became mired in a child abuse case. One of the members ran a day care facility in Long Beach. Being a new recruit, Damien was not privy to the high-level activities, but he did hear of the deflowering rituals the Church of Baphomet engaged in, and put two and two together. He had been so looking forward to participating in the rites.

Satan appeared to Damien in a dream. *Go forth, and start your own Temple,* Satan had commanded. The next day Damien liquidated what he could and left behind what he could not, and made arrangements to move out of state. Among his holdings were a rental house east of Albuquerque, currently vacant, and a small adobe on ninety acres south of the city. That property included an unused gravel pit. *A good enough place to start the Temple of Satan as any,* he'd decided, and set out for New Mexico.

It all seemed so long ago, Damien thought as he peered from his living room bay window, regarding the moonlit valley that ran past the Sandia Mountains as if it were all his very own. He had worn his "Sunday best," the black silk Catholic priest's suit with one minor alteration: the white collar insert had been replaced with a jet black one, to reflect his role as group leader, the high priest, the Ipsissimus of the Temple of Satan.

So Panic has found a new one, after all, Damien thought. The high priest had just re-dyed his goatee and hair jet black. Already naturally pale, Damien had applied a thin layer of white to his face to enhance his undead look. He picked up an old fashioned doctor's bag and, in his black Lexus ES300, took off for the suburbs of Albuquerque.

Panic drove like a maniac, urging the Escort up to eighty. Conversation was impossible over the wail of the tortured engine. An old ghetto blaster bounced around on the back seat as they listened to fuzzy old tapes of Black Sabbath and Ozzy Osborne, music that had been around long before either of them had been born. And the higher he got on the fat cigarette they passed back and forth, the less Lucas cared what happened to him.

This may not be so bad, after all, he found himself thinking. The blackmail pictures weren't bothering him anymore, because they weren't *for* blackmail. They were to document his own willingness to serve the Master, Panic explained.

Panic took an exit ramp that didn't seem to go anywhere, and turned down a gravel road. "This is it," Panic said, parking the Escort and turning it off; they were in total darkness. A short distance ahead of them a pair of headlights cut through the dark like a knife, then went out. "Let's go," Panic said, getting out and lighting the ground before them with a flashlight. Lucas followed him to a rocky clearing where a huge slab of concrete had been set up as an altar. On it was some kind of skull, a goblet, and a row of candles, which Panic lit with his Bic.

When he regarded the thirteen black candles, lined up in a row behind what he now perceived as a cow's skull, the full understanding came to him: *These people are devil worshipers, and I'm about to become one of them! Wouldn't father just shit if he knew!* The thought added a rosy glow to the bizarre little ritual.

"Behold, the *Master*," Panic said, getting down on his knees and bowing. A dark form appeared behind the altar, and Lucas repressed a shudder. *It's a damned vampire!*

"*Get down, you fool!*" Panic hissed. "Show proper respect!"

Lucas got down, cowering.

"You may rise," a deep voice said, and the form behind the altar opened a dark cape and allowed it to drop to the ground. At first Lucas thought he was a Catholic priest. Then he saw the white collar was missing . . . or rather, the collar was all black. The "Master" was as pale as a ghost, and for an instant Lucas wondered if he *was* a vampire after all. Slowly, Panic got to his feet, his head remaining bowed. Lucas followed his lead.

"Who wishes to become a member of the Temple of Satan?" the Master bellowed.

Lucas stood there, feeling stupid. Panic elbowed him, hard, in the ribs.

"Uh . . . I do," Lucas stammered.

The Master rolled his eyes. "And who *are* you?"

"I am Lucas," Lucas said. *That's what he wanted, wasn't it?*

"Not so far as the Temple of Satan is concerned, you're not," the Master said. "Let's see, you are . . . let's make you *Helter Skelter.*"

"Yeah!" Panic whispered. "Way cool."

"That is your new name. I am the Master, and you are always to refer to me as such."

"Yes, Master," Lucas said, wondering if he was supposed to look at the "Master" when he said it. *Dammit, they're not telling me anything, letting me screw up before . . .* Before the anger took hold, he realized that he didn't care, that he wanted in this group, and he would jump in a river if they told him to. Finally, he was *belonging* to something, and it felt rather good.

"Now drink from the chalice of hate," the Master said, "and be one with us!"

Lucas took it and, without question, drank. Whatever it was, it tasted horrible, like something had died, or maybe sour milk. Only when he spilled some on his hands did he realize what it was: blood.

Lucas suppressed an urge to vomit, and realized these people might appreciate something like that. But nothing came up. Panic took the cup, drank deeply, and handed it to the Master, who drained it.

"Very good," the Master said, blood dripping from the corners of his mouth. "You are one of us. You will not betray us, for if you do we will kill you, and drink *your* blood at future ceremonies."

This is what I was looking for, he thought giddily, trying not to think about the blood he'd just drunk, or its origins. The Master retrieved his cape from the ground and walked away, disappearing into the darkness.

Chapter Nine

King Aedham Tuiereann stood before the tall window overlooking the fork of the two mighty rivers; he imagined himself on the bow of a large ship, its prow splitting the river in two. Watching the swift flow of the mighty Arannan and Gruac rivers had a profound calming effect.

When will Avalon dispose of this scourge once and for all? he wondered as he gazed into the deep currents.

He walked over the floor's chilled flagstones to the display cabinet against one wall. Inside were gifts from neighboring elfhames: jewels and gemstones, each coded specifically to him to allow instant communication to the gift's sender. Though some he could not name, he did recognize several examples of *diaspar* or elvenstone, the most precious gem of Underhill. Diaspar was rare and powerful, and as a gift of this nature its value was beyond measure.

Set off to the side of the case was a small box of inlaid wood, its lid open to reveal a four-faceted blue crystal. It was, among other things, a memory crystal, a depository of his father's last thoughts. Niamh had identified it as being a specimen of *amene* crystal, a perfect stone for concentrating node energy. The stone had been used in the weapon Aedham had slain Zeldan Dhu with.

That weapon, a long aluminum and magnesium rifle,

complete with a backpack battery, hung on the wall of the solar. It had been dubbed "Madame Photon" during one of their celebratory castle-warming parties. In Underhill it was useless, with or without the crystal. In the humans' world, however, it amplified node power as it amplified light, and in a mage's hand was as powerful as a levin bolt, with a much longer duration and more easily aimed. It was kept as a trophy of the final battle . . . a battle which was turning out to be less final than he had thought.

Aedham reached for the blue crystal, his hand hovering over the box. After all it had been through, he wondered if it still retained his father's message. That was why he had retired it from service, to preserve what might still remain recorded on it.

One way to find out, he thought, and carefully picked it up. Holding it between his hands, he *reached* as if it were a node.

He was only vaguely aware of the bright blue light which found its way through his fingers. In moments he was in touch with the stone's message. Closing his eyes, Aedham saw the flickering mage light, the tiny room, the few survivors of the attack. His mother, dead, under a blanket . . . himself, asleep on the floor, looking no more than twelve. The ceiling thundered with the levin bolt pounding. Falling dust, the walls that threatened to collapse. He saw it all, remembered it all . . .

. . . this is the last message I will ever send you, dear son. All is lost here, as I record this crystal. Your mother has died and soon I will, too, but what is important is that you take the clan to safety. Zeldan Dhu will pursue you until he finds you and kills you, and once that is done he will kill the rest of the others, and there will be no Avalon. Do not misunderstand me, my dearest son. I want you to find safety in the humans' world, but once you've established yourself there, you must make yourself

strong and attack Zeldan. Soon, and quickly. If you don't attack, he will surely kill you. That is the only way you will survive, and this request is the only gift I can give the elfhame, in my dying breath. Find Zeldan and—

The message ended, suddenly, and Aedham found himself kneeling on the flagstones, trembling. Collecting himself, Aedham got to his feet and returned the crystal to its box, and closed the lid.

How he yearned for Japhet's severed head on the end of a pike, to post just outside Avalon territory as a warning to other Unseleighe who might try to subdue them!

The fire in the solar's hearth had dimmed, and with a touch of magic Aedham gave it new life. The King had felt a chill spread throughout the castle the moment Petrus had returned with news of the Unseleighe. In his mind's eye he saw another Unseleighe army, larger than Zeldan's, massing on the other side of the rivers, with the familiar black eagle banners that had heralded so much disaster in his elfhame's past.

Are we ready this time? He'd awakened many a night with that question burning in his mind.

He wanted to accompany his men to the humans' world and slay Japhet himself, but his first obligation was to his people. His father's message, still impossibly clear after all this time, had convinced him of this.

I must protect the clan, he thought, the decision slamming down like a hammer, *and send my best men to hunt down Zeldan's son. That's what Father would have done.*

Petrus was sound asleep now, but when he awakened the King would tell him he would be in charge of the small unit; Aedham hoped the youth was up to it. *If not, there's always Odras,* Aedham thought, knowing the wise old mage would work his magic in ways no one would see, if necessary, no matter who was officially in charge.

Petrus is a capable warrior, and a leader. We're ready for you, this time, Unseleighe vermin!

While he was fantasizing about the slaughter of an Unseleighe army, his mage hearing picked up the faintest cry. The vision shattered. Aedham turned, pulled his royal robe around him, and started for his bedchambers, two floors up.

I'm coming, young Traig, Aedham sent, though he knew the words would only be buried in the baby's wails.

He'd posted one guard on the floor of his bedchambers, and she snapped to and stood at attention as soon as he was in sight. On his way, he passed the mages' workshop, where Niamh and Odras were conducting a peculiar experiment with crystals and stones; mesmerized by their work, they didn't even look up. Down the hallway to the bedroom, he heard the baby's cries quite clearly.

Ah, the joys of fatherhood, he thought, meaning every word of it.

"I'm coming, Traig!" he shouted, opening enormous oak doors to the royal bedchamber. In the far right corner a nursery, furnished with gifts from the other elfhames, had been set up. The gold and silver crib came from Outremer, and the elaborate mobile of wooden Keebler elves which dangled over it was a gift of the Court of Joyeaux Garde. They were real, solid items, not kenned, the proper thing to surround an elvenchild with.

The moment Aedham's face appeared above the crib the crying ceased.

"So what is it this time?" Aedham demanded with mock sternness, but he saw right away what it was. Prince Traig had wriggled out of his diapers, and lay there as naked as the day he was born.

"Young man, this will never do," Aedham said lovingly, picking up his son and giving him a kiss on the forehead. "What will Mommy say if she sees you running around like this, hmm?" He held his baby son up, as if offering him to the gods. Traig's fat little arms and legs wriggled, as did his small pointy ears. Holding the child aloft brought laughter and goo goo sounds; but this time it also brought a stream of wet warmth trickling down the front of the King's robe. Traig laughed, amused at dousing Daddy with the fountain of youth.

"Oh *shit*," Aedham said as he gently lay his son back in the crib, and began looking for something to clean up with.

"No, actually it wasn't *that*," a thin female voice said from behind him, followed by a sharp giggle. Ethlinn came up behind him, wrapping her arms around him, then, evidently rethinking the move, withdrew. "Peed all over Daddy, did he?"

"Yep, he sure did," Aedham agreed. "Is this what they mean by the 'royal wee'?" He gave up on the robe and took it off. Underneath he wore cutoff jeans, much to Ethlinn's amusement.

"What was that about running around improperly? You look more like a beach bum than a king," she said, deftly rediapering the prince, who was already starting to doze off.

"Well, I had the robe on *over* it," he protested, but still felt half naked in the skimpy cutoffs. Which, in the bedchamber, was not such a bad thing.

"I think I'll get cleaned up," he announced. "Join me?"

"In a moment," Ethlinn replied, her attention focused on the prince. She wore an emerald green dress with ruffles, and a large elvenstone pendant he had given her at their wedding, looking every bit the Queen she was. He regarded his wife and son with nothing short of awe; she was as beautiful today as she had been when he met her in Dallas, when she was Moira, cutting hair at Skary Hairdos, and he was Adam serving coffee at the Yaz. Her glorious hair cascaded over her shoulders with its own wild aura. Tall and thin, she was a leggy girl, which had immediately attracted eighteen-year-old "Adam McDaris."

We should go back there someday and visit Samantha, he thought. His sister, Lady Samantha, lived among the humans as a homicide detective in Dallas, where his family had hidden him from the Unseleighe. He had grown to manhood as a human, oblivious to his elven heritage. Others of the clan, Moira and Samantha among them, had watched over him until the time came to assume the crown of Avalon. Whether it had been luck or intuition, it was no small relief to the Seleighe of Underhill that he had fallen in love with and married a member of the elvenblood.

From the rear of the bedchamber he entered their private sanctuary, the grotto. Walking into the misty tropics one easily forgot there was a castle beyond all of it. From the ceiling of the cave a warm waterfall splashed into a pool. Limestone stalactites and stalagmites formed columns, surrounded by a jungle of fern and mosses. The cutoffs dropped to his ankles, and with a nudge of his mage powers he increased the water's temperature a tiny bit. He stood under the waterfall, the warm water washing over him, wishing he weren't alone.

When he stepped down into the pool, his wish was granted. Ethlinn entered the grotto, wearing only a smile and a sultry, hungry look that turned his spine to Jello.

She eased into the hot water, the steam forming a thin fog on the surface, and drew up behind him, her long arms folding over his chest. *If there is a true heaven for an elf,* Aedham thought, *this is it.*

He lay there, against her soft breasts, watching the waterfall spill down.

"Would you like it any hotter?" Aedham asked softly.

"Any hotter than this, my love, and our second child would be on the way in no time," she said, nibbling on his earlobe.

"No, I mean the water," he said, with a giggle. "I needed to relax."

"Oh, it's fine, love," she said, pulling him closer. "Are you worried about the Unseleighe?"

He didn't answer right off, wishing the subject would just go away. "I have to be," he said. "But I've decided to stay here, and send Petrus after Japhet Dhu. I'm not leaving you and Traig."

Her reply was a tight hug that pulled him closer to her.

"Are you sure he can handle it?" she asked. "I mean, he's only what, seventeen?"

"He's old enough," Aedham insisted. "And he is a born leader."

"But would he ask for help if he needed it?"

The question hung in the air for what seemed forever. It appeared to be a trait among the Avalon elves, his father King Traigthren included, to stubbornly refuse assistance until it was too late.

"Yes, I believe he would ask for assistance," he answered. The King regretted appointing his best warrior, Marbann, Ambassador to Outremer—and to all the other clans as well, for the time being. He'd needed someone mature in whom he could trust and Marbann had volunteered for the position. Through him they had brought some of the best from the other elfhames, as much as the tall elf seemed to impress all who came in contact with him. *Still, I miss him.*

Aedham continued, "And until Marbann returns from Outremer, Petrus is the highest ranking. Besides, I'm sending Odras along. If anything happens, he can work his magery behind the scenes. That old mage has seen more battles than any in Avalon."

Far more, he thought, remembering the mage's colored past. Odras had begun his life as an Unseleighe, and had found their ways unacceptable. Once he renounced the Unseleighe court he spent his life trying to make up for the wrongs his brethren had committed by helping wherever he could. He continued on his path even though no Seleighe would associate with him . . . until Aedham had recruited him. It was a delicate fact the King had kept between himself and Ethlinn.

"I suppose," Ethlinn replied, not sounding entirely convinced. "Where did the vermin go, anyway? I hope not back to Dallas."

"New Mexico," Aedham said. "Odras got a good reading from that Gate they left open."

"I wonder why there," she said. Then, "I'm glad you're staying."

"I am too," he said, turning around and facing her. Ethlinn's legs drew up and encircled his waist.

"What was that you were saying about a second child?" he whispered playfully into her neck, knowing full well Ethlinn could choose whether or not she conceived.

Though distant, the baby's wails sounded in the bedchamber.

"That was a short nap," Ethlinn said, her disappointment obvious.

"Traig can wait, can't he?" he asked, too late realizing how selfish the words sounded.

"Yes, he can," Ethlinn whispered. "You obviously *can't*, my love."

What at first seemed selfish turned out not to be selfish at all, but practical.

Brandishing an M60 machine gun, Rambo the Elf stalked the jungle in search of the enemy. He had just risen from the slime of the Amazon river, and after single-handedly breaking the backs of several alligators the Superelf walked silently on the muddy ground, ears pricked and alert for danger. The M60 was like a big cold iron battering ram, its barrel big enough to fit his fist in.

A snake fell out of the tree, wrapping itself around his bare torso, but this was a trifle; despite its size, as big around as his thigh, Rambo the Elf brushed it off casually, as if swatting a fly. Then, a noise. He held his weapon tightly, his trigger finger poised, ready to discharge the bullet hose.

Aha! So this is where the munitions plant is! he thought, elated that finally he had found his objective. He peered through the leaves of a giant banana plant. Sure enough, the munitions plant, cleverly disguised as a cookie and cracker factory, was operating at peak production. The cartoon elves in little white chef's hats tended the assembly line carefully, oblivious to the firestorm about to descend around their pointed ears.

Look at them, Rambo thought acidly to himself. *If they only knew what fate awaited them!* White creme filling squirted from animated nozzles, landing on slabs of chocolate wafer as they chugged through the works on a conveyor. But Rambo knew this was no ordinary creme filling, it was *plastique*, a high explosive that could be molded into *any* shape. Rambo was about to foil a plot to destroy Avalon; the chocolate cookies were to be offered as a present to King Aedham, but spies within the enemy's ranks had leaked the information before any harm could come to the elfhame. And King Aedham had sent Rambo in to do away with the enemy, "any way he saw fit."

If that's not carte blanche for a slaughter, I don't know what is, Rambo thought, leveling the M60 at the factory.

With a war cry that would have made the Tuatha De Danaan proud, Rambo leaped forward, discharging his own special form of carnage. The elves jerked and spasmed as he spat fire at them, their bodies riddled with armor-piercing ordnance.

Ah, the joys of battle! Rambo thought, at home in his element.

"*Aaarrgh!*" Petrus shouted as he leaped out of bed. Gradually he realized something was amiss with his weapon; he wasn't clutching the solid stock of an M60. It was something soft, and spongy.

He opened his eyes and saw not the factory but the wall of his bedroom, papered with Rambo posters. In his arms he clutched not an army issue M60, but a green and red stuffed dragon, with eyes that jiggled.

Wow, Petrus thought, tossing the dragon on the unmade bed. He had actually worked up sweat during that dream. *That was weird.*

The long hot bath he had taken just before catching some much needed rest had knocked him out but good. Lying over a heavy oak chair was a tunic that looked clean, and he slid it on, wondering where in the castle he could find something to eat. *I could even eat one of those alligators I killed.* His stomach roared loudly at the thought.

But he had no need of alligators; on a stand by the door was a large plate of bread, cheese and slices of beef.

Petrus finished all but a large handful, which he took with him to the mage's workshop. Ensconced oil lamps lit themselves as he approached, and extinguished themselves after he had passed. At the end of the hallway the guard snapped to attention, her eyes wandering ever so slightly to Petrus' developed torso. Though not as large and muscled as the King, he had put on substantial lean weight, and was still enjoying the reactions he got from both the female and male members of the young elfhame. The females vied for his attention, and the males, most of them anyway, found his new bulk somewhat threatening. When he wasn't blasting away at cartoon elves with stuffed dragons, Petrus could wield the heaviest broadsword in the elfhame, though with some effort.

Now all I need is a little experience. . . . he thought, savoring the prospect of the coming campaign. King Aedham had planned to lead it, emphasizing the importance of ridding the worlds of the Zeldan clan once and for all. Petrus loved serving under Aedham, and even if he had served under no other king he knew intuitively that none would be as fair and noble as his king had been.

As expected, Odras and Niamh were hard at work, and seemed excited by what they were doing. During their recon of the old palace grounds, Odras had unearthed some *topolomite*, a crystal used in magical workings. The old mage had mentioned something about some unique qualities in the combination of certain stones.

"Aie, Petrus," Niamh said brightly, looking up. He was easily the shortest adult Petrus had ever seen, as well as the ugliest, with an enormous round spudlike nose and teeth like a rat's. But Niamh was a brilliant engineer, adept at blending elven and human technology, which is what he and Odras appeared to be doing.

"You're in time to see a little demonstration," Odras said, leaning over a long wooden rail, inclined at a slight angle to the table. On the rail was a small wooden cart that could fit in his palm, with crude wheels that didn't look quite round enough to work. In the cart was a huge piece of elvenstone, and at the bottom of the ramp were two other stones, one the topolomite Odras had collected.

"When diaspar, commonly known as elvenstone, is held close to certain other stones, a brief spark of node energy erupts," Odras said. Any elven child knew this, however, and the resultant spark was weak but dazzling. Then he saw what they were up to.

"That's topolomite *and* amene," Petrus observed, studying the two jewels at the bottom of the ramp closely. They were in holders on either side of the wooden rail, about level with the diaspar in the cart.

"I think you should stand back, you should," Niamh said, and Petrus put a little distance between himself and the table.

Niamh released the little cart which, despite its slightly lopsided wheels, rolled down the ramp. When it passed between the other two stones, a large blue sphere flashed for an instant, making a *pffffft* and *buzzzz* as it flared and faded. Petrus jumped back, startled. This was hundreds of times brighter than what he'd expected.

"Whoa," Petrus said, blinking his eyes. The light had left blue ghosts dancing in his vision.

"It's more than just light, too," Odras said. "It's the same energy stored in the nodes. Only here it's not stored, it's generated. We may have just discovered the secret of the nodes."

Now Petrus understood why they were so excited. The nodes, large collections of naturally occurring power deep in the earth of Underhill, were the source of the elfhame's power. But they were like stored pools or wells, and didn't seem to be renewable.

This was altogether different. *If we can make node energy, instead of just dipping into stores of it . . .*

His thoughts were interrupted by the King, who had just appeared in the doorway.

"Aie, King!" Niamh said. He was already putting the wooden cart at the top of the rail. Then, "Watch this."

The cart rolled down to the stones, with the same result.

"Whoa," the King said. "That's node energy."

"That's correct," Odras said.

Aedham walked up to the worktable and picked up the diaspar stone. "That means . . ."

"That *means*," Odras continued, "that with this combination of stones we can generate that which has never been generated before. At least, by elven hands."

"Do it again," Aedham said, grinning from ear to ear.

The blue sphere flared predictably, this time with Aedham visibly concentrating on the resultant power. The sphere contorted to an egg shape before it dissipated, a sure indication the King had touched it somehow. Yet Aedham looked disappointed.

"It's wild energy," the King said. "I mean, the node energy is, well, *tame*. Easily controlled. Perhaps it is a quality it assumes when it ages, or something. This stuff, it's impressive, but I don't know how I could use it, short of a flashy fireworks display." He turned to Niamh, "That doesn't mean we *can't* use it. Keep working on it, Niamh. Odras, experiment with it. You have a great deal more experience with these energies than I have."

"Aie," Niamh said, and Odras bowed respectfully.

"Petrus, I wish to discuss something rather important with you," the King said. "You can finish your sandwich while I talk."

Embarrassed, Petrus realized he was still holding the last sandwich. But he was still hungry; with his ear turned to the King, he wolfed down the remainder of it.

Aedham led him to the spacious hallway, which was more of an informal gallery, where several examples of kenned human art hung; Warhol, Max, Haring and Ernst on one side, and Rembrandt, Manet, Renoir and da Vinci on the other. At the end of the hallway was the King's bedchambers, from where Petrus heard the faintest cry of Prince Traigthren.

"I'm not going to be chasing Unseleighe with you on this quest, much as I would like to," the King began, getting right to the point.

If Petrus hadn't already devoured his meal he would have choked on it at this news. Aedham's casual delivery of the information also stunned him.

"But, Sire, who will lead us to Japhet Dhu?" Petrus asked, but he already had an uneasy premonition of who that someone would be.

"Your performance on this latest expedition impresses me," Aedham continued. "And it also convinces me. I feel you are more than capable to lead. Don't you agree?"

Petrus didn't know what to say. Less than half a candlemark ago he had been trying to bore holes in his wall with a stuffed dragon; now the King wanted him to lead a military action against the most hated Unseleighe enemy of Avalon, and of most of Underhill.

"Odras will go with you, as will Wenlann." The news brought mixed feelings. While he welcomed the experience and magical expertise of the mage, Wenlann would only get in the way.

"I know you've had your differences with Wenlann," the King said, as if reading his mind. "But as you are the adult leader I know you are, this will not be an issue." Into the silence, the King amended. *"Will* it?"

"No . . . of course not, Sire," Petrus said, stammering despite his efforts not to. *I'm just not awake enough for this conversation,* he thought, and turned his energy to finding something noteworthy to say. "Wenlann and I . . . well, we're not exactly siblings . . ." *Thank the gods.* "But we have more or less grown up together. I'll see about reducing the friction."

Aedham smiled, a sure sign that he had, after all, said the right thing. "I knew you would come through. The most important thing I wanted to tell you is, this is to be a reconnaissance only! Do not engage the Unseleighe."

"Aie," Petrus said, trying not to let his indignation show. *He doesn't need a warrior for this, he needs a spy. I am no spy. But it is as he commands. I will do it, and I will do it well.*

"If I had Marbann at my disposal he would go with you," the King said. "He is in Outremer, and will not be back for some time. Your mission is to Gate to the humans' world, locate Japhet Dhu and his clan, determine what damage if any he has done to the human race—remember what Zeldan did—and as soon as you do this contact me on the Net. The Avalon account on AOL is still active. Send me E-mail. Do handsprings. Sharpen your sword. But do not, under any circumstances *engage Japhet Dhu!*"

The inflection he gave on the last of his statement told Petrus what his battered ego wanted to hear. *It's not that he doesn't trust me to do the job,* he thought. *He wants the privilege of beheading the bastard himself! And if anyone deserves the honor, Aedham does.*

"Aie, King!" Petrus said enthusiastically. "When will we depart?"

"As soon as you feel fit," Aedham said, casting a glance toward his bedchamber. "If you'll excuse me, the prince requests my audience."

As the King hurried off to tend to his son, the realization of what he was being sent to do came crashing down on him.

The King is sending me after the Unseleighe.

Bloody hell!

Those two elves back there seemed rather persnickety when I mentioned Avalon, Thorn thought. *I think I'll try them first.*

Underhill folded in around him, looking like the Irish countryside, without a sun and not much of a sky. Here the light was everywhere. The gently rolling green hills created no shadows in the valley, and neither did he. But a ghost didn't cast much of a shadow anyway.

The Guardian allowed the sound of his motorbike to flow ahead of him, to let the inhabitants of this place know he was coming. They probably wouldn't appreciate a surprise, he guessed. Valerie seemed a bit wary in this new place, but purred on faithfully anyway.

It's okay, Valerie, Thorn soothed. *These are the good elves. They'll help us. I hope.*

❖   ❖   ❖

The long rest had more than recharged Petrus' batteries, and the prospect of leading an action against the Unseleighe added a nervous spring to his step.

I'm ready to go now, Petrus had thought. He was in his quarters packing away his IBM ThinkPad when he heard a sound that was most assuredly out of place in Underhill.

What the hell? Laying his computer on his bed, he went to investigate.

The sound penetrated the castle. Odras, the King and one of the guards were descending the grand staircase as Petrus came down behind them.

"Sire, what is it?" Petrus asked. The sound was vaguely familiar, but he couldn't quite place it.

"It sounds something like a motorcycle," the King said. "But in *Underhill?*"

"It seems to be at the gate," added Odras.

"Petrus, find out what the *hell* is going on down there," the King said. "Odras, please recheck the security of the castle and nodes."

"Of course, Sire." Odras dropped into a light trance.

"Aie," Petrus said, and set off for the gate house at a run. Halfway down he realized he was unarmed.

"Lower the drawbridge," Petrus ordered.

Scoriath nodded and gestured to a guard. After some awkward clanks and rattles of the chain and a deafening creak of the massive wooden hinges, the drawbridge settled into place with a dull *thwumpp*.

The rider had dismounted and now stood patiently with his hands folded in front of him.

"Welcome to Avalon," Petrus said brightly, offering his hand. "How may we help you?"

The man took Petrus' hand, and immediately the elf knew this was no incarnate human, but a ghost. *A special ghost, to be able to look the way he does, and find Underhill, much less Avalon!*

"Avalon," the man said, his eyes drifting past Petrus, to the elven community beyond. "I'm glad to see that you are doing as well as you are," he said, returning his attention fully to Petrus. "I recall hearing of the . . . unfortunate fall of your home some time back. I am Thorn, and I am a Rider Guardian. I serve the Lord of the Land of Shadows."

Petrus' estimation of the stranger rose by several notches. *The Guardians, of course,* Petrus mused. *Odras told us about them. I never thought I would actually meet one.* Everything about Thorn, his aura, his composure, his total absence of malice, seemed to confirm his claim.

"I am honored," Petrus said, slightly humbled in the presence of this spirit. "Please, come with me back to the castle. Our King will want to meet you."

Thorn walked the bike alongside Petrus. When they reached the gate house, Petrus said, "It's okay. He's a friendly." Scoriath nodded.

"If I didn't know any better, I would say that motorbike is an elvensteed. She seems to have the spirit of one."

This was clearly the right thing to say. Thorn beamed, his broad grin like a splash of sunlight. "She's my girl, Valerie. She has her own soul, but she's a bit nervous in Underhill. Unfamiliar territory, and all."

After meeting Thorn, Aedham seemed completely at ease with the visitor, and afforded him the same respect he would a visiting King.

After the formal introductions, Thorn spoke respectfully to Aedham. "I have encountered elves in the world of sun and body. They intruded on my domain by assuming the form of motorbike riders. They seek to subdue one of my charges, a man named Wolf who is in great danger."

"Elves?" Aedham said, his ears pricking noticeably. "What did they look like?"

As Thorn described the two in detail, the King's face

darkened. "One of them was named Nargach, but he was not the leader. I take it you know of them?"

"It's Japhet Dhu," the king said. "The son of the Unseleighe who destroyed Avalon." Aedham turned and faced the valley beyond the moat, his expression betraying deep, grim thoughts. When the King bathed himself with darkness like this, Petrus got nervous. Everyone remained silent.

Odras stepped forward, curious about the motorcycle. "May I?" he asked before approaching Valerie.

"Certainly," Thorn replied.

Odras examined the bike. "What is *this* called?" he asked.

"The front fork," Petrus provided.

Odras looked up from the bike, his face on fire with a new idea. "Petrus, imagine, if you will, amene and topolomite crystals located on the 'front forks.' "

Of course. "And an elvenstone on the wheel."

"No, several elvenstones," Odras said. "This could get rather exciting."

Thorn looked confused, but didn't ask for clarification. The king spoke, drawing their attention away from the bike. "I would like to offer an alliance," he said to Thorn. "With *you,* if it is within your domain."

"I was going to suggest the same," Thorn said, smiling shyly. "But I didn't feel bold enough. I don't know what help I would be, as I am no warrior, and my powers are limited. I am not a violent spirit."

"That's all right, we'll make up for it!" Petrus blurted without thinking. Odras flinched, then grinned, a eerie sight on an old elven mage. The King visibly suppressed a laugh. Petrus shrugged, as if he had only stated the obvious.

"Petrus speaks for us all," the King said, "And I must tell you up front, I intend to kill this clan of Unseleighe."

"I have no problem with that," Thorn said. "They are

a threat to Wolf, and it is my duty to protect him." He extended his hand. Aedham gripped it.

"Done," King Aedham said.

Lucas woke with images haunting him from the night before, feeling a little sick and nervous. As he stared at his bedroom ceiling he wanted to feel the same elation he'd experienced the night before at having been admitted into the secret, mysterious cult. Instead he felt tainted, an unnerving feeling after having pledged himself to this thing.

Yet, he felt stuck in it. *They threatened to kill me. For what? Turning them in? What would they do that would* . . .

His thoughts trailed off into fear as he recalled the blood he'd drunk during the little ritual. It'd had a strange taste to it, but what was he saying? He didn't know what blood tasted like, except for what he might have had in a rare steak, or . . .

From my own cuts. When I was shaving, and whacked myself good on my upper lip. He'd tasted blood then.

He started feeling nauseous, and got up to go to the bathroom in case he had to puke. But once he got there the feeling went away. Still, he felt dirty, and got into the shower, where he washed himself until the hot water ran out.

Afterwards he decided to do something about this, instead of just feeling scared. The next logical step was, *get out of this thing. How much of a hold do they really have on me?*

Chapter Ten

The Creator roused Ha-Sowa from a long , fitful sleep, and said: *Another Chaniwa medicine man has come of age. A Chaniwa* chakka.

It had been the reason for his being, Ha-Sowa recalled in the deep, misty recesses of his memory. The creator, *Nargak*, had summoned him from a mire of other demons, some formed, some not. The creator had pulled him from the chaos and given him a purpose. First, to kill the chakka. Second, to harass and torment the Chaniwa. Ha-Sowa had learned from the world of matter, and the strange beings who lurked there. He, like other spirits, had been attracted to this desert land of pinyon and juniper; the veil between the worlds was thin here.

Ha-Sowa felt other stirrings. Nargak, the creator, was near.

The demon stood in a typical feline stance, tail flicking, eyes narrowed.

The hibernation was over.

Ha-Sowa was fully awake, and restless.

Damien kept a black Ford van, circa 1977, in a rented warehouse near downtown Albuquerque. He used the van for special errands only, when Satan's work promised to be dirty. Tonight promised to be dirty indeed, and he didn't want anything traced back to the Temple of Satan.

"Keep it *down*," Damien said irritably as he drove the van down darkened streets, toward Highway 60. Heather was trying to snort a line of heroin straight out of a one-zip baggie using a soda straw, in plain sight of the sparse traffic around them.

Marvin and Edwin sat rather quietly in the back, a quiet he decided to savor. Satanic Panic was not going to be with them tonight, for which he was grateful. Damien had never seen anyone ramble non stop, for hours, and end up saying absolutely *nothing*.

Damien had ordered street clothes, rather than robes, in case they did get pulled over. Heather passed the bag of heroin back to Marvin, who did his share and passed it to Edwin. Damien no longer needed the drug to do the work.

That kid had better still be gone, Damien thought, not looking forward to canceling tonight if the son had decided to show up. During a brief drive-by at sundown Damien had seen that the bike was not there. On this trip he had brought a small but costly infrared scope. A half hour later they were parked on the highway down from the old Indian's trailer. Damien looked through the IR and saw that the Harley was still gone. He checked his tools; ritual blade sheathed at his belt, the baseball bat on the floor between the seats, the Ruger in the cross draw shoulder harness, should things go awry. His last precaution was to put on surgical rubber gloves, and then to watch over the others to make sure they got theirs on.

Looking good, he thought, driving the van up the short dirt drive. In the trailer was a single dim light, perhaps a TV. He pulled the van up and stopped, letting it idle, and put on the brights. Experience had shown him that it helped when the sacrifice was somewhat blinded before the first blow.

Ah, but he is a frail old man, Damien thought. *Must be careful not to kill him right away.*

It bothered him that Satan was not in his head this evening, but such was often the case in times of the Sacrifice. The first few times the Master'd had to coach him through the routine, but now he knew what to do. That the others were watching, letting him do the work, gratified him to no end. *I am, after all, the Ipsissimus. The leader. It's my* job.

For a time nothing happened as they sat in the van, the headlights illuminating the dingy little trailer perfectly. Damien had started to wonder if anyone was home when the trailer door opened up, and the old Indian stood framed in the doorway, wearing some kind of robe, holding a double barreled shotgun and aiming it toward them at waist level.

"*Shit!*" Marvin exclaimed. "Let's get out of here."

"Just hold on," Damien said, feeling bold. He turned the engine off, but left the brights on. Then he got out, but remained behind the van's open driver door.

"Uh . . . excuse me. We're lost," Damien said, projecting as much innocence as he could. "Sorry to bother you, but do you know where Mountainaire is?"

The Indian stood there momentarily, then lay the shotgun down and stepped down from the trailer. Slowly, as if he'd just wakened, he walked toward the van, holding his hand up against the light.

"*Now,*" Damien told his group, reaching for the ball bat. "Look sharp."

"You go . . . up the highway. About twenty miles . . ." the old Indian began so say, but the baseball bat slugging him in the stomach prevented any more words. He doubled over, groaning, and fell to his knees. Damien smacked him in the back of the head. The Indian collapsed on the ground.

"Oh, hell," Damien said, disappointed. *I hope I didn't kill him.*

Damien turned him over. His mouth was hanging open, but he breathed ever so shallowly.

"The ritual has *begun!*" Damien shouted to the rest, the signal to begin unloading the few odds and ends they had brought to add atmosphere to the ritual. What ensued became a bit of a blur, but strangely organized as they methodically set up thirteen black candles in a circle around their sacrifice. Heather giggled hysterically.

The candles were lit, and Damien reached in and turned the van's lights off. The group was standing around, waiting, expecting. Edwin handed him the goblet, reminding him what he had to do next.

"In the name of Satan our master, I do sacrifice thee!" Damien intoned.

Without really thinking, or feeling, he unsheathed his knife and cut the old Indian's throat, deep into the artery. A fountain of blood spewed momentarily, caught in the light of a candle flame. Damien caught it in the goblet. When the goblet was half full he stood to his full height, holding it aloft.

"From this we drink our reward from the great one," Damien said, trying to remember the ritual he had prepared for this event. It was to be a condensed version of what they normally did; they had almost been caught last time. *Oh, to hell with it,* he thought. *We've done what we came here to do.*

"Here, in the fourth hour of darkness, we have made our sacrifice. We have served the Master!" He drank and passed the goblet to Edwin.

"We have served the Master . . ." Edwin said.

"*We have served the Master . . .*" Heather said, and giggled.

Damien waited until Marvin had drunk. "Okay, we're finished. Get everything back in the van. Marvin, help me move him inside the trailer," he said, grabbing the Indian's arms. Marvin obediently opened the trailer door and took up the feet, and without much effort they moved the body inside. Leaving him out in the open, with the black candles still burning, was tempting; it was always a thrill to see his handiwork splashed across the front page of a newspaper, with captions including such hysterical phrases as "Devil Worshipers" or "Satanic Crime." But the sensible thing to do was to conceal the body somewhat, to delay discovery a bit.

The shotgun caught his eye as the flickering gray light of a black and white television passed over it. The sight made his blood boil; the weapon had been intended for him.

Marvin eased out of the trailer as Damien picked up the weapon.

Wait. Kill the son, too, a voice in his head said, faint like a whisper . . . then it was gone.

Was that you, Master? No answer. *Must be the stress,* Damien considered, before turning his attention back to his work. *No neighbors, no concern,* he thought, calculating the amount of sound the gun would make. He pressed the barrels against the center of the old Indian's chest and pulled both triggers.

"He's meat for sure now," Damien whispered, dropping the gun.

Now it is time for us to get the hell out of here.

The van was already running, the lights back on. Damien climbed in, did a three point turn around and drove sedately, as he always did, back to the highway.

"Uh, Damien?" Marvin said from the rear of the van.

"Not now," Damien said, miffed he hadn't used his proper title.

"Ipsissimus?" Edwin's voice ventured from behind him. "There's . . ."

Now that's better. "There's *what?*"

"Well done, my human minion," a voice to his right said. "What do you do for an encore?"

This one was not a voice he knew. At all. Puzzled, he looked to his right and saw sitting on the passenger's side a short but impressive looking creature with long, pointed ears, wearing a long, satiny red robe, holding a short pitchfork upright between its legs, phalluslike.

"Holy shit!" Damien blurted, despite himself, and slammed on the brakes. The vehicle skidded to a stop. The engine made a sad, whining sound as it died.

"What the hell are *you?*" Damien asked, convinced that *whatever* it was wasn't human.

The critter frowned. *"What's this 'what' business? Who do you think I am, Damien Szandor?"*

"I, um," Damien stammered. Then he became acutely aware of his followers, all of whom had chosen seats in the back of the van, looking at him. *Was this a joke?*

"I am the *Master,* you fool. You just committed an atrocity in my name, dumbshit."

"You are?"

"Yes, I are," Mort said, speaking with Damien's voice. The effect was spooky. "Forgive the stereotype," he added, indicating the pitchfork standing upright as his forked tail flicked back and forth. "But sometimes tradition has its uses. I could appear as a chimpanzee if I wanted to, but somehow I don't think it would have had quite the same effect."

"Well, I suppose not," Damien said, now starting to regain some of his lost composure. "Please excuse my . . . surprise. You have never appeared to me in this form. In fact, you have never appeared *at all.*" The importance of what was happening began to sink in. "This is a momentous occasion!"

"You bet your sweet patootie it is. I have a special task for you," said the little Satan. "Now, that man you just killed back there. I mean, that was good . . . really good. But it's his son we're interested in."

So he was trying to reach me, Damien thought, cringing at the memory. "I should kill the son?"

"Oh, no. We want him captured. You think you can do that?" Satan winked, and adjusted the red fabric around him.

"Of course I can," Damien said. "But you didn't ask me to kill him back there, did you?"

Satan looked momentarily puzzled. "We don't want Wolf dead." He reached over, and touched Damien's right arm. "Just so you know I'm real." He leaned back in the chair, added, *"Ciao,* baby," and snapped his fingers. In a puff of sulfuric smoke, Satan vanished.

The followers in the back seemed too stunned to comment, and so was Damien.

The leader started the van and slowly accelerated west on Highway 60.

Nargach is becoming a problem, Japhet Dhu decided. *No, he's been a problem all along. He's now becoming a bigger one.* He assigned himself guard duty that night. It was just as well he was here, at the peak of a barren hill, watching over the ravine from a safe distance; this made a confrontation less likely, and right now he doubted he could defeat the mage in a magical battle. As his doubts continued to nag at him, he wondered if he would *ever* be powerful enough to defeat him.

To provide some sort of diversion for his men, who had long since recovered from the exhausting battle Underhill, he and Nargach had kenned a female. Nothing fancy, simple but functional, and with the kenned Persian tents and carpeting to complete the effect, the men were able to forget they were in the middle of a big nowhere.

At least, for now. Something is going to have to happen, soon. The men are getting restless, and so am I, Japhet thought, regarding the moonlit desert in silence, admiring its bleakness.

Japhet had thought the Mage had never been to this world before. Now, he wasn't so sure. Nargach's whole attitude changed soon after they'd arrived; began dropping sly comments to the effect that something big was about to transpire, and that maybe Japhet's hold on the group was not as powerful as he would like to think. But he knew that the Unseleighe had a tendency to change alliances as it suited them, and Nargach was maneuvering into a position to take over.

But then, Mort has yet to return, he realized, and saw the advantage of being where he was: out here, away from the rest, he would be the first to speak with Mort, and find out what, if any, progress he'd made with these thrice damned "Satan Worshipers" before anyone else did.

His eyes unfocused, and he slipped into spirit mode, one foot on the sand and the other on the ether. Imposed over the gray landscape was the familiar horizon of the spirit world, where he and Nargach had confronted that demon of a motorcycle rider. That was another enigma: *How had that little rat escaped from them?* Japhet had never seen *anything* move that fast before, in any world.

There is something else lurking here, something more powerful than mere human ghosts, Japhet mused. His new fear was that he would encounter one of these super spirits, and he would *not* be their equal.

Is this what Nargach knows? he thought, and a new fear came over him. The more he considered this, the more likely it seemed. Getting rid of Nargach altogether might be his only option if this paranoia became reality, and that was *not* something he was prepared to deal with in this place.

Japhet sensed something approaching from the spirit horizon, and with some relief he saw it was Mort. His relief turned to apprehension when he saw that Mort seemed to be *fleeing* something.

Mort was virtually flying; as he drew closer the Unseleighe saw what was chasing him. A black, four-legged animal *spirit*.

Mort's stuttering voice came into hearing range, and Japhet barely made out his frantic words.

"*Cat!* Cat, *big cat*. Big *Big* Cat. Big kitty, take cover!"

Mort flew by in a blur of red satin, the tips of his three pronged pitchfork leaving a tracer as he sailed past, toward the camp. "Big Big *BIG CAT!*"

"Mort! Come here and *report!*" Japhet commanded, but the little demon didn't look like he was about to stop.

Japhet summoned the energy to bring up some low-level shields. The shields snapped into place a good distance away, but the cat broke right though them. Japhet summoned a little *more* power, putting up the kind of shield that would stop an elf, but this only slowed the cat down; as if running through water, it continued its steady lope, straight for Japhet.

Levin-bolt? Japhet wondered. *If this creature just walked through those shields, what can it do to . . .*

Then Japhet saw why Mort was making such a spirited escape. The cat was a powerful demon, and he had not the time nor the resources to prepare any effective defense against it.

Japhet was considering his own escape route when a familiar and irritating voice called from behind him, "Ha-Sowa! I am Nargach, your creator. I order you to stop and await my commands!"

Japhet whirled. "Nargach, what *is* this?" he demanded. "One of your little surprises?"

"Perhaps," Nargach said, with a sardonic grin. The

others were coming to investigate as well. Now they were witnesses to this shift in power. *I should challenge him right here and now! How* dare *he humiliate me like this!*

But the cat had obeyed Nargach's command. *Did he say he was the demon's* creator? Challenging Nargach to a duel right here and right now seemed rather silly.

"Japhet Dhu, I would like you to meet Ha-Sowa. Ha-Sowa, Japhet Dhu." He omitted Japhet's title.

"You are . . . the Creator?" Ha-Sowa said, with a disembodied growl that came from deep within the cat's chest.

Its massive black head tilted as it studied Nargach, who reached up with one hand and drew a series of complicated sigils in the air. "Do you remember these, my child?"

The sigils vanished quickly, but apparently their ghostly image had lingered long enough for the creature to read them.

"And this?" Nargach said, and with a tiny spark of magic touched the cat's nose.

"Yes I do, my Master," Ha-Sowa said, and seemed to radiate content, its loud purr sounding like the growl of a motorcycle. "It has been so long. And my purpose remains unfulfilled. Do you wish something else of me? Have I failed you in some way?"

"No, you have not, my Ha-Sowa," Nargach continued, and turned toward Japhet, expression intense and daring. "This is not my first time to this land, *Lord,*" Nargach said with undisguised scorn. "Or did I neglect to mention that?"

"Perhaps you did," Japhet replied, feigning nonchalance with great difficulty. "I must have forgotten."

"The human you call Wolf," Ha-Sowa said to his creator, changing the subject. The creature sat on its haunches like a proud lion, relaxed but attentive, its tail swishing back and forth urgently. "There are others who attempt to subdue him. He is a *chakka,* and he is mine to kill, is he not? I intercepted and chased one of them here."

"So you have," Nargach said, glancing back toward the camp, where Mort evidently remained. "It was my way of leading you back to me. You did well to chase him back here, but you are not to harm the demon, or any of these comrades of mine, in any way. We have a purpose designed for you. Listen carefully . . ."

Japhet had not known he was capable of such hate. Glaring at Nargach, he watched helplessly as the power of the clan began to shift.

Not if I can help it, Japhet thought, temporarily setting aside his original goals. If he were to gain any ground in this new world, or even remain Lord of the clan, *Nargach must die!*

From the brief chaos of the Gate, Petrus led Moonremere into the hot dry desert air, touching down lightly on red sand. The hills of New Mexico, splotched with green shrublike trees, folded in around him. Petrus searched for the power to conceal his party.

Next came Thorn, who didn't need the Gate, but used it to ensure that they stayed together. He pulled away from the Gate, circled around, and began immersing himself in the trance needed to contact another Rider Guardian.

Next came Wenlann, then Odras, right behind her. By the time they arrived Petrus had located the energy they needed. Odras took over, following the traces down to the natural Earth to cast the concealing spell about them like a net.

"Well done, Odras," Petrus complimented. Odras quickly dismissed the gate, lest it attract unwanted attention. No sooner had they arrived than Petrus sensed something amiss. The earth energies felt tainted. He was no mage, but every Avalon elf knew the stench of the Unseleighe. And if their foul odor was here, however faintly, they could not be far off.

"Easy, girl," Petrus said to Moonremere, who seemed jittery in this new world. He nearly asked Thorn about his progress, but had been warned against distracting him. Odras pulled his 'steed closer to the young leader.

"I sense them too," Odras said. "They are here. But I know not where, yet," he said, regarding the horizon. Then he saw movement; a distant figure approached them swiftly.

"That's our man," Wenlann said. "Looks like he's on a beemer."

"Boxer," Petrus corrected, though both terms were applicable to this BMW motorbike. The rider wore a full white Bieffe helmet with visor, a black leather jacket and chaps. The white, red and black racing boots seemed more appropriate to a sport bike, which this was not, but still provided maximum protection.

"There's Hans," Thorn said. "What do you think?"

Hans came to a stop in front of them, pulled the bike up on a center stand, and dismounted. After taking the helmet off and hanging it on the handlebar, he walked over to Thorn, and the two exchanged hugs.

"Not much cold iron at all," Odras commented, who had been probing the machine for its constitution. "Most appropriate."

The two riders came over to the elves, Thorn's arm around Hans' shoulder. "Hans, these are the elves I told you about. This is their leader, Petrus."

He immediately dismounted and walked over to them, bowing slightly as he extended his hand. "Thank you for coming, Hans."

"My pleasure, Petrus. Good to make your acquaintance," Hans said in a German accent, and shook Petrus' hand.

"We needed a very special bike to emulate, and while we don't pretend to be true riders, we wanted to consult the best," the elf said, hoping he wasn't laying it on too thick.

"Well, you won't be the first to make copies of this bike," Hans said good-naturedly. "This is Nina. Will she do for your purposes?"

"Oh, yes indeed," Petrus said. Nina was a beautiful bike, though looking older than he had expected.

"Nina is a 1976 R75/6 touring bike. 750cc. Continental tires. Air cooled," Hans said proudly. As well protected as Hans appeared to be, Petrus was curious about what kind of accident could have possibly killed him. Thorn had warned him against asking such questions, though he had filled him in about his own demise with some pride. With other Rider Guardians this was considered bad manners.

Petrus admired the beemer, nicknamed a boxer because the small working parts of the engine were contained in a cast aluminum, aerodynamic box; on other bikes one saw the generator, wires, everything, exposed to the elements. Even though cast wheels were coming into their own in the seventies, BMW stayed with the wire-spoked wheels, along with the fiberglass fenders and handmade, black teardrop gas tank. All told, it was a style that had been in use by BMW since the thirties.

"She can top out at two hundred twenty," Hans provided.

Petrus stared at him. That was fast, even for a motorbike.

"Two twenty *kilometers* per hour," Thorn said, visibly cringing at having to temper the specifications with the correct measuring system. "That's about one thirty *miles* per hour."

"That's still fast," Petrus said, still pleased with the bike's performance. "But as elvensteeds, we could go considerably faster."

"You could," Thorn said. "But touring bikes, they usually stay within the speed limit. They're not in much of a hurry to get there. It's the slower, continuous ride they're after," he added.

"I see," Petrus said. *Perhaps, when all this is done, I can come back and grab onto a really fast bike, a real one. Like maybe a Ducati or a Triumph. Or a Katana or a Ninja or a K . . .* The elf didn't realize he had so much trivial bike information in his head. *Guess it comes from watching too much Speed Vision.*

"I think I have absorbed all I can. I will begin now," Odras said, climbing off his 'steed. "The BMW will make a most suitable conveyance."

Within seconds, the three elvensteeds morphed into BMW motorbikes, each identical copies of Nina, sitting upright on their center stands.

"And now us," Wenlann said. "We can be a little more creative, can't we? How 'bout something in *blue* leather?"

"Of course, milady," Odras said, and with what looked like a little more difficulty, gave Petrus pretty much a carbon copy of Hans' attire, which writhed into place around him as if alive. He was glad his sword remained in place, shrouded in concealing glamorie, and completely functional. Wenlann wore a different sort of gear altogether, a blue and white touring suit with matching helmet and boots.

Where did Odras get the idea for that riding outfit? Petrus wondered, casting an inquisitive eye in the Mage's direction.

"I watch Speed Vision," Odras replied to his questioning look. Then he focused on himself, and ended up with a full black leather touring suit with the BMW logo on the shoulder.

"Hey, spiffy," Petrus said, considering asking for more stylish change to his own gear, then opting to take care of this later. The scent of Unseleighe in the air had left him feeling anxious about getting under way.

The riding bags they had brought became, without

much alteration, luggage for the motorcycles. Petrus checked to make sure the laptop was still there. It was, along with what looked like a comfortable change of human clothing.

"Most remarkable," Hans said as he admired Japhet's handiwork. He climbed back onto his bike. "I must go now, Thorn. Good luck, to you all." Before slipping the helmet on, he added, "And have a *good ride.*"

"Will do," Petrus replied, sitting on Moonremere, who seemed quite content to be a motorcycle for the time being.

"I must be off too," Thorn said, and rode off in the opposite direction.

Petrus moved to put his helmet on, but immediately found a problem with their disguise.

"Uh, Odras?" Petrus inquired.

"Yes, Petrus?"

"Did you forget something?"

Then Odras moved to put his helmet on, and made the same discovery Petrus had.

"I'm afraid I did," he said, and, with a brief touch of magic, transformed their three sets of pointed ears to rounded human ones.

On the highway they watched their speed, keeping it just under 65, but it was an effort. The bike wanted to go faster. The New Mexican landscape filled the horizon around them, a beautiful desert land with a clear, blue sky, touched with one or two clouds, and a bright sun he was *still* getting used to.

Ah, this is the life! Odras sent.

Indeed, Petrus replied, but his riding euphoria was suddenly tempered by a blast of Unseleighe magic, somewhere close by.

Yes, I sense it too, Odras said. *What is that up ahead? A metal shack?*

To the left of the highway was barren scrub, but they

were coming up fast on a dirt road that led to a tiny trailer. The power he sensed was not quite Unseleighe, but was familiar, and this trailer was the source of it.

Investigate? Odras inquired.

Yes. We're turning off here, Petrus said, shifting down and slowing Moonremere. It was a bit of a letdown, stopping already, but this was important—and it was the reason they were here.

The black feeling became darker and stronger as they pulled up at the small trailer. Petrus parked, took his helmet off.

"Blood," Wenlann said, getting off her 'steed. Indeed there was a large stain on the ground, and Petrus drew his sword.

"The source is long gone. This is residue," Odras said.

Petrus was following the trail of blood to the door of the trailer. He didn't bother to knock, sensing no life on the other side.

The door opened with some difficulty, and looking down he saw why. Blood had coagulated at the bottom of the door, and the dark ooze dripped to the ground. Lying on the floor and looking up at the ceiling was an old Indian man, quite lifeless.

"Wax," Odras said, examining the blood outside. "This man was killed out here."

"Unseleighe?" Petrus said, but he knew the feeling wasn't the same. *If not Unseleighe, then what?*

"Not Unseleighe precisely," Odras said. "Someone, or something, trying to emulate the Unseleighe. Peculiar." He walked over to a set of tire tracks. "It's stronger over here. Where the blood *isn't.*"

Petrus was convinced they were the first on the scene, and it looked like it had happened within a day, or perhaps the night before. "There's nothing we can do here," he said, and even Wenlann, looking grim, nodded in agreement.

"I think this is going to involve us," Odras said. "I don't know how, but I think we will encounter who is responsible. It may even be Japhet Dhu. Or someone working for him."

"We can't just leave this, can we? And what about *our* tracks?"

Odras was reaching for something in his bag when he looked up, grinning. "What tracks?"

There were none . . . not even footprints.

"I think we should call the police," Wenlann said, glancing at the old Indian's body reverently. "We shouldn't leave him." For once Wenlann was agreeing with Petrus, and he didn't know what to think of that. This man had been around a long time, and touched the spirits more than most people ever did, Petrus saw in his face. *But who murdered him, and why?*

Petrus heard an electronic beep, and looked up at Odras, who was holding a cellular phone. "Spock to *Enterprise*," Odras said as he flipped the receiver open.

"You thought of everything," Petrus said.

Odras dialed 911 and spoke briefly into the phone, then pushed the telescoping antenna back into the device and returned it to the pack. "Thank Niamh, It was his idea. And his doing. I think we should, as they say, 'get going while the going's good.' "

In no time they had mounted up and ridden off, seeing no witnesses anywhere. It was the perfect place to commit a murder; there was absolutely nothing around.

When 60 connected with Highway 25, they turned north, where a sign directed them toward Albuquerque.

Chapter Eleven

Whatever it had been, it was the kind of dream that evaporated at the moment of waking. If it had been the girl again, she was gone now. He was in an alien environment: the sheets on top of him and beneath him were clean and white as lilies.

But where the hell am *I?*

Looking through a window, Wolf he saw he was up high somewhere, and it was still daylight. And he felt strange. Bits of memory floated to the surface: Grampa, riding his beloved bike, then the horrific death, her death at *his hands. . . .*

Then the pain, when he tried to move, made him catch his breath. It hurt to breathe, to move his arm, to scratch himself, even to yawn.

Footsteps drew his attention to the door, where he saw a nurse and a doctor in white. "I'm Doctor Vaughan," said the doctor. "Do you mind telling me how you dropped a hog doing almost a hundred miles per hour, and not break a single bone in your body?"

"Huh?" Wolf said. "Soft sand, maybe," Wolf said. *Guess I didn't mess myself up as much as I thought.*

"I saw a Polaroid of the bike," the doctor continued. "What was left, anyway. Was that a Sportster?"

"Yeah," Wolf said sadly.

"It's okay to come in, deputy," the doctor said to someone, unseen, in the hall. A sheriff's deputy stepped into the room, holding his hat in his hand. There was something disarming about the gesture, and something wrong. The man's expression bore straight into Wolf's soul.

"I'm Deputy Clarke," the cop said. "Are you Paul Laner?"

Wolf cringed. His foster parents had been the Laners. "Yes, sir."

"You sure were riding down Highway 60 in a big hurry," the deputy said casually. Then Wolf knew where he'd seen him before; his vision, after the wreck. This was the deputy who had pulled him over yesterday. "Was there some kind of problem back at the house?"

What *was* it? Hell, he had to think about that. "I just wanted to get out of there. I didn't realize I was going as fast as I was."

The deputy's face had gone neutral, and it looked as if this had come with an effort. "Do you live with your grandfather in that trailer you rode off from?"

"What is it?" Wolf said suddenly. "Is he okay?"

The deputy stared at him for a long, long time. Wolf did not let his eyes drop from the deputy's. He wanted to *know*, now, what was going on.

"No, I'm afraid he's not. We got an anonymous call this afternoon. Took us a while to figure out which trailer on which highway, but we found it. Your grandfather was murdered."

Wolf wasn't listening anymore. He had drawn inside himself, fighting the tears, afraid to cry.

"I'm sorry, son," the deputy said, and said nothing more for a long time.

There were only about a dozen reasons why this had to be his fault, his riding off and leaving him alone being the primary one.

"When?" was all Wolf could manage to say.

"Late last night. It was around midnight, maybe one o'clock in the morning."

The rest went unsaid: *Yeah, happened while I was in the hospital, unconscious.*

The deputy continued, "Son, did you have any enemies? Or any harassment, because of your blood? *Anything?*"

"Out there? No, not at all," Wolf said, but he had zeroed in on what the deputy had said: *Your blood.* For the first time, he thought of himself as a Chaniwa, on the day he had become the last surviving one. The grief pressed in on his throat, his chest, his own pain forgotten. "Who did it?"

"We're not sure. We're following some leads. What might have been a van or a truck had pulled in and stopped. The tracks of four people were all over the place. There were signs of burning candles, in a circle, around where his throat was cut. It looked like it might have been a ritual, or something." He cleared his throat, seemed hesitant, but resigned, about asking his next question. "Do you know of any devil worshipers who would want to hurt your family?"

Wolf shook his head. He didn't have to think very long about that one. *Satanists? Here? He's got to be kidding.*

But clearly he was not, and pressed on. "Do you know any at all?"

"No, none," Wolf said. "What makes you think they were devil worshipers?"

"Around the site of the murder we found traces of black wax. There were round impressions. And, there were thirteen of them. Thirteen black candles burning in a circle around the murder victim. Of course, it don't prove anything. But it is a strong sign that Satanic ritual was involved."

Wolf shook his head, again, mystified. "It just doesn't make sense."

"No, it don't," the deputy agreed. "That's why I was hoping you could tell us something."

"We hardly know anyone, at least that would come all the way out there. I'd been here for about six months. Before that I was in Iraq. Desert Storm."

The Deputy's eyebrows arched at this news. "Army?"

"Rangers," Wolf said. "Where is my grandfather's body?"

"The coroner will have to do a full autopsy. We can release it in a few days if nothing unusual shows up. The cause of death appears to be a shotgun blast to the chest."

Wolf closed his eyes at the news, and felt his lip tremble. *No. I'm not breaking down just yet. I'm getting out of here.*

"You can leave now, if you want to," the doctor said.

While the nurse helped him put on his ripped-up clothes the deputy waited outside. Wolf refused the wheelchair she had in the hall. Every footstep seemed to be a bit less painful, and it felt good to be moving around on his own, even if his entire body groaned in protest.

Deputy Clarke was kind enough to give Wolf a ride back to the trailer. It was late afternoon by the time they arrived, their shadows long and ghostlike on the red and yellow sand. Everything looked normal except for the closed trailer door. Grandfather always kept it open this time of day. The police tape had gone when the crime scene people were finished, but Wolf did find little lengths of coat hanger with little flags of plastic fluorescent tape.

Clarke explained the scene to him. "Those markers there, that's where we found the van tire tracks. Those over there, in the circle, is where the wax was. Most of it's melted into the sand."

Wolf wasn't looking at the wax; what drew his attention

was the large black stain in the center, where Grandfather had bled. He went to the trailer and opened the door, and nearly gagged on the smell. The bloodstain at the bottom of the door had clotted, and filled the cabin with the stench of spoiled meat. Blood covered the entire floor, and had dribbled down the cavity made by the shotgun blast after it had traveled through Grampa's body.

"You plan on staying here tonight?" the deputy asked.

Where else would *I stay?* It had never occurred to him to go anywhere else, this was his home.

"I'm not going anywhere for a while," Wolf said, estimating he had enough food to hold out a week.

"We took the shotgun in as evidence," the Deputy said. "Do you have any other firearms?"

"Yeah. A .357 Ruger."

The deputy nodded, apparently satisfied he wasn't defenseless. "I'll be back in a few days to make sure you're still alive. Do you need anything here?"

Wolf grinned, the brief amusement tempered by grief. "Coffee," he said, trying to forget that's what he'd gone after in the first place.

"You got it," he said, and climbed back into the car. "Take care of yourself."

It was a bit strange to see the cop car, which only a day before had filled his rearview mirror on the Harley, drive slowly off. The world was truly fucked up in a lot of ways, but people like this deputy gave him hope.

Wolf wanted to sleep, but he had work to do. With the few hours of sunlight left, he moved everything that might have some use out of the trailer, starting with the small twin bed in Grampa's bedroom. The coffee pot was high on the list as well, along with an old tortoise shell rattle that was at least two hundred years old. The old knife was still on the table, and he checked to make sure the coin was back in the bone handle. There were odds and ends including the TV and portable lights. He even discovered a whole pound of coffee stashed away behind some flour and sugar. Everything went into the shed. It would become his new home, and sharing it with the old Indian motorcycle warmed his soul somewhat.

The electric meter was barely connected to the trailer as it was, so it came off easily. Inside it were four 120 volt outlets, all he would ever need. He removed it from the trailer, and for the time being he propped it in the shed's tiny window. A corner of the shed used the power pole for support, so he took up the slack of the power line by wrapping it carefully around the pole. With a huge monkey wrench he turned off the water to the trailer, leaving the outside tap over the crumbling water trough as his only supply. Without a second thought, he poured what was left of the precious gasoline throughout the trailer, and with his Bic lighter set it ablaze.

Wolf watched the flames consume the trailer; it went quickly, as it was old and there wasn't a bit of fire retardant material in it. He watched in grim satisfaction the result of his work; the Chaniwa always burned the home of the dead, to eliminate all bad spirits lingering there.

And there are bad spirits indeed, Wolf thought, wondering if he would ever know who killed his grandfather. *Yes, I will know. As certain as this trailer is burning right now.*

The trailer burned down to the thin skeleton of a steel frame; there wouldn't be much for him to deal with. As he was about to turn and collapse on the bed, he saw a vague image forming in the flames.

He lit a cigarette and blew the smoke toward the image. Tobacco smoke would bring the truth out, whatever the truth might be.

But he really needn't have bothered. Grandfather was determined to talk to him. From coals of the simmering trailer, Fast Horse stepped forward, his image thin and transparent. *He looks pretty good for being dead,* Wolf thought, drawing on the cigarette.

So much I have left to teach you, Wolf heard in his head, as if his grandfather were talking to him from across a formica table as they drank their morning coffee. *No more time left, so I must tell you the important thing. Ha-Sowa is near. You did well to burn the home of the dead. That is the first step. But you must return to the ways of the Chaniwa, as that is all that will save you.*

Something popped loudly in the flames, but he hardly noticed it.

But how will I learn the ways when you are gone? Wolf asked.

The glimmer of a smile passed over the image. *I will not be gone, not as you think. You will have my knowledge. My memories. My soul will continue, but you will have everything else.*

You will also have a gift, a red Indian gift . . .

The image flickered, seemed about to disappear. Then, with the speed of a striking rattlesnake, the image shot toward Wolf and drove itself directly into him. Wolf wasn't ready for this. The impact of Fast Horse's soul colliding with his own knocked him backwards. Then, Grampa was gone.

Or is he? Wolf wondered, sitting up. He was still in pain, but there was something different about himself. *Monkakchi! Kika wama mi Akaniwa . . . Goddamn, I'm thinking in Chaniwa!*

"Foyimi okchaa afo si!" Wolf shouted, lying on his back. "Grandfather still lives!" he repeated. "Foyimi akshocki, avi bavanamai: or at least his memory is still alive."

Do I know everything? he wondered. *Or just what I should know. . . . I don't understand. There must be more than just the Chaniwa tongue. Something new, something that . . .*

Before his thoughts took another excursion, Wolf got

up and hobbled over to the ground where Grampa's blood had stained it, the place where these murderers had cut his throat.

The images came fast, and sharp, and painful. He fell over on his knees, and with his right hand, held himself up. With his left hand on the bloodstain, he closed his eyes.

. . . Headlights filling the window. They turn their brights on. This is a bad sign..Fetch the shotgun from the bedroom, open the door, see who it is.

Just some foolish people looking for Mountainaire. Put the shotgun down. Big black van, a man standing behind the door. His hair is deep black, like an Indian's, but is not Indian. Get a good look at his face. This is not an honest face. What's that . . . behind him. Awwrfmmmmmph. . . .

Four people, standing around. I'm hearing their voices. . . . They say, "The ritual has begun!" Doesn't look like a ritual to me. Looks like they're just kicking an old Indian's ass.

Knife cuts throat, hard, blood flows. They're drinking my blood. "In the name of Satan our master, I do sacrifice thee!" they say. It's getting dark. It's getting so dark, great Hand hold me . . .

Then nothing. A light, a voice. Too dim.

Wolf opened his eyes, blinking back the tears.

"I saw them," he thought, amazed. "God dammit, I *saw them!*"

The sun had set, and the chill of the night had begun to move in. *Have to get up, have to get under the blankets.* But he wanted to stay here, by the stained ground, he wanted to know everything his grandfather had given him, all of it, right now.

It's not that cold. The sand is soft. I'll just sleep here, on the bloodstain. I'll sleep here all night . . . all night long. . . .

✧   ✧   ✧

The sleep became a tunnel, pulling him from the now to the then. *Shilombish Hoshontikatchi Yaakni*, the Spirit Shadowland, the place you go when you die. Only the Medicine Men could go to this place without dying, and they often did so when they wanted to know something. Here, they spoke to the spirits. Fast Horse knew this, and now Wolf knew. But he wanted to know more, as it pertained to *his* now: What was the bad magic that killed his grandfather, and what was it planning to do next?

The tunnel became a river, and Wolf saw a vast land, wild and natural. Entering from the sea the winged canoe sailed upstream, slowly, fighting the mighty current with the breath from the sky.

Okoshi, the medicine man, followed the canoe with the rest of the tribe, and after the gods had argued and warred among themselves he came across the first, a *chi-en* and an evil one. Though the warriors were with him, Okoshi was afraid of this *chi-en*, who looked more godlike up close.

You will let me pass you worthless human! the *chi-en* spat, using the wind to carry his venom. *I am Nargach, prince of the Unsaylee, and you will get out of my way now!* The warriors heard this as well, and raised their loaded bows; Okoshi raised his hand, stopping them.

"*I hattak taha ishtimanokfila. Apiilachi ilhokoffi.*" Okoshi said.

(*This one is too much to worry about. Let him go.*)

The warriors obeyed, but they kept their arrows trained on Nargach, who walked away laughing. The *chi-en* continued walking into the fire, and Okoshi knew the *chi-en* was no more. The ring of fire disappeared.

Wolf woke with a start, not knowing where or who he was. Then he caught the unmistakable stench of burnt plastic and fiberglass, saw the smoldering coals of the trailer glowing dimly in the dark. A waning, near-full moon burning orange on the horizon had begun its ascent. Wolf had seen the moon rise and set on this barren landscape many times, made all the more brilliant by the Milky Way, a single, violent brushstroke of light across the clear sky. But this time things were different, the full moon spoke to him . . . or rather the goddess she represented beckoned him from the future, and the past, intersecting on the now.

The moon is different tonight, Wolf thought as he lay back down, slowly, on the bloodied sand. *I am different tonight.*

Fast Horse's spirit, still lurking in the darkness, whispered, *There's more. Go back to the Land. Ask the Hoshontikatchi, the shadows themselves, what became of us, what became of the Yaakni Alackchi, the medicine men . . . and why we brought the chakka to us, made them what they are now.*

Wolf closed his eyes on the brilliant Milky Way, and did as he was told.

A bear had probably killed the wolf; there was nothing else around that could have done so complete a job. Okoshi had no doubt that it was a bear, with its tracks left all over the place. But the wolf had put up a good fight, and even managed to draw blood; Okoshi knew the difference between wolf and bear blood, knew it by scent.

Okoshi carried the wolf's carcass to the circle, where the white woman wanted to work her medicine, *wikka*. She had *cast circle* and consecrated the ground with her blade, and awaited Okoshi. The elders waited as well, along with the *chi-en* boy who had taken a wife already, who was now pregnant; the circle was to help her too, though Okoshi didn't know how. The woman, Margot Jameson, knew the medicine the woman would

need to give birth to a healthy baby. It would be the
first *chi-en* and human, though *Akaniwa* was what they
all called themselves now. For a time the *chi-en* clung
to the name of their former tribe, the *Saylee*, to which
they had belonged before Nargach had conquered and
enslaved them. But soon they realized they were not
going back; their tribe was here, with the new *Akaniwa*.
The tribe's power was in the five pointed Hand; it became
their symbol, their doorway to *Hoshontikatchi*.

It was a medicine working for two purposes, combined
on the night of the full moon since both were essential
to the well-being of the tribe.

The wolf's body was slung over Okoshi's shoulders,
but it was getting heavy. He wished he'd brought the
young *chi-en* along, Alin, who had the strength of ten
braves. Obviously, their child would be strong too; all
the *chi-en* would add their strength to their blood. The
Chaniwa would be a stronger people.

But not with the Ha-Sowa ready to attack, Okoshi
thought, remembering the vision of the demon the evil
chi-en had left behind. Margot had agreed with him,
the Ha-Sowa was a threat, and was real, even if they
didn't know when the demon might strike. It may wait
a generation, it may wait two. It may strike tomorrow. . . .

So together, Wikka and the Yaakni Alackchi, they would
protect the tribe by protecting the child.

Okoshi arrived with the wolf. Margot instructed him
to put some of its blood on a staff she had prepared for
the ritual, and then put the wolf's body in the fire. Earlier
Margot had jumped over it, to the amusement of the
tribe, who joined her in jumping over the fire. It was a
cleansing, she had said, and the tribe felt its power. The
Chaniwa would also pay respect to the wolf, not only
for what it had been in its previous life, but for what it
would become. They would ask its spirit to protect them.

The *chi-en* knew of a way to incorporate the spirit of

animals, the stronger the better, into their own; they knew already the child would be male, so they needed a male wolf. Margot had sensed the wolf's death earlier that day, and declared tonight the night to make this happen. The moon was full, they had harvested abundant food, and they were in celebration. Now all they needed was protection from Ha-Sowa, and their future as a people would be secure.

They began the dance, and Margot used the power they had raised to talk to the spirits, and the goddess of the moon. The pregnant wife had become tired, and she lay on a deerskin within the circle, and everyone danced around her and the fire.

Okoshi entered trance with Margot, and together they sensed another wolf, a living wolf, outside the circle. It was a she-wolf, and it was mate of the wolf the bear had slain! She had followed its scent, and she was watching the circle from afar.

This was all meant to be, Margot had said to Okoshi, and the medicine man agreed. Together they molded the magic raised in the circle, and with the *chi-en* they cast the spell.

The newborn would be a new Chaniwa, neither human nor *chi-en,* and he would pass his power on to future generations. With the wolf's spirit a part of his own, he would shapeshift. He would be the first *chakka.*

As the flames died down, the wife lay peacefully asleep. The tribe sat, savoring the power of the circle, talking about their two different kinds of medicine, and it was all one medicine now.

Margot heard the she-wolf, beckoned her to come. *"Animals can cross the circle,"* she had said. *"People cannot. She won't harm us."*

Even the elders didn't become alarmed when the she-wolf came into the circle cautiously. She walked to Alin, then to his wife. She licked her swollen womb; Okoshi heard her say goodbye to her mate. The she-wolf turned, and walked slowly away, back into the forest.

The Chaniwa were crying at the sight, touched by the feelings of the she-wolf, but it was a rejoicing as well. It was a new beginning for them all, the elders, the young couple, Margot and Okoshi. And for the *chakka*. They slept around the fire that night, around the coals that warmed them all the way till dawn.

They woke to the sunlight of a new day.

This morning in the desert fall arrived early; Wolf opened his eyes, finding himself laying stomach down on cold ground beside the remains of the trailer.

Bit by bit the images of his dreaming came back. Instead of fading away, like they usually did, they became stronger, permanently affixing themselves to his memory. It was some of the most vivid dreaming he'd ever experienced, and a part of him knew it was more than a dream . . . it was a vision. He had relived the beginnings of the Chaniwa.

Enough thinking. Now for action. Wolf gathered loose boards, a couple of cinder blocks, and made an altar against the side of the shack. *I must turn to the Chaniwa ways,* he thought. *Grandfather said that's the only way I will survive.*

The dream catcher Hand of the Chaniwa went on the altar, along with a few chunks of quartz crystal in matrix, rough jasper, the old rattle. For a terrified instant he'd thought the pinyon carving of Ha-Sowa had gone up in flames, but he had saved it with everything else that was important. It went on the altar too; on top of the Hand. Next to the carving went grandfather's knife, which was also a medicine man's ritual tool called the *atami*. A half carton of Marlboros had been another find in the trailer, and he put a fresh pack on the altar, with a pack of matches. Wolf had heard once that the Chaniwa was the only tribe to use an altar; furniture of this type was a white man's creation. *Margot's magic must have impressed them for the tribe to embrace her tools so totally.*

In the center of the altar went the most sacred thing of all: The Mr. Wake the Hell Up took its rightful position as the centerpiece. He filled it with water from the trough, and coffee from his recently found stash, and after plugging it into the meter, turned it on.

Damn, it's cold. He went into the shed and found one of Grandfather's *konsaintas,* the one made of deerskin, and put it on. From the pile of dishes he'd salvaged he pulled out his coffee cup, went back out to the altar, lit a cigarette, and sat.

"I miss him already," he said to the horizon, letting the ache in his throat rise up and become a full sob. As he sat there, he realized, with a horrible sickening clarity, his true position in the universe.

I'm the only one left.

He thought he had known what loneliness was, but sitting there, waiting for his coffee to finish brewing, contemplating his shack, the pile of pathetic possessions, and the scrub land around him, he discovered a level of loneliness he hadn't thought was possible.

Wolf knew sadness, and he knew pain, and he also knew the conditions didn't last. He tried to meditate on the gift Grandfather had left him, an instant awareness of a fully trained Chaniwa medicine man . . . or perhaps a partially trained one . . . and tried also not to fill his morning with hatred for the ones who had killed Grampa. Hate was not a feeling he liked, and he decided then that he wouldn't nurse it into being every time he thought about Grampa.

Grampa . . . Fast Horse . . . Okoshi . . . he thought, remembering something from the dream, something he had missed while experiencing it. The medicine man who encountered the *chi-en,* the one who led the tribe to the children of the gods. *He acted just like Grampa,* he thought. *It was as if he was Grampa.* It was a strong belief that medicine men were reincarnated as future medicine men throughout the history of the tribe.

Then it hit him. *Okoshi means fast running horse.*

With that comprehension the desert, and the entire universe, got just a little bit smaller.

The coffee maker's loud blurt disrupted his thoughts, shaking him from the half trance he'd fallen into; he reached for the coffee cup, an automatic morning reaction, as involuntary as breathing. The carving of Ha-Sowa stood on the altar, imprisoned by the Hand. It looked like an animated cat, something that might have come out of a Warner Brothers cartoon. *Nargach, Nargat, whatever his name was. It's the same one, the same* chi-en *in the vision. He made Ha-Sowa.* When he thought the demon's name, he made certain to be looking in the Hand.

I believe everything else, now, he thought. *Now that I've had the Vision. Perhaps shapeshifting is meant symbolically, that the chakka had the strength and ferocity of a wolf? No, the legends were specific.*

Wolf-man, man-wolf.

A warm breeze drifted through, announcing the arrival of mid-morning. The *konsainta* felt good against his skin, soaking up the sun's warmth. Barefoot, Wolf gathered up the coffee pot, his cup, cigarettes and lighter, and walked a fair distance into the property. At the north end of the property was a range of juniper-spotted hills. After he'd walked a distance he stopped, and sat down cross-legged, his knees sticking out of the open slits of the *konsainta.*

At the edge of his vision, he caught movement. He looked up to see a distant motorcycle and rider poised at the top of the hill. Three more cycles appeared beside him, and they stood regarding Wolf for several moments.

Strange, thought Wolf. *I didn't hear anything.*

Apparently uncertain of their welcome, the riders picked their way through the rocks coming down. Only when they had come a certain distance did Wolf see this was Thorn with his old Harley, with three other motorcyclists he didn't recognize. Wolf surmised the Rider Guardian was just being polite as he descended the somewhat steep hillside in a leisurely manner, hovering about a foot above the ground. The other two did not appear to be spirit at all, but negotiated the rocks with skill, as if the motorcycles, the makes of which he didn't recognize, had minds of their own. They wore modern motorcycle garb, nice full visored Bieffe helmets. Wolf's curiosity was definitely aroused.

"Po-kwa-te, Thorn," Wolf said amiably, getting to his feet, with some effort; he wasn't entirely used to wearing a *konsainta.* "It's good to see you under better circumstances."

The other three bikes pulled in around him, and stopped. They were old beemers, each apparently the same make and year. The bikes looked old; sixties, early seventies maybe. Thorn was, as always, slightly transparent, betraying his ghostly identity. But he was still the shy country boy he remembered, the aspect of personality they both shared.

"Hi, Wolf," Thorn said, after pulling off the ever-present leather helmet. "I, uh, took the liberty of inviting some friends along. I hope you don't mind."

The other three had dismounted, and had begun taking off their helmets. One was taller, and darker of skin than the other two, who were, well, goodlooking young kids, apparently out for a ride in the hills on machines far from suitable for the purpose.

The girl especially . . . their eyes locked, and in that moment he remembered the dreams of her, the ones he'd wakened to nearly every morning since his return. But something was missing, the identification was incomplete.

The boy stepped forward, looking normal in just about every way, but something was shouting at Wolf that they were anything but normal. Their eyes seemed peculiar, a brilliant green, with oddly shaped pupils.

"Wolf, I'm Petrus," the boy said, but his smile seemed forced, and his eyes were darting possessively back and forth between Wolf and the girl. "This is Wenlann and this, over here, is Odras. We are . . . Well, Thorn, should we tell him?"

"Oh, go ahead and *show* him. I don't think it will surprise him too much. Well," Thorn corrected, looking slightly chagrined. "Maybe a *little*."

"What are you talking about?" Wolf asked, not at all alarmed. "What am I missing here?"

Around the head and face of all three of the newcomers a brief cloud of distortion formed, then vanished.

Wolf rubbed his eyes, saw three *chi-en* in motorcycle garb standing beside beemers. The girl, Wenlann, smiled at him, and his heart missed a beat. Now, with the missing element of the pointed ears present, identification was complete—this *was* the girl he'd been dreaming of, and now she was standing before him, smiling seductively.

"*Okaayopi chi-en,*" Wolf muttered, dropping his cigarette.

"Hmmm?" Thorn asked. "Sorry. I don't speak Chaniwa, and I'm afraid our guests don't either."

"You're elves," Wolf translated, vaguely aware of the lit cigarette smoldering on top of his right foot.

Chapter Twelve

"You know," Wenlann said, after a moment of awkward silence. "I think he's taking it pretty well. I mean, didn' the King like pass out or something when Marbann delivered the same news to him?"

Petrus regarded Wolf with distaste, and tried not to let it show. *He sure is looking over Wenlann,* he thought, holding back his anger, and the sharp tongue that usually came with it.

Wolf realized the cigarette was burning on his right foot, and shook it off.

"Why don't you come over to my home? That shack just over there," Wolf said, picking up his coffee po and cup. "Please excuse the mess, but I just did some rearranging."

Out of politeness they walked their motorcycles over to the homestead, the elvensteeds more or less navigating themselves. Wolf didn't seem to take notice. As much as Petrus tried to deny it, Wolf had an aura differen from what he was accustomed to seeing in humans. I was as if Wolf were part elf, the way the edges of the field shone, leaving no doubt in Petrus' mind that Wol was at least a mage. Wolf looked somewhat effeminate in the animal skin robe he had on, and Petrus wondered what Wenlann could possibly see in him. Yet she wa

awking, in undisguised pleasure, at this human whom
he Unseleighe wanted.

Well, the Unseleighe can have him! he thought in a
noment of ill-feeling . . . which promptly turned to guilt.
*Volf didn't murder my family, the Unseleighe did. And
f the Unseleighe are his enemy, then Wolf is our friend.*

"This is not exactly a social call," Thorn said once they
ad arrived at the shed. Petrus glanced over the burned
emains of a trailer—and in that second, realized he
ad been here before.

This is where we found the victim. . . . Petrus thought
rantically, wondering what the link between them and
his human could be.

Wenlann appeared to recognize the place as well. *Why
'id he burn the trailer? Did someone do it to cover up
he crime?* She gave him a knowing look, but sent no
houghts; just as well, as they didn't yet know how sensitive
his human was. *Would not do for him to intercept a
ordless message.* Odras' expression was as neutral as
ver, but Petrus knew he must recognize the place as
ell.

"As you can see," Wolf said, lighting another cigarette
nd motioning toward the burned remains of the trailer,
I'm not exactly set up to entertain guests. After my
notorcycle wreck someone came here and murdered
ny grandfather." Wolf tore his attention away from
Venlann, who had parked the bike on the side kickstand,
nd looked Petrus directly in the eye. "Do you know
nything about it?"

Why lie? "We found him, yesterday morning," Petrus
dmitted. "We sensed some wrongdoing here, and we
ame to investigate. We found him dead, he'd been shot
n the chest. Odras had a cellular phone. We called the
olice, but didn't stick around." Petrus shrugged, feeling
he burning of embarrassment on his face. "There was
ot much we could tell them."

Wolf's eyes drifted over to a large dark stain on th sand. "I see," he finally said, and the elf had no idea he was angry or not. *It was as if he could hide his thought and feelings as well as Odras can.* The prospect chille him.

Wolf looked up, glanced at Wenlann in that maddenin way, then looked again to Petrus. *Well, at least he accepting me as the leader of our little party. I must a least give him that.*

"This isn't exactly your home, is it? I mean, our legen tells of another land, that is like an alternate dimensio or something, where the *chi-en* live. Is that where you'r from?"

"In a sense, yes," Wenlann said, before Petrus coul speak. "We've come here for a reason." She stoppec glanced up at Petrus, as if suddenly realizing she'd spoke: out of turn. "Petrus, you should speak for the group You are in charge, after all."

"You know something about my grandfather's deatl don't you?" Wolf asked, more as a statement, thoug not an accusing one.

"No more than we have said already," Petrus saic flustered. Yes, he felt like he should know more abou this murder. It and the dark power lingering after it ha attracted them the moment they arrived in this lanc even if it hadn't been directly linked to the Unseleighe *A close facsimile of Unseleighe power, perhaps,* h speculated.

"My people, the Chaniwa, we have a long history, Wolf said, taking a nervous drag off the cigarette. "I the early days of our tribe, we came into contact with group of *chi-en*, or elves, such as yourself. They wer once the slaves of Nargach, an Unsaylee being of you kind. Don't ask me what Unsaylee means, I don't know I do know that our ancestors, the ones who joined th tribe, were not the same." He paused momentarily, th smoke trailing up past his face, looking as if he were trying to remember something. "They were Saylee, the opposite. Enemies of the Unsaylee."

Wenlann gasped, but said nothing. Petrus stared at him, hardly believing what he was hearing. Without any prompting Wolf had described the core of the elven conflict Underhill, the Seleighe, the Unseleighe.

"If I'm hearing this correctly," Wenlann said, "Your ancestors are *elves*?"

"We, the Chaniwa, I mean, call them *chi-en,* but yes they are indeed elves, such as yourself," Wolf said, moving a little closer to Wenlann. Odras gave Petrus a warning look; the mage wasn't missing any of this exchange. "I feel like I've met you before," Wolf said to Wenlann. "Have we met? Do I know you from somewhere?"

Wenlann blushed, her gaze falling to the ground. For a moment Petrus felt like he was eavesdropping on a lover's conversation. Odras stood by his 'steed, patiently waiting for the conversation between Chaniwa and Seleighe to run its course.

"I don't think so," Wenlann said, "but I have to admit, I have the same feeling of, well, that I know you from *somewhere.*"

Well, as Thorn pointed out, they weren't here to socialize. They were on a mission for the King, and this line of discussion wasn't getting them anywhere. The Rider Guardian remained in their company, but Petrus sensed he was growing more distant as time passed. *And if Thorn knows more, he isn't saying, yet.* So far the alliance the King had made with this spirit had only led them to Wolf, which so far had been inconsequential, and unpleasant as well. *Perhaps we don't need Thorn after all.* But it wasn't up to him to dissolve the alliance, that was the King's duty, and Petrus' duty was to serve the King.

"Did you say the Unseleighe *Nargach?*" Odras inquired.

Everyone turned to the mage, including Thorn, then back to Wolf.

"Yes, it was Nargach. Or Nargat. This was the *chi-en* who enslaved the Saylee."

A shadow fell over the mage's face. "That explains quite a bit. I feel we might have stumbled onto something more powerful than any of us bargained for."

Now Thorn looked excited. "Nargach? *Nargach!* Are you certain?"

"As certain as anyone can be. But that was centuries ago. My guess would be even a thousand years ago."

"That length of time wouldn't matter to an Unseleighe, for two reasons," Petrus said. "Elves live *much* longer than humans. A thousand years relative to this world is a long time, but not beyond possibility. And second . . ."

"Second," Wenlann said, interrupting again. Petrus bristled. "There's the time rift between Underhill and this world. Time passes differently here." She looked to Odras, asked, "Is it possible this is the same mage?"

"Possible, and probable," Odras replied. "In fact, I'm certain of it."

"But Nargach," Thorn said, struggling to get their attention. "Nargach was the Unseleighe that I encountered recently. This is the reason I went to Underhill in the first place, to find Avalon."

Wolf looked like, well, that he'd seen a ghost. "When, Thorn?" he asked. "When did you see Nargach?"

"When I first made contact with you, after your bike wreck," the country lad said. "Two Unseleighe intercepted me, one of them was named Nargach. They wanted to bribe me to help them."

"Help them what?" Wolf said woodenly.

"They wanted to capture you," Thorn said. "They said they wanted to use your power, that was their interest in you. It's my purpose to protect you. Did I do well?"

Wolf looked at the Guardian incredulously, then cracked a smile. "You did fine," he replied, casting a glance toward Wenlann, who looked away coyly. "You did just *fine*."

"Something doesn't quite mesh," Petrus said, gritting his teeth. "What is the big connection? I can't believe this is all one big coincidence. Odras, do you know Nargach from somewhere?" *Of course he does, he must. And Odras is old, older than my father, older than I imagined. It's beginning to look like Nargach is manipulating Japhet, instead of the other way around. Ooooh, boy. What an Unseleighe mess!*

Before Odras could form an answer, which didn't appear to be forthcoming anyway, Wolf spoke up. "I know what the connection is," he said, sounding what, guilty? *About what?* Petrus wondered.

Wolf looked at something on the altar, then said, "It's Ha-Sowa."

Thorn, Wenlann and Petrus all replied, "Who?"

"A spirit . . . no, a *demon*, something evil," Wolf said, sounding miserable as he walked over to a long table with a coffee pot.

Wolf picked up a small wooden carving and held it out to Odras. "My grandfather made this. My grandfather . . . had intimate knowledge of this spirit. He knew what he was talking about."

Odras took the carving in both of his large, dark hands. "Long ago, the Unseleighe court knew more about demons than they do now." He paused to examine the carving in detail, then grimly handed it back to Wolf. "Some have lived to the present. Nargach is one of these ancients. I thought him dead long ago, until I felt stirrings in Underhill, deep, dark stirrings that reached beyond the depth of the typical Unseleighe. Then I knew he still lived, but I didn't know where. He must have insinuated himself in Japhet's remaining clan sometime shortly after Zeldan's defeat." The old mage took a few steps toward the table. "May I approach it?" he asked and Wolf consented. "I had heard rumors about the Chaniwa. And also of the brief slave trade the Unseleighe indulged in when the Seleighe were at their weakest. This altar," he said, scrutinizing the various items on it but not touching. "This is not typical of the human tribes of this continent, is it?"

"No, it is not," Wolf said. "It comes from the white man's land, from long before they settled here."

"The Celts," Odras said. "Celtic magic, in particular. This is the *pentagram*."

Wolf picked up the dream catcher, with its uneven five-pointed star made of sinew. "It's called the Hand of the Chaniwa. It is a symbol of our religion, as well as our tribe as a whole."

"You said 'tribe,' " Wenlann said, moving beside him to examine the dream catcher. "Where are the rest?"

"There are no others," Wolf replied, sounding sad. "Me and my grandfather, Fast Horse, we were the last. Now it's just me."

Despite his jealousy Petrus found it in himself to feel pity for this human, if only for a moment. *How sad he must be.*

"Here," Wolf said suddenly, placing the carving back on the altar and reaching for something else. "I want you to have this." He held out a necklace, which looked extremely, well, primitive. It was strung with what looked like animal teeth of some kind, with several hand-carved beads.

Wenlann looked overwhelmed. "This is . . .this must be a family heirloom," she said. "I can't—"

Wolf wouldn't take no for an answer. "Yes, you can. Please. Let me give this too you. It's important that you have it."

She looked as if she would argue further, then she

reached for something around her neck. "On one condition. That you take this in return."

It was the silver, heart-shaped Celtic knot. As they exchanged necklaces Petrus knew from that moment on that the situation had changed drastically in their small group, and he was certain he wouldn't like the results. However, he was powerless to do anything about it. *Remember the mission,* he thought frantically. *Remember the mission, that's the only thing that's going to keep me from going nuts!*

"It's beautiful," Wolf said. "And there's a . . . is that a wolf in the design?"

Petrus leaned over to see what he was talking about. Wenlann said, "I never noticed that before, but yes. The ears, the snout." She shook her head. "It's like it was invisible, until I gave it to you."

Petrus sought to change the subject. "How did a demon from our world get loose here?"

Odras replied, "Ha-Sowa is not a demon from Underhill."

Wolf looked up. "But I thought—"

"The Unseleighe are masters of turning the demons that haunt the humans' land to their own use; at least, they used to be. Nargach is one who still knows how to do this."

"The early tribes had no such spirit. Where did Ha-Sowa come from, then?" Wolf asked.

"The Egyptians called her *Hat Sotor,*" Odras answered. "Indeed, the cat was said to be a lioness; as the Unseleighe's goddess-slave, this lioness aspect seems to have embraced her entire appearance."

Odras sighed and contemplated the altar, as if the carving of Ha-Sowa would jump up and give him the answer his puzzled expression seemed to be requesting. "I would guess that she had weakened, not just with time, but with the passage of the culture that worshipped her. The Unseleighe would find such entities and give them a new purpose. *Their* purpose. Fortunately most of the thrice-damned Unseleighe clan lost touch with the ability to do so."

For Petrus the news raised another question: *How does Odras know so much about this?* The Avalon clan had been rather isolated before even Zeldan had attacked, and Odras was from a distant Seleighe Elfhame he couldn't remember the name of. At any rate, he supposed he was glad for Odras' knowledge. It could only help them in the long run.

If it could only help us now, he thought.

"We are here to locate the Unseleighe, led by a lord named Japhet Dhu," Petrus began, but Wolf seemed to be only halfway listening. "Nargach is with them. What about Ha-Sowa? Have you seen or felt her presence?"

Wolf looked at Petrus with a dreamlike expression, as if he were looking right through the elf.

"Ha-Sowa is near," Wolf said, at length. "My grandfather told me she was, and now I feel her. But she is my problem."

"No, she is *our* problem," Wenlann said emphatically. "Perhaps Ha-Sowa is the common link that's pulling all of us together. I'm not much of a believer in coincidence."

Petrus had to admit, neither was he. *So, now what? Contact the King, tell them what they had learned?* "Do you have a phone?" he asked.

Wolf looked around the remains of the trailer, the shack that looked ready to fall over. "What you see is what you get. No phone here." The human grinned, somewhat condescendingly. "What do you need to do, call your King? I'll bet the price of long distance is outrageous."

"Not with MCI's 'Friends and Family'," Petrus replied, not missing a beat. "Actually, what I wanted to do was drop him an e-mail message. It's even cheaper that way."

"Oh," Wolf said, but he had that polite but uncomprehending expression that humans and elves, who knew nothing about computers, both shared whenever the subject came up.

"Well, then," Petrus said. "Perhaps we should go on in to town, *as we had planned*," he said, moving to mount Moonremere.

"Well, ex*cuse* me while I pry that hint off my forehead," Wenlann replied sourly.

"Where we can contact the King, and perhaps find . . ." Petrus continued, but his voice trailed off, as he was about to say "find suitable digs," but that would have been most impolite. He made do with, "A place to stay."

"I would offer my home, but I think it would be a little cramped. Everything I have is yours," he said, but he was looking at Wenlann. "If you're looking for a good, inexpensive place to stay, try La Puerta on Central. *They* have phones."

"Thank you," Petrus said, and as Wenlann prepared to ride, he asked Wolf, "Are you, uh, going to be all right out here?"

"This is my home," Wolf said. "I am armed, as well. And I've got Thorn here to look over my shoulder."

"Be that as it may," Thorn said, who also appeared to be ready to ride, "perhaps you should consider staying close to these folk? I doubt I could handle much in the way of demons, short of fleeing them."

"I'll consider it," he replied, "but right now I must stay here."

"I'll be back soon," Wenlann said, without so much as a glance toward Petrus, who sensed the unspoken *"when I'm alone."*

Helmeted and ready to go, the three elves rode out of the homestead in single file, and made a right on Highway 60.

Traffic was light when they turned north on 25, which was fortunate since Petrus found the cold iron content in the cars and trucks they passed to be very uncomfortable, even through the leather he wore. It wasn't all that cool to begin with, and he was still getting used to having a bright, blazing sun in the sky. Moonremere seemed nervous around some of the larger vehicles, the big semi-rigs in particular, who not only made a horrendous noise but churned up air currents that made passing them on a motorcycle an adventure.

Albuquerque wasn't a big city, especially by Dallas standards. As they approached it from the south the skyline was limited to a handful of office buildings, multilevel garages and a few large hotels. Not an enormous metropolis, but not a little town, either; more than large enough to vanish into. What Petrus found so striking was the Sandia mountains and the infinite sky, clear and blue, that seemed to go on forever. And the comfortable dryness of the air was nothing like Underhill, which tended to be damp in Avalon.

And the *energies* . . . in the ground, all around them, unused, untapped, wild. There was the hint of a node somewhere near, but most of the power seemed to be a part of the wind as well as the earth. *Dallas was nothing like this*, he observed, wondering what Odras thought. He also wondered if the Unseleighe would be able to use this type of power against them. He suspected they would have trouble with it, and didn't want to distract Odras by asking about it now.

They took the Central Avenue exit and proceeded east, seeing a number of motels along the way. Along this stretch of street it looked like the main industry of the area was mobile home dealers and Indian crafts . . . any of the motels would have likely been suitable, but Petrus felt compelled to follow Wolf's advice and find *La Puerta*.

The long white adobe motel came up on their right, a large brick-pillared sign announcing *La Puerta Lodge*.

They pulled in just after the sign and stopped in front of the office.

Petrus glanced over at Odras, who had the honor of carrying their freshly kenned cash.

"The King said to prepay for a week," Wenlann reminded him as he took the bills from Odras.

Fighting annoyance, he said, "Yes, I remember what the King said." He caught a glance of the wolf's-tooth necklace, which enhanced his annoyance by a factor of ten, then started for the front door of the office.

A very small, frail woman stepped into the office. She had a little tuft of blue hair, pulled into a bun, with square bifocals, and wore a rather dated but functional blue dress, which went all the way down past her ankles. She stepped lightly over to an old, solid wood counter, greeting him warmly with a dentured smile. Just beyond the office he caught a glimpse of a quaint, comfortable living room, with an rather old console television blaring away with what sounded like a stock car race. The place had an old smell, of mothballs and cedar, not unpleasant, but warming. *No corporations here, just a mom, and a pop, and maybe a dog.* Petrus relaxed as he smiled at the woman.

"Lovely riding weather it is," she said, glancing out the window at the three motorcycles. "My husband and I used to tour on Indians, just after the war."

"Oh, it's been a nice ride," Petrus said. "Beautiful country as well."

The woman was studying the bikes further, which was starting to make Petrus nervous. Her brow wrinkled. "Are you folks all the way from Germany?"

Huh? What is she . . . Then he saw what she was talking about. *The license plates! Oh* sheisse, *Hans is from Germany, and so is his beemer!* Fortunately, only one of the plates were visible, the one on his bike, closest to the office. Otherwise she would have seen three identical plates.

"Those are beauties," she said, turning reluctantly from the window and pulling a card out of the drawers. "A friend of ours has an old slash two. Lovely shaft-driven machines, just *lovely*." She handed him a card and, thankfully, a plastic Bic pen instead of a metal one.

Petrus filled out the card with their "address," Box 11, Rural Route Nineteen, Kingman, Oklahoma. "I'd like to prepay for a week," he said.

"Oh, how nice," she said. "That's . . .oh, I can give you a discount. Seven days? One thirty, with tax."

"Thank you, ma'am," Petrus replied politely as he handed over the bills. "That's very kind of you."

"Oh, never you mind," she said, her eyes twinkling. "I've ridden motorcycles for years. We're practically family!"

Which explains why Wolf recommended this particular motel, Petrus thought, maintaining a sincere smile. She handed him two keys, each on big green plastic tags that said "La Puerta Lodge." "It's number seven, on the end. There's even a carport where you can park your bikes. You just let me know if you need anything. And you can call me Mattie."

"Thank you, Mattie," Petrus said as she rang up the money on an old, non-electric cash register. "We were hoping to find a nice place like this."

If I stay here any longer, she's going to start feeding me milk and cookies, he thought as he closed the screen door behind him.

The room was small but suitable, though the bed would be a little cramped for three. Looking over the room, deciding where the cold iron was, and determining there wasn't much they would have to watch out for except for the fixtures in the bathroom, Petrus realized there wouldn't be much time for sleeping on this mission, so the bed's size was irrelevant.

Odras brought in the bag with the laptop and set it beside the telephone on a small, imitation woodgrain table. Petrus began setting up the machine to dial in to America Online. Meanwhile Wenlann stood behind him, in front of the mirror, admiring the necklace Wolf had presented her.

Crap! I'd almost forgotten about that, he thought as he plugged in the adapter and began the brief booting process. He tried looking away, but it was impossible; the mirror was on the wall right in front of them, and the necklace, which she fondled lovingly, appeared right above the laptop's screen. It was as if she were taunting him with it.

Well, if she is, she's not going to win! he decided, and plugged the phone line into the internal modem.

"You know, this must be very old," Wenlann said. "These are real wolf teeth."

Petrus ignored her, concentrating on the screen. Then, a moment later, "Did you say something?"

"This necklace," she said, and Petrus had to glance up. "Some sort of power is connected with it. Do you suppose Wolf is a mage?"

"It seems possible," Petrus replied neutrally. "His grandfather certainly must have been. But that doesn't mean *he* is."

Odras spoke from near the door. "If you'll permit, I am going to place some protective wards around the perimeter. Then I might pursue this idea with these gemstones."

"Go right ahead," Petrus said. *We're about to have a hell of a fight anyway. He must have seen it coming.*

The mage nodded and slipped out of the room.

Petrus turned to the laptop, hoping the conversation would just end. Pretending to be busy wasn't much of a pretense; he hadn't used the AOL account in a while, and he was trying to remember how this machine was set up.

"You're not changing the subject on me like that," Wenlann said, from just behind his right ear.

"*Wenlann,*" Petrus said, making no attempt to conceal his irritation. "Do you *mind?*"

He typed a brief message to the King, giving their location, and a short summary of their encounter with Wolf.

"He was *not* insensitive to magic!" Wenlann protested, reading over his shoulder.

"Do you want to write this?" Petrus said, but sent what he had composed before she could answer.

"Well, I suppose it doesn't matter now," Wenlann said, and sat on the edge of the bed, the necklace now cradled in both of her slender hands. Petrus turned around and glared at her. "This bothers you, doesn't it?"

If she hadn't been smiling, mocking him, he might have held his tongue. But the situation suddenly made remaining civil an impossibility.

"*Yes, it bothers me!*" Petrus said shortly. "There! You wanted a reaction out of me, you got it."

"But why?" Wenlann said, this time sincerely.

"I . . ." He began, and stopped himself short. *Admit I'm in love with her? Now? No way!*

"We are Elven!" he ranted. "Not only are we Elven, we are *Avalon.*" Brief image of elf and human, in bed, making love. "It just doesn't . . . I don't know."

Wenlann looked like she was ready to laugh, which infuriated him further.

"I think you're afraid you wouldn't, how should I phrase this . . . *measure up?* Wolf is a human, and although he is a young man, he is a man! Is that what it is?"

And I'm not?

"You're still a virgin, aren't you?" Wenlann observed, accurately.

"It is not proper to discuss such things!" Petrus said, wondering just where in hell all this prudishness was coming from. *Was it a trait of the Avalon clan, fall back on propriety and decor when the argument is in trouble?*

Petrus felt his face burning. He felt his *ears* burning. Wenlann sat seductively on the edge of the bed, her legs crossed. *Laughing* at him.

"I'm going to go for a walk," Petrus announced, standing up. "Maybe Odras has a few ideas on how to find the Unseleighe."

His sudden calm amazed even him, he mused as he left the small hotel room. With a start he saw only two steeds, instead of three. From somewhere behind the hotel, he heard the purring of the third one. *Odras. What is he up to?*

Grateful for the sudden diversion, Petrus picked his way through a gaping hole in a chainlink fence, walked over a gravel lot and found a wide side street, flanked on either side with warehouses and industrial businesses. None of them seemed to be open, and except for Odras on the beemer 'steed, the street was deserted.

The mage dismounted the bike and pulled a half used roll of gray duct tape out of the saddlebags; Petrus saw pieces of duct tape wrapped around the spokes, and the front forks.

This looks really bizarre, Petrus thought, wondering if he should disturb Odras at work. *No, I've gotta see what this is.*

Odras looked up as Petrus approached, clutching a small leather bag and the tape.

"Whatcha doin'?" Petrus asked conversationally.

"Pursuing an idea," the Mage said, glancing around. "This seemed an ideal place. No humans about." He pulled a length of tape, ripped it off, and from the leather bag extracted a crystal Petrus recognized as diaspar, or elvenstone. "Do you recall the experiment in the workshop that produced such amazing results?"

"Of course," Petrus said, then saw what he was up to. "That's elvenstone on the spokes."

"Amene and topolomite on the forks. Admittedly, this is rather crude. But the duct tape has done well."

"The tape doesn't affect the crystal's field?" Petrus asked, leaning to examine the configuration of crystals on the fork.

"Amazingly, not. In fact, it acts as a sort of buffer. Takes the edge off the generated field, as it were."

Odras completed taping the elvenstone into place on the front wheel. Now Petrus counted five stones, equally spaced around the rim. "I've discovered that the elvenstone needs to be at even intervals. Otherwise the field pulsates unevenly. Difficult to work with."

"I see," Petrus replied, not sure if he did.

"Observe," Odras said, mounting the bike. The elvensteed started of its own accord, and the Mage rode off at a leisurely pace down the street. Immediately he saw a flashing of yellow and blue light near the motorcycle's forks as the five elvenstones passed between the amene and topolomite crystals. Though not a mage, Petrus knew this was an exciting advancement in elven technology. *This is not stored node energy, this is generated node energy! Just like in the workshop at home.*

At the far end of the street Odras was a mere spot. The mage paused briefly, then began riding swiftly toward Petrus, the 'steed's two-banger simulacrums increasing in pitch and volume as it approached.

The bike was traveling at a considerable speed as it passed, but not so fast that he couldn't see the white circle of power that had formed before the bike; tendrils of power streaked off the disc's edges and down past Odras, resembling licking flames. The mage seemed to be in full control of matters as he decelerated, turned, and rejoined Petrus.

"The optimum speed is right at fifty two miles per

our. Any slower and it doesn't stay together. Any faster,
and it falls apart."

"What falls apart?" Petrus said, still uncertain of what
he saw in front of the bike.

"A Gate!" Odras said, his eyes on fire with the discovery.
"Or a concave disc of node power that can easily become
a Gate with a little push."

Petrus smiled with satisfaction, a short lived feeling
as a complication occurred to him. "But what if we don't
want the Gate, or any energy coming from the front
wheel? I don't think we'll want that white disc preceding
us as we tootle around Albuquerque."

Odras untaped one of the crystals from the front fork.
"Remove the amene, put it away. The other two jewels
become inert. Nothing happens. The machine doesn't
work."

Petrus thought feverishly. *Do we really have time to
develop this? This is supposed to be a recon, not an
assault, or even a scientific expedition.*

Still, the possibilities . . .

"Nargach, what *was* that? That's the second one now,"
Japhet said, rising from a dubious state of slumber. Dry
wind wafted through the tent, the tassels over the
doorway dangling silently in the breeze. The other
Unseleighe, some still drunk from the evening's revelry,
had evidently sensed it too. They were struggling to sit
up, looking confused.

Nargach appeared in the doorway. "Node energy," he
said softly. "Toward the city."

"Human mage?" Japhet asked hopefully.

"Unlikely . . . not like this," Nargach said, his gaze
turning away. "A short flash, then it was gone."

"A Gate?" Japhet asked fearfully, before he could mask
his emotions.

"More powerful than a Gate," Nargach replied, his

eyes narrowing. "I think we may have Seleighe visitor soon."

Japhet Dhu stared at the horizon, wishing he coul just go back to sleep and forget this nightmare. But wit Seleighe in the area, the whole situation had changed again; first with the arrival of Nargach's blasted demon Ha-Sowa, now *this*.

It's time to change the conditions of the game, Japhe thought. *Time to return to Underhill, where the Seleigh will least expect us to go. And a place, if my guess prove correct, where Ha-Sowa has no power.*

This place was getting boring anyway.

Chapter Thirteen

Lucas was supposed to meet Panic that afternoon, for reasons that were still unclear. There was a bookstore and coffee house near the University that was supposed to be their contact point; the meeting was in half an hour, and if he walked west, he would be there in time. But he was having second thoughts about the whole thing, and before he could change his mind he started walking east on Central, toward home.

He looked up to see a black van going west, the driver gazing intently at him. He glanced behind him as the van passed, and his heart skipped a beat when he saw it was making a left turn into a parking lot. Fighting an urge to run, he made do with a swift walk. A second glance behind him revealed that the van had turned around, and was coming up behind him slowly.

Too slow, he thought. *Too damned slow.*

The van pulled up beside him, slowed to a walking pace.

Lucas hazarded a glance up, and stopped in his tracks when he saw Satanic Panic sitting on the passenger's side, grinning from ear to ear.

"Where ya goin'?" Panic asked, as the van stopped altogether. "We have a meeting, remember?"

Now what? "Oh, yeah. That's right. Look, I can't make it. I've gotta . . ."

Panic's expression changed to sullen disapproval, and Lucas felt weak all over again. "Come here a second. I want you to meet someone."

Feeling powerless, he went over to Panic's window, sensing someone moving around inside but not seeing anyone in the driver's seat.

Panic extended his hand, as if to shake Lucas'.

"For you to leave we have to shake on it." Panic's eyes narrowed, to slits. "You do want to leave the group, don't you?"

"Yes, I want out. This is sick shit. I don't care what I promised, I was stoned out of my mind." He reached for and grasped Panic's hand. "I want out."

"It's a *deal*," Panic said, rather loudly, but he wasn't letting go of Lucas' hand. His grip tightened. Lucas tried pulling away.

The van's side door flew open, and he saw a large man, wearing a hockey mask, holding a white cloth in his right hand.

It happened quickly, suddenly, and Lucas' last thought as the cloth closed over his face was that these assholes must have done this before.

Dammit to heaven and back, I knew the kid was going to flake, Damien thought. *Oh well. Such things happen. Not everyone is ready to be enlightened. Not everyone has what it takes. Very very few, in fact.* In the long run it all worked out. Those who didn't quite cut the satanic mustard were often loners anyway, making them excellent gifts for the Master.

He pulled the kid into the van and dropped him on the floor, then slid the door shut. The boy was limp but he was still breathing, however shallowly.

"You know what to do," Damien said to Panic as he returned to the driver's seat. As Damien pulled away he heard the familiar rip rip rip of duct tape being sectioned off. "Get the hands and feet real good. One long piece is usually enough for the mouth," Damien prompted, but he needn't have worried.

For a second or two Damien caught a glimpse of the Master sitting in the van's far back seat; his face was calm and approving. He must have been sitting there the whole time, invisibly watching his work. This had happened before; it was the Master's way of testing him. Then the Master vanished, but Damien knew he wasn't seeing things.

To the cabin, he thought gleefully. *There is much to do.*

Once Nargach dismissed the kenned tents of their temporary homes, the ground beneath them looked as if nothing had touched it. The mage also refreshed the glamorie on the 'steeds, renewing their sharpened image as Harley Davidsons, before they set out on their short journey to Damien's cabin. Mort rode on the back of Japhet's 'steed.

It will be most gratifying to return home, where Nargach cannot toy with my clan. I may even suggest that Nargach stay here, to make his own way. I can do without a mage for a time, and sooner or later I will come across another. Nargach must go.

But to rid myself of him as only an Unseleighe might, that is the challenge. Short of destroying him outright, I must cast him from the clan without his even knowing, while not losing face in the process. Let him stay here with his feline plaything. I'd rather he make his own kingdom than try to take mine!

Such as it is. . . .

"Turn off here," Mort said, indicating a dirt road that seemed to go nowhere. "It's a large section of land."

Indeed it was a vast place, Japhet discovered as his 'steed deftly negotiated the dirt and gravel, something an ordinary two wheeler would have found difficult. Vast and hilly, the land would conceal them well, better than the ravine they had just abandoned. *And we may stay here with the blessings of the owner. I can't think of a better stage upon which to fortify my forces.*

An unassuming adobe building appeared ahead of them. A black vehicle was parked in front of it, a nasty construct of cold iron the elves went out of their way to avoid. Their clan of five pulled up and parked in front of the cabin as if they owned it, while Mort disappeared temporarily, apparently to alter his appearance.

A human appeared in the doorway, looking frightened as the bikers dismounted, regarding their surroundings with displeasure.

Japhet waited for some time, eying the human suspiciously, noting that he didn't seem all that impressive. *Has Mort finally erred in selecting a weak partner for us?* He reminded himself that their choice was limited by the sparse population of this land.

After a long moment, during which nothing had happened, Japhet grew impatient. *Where is the little devil?* he wondered.

Still, no Mort. The leader was considering taking the matter into his own hands when a cloud of acrid, sulfuric smoke appeared between the elves and the human. From the cloud stepped Mort. The Unseleighe stifled a laugh when he saw that Mort had become a larger, taller version of himself, wearing a black suit. He had even assumed the pointed ears of the Unseleighe. *Such a handy little helper Mort is.*

Yet after Japhet had briefly studied the demon's new form, Mort's size surprised him. It was not mere illusion. but an accurate depiction of what he had made himself. which told Japhet that he had gained considerable power. In fact, in this form, and with the power he saw lurking beyond it, Mort could have challenged

Ha-Sowa instead of running from her like a coward.

No time to muse over what this means, Japhet thought, and turned his attention to the exchange between Mort and the pathetic human.

"M-Master," the human stuttered. "Is this your true image?"

Mort hazarded a wry look back at Japhet, one which both assured and amused the leader. *I know that look. He's going to toy with him.*

"Close enough, for talking purposes," Mort replied, but his voice was deep and amplified, the voice of a god. "These are my demons, my makers of evil. You will afford them the same respect you afford me, always, and absolutely. Do you understand, Damien?"

"Yes, Master," Damien said solemnly. "I am your servants' servant."

Mort nodded appreciatively, while Japhet suppressed outright laughter. *Ah, so this is the mysterious Damien,* Japhet thought, somewhat disappointed. *I'd expected more.*

Mort continued, in his grand way, "I have summoned you to do my bidding. Have you the gift I requested?"

With some irritation Japhet saw that he had not been kept informed of the deals Mort had made with him. *What gift?*

"Master, we have not succeeded in fulfilling your request," the human said. "Until we do . . . we have this to offer. Please, come inside."

Japhet noted with further apprehension that Mort easily decreased his size just enough to fit in the dwelling's doorway. Again, another display of power the Unseleighe didn't think he had.

So let's see what gift they have for us, Japhet considered.

The cabin was deeper than it was wide, and much larger inside than he had expected. A stench filled the cabin, which the leader found refreshing.

"I'm afraid I'm lacking in electricity and water," Damien said, as Mort examined the cabin as if he were a military officer inspecting his soldiers.

"I am not concerned with such trivial matters," Mort said, in that deep, booming voice. "What do you have for me, my servant?"

"In here," Damien said quickly, pushing open a door. Inside was a crude table and a soiled mattress, upon which lay a human boy, bound with gray cloth around arms, legs and mouth. The boy was sleeping soundly, and Japhet had the distinct impression he had been drugged into that condition.

"What's this?" Mort exclaimed in obvious displeasure. "Do you mean to say this *child* is your gift?"

"Master, it is what you always wanted. . . ." Damien said, then looked as if he wished he could recall the words. "Of course, if there's someone else, we can of course—"

"I have already *made* my request," Mort said, in a low, threatening voice. "What has delayed you in obtaining the human known as *Wolf?*"

"But, Master, we must wait for the proper time," Damien replied weakly.

"The proper time is *now*," Mort said. "And I can wait no longer. You will obtain that which I desire, or I will find someone worthy of my favor. Do you understand?"

Damien bowed his head submissively. "Yes, Master, I hear and I obey."

"Before midnight," Mort said, as Damien made his way for the front door. "Meanwhile my demons will remain in this humble trash heap you call an abode until your return. *Then* we will decide your worthiness."

Already Damien was stumbling toward the van. "Yes, yes I will. . . ." he said, the vehicle's wheels kicking sand and gravel as he drove off.

"Well done, Mort," Japhet replied, with a chuckle. "I

don't think I could have done better myself. Perhaps you would do well to stay here."

Mort turned, changing back to his original appearance before he addressed his leader.

"You mean here, in this world? What have you in mind? Are you taking the clan elsewhere?"

Semion and Domnu were listening with interest, as were Ruadan and Nargach, who seemed appropriately surprised and suspicious.

"It is time to return to Underhill."

"Is that so," Nargach said. "What has prompted this . . . swift decision?"

"By no means did I come to this conclusion hastily," Japhet said, returning the mage's hard look with one of his own. "I have a plan. Until now, we have reacted to the Seleighe's defenses."

"You mean *fled*?" Nargach said.

" 'Tactical retreat' is the phrase I would choose. You may call it whatever you like. This time, however, we have an advantage. We have an opportunity now to take hostages, starting with that child in the cabin."

"The Seleighe have arrived," said Nargach. "Taking a hostage will only give them a reason to intensify their chase. What strategy is that?"

"You're not afraid of these lesser elves, are you, my dear Nargach?" Japhet chided mockingly.

"*I do not fear the Seleighe.* They are all children compared to us. I simply question whether we should lie low in this land, consolidate our power as originally planned, and then act."

You mean, Japhet thought, *you wish to remain here so that you can consolidate your forces, using Ha-Sowa as a foundation!*

"Your father did quite well here," Nargach continued. "Why do you question your own abilities to do the same?"

No, Nargach, you will not shift the topic that easily.

"If it is your precious demon you are concerned about, she is more than welcome to accompany us to Underhill."

The mage replied with stony, hostile silence.

"That is, if she *can* go with us. You created her. You did allow for contingencies like this, did you not?"

"Ha-Sowa is tied to *this* land. If we return to our rightful home in Underhill, she will remain here."

"I see," Japhet said. "So it is not an issue."

"*Gentlemen*, gentlemen, gentlemen," Mort said smoothly. "Forgive me, but I have neglected to mention, there are only three Avalon Seleighe. I have been so preoccupied with handling this human cretin Damien that it completely slipped my mind."

Japhet stared at him, going to no trouble to conceal his irritation. *This is not like Mort. Is he becoming more independent than is comfortable for us?* "Why didn't you tell us before?"

Mort said, submissively, "As I have said, I was busy dealing with these silly humans. That blast of energy you felt, it attracted my attention as well. I went to investigate, and keeping a safe distance I spied three Seleighe elves I recognized from Avalon. Two young elves, and a mage. Odras, I believe his name is."

"*Odras?*" Nargach exclaimed. "But he's . . ."

"He's what?" Japhet asked. *He sounds like he knows this Seleighe.*

"He's in the employ of Avalon," Nargach continued, but Japhet suspected this was not his original thought. *Something to pursue later, perhaps.* "I'm not very impressed with his talents. If he had stumbled across something powerful, which apparently he has, he probably doesn't have the skill to make use of it. I would call what we felt an anomaly, and something we shouldn't concern ourselves with."

"I know where they are," Mort said smugly.

Japhet considered this carefully, but quickly. *Only*

*three Seleighe, and one is a mage. We outnumber them.
If we attack, their mage will likely attack Nargach
first, and perhaps kill him, which would solve one
problem for me. And it would avenge me, for the time
being.* This last consideration seemed the most
gratifying, and it would reassert his power in his little
clan. Leading victorious battles had a way of doing
that.

Japhet smiled broadly, an unfamiliar contortion on
his Unseleighe features. "Show us, my little servant,"
he said to Mort, barely able to restrain his elation.

The clan was clearly pleased at this turn of events; at
last, it was something to *do*. Kill Seleighe. Before they
left, however, Japhet suggested a few arrangements
should the campaign go as badly as the last one had.
Even Nargach agreed it was best to leave a magical escape
route, which had saved their hides in their recent defeat
in Avalon.

First he instructed Nargach to set a trap of imprisonment on the cabin, should the Seleighe come and try
to rescue the little human fungus in there. The spell
was carefully laid and tuned to freeze any Seleighe in
their tracks should they come near the cabin. Then, a
short distance down the dirt road, Nargach drew up the
power to create a Gate.

It had started out as a simple job of organizing the
contents of the shed a little more efficiently, so that he
didn't bump into the old Indian motorcycle every time
he moved; he didn't want to risk dinging it up any more
than it already was under the inch-thick layer of dust.
When he removed the cover, he stood in absolute awe
of what he found underneath.

What he remembered as an old, dirty and neglected
non-running machine was now an immaculate 1946
Indian Chief, with whitewall tires that were actually

white! Its fire engine red paint shone even in the shed's dim light, as bright and glossy as the day it rolled off the factory floor. When he pressed the front tire, he expected the rubber to collapse under his hand, but the tire was firm and fully inflated. The skirted fenders curved gracefully around the top half of the wheels. Hadn't the first one been removed, and sitting in the corner? He checked the oil, full and recently changed. The tank was also full of gas, when before it had been drained. *And this smell. New oil, new paint, new rubber. New motorcycle? But how can this be?*

Then he remembered Grampa's parting words: *You will also have a gift, a red Indian gift.* The message made no sense then. It made perfect sense now.

"But do you run?" he said to the beautiful beast.

Wolf eased it carefully out of the shed, flinching every time it came close to *touching* something unclean. In the shed it was a gorgeous machine, but in full sunlight it was a dazzling work of art.

And it started right up.

"Monkakchi!" he muttered. *"Goddamn."*

In a daze, he slipped out of the awkward *konsainta* and found jeans and his old boots. In the pile of stuff he had salvaged was an old t-shirt, and a thick jean jacket. He also found a pair of old riding goggles. Once everything was on, he turned to regard the two-wheeled miracle. The Indian purred as it idled, with hardly a vibration through its leather saddle seat as Wolf parked his bony posterior on it.

Though he had never ridden an Indian before, he knew the shift pattern, the brakes, everything about it. *But I'm still an injured rider,* he reminded himself. *Nothing fancy, now.*

He eased the clutch out and rolled down the dirt road, then eased to a careful stop at the highway. In spite of his recent wreck, the asphalt beckoned once more.

Just a short ride, he thought eagerly as he rode out onto the highway.

He rode perhaps a mile down the highway, shifting through its four speeds as if it were his old Harley. It was a bit wider and longer than what he was accustomed to, so it was a challenge to make a slow, wide U-turn on the highway, using part of the desert to accomplish the feat. But he brought the Indian back home in one piece, after riding maybe two miles on it, and reaching the phenomenal speed of 48 miles per hour.

He parked it alongside his mattress in the shed, half tempted to lay her down on the mattress beside him so he could sleep with her. Then he remembered Wenlann, and her promise to come see him.

I'm in no shape to entertain ladies. I've got to rest up, heal up, and get better. I've got a motorcycle, and a real potential girlfriend, all on the same day. Life is good.

He drifted off listening to the cooling Indian engine go *tic tic tic,* a lullaby that sang him to sleep.

Danger, Thorn sensed, at the edge of his domain. *Wolf is in danger.* The screaming warning brought the image of a black van driven by a very dangerous person.

Thorn set off in haste, pushing Valerie to her limits, but when the distance to Wolf shortened, a fog of haze and confusion greeted him; it was like trying to ride through a snowstorm, against a sharp wind, with no clear road ahead.

Then he remembered the pain Wolf was in. Pain did this, made this storm happen. Yet the impending danger, no, *doom,* that was about to befall Wolf kept him going. He had to find him, it was his duty. Through the storm Thorn caught the outline of the shed, and of another vehicle. *The black van.* They were going after Wolf.

Wolf, wake up! Thorn shouted against the storm, but could not penetrate it enough to reach his charge. He tried riding Valerie past the dangerous people who were now carrying Wolf into the van, but was simply not skilled enough to reach through the levels without Wolf to lock in on. *These are the people who killed his grandfather. They must be considering the same with Wolf.*

He was helpless to do much except observe the van's progress. Then up ahead, a cabin. The dark power of the Unseleighe lurked in this dwelling.

Contact the Seleighe. He turned Valerie around and rode downwind instead of against it. As his speed increased, the storm receded behind him.

Petrus had gone out of his way to show how angry he wasn't by lying back on the bed and turning on the TV. Maybe there was some local news about the Satanic group. Wenlann lay down on the bed next to him, not saying a word, and promptly went to sleep. Her deep breathing not only made his heart ache for her even more, he felt the beginnings of his own fatigue coming on. He was ready to doze off, sitting up in the bed, when Odras rolled past the window and parked his beemer 'steed, then entered the room with a flourish.

"It *works*," he announced proudly. "We can Gate when and wherever we want to without tapping into stored Node reserves."

"No foolin'," Petrus replied, too tired to say more. Odras sat cross-legged on the floor in the corner of the motel room, closed his eyes, and became absolutely still. This was a routine Petrus had observed many times before. *He's meditating.*

Petrus had been dozing for half a candlemark or so when the roar of a motorcycle just outside their open window jolted him awake. Still groggy, he grabbed his sword, and was at the door before someone knocked.

Odras came awake also, and peered out the window.

"I don't recognize this rider, but he appears to be unarmed."

"Appears" isn't good enough, thought Petrus, holding the sword behind the door as he opened it.

"Good afternoon, hon," greeted the rider, clad in a one-piece leather riding suit similar to Odras'. Petrus didn't recognize her immediately because her bluish white hair was pulled back, a style suitable for wearing helmets.

"Mattie?" Petrus asked.

"I just thought I would drop these off before I left," she said, balancing a Tupperware container on a red Shoei helmet.

"How *sweet* of you," Wenlann said, joining Petrus at the door and accepting the gift.

"Please, come in," Petrus offered, once he had regained composure.

"No thank you, sweet," Mattie said, returning to an idling sport bike, a sienna red BMW R1100RT. "I was just on my way out for a little spin, then it's off to the quilting bee at the church. If you need anything, just call the front desk."

Petrus watched, thunderstruck, as she tucked away a bungee net, then put on the helmet. She mounted the sleek machine and pulled out of the parking lot, hunched over the cycle like a nineteen-year-old kid. But when the bike hit asphalt she was gone in an instant. The roar of the 1100 dopplered away like a receding bullet.

Petrus stood at the door for some time, stunned. Wenlann's laughter shook him from his trance.

"Here. Have some oatmeal cookies," she said, offering the opened gift. "They're still warm." He bit into the gooiness with pleasure, as Wenlann remarked, "The look on your face."

"Humans," he said, around a mouthful of cookie. "Never a dull moment."

He was about to suggest dinner when the roar of another, quite different motorcycle drew closer.

Thorn.

Petrus and Wenlann were both outside by the time he pulled Valerie up on her center stand. Thorn's expression told them right away the news was bad.

"They have Wolf," he said breathlessly.

"*Who* does?" Petrus asked.

"The Unseleighe, you fool," Wenlann said, distressed.

Thorn nodded. "Yes, the Unseleighe. And Damien, the Satanists. The ones who killed his grandfather. They abducted him and took him to a cabin."

"Oh, great," Wenlann said. "I knew we shouldn't have left him alone!"

"Are you certain they were Unseleighe?" Odras asked, stepping out of the motel room.

"No doubt. I've met them before, I know what their power feels like. They have made that cabin their own."

"They must be planning on staying here a while, then," Petrus said, trying to take control of a situation that was becoming quite uncontrollable. "Five Unseleighe, one a mage. One, Japhet Dhu. The humans we can handle easily. And three against five? The odds could be better, but . . . Odras, are you with me?"

"Certainly," the Mage replied. "That is, if you insist on this course of action."

Petrus studied him, and in the mage's relaxed, ambivalent look saw that he didn't really think going after the Unseleighe was such a good idea.

"I know they have humiliated you," Odras said, apparently sensing his indecision. "And granted, the human Wolf is in a great deal of trouble. But we are only three. Even in the best light the odds are not in our favor."

"All right, then," Petrus said. "We will go and verify the location. Wenlann, would you stay and try to contact the King on the net, and tell him we're ready for reinforcements?"

"Thank you," Wenlann said, more to Odras than to Petrus, and went back into their motel room.

Petrus turned to the Rider Guardian. "Thorn, would you kindly show us the way?"

Chapter Fourteen

With a start Lucas awakened and tried to sit up. It was dark. He couldn't move: he was bound by something strong and sticky. He tried yelling, but a strip of tape turned the shout into a *mrwwwmph*.

Rolling onto his side, he faced a long, horizontal slit of light. As his panic subsided, he realized he was looking at the bottom of a door. He heard nothing except for a whistle of wind coming from somewhere above him. He lay there for an eternity, willing his breathing to slow down.

He lay on a mattress, which had a cloying, metallic odor. Like someone had soiled the mattress, or had even bled and died on it. His stomach roiled at the thought. He closed his eyes, and with everything he had, summoned calmness. As he relaxed, his heart hammered a little less at his ribcage. *Okay, let's try this again.* A second attempt at sitting up succeeded, but something around his ankles hindered his standing up.

He rolled over on his knees and rocked back until balanced on his feet. The strip of light now illuminated his Nikes, and he saw duct tape wrapped around his ankles. The door was not that far away, but required careful hops to reach it. He lost his balance, and shoulder and head slammed loudly into a metal door. He froze, waiting to see what, if any, response the sound would get. Nothing stirred. Righting himself, his hands brushed against a doorknob. He turned it, but it didn't yield. *Locked. Great.* The doorknob was smooth and featureless. The lock was on the other side. Inching his way along the wall his arm connected with something sticking out of the wall.

A switch. Light flooded the room when he pushed the switch up with his arm.

He wished he hadn't.

Lucas screamed against the tape over his mouth, and backed into a corner where he collided with a work table. But his eyes were on the ceiling and opposite walls; any calm he'd achieved earlier was gone, as he started to hyperventilate through his nose.

Why don't they just kill me and be done with it? he thought as he tried to push himself deeper into the corner.

The mattress was indeed blood-soaked, the stains having dried to a blackish brown. In the far corner was a board set up on two cinderblocks, upon which were the bare skulls of what looked like dogs, cats and people. At least five full human skulls grinned silently at him, some small, as if from children, and some with an occasional patch of flesh or hair still intact. Hanging on the walls were several metal wires, with bones strung on them like a necklace. On the cinderblock walls were pentagrams, baphomets, inverted crosses, and other symbols he didn't immediately recognize, all drawn in blood.

Dear God, Lucas thought, wondering what, if anything, might save him from this. Wind blew through a tiny rectangular window overhead, and beyond it was the darkness of nightfall. The table he was leaning against had a few odds and ends on it. There were a few gallon cans of paint, a jug of mineral spirits, some paint brushes.

Then his eyes caught a square can of something marked "solvent," and he had an idea. He hopped over to the other end of the table, tipped the can over with his nose, to where it was hanging over the edge of the table. With difficulty he bent over and reached up with his bound hands.

A truck or something pulled up outside, followed by a loud slamming of doors.

"*Shit,*" he muttered, almost dropping the can. He had it in one hand, but it was too big to fit in his hip pocket. Instead he slipped it down the back of his pants, inside his briefs, and pulled his long t-shirt back over his backside. He hopped back over to the light switch, turned it off, and fell back on the mattress.

A door some distance away opened with a loud squeak.

"Finally we've got the sonofabitch," he heard someone say, followed by the sounds of shuffling feet, as if a two or more people were carrying something heavy.

"Leave the handcuffs on," the voice said again.

"What about the little shit in there?" That was Satanic Panic.

"Check him."

Lucas closed his eyes and feigned sleep. The door opened briefly, then closed.

"He's still out," Panic said. "You gonna give me the bag now or what?"

"Here," said the voice, then came the rustle of plastic. "Same as the last. Be careful with it."

"I'm always careful," Panic replied, and giggled like a schoolgirl.

The door opened again, and an engine started. Lucas waited until the van was long gone. Whoever or whatever they had brought in wasn't moving. He got back on his feet, turned the light back on, and began peeling the tape off his mouth using the corner of the table. Nearly all of it was off, the long strip hanging off his right cheek, but he could finally breathe freely through his mouth. Then he studied the window at the top of the wall, a horizontal strip of space that looked about six inches high. If he pulled the table over, he would be able to get up to it. But first he'd have to get unbound.

Before trying the can of solvent he tried the worktable's corner to free his hands. Lucas hacked away at the tape, cutting his hand a few times in the process. The blood running over the tape made it slick, and well nigh impossible for the table corner to gain purchase. Then he heard something outside, and froze.

Something was just outside the window. Then came a long throaty growl, the kind of sound that only comes from very large animals. The sound shook the glass in the window and reverberated against the cinder block walls like a mufflerless motorcycle. A mountain lion. Had to be. It was *huge*.

It wasn't leaving. *What is it finding so attractive?* Perhaps it was the blood on the mattress and walls, not to mention the fresh blood on his hands. But he wasn't ready to die yet. He considered the stuff on the table, wondered if something there would hide the smell of the blood. The mineral spirits might make this an unappetizing buffet after all. The solvent was still in his pants, cool and clammy against his left buttock. *I could use the table corner to open it. . . .*

In the midst of putting this plan to action, he heard the cat scream again. Then another wild animal sound: A wolf, in the room next to him. *What is this, a goddamn zoo?* he thought, staggering backwards, away from the sound. *Maybe I don't want out of here after all.* The metal door holding him in looked pretty stout. Now he was glad it was. The Wolf's bark rattled his diaphragm.

Big dog, big cat. Great, maybe they'll fight it out and leave me alone.

The ruckus sounded like the mountain lion and wolf

were trying to disembowel each other. The fight traveled outside, as he heard a distant version of it from beyond his window. Soon, the fight faded to silence.

Then he remembered, *The others. Panic. Whatshisface. They're going to be back.*

They will kill me.

In the darkness Japhet Dhu and Nargach observed the lone Seleighe through the motel window, keeping their distance from a set of subtle but effective wards protecting the room. Nargach had muttered something about this being the work of Odras, but had failed to elaborate if this was a problem for him or not.

"She's reading a book. Sideways," Japhet observed.

"That's not a book," Mort informed them. "It's a laptop. She's probably on the Internet."

"Which means?" Nargach asked, saving Japhet the trouble.

"Which means," Mort said, brightening, "the phone is unplugged, and she can't call 911. How *convenient.*"

"Well, where are the rest of them?" Japhet said, annoyed. Everything the demon said was gibberish.

"Off somewhere else," Mort replied. "There is only one elvensteed."

"That conveyance?" Nargach asked, squinting at the space next to the room.

"Do you know the Seleighe to use anything else?" Japhet replied shortly.

"As a matter of fact, I do. That's a motorcycle . . . No, wait. That is an elvensteed, in disguise. How clever of them," the mage said sardonically. "Too bad it won't do her any good."

"Does she suspect anything?" Japhet said before thinking.

"Of course she doesn't," Nargach replied shortly. "Can't *you* see that?"

Japhet held his tongue, focused instead on the task ahead of them. *Capture the Seleighe, take her Underhill. I wanted a bargaining chip, now I have one.*

Presently Rochad returned from his brief recon around the other side of the motel. "I had to negotiate a gate of cold iron, but I was able to observe the far side of yon dwelling. There is indeed an exit, a large wind hole with panes of glass over it. The frame is cold iron, which any elf might overcome if desperate enough."

And she would be, to get away from me, Japhet thought with grim satisfaction. "And the wards?"

Rochad looked down, as if afraid to relay the news. "As Nargach said, they surround the inn."

The mage waved the observation away. "The wards are not a problem. I can eliminate them rather easily, I just can't do it without the Seleighe's noticing."

Japhet shrugged, "Then, what is the problem? I think our concerns were of giving advance warning to a party of three." He spied the dim figure, still sitting at the book. "We will not have a better chance. What have you in your bag of tricks to make this wench more manageable?"

The mage's eyes furrowed, more a look of concentration than annoyance, which is what Japhet was after. *Well, perhaps later.* "A version of the trap I set back at the cabin."

While Nargach summoned the forces for his work, Japhet dispatched the others to cover the rear exits, in case the wench tried to get out the back way. The prospect of a real female prisoner seemed to add spring to everyone's step. *So be it. If it helps morale, then all the better. Provided she doesn't become a liability, if we are overestimating our bargaining power with her . . . then it's execution time.*

She had hoped to catch the King on one of the chat lines, where he often lurked as a matter of course, but there was no sign of him there tonight. *Could well be it's daytime, or he's preoccupied with other matters.* The time difference between this world and Underhill had never been constant, and that the two realms could communicate in this manner was a miracle. Wenlann made do with a detailed letter describing what was happening.

She had removed the wolf tooth necklace and set it next to the laptop, its white teeth shining brightly in the lamplight. Still, it fascinated her. Or was it the previous owner that had her interest? Whenever she thought about him a chill ran down her back and other places, this humble, fragile human with the power of a mage lurking just beneath the surface of his thin defenses, the shields of a child. Granted, his rounded ears and strange eyes were at first a slight turnoff, but everything else about him compensated for this threefold. His immunity to iron added to his alien appeal, and to see him on a motorbike, a real motorbike, in leather and boots . . . Well, this was not something one saw in Underhill. But it was something a maiden might *dream* about.

You're being ridiculous! she chided herself. *An elf and a human? What about the in-laws?*

Wenlann pushed the thought aside, a bit annoyed at herself for such silly thoughts. *It just isn't done!*

But the moment she turned off the laptop and closed it, she knew something *else* was wrong. Her 'steed seemed to be spooked by something. She went outside to check on it. *There, there,* she soothed, but the 'steed was not being very communicative.

She noticed nothing amiss in the darkness, except for a nearby streetlight that looked like it was about to go out. Odras' wards were still firmly in place. *If anything unfriendly tried to get past those wards, I'd know in an instant.* After all, they were among humans. Perhaps one of them was considering ripping them off.

Wenlann laughed at the prospect of a thief trying to steal her 'steed. *Now that would be a rude surprise. They'd be lucky if they got away without a pair of hoof prints embedded in their forehead.*

Frayed nerves, that had to be it. She returned to her room and locked the door behind her, then opened the front window a crack before pulling the curtains all the way closed. The one small window in the back afforded a cool breeze, a little stronger now that the front window was open. Wenlann suspected the little air conditioning unit, which looked to be about a hundred years old, would blow tainted air.

Perhaps her anxiety had to do with Petrus and Odras, but no, she would have *really* sensed something then. The old mage was somewhat of an enigma, and while parts of his past were a bit blank she trusted him implicitly. *It was rather sly of the King to make sure Odras came along,* she thought with a half smile. *No matter what kind of trouble Petrus got into, the mage would likely be able to compensate for it.*

Whatever she was sensing, it was real, and it was close. *Just as long as the human isn't wielding a cold iron blade.* The possibility made her shudder.

Maybe I should shut all the windows after all, she thought, getting up.

In mid stride to the front window, the universe froze for perhaps a second. It was as if a pulse of negative time had been sent through the land, holding everything in place for an instant, then moving on.

Then, beyond the thin curtains, she saw and heard the wards scream in alarm. *This is no human,* she thought. Some yards away, beyond the front window, a circle of light reminiscent of a Gate formed momentarily. And when it went out, so did the ward on that side. Indeed, they were Unseleighe.

Something scratched at the rear window. She turned,

saw a dark Unseleighe face gazing back at her, the tip of a bronze sword scraping the glass.

There were what, five of them? She had to assume they were all out there. Too many to fight, especially when one's a mage.

Act now, or you're done for!

She made a run for her elvensteed, the only thing at her disposal that would put her at any kind of advantage. *The second I'm on her, we could be out of here,* her thinking went. She ran outside, reaching for the 'steed which was only a few feet away. Her body hit something magical, like an invisible glue, or a strong, unseen spider web. She tumbled over on her side, unable to move anything, not even her head so she could see the bastards walking up to her.

Two towering shadows stood above her, their faces grinning like skulls. Unable to do anything except observe, she recoiled inwardly as they picked her up, and placed her over another 'steed-as-motorbike. At one point she caught a glimpse of her own 'steed, evidently imprisoned by the same paralysis spell.

She rode draped over the back of the seat. The mage cast some manner of glamorie over her, and when she saw that she was riding through Albuquerque cloaked as motorcycle luggage her resolve to kill each of these rodents solidified. During the ride into the darkness, away from the comforting if garish electric lighting of Albuquerque, she caught herself fading into unconsciousness, and back again; while awake she probed the working that had immobilized her, but found herself unable to break through it.

At least I still have my mind, she thought in a frenzy. *I have something to work with, some chance to get out of this mess. Listen. Observe. Look for weaknesses.*

The 'steeds decelerated, the simulacrum brakes even emitting a faint, scorched rubber scent. Beyond her periphery was the unmistakable vibration of a Gate, its yellow light reflected on the sand around them.

"Just carry her," someone ordered as he climbed off the bike. "She's a weak, light thing. You should have no trouble with her."

We'll see about that, she considered, careful to keep her thoughts to herself.

"Take her to the place," the voice said, the vaguely familiar face drifting in and out of her limited view as the other slung her inelegantly over his shoulder. Even though they had dismissed the luggage glamorie, she still felt like a sack of stolen goods. "I will go and gather Wolf."

Wolf? Have they captured him too? She pushed vainly against the paralysis, her determination now fueled by her need to help Wolf.

As the Gate's field closed in around her, she saw that the Unseleighe were already riding away; the motorcycles' roar sounded like a large hornet in a long hollow tube. Then, sudden silence as the Gate closed in around them.

At the dream's edge, Wolf was in full wolf costume, face whitened with chalk dust, eyes blackened with charcoal. He wore a large wolf's hide, the flap of its skinned head hanging over the top of his face, and the rest reaching all the way down his back.

Grandfather was there too, with the circle of Chaniwa, pounding on drums and shaking turtleshell rattles, the beat rising in power and speed. Wolf danced around the fire, alone but not alone. There was the spirit of his soul's mate, the she-wolf his ancestors knew who had come to the circle. Then there was the soul of the white witch, wearing the Hand around her neck on a leather thong. Above was the Moon Goddess, looking down on the fire with the loving expression of a mother. The Horned God lurked in the woods, his naked flesh reflected briefly as he stalked the forest.

Wolf was not alone as he danced around the fire, the white witch and she-wolf following him as he went deosil. He walked barefoot on the few coals that dribbled off the intense fire, feeling nothing but the Horned God's warmth. . . .

The dream dissolved in an instant as he flashed to wakefulness.

I'm a prisoner.

On a cold cement floor in a strange room, he lay with his hands and ankles in what felt like handcuffs. Moonlight from the window was the only illumination. The cuffs had been clamped tightly around his boots, and the resultant folded leather crimped painfully against his legs. A rag tied around his head covered his mouth. From somewhere beyond the four walls he heard a truck or a van driving away, with the rattle of gravel announcing its departure.

He smelled blood, lots of it, intermingled with the stench of rotting meat. Something went *clunk,* then *rustle,* on the other side of the wall. He listened for more, sensing someone else over there, possibly in the same mess he was in. Whoever it was they weren't talking.

Then he felt it, far beyond the walls.

First was the awareness of something dark, *out there.* Wind blew against the building, poking through the narrow window, bringing with it the scent of . . . *cat.*

He remembered grandfather's woodcarving, now sitting on his altar, at home. *Ha-* his mind began, but he dare not even think the name. With imminent danger at his doorstep, this was easier to do than he would have otherwise thought.

Not unless I'm looking into the Hand, he thought. How things have changed; a few days ago, he was laughing at the concept of the cat spirit. Now, the cat spirit was here.

Cat spirit, cat spirit, cat spirit, he thought frantically, forcing her true name out of his head. *Cat spirit, begone....*

But the cat spirit was still out there. It screamed, loudly, like a mountain lion. Like a woman in pain.

It's out there. It's coming here.

Then it began to happen.

The first wave hit, bringing nausea, cooling quickly to a heightened alertness. He closed his eyes, praying he didn't vomit with the gag in his mouth, and saw the wolf spirit within him. It burned like a bed of white hot coals. It was starting to happen, but he was hanging onto his human body. *Let it go,* the wolf spirit said. *Let it happen.*

Then, *Let me rise. I can fight Ha-Sowa. It is my purpose, and I have done it for a long time.*

With one, loud exhalation through his nostrils, he relaxed on the concrete, closed his eyes, and let the spirit take over. The nausea came again as his insides shifted, making a squishy, wet noise. Across his skin, from head to toe, something wriggled and stuffed itself against his clothes. He ventured a peek out of one eye; he looked down a long, brown snout, growing longer and furrier. With his now overly long tongue, he licked the long teeth that had sprouted from the top of his mouth. The scents around him became razor sharp, as if all along he'd been smelling in two dimensional black and white, and his senses had suddenly become three dimensional color, with surround sound; the odor was about to knock the wind out of him. But the blood and the other stenches were the loudest of all, and he now knew with certainty this was human blood, human meat. People had died violently in this place.

The change continued with a vengeance throughout his body, and he felt his arms and legs grow thinner. Feet and ankles slid easily out of the handcuffs, and the shackles fell with a loud rattle to the concrete floor. He looked at his hands, and as he watched the fingers became shorter, the ends morphed into tough pads, and fingernails became round, long and pointed. He watched the hair grow rapidly across the surface of his darkening skin, reminding him of a high-speed movie of flowers growing in a field.

The change was not happening in his clothes, which were becoming tight in certain places, and about to fall off in others. Something told him to take them off, while he still had the dexterity to do so. The gag had fallen off on its own, but his thick, canine shoulders were squeezing through the collar of the t-shirt, painfully. The jean jacket had slipped off with the cuffs, and he reached around and pulled off the t-shirt bunching around his shoulders. As he worked the shirt and jeans off, he felt the heart pendant Wenlann had given him, hanging around his neck. Once he had all garments off he stood on all fours, panting.

I am here, I am the wolf, the spirit said from within, joining with his own thoughts symbiotically, the human part of him now taking a back seat in the situation.

Fur and muscles thickened, his vision sharpened; he lost some of the color of his human eyesight, but gained much more definition. But while exploring his new senses and shape, a loud scream, along with the stronger scent of cat, drew his awareness away.

Ha-Sowa. He was no longer afraid to think the word.

Wolf was all wolf now, and he let his new self have control. His vision turned red, and he growled deeply with the rise of his hackles, seized with death-fever, the soul of the hunt. Wolf lunged at the door. It broke under his weight, and as he forced his way through it splintered into a dozen pieces.

Ha-Sowa crouched before him. Wolf landed on all fours, back arched, teeth bared. The cat hissed, and turned loose another scream, then the two animals were upon each other.

Wolf went for the throat, missing the huge claws by a heartbeat, but the cat was too fast. Both swirled around one another like a cyclone, Wolf nipping but not gaining purchase on anything, until a hind leg came into view. With his huge jaws, he clamped down, hard. Something went snap between his teeth, just as fangs sank into his rear haunches. Locked in this mutual death grip, the wolf spirit within fought against pain. Finally, the cat released, and Wolf pulled away.

The two beasts regarded one another in mutual hatred, pacing back and forth, not in the desert but on a wide plane, with darkness on one side, and light on the other. Pacing, pacing, circling each other, wolf and cat tested the other's motions, Wolf noting the limp the cat had. His failure to break the bone enraged him, and he crouched for another attack.

Wolf had been here before, he knew the scent of the place, which was a total absence of odor, save for the musky cat scent, the smell of a wounded, angry animal.

Wolf made ready to leap at the cat again, finding a split second when the cat's neck was partially exposed toward him; Ha-Sowa turned its massive feline head toward him, her eyes now brilliant white orbs within the black skull. The light spread through the body, and the body changed like he had changed, only instantly. The light faded back into the eyes.

The eyes were still that of the cat. The face was not.

The cat eyes were Wenlann's eyes, staring back at him seductively.

No! Wolf thought. *It's an illusion, it's trying to trick me!* Ha-Sowa had become the beautiful *chi-en* of his dreams, dressed not in motorcycle gear but buckskin, like that of a brave. But this was no Chaniwa brave; her beautiful, rounded breasts filled the buckskin nicely, the twin nipples announcing their pointed presence. Her hair cascaded down her shoulders like a waterfall, longer and deeper brown than he'd remembered.

This can't be he thought, but his resolve to attack the cat dwindled, replaced by a longing in his loins.

Wenlann looked down at his excitement, turned her head delicately, and laughed piercingly.

At the moment of maximum humiliation, Wenlann turned her head back, her eyes now orbs of light again. Their eyes locked, and Wolf was caught in an instant of indecision.

In that instant, Wenlann vanished, replaced by the angry black cat, in mid-leap.

Wolf dodged out of the way, finding himself again in the desert. *Ha-Sowa!* he thought, looking around; the cat had vanished, but no, wait, there she was, silhouetted by the rising, full moon. Some distance away, she stood and shrieked at him, turned, and dropped behind the rise.

No, she's not getting away! he thought, the animal rage filling him again. He caught sight of Ha-Sowa again, moving at a slow lope, the limp in her hind leg much more pronounced now. She was apparently more injured than he'd first perceived. Again, another illusion. Wolf bolted after the cat, ignoring the pain in his right paw.

You are not getting away! his thoughts raged on, but as he ran after Ha-Sowa, her image faded, until she was no more. He wanted to chase her into the spirit world, where she had certainly gone, but try as he would he didn't know how to reach it. That she was able to pull him into it, and discharge him from it at will, lent a disturbing advantage to her.

Home, his instinct told him. *Go home. It will be safe there. For now.* Without thinking twice about where home was, he turned toward it and began a slow ambling lope, the ancient motion of a wolf in transit.

✧   ✧   ✧

Presently Wolf arrived at his home, avoiding houses, farms and highways. Humans shot wolves out here, to protect their sheep, or just for the hell of it. During his journey the moon crept higher, then began her descent, lighting the ground around him so brilliantly that he feared his own visibility. Someone with a scope could pick him off, and with this light they wouldn't need IR.

He didn't feel completely safe until he saw his altar, standing in the full light of the moon as if a lamp were poised over it. Everything remained in its place, including the carving of Ha-Sowa, which no longer seemed as threatening.

Wolf sat back on his haunches and started nibbling at a small cactus thorn that had planted itself in one of his rear paws. In the comforting environment of his home, the wolf spirit seemed to be at ease again. Wolf heard it, whispering within his soul.

The danger has passed, but do not deceive yourself. Now Ha-Sowa knows who and where you are, wolf-self said.

As if on cue, he felt the changes again, his shifting organs, the ripple of his skin. Hair that had only recently grown out withdrew back into the skin. He lay on his side, to let the change happen more easily. He welcomed the cage of his humanity, the familiar touch of hairless skin, of limbs, and of opposing thumbs.

She will return. I will keep watch. While you're awake, while you sleep. I will protect you. I will be with you always.

As wolf body turned to human body, he braced himself for the pain he remembered before the change. Oddly, the pain didn't return. He looked down at himself, his nude body now lying prone in the bright moonlight. The bruises were gone. His muscles were a bit stiff, but far from the agonizing soreness he'd known before.

As the wolf-spirit retreated into the core of his soul, it had one more parting thought for him.

Your desert sickness is healed, also. You are well.

He blinked at the star-filled sky, and a grin spread across his now-human features.

No Gulf War sickness, he thought. *I'll be goddamned.*

He sat up, feeling giddy. The impact of what had just happened was starting to sneak up now, giving him goose bumps. *If only I had more control over it . . . My wolf self seems to have a mind of its own.* He listened for the wolf spirit to answer, but it was a dim spark, dormant but awake, and listening. *It will tell me what I need to know when I am ready,* he knew, the thoughts emerging from that formerly hidden pool of ancestral knowledge.

The old coot was right.

But the trouble was only beginning, he knew; Ha-Sowa was injured, but not out of the game. *She will be back. Then the Unsaylee, to muddy matters.*

He stood and stretched to his full human height, feeling something metal, and heavy, against the top of his chest. The pendant hung there from its frail-looking chain. Now he was confused. *How did this silver chain survive that fight?* he wondered, taking the chain off. It felt different from the pendant. He pulled on it tentatively. The chain gave no sign of breaking. Again he pulled, harder. The chain was solid, more solid than steel. His muscles strained against it, the chain leaving a line on his palms. The chain remained intact.

"Strong stuff," he said to the pendant, in admiration. The Celtic knot shone back at him, catching the moon just right.

Wenlann, he thought, his heart aching. *I must go to her. . . .*

The moment his longing for her crystallized into the thought, he felt a vibration, a singing of pain course through the chain to his fingers. *Wenlann is in trouble,* he thought, knew, from what this pendant was telling him. He held it directly in his palms, the chain looping back over his hands.

He held it, and *sent* . . .

His thought sailed through time and space, and ran firmly into a black wall, a layer of bad magic that he'd tasted before.

The Unsaylee. He released the thought, lest the dark elves follow it back to him. It would not do for them to know he was back in action again.

I've got to go there, came the frenzied thought. He went for the Indian motorcycle, which was nestled safely in his shed, and was prepared to start her up and take off for Albuquerque when he remembered something.

I'm naked.

It would get a little breezy, riding the Indian in the nude. He rushed back into the shed and rummaged for yet another set of riding clothes. He was running out of things to wear.

Damn, even the boots are gone. Back at that cabin. He picked up an old pair of air conditioned Nike high tops. *They will have to do.* Grandfather's old hunting knife and sheath glinted at him in the moonlight, and he hurriedly strapped it onto his belt.

The goggles were still hanging off the handlebars, and like a champ the Indian started right up. Wasting no more time, he put her in gear and hit the gravel drive a little faster than was safe.

I told them La Puerta. I hope that's where they went, he thought, but something in the information he'd received when sending the mental probe to Wenlann told him that was precisely where they had gone; perhaps it was a flash of the motel, of the single elvensteed parked in front, masked in some sort of magical goo. Then the image was gone. Just as well, he had to concentrate on the road, and getting there quickly.

Where the hell is Thorn, anyway? he wondered, not knowing if the angel was with him or not. Then he caught himself, between third and fourth gear. *Thorn is my guardian, and he saved my life. I owe him. It's not the other way around.*

Ahead, on the highway he saw what at first appeared to be a large car or truck approaching. Then he recognized it for the illusion it was, two motorcycles riding in side by side touring formation.

"Thorn and the Saylee?" he said aloud, slowing down himself, looking back, then turning around. It was Petrus and the tall dark one, Odorous or something. *But where the hell was Wenlann?*

They met on the median, facing opposite directions.

"You've escaped," Thorn said, sounding slightly puzzled. "How—?"

"I'll tell you later," he told the Guardian Spirit. "You were coming for me, weren't you?"

"Of course I was," Thorn said, falling into his country drawl. "It's what I'm best at. You okay?"

"Like I said, later," he said, turning his attention to the elves. "We got another problem." Petrus yanked his helmet off, looking very accusingly at Wolf.

"Where's Wenlann?" Wolf asked the young elf.

"Why?" Petrus replied, his eyes flashing with jealousy.

Wolf tried not to roll his eyes too obviously. "She's in trouble. This pendant—" he said, reaching for it.

"We're going after Japhet. The Unseleighe," Petrus said. "Why do you think she's in trouble?"

Petrus might be an elf with some degree of magical ability, but right then, sitting on the beemer, he looked like a little rat-faced punk. The other one, who had a thick aura of magic about him, was entering into some kind of trance. It occurred to Wolf that this older elf might be the one actually pulling the strings in the little group, however inconspicuous he might be.

"He's right," Odras said, emerging from the trance as if from a light nap. "The wards have been violated. And . . . there's trouble. The vision is unclear. The Unseleighe were there, and they've hidden their work well." He looked directly at Petrus. *"We must go back. Now."*

Petrus looked chagrined, and in pain. Without saying a word the young elf donned his helmet, turned the beemer around and headed back for Albuquerque.

At least, Wolf considered, as he and the other elf fell in behind him, with Thorn bringing up the rear, *he can think he's the leader if he rides in front of us.*

Chapter Fifteen

Lucas was about to give the duct tape around his hands another good pull when he heard, in the distance, yet another unwelcome sound.

A *motorcycle*. Now *what*?

A motorcycle, then another, pulled up in front of the house; then someone entered the cabin.

"Where is he?" a tinny, metallic voice roared through the building. The door to the room flew open. The thing was tall and dark and freaky looking, with pointed ears, a pointy face and clothing straight out of the middle ages. His words sounded artificial, like a chip voice. It was not human. God only knew what it was.

"Where is he?" the creature repeated, kneeling down on one knobby knee. It held up a hand, each finger having a long, sharpened claw.

"I-If you're talking about the wolf and the cougar, they're long gone," Lucas stammered out.

The creature regarded him curiously. He stood to his full height and folded his arms behind him, cupping his elbows.

"Wolf. And *cougar*?"

One of the creatures explored the wrecked room. "Gods dammit, Japhet, it smells like cat piss in here," it said. "And there's no way that kid could have gotten out of those cuffs."

"Wolf," the creature said, his face darkening, if such were possible on the already grim expression. "And . . . *cat.*"

"Blood," the other said, looking at the floor. "Here, here . . . and here."

"Nargach's pet," the one named Japhet said bitterly. "I needed Wolf to defeat him, *and he knew it.*"

Lucas had no idea what they were talking about, but whatever it was he hoped it would distract them enough to leave him alone.

"You," the creature said. With one swipe of a claw he cut the duct tape around his ankles. "On your feet. You're coming with us."

Lucas felt weak in his knees as he stood up.

"If you try to escape we'll kill you," Japhet said. "My patience is expended. Don't test it further."

"Where are we going?" Lucas asked conversationally as they led him outside.

" 'Where are we going?' " the creature mimicked, with a generous helping of sarcasm. "To *Hell.* A place you've never been before."

Don't count on it, Lucas thought as they shoved him forward.

The Unseleighe mage carried her with little trouble through the Gate to Underhill.

Where are we? Wenlann thought. Right away she noticed the absence of a marble slab, the customary flooring for a permanent Gate, and wondered how long it would remain open.

This was not a portion of Underhill she knew; but she had heard of this place, recognizing it by the featureless mist that spread across the land. This place was a pocket of the Unformed. They came across a cluster of boulders, then entered a cave. Inside was the subdued, ambient light one found throughout Underhill. Then the mage stopped and lay her on the ground roughly. She was still paralyzed, and unable to break her fall. Her head hit the floor with just enough pain to rekindle her anger.

Now what? she thought, considering a number of unpleasant scenarios: rape, torture, mutilation, more rape. The Unseleighe were famous for it all, and she hoped *this* mage would be the exception. Her paralysis spell began to loosen, and she sat up slowly, rubbing circulation into her arms.

"Those wards that were supposed to protect you did nothing of the sort," the mage began. "You may call me Nargach. And I am not the evil mage you think me to be."

Yeah, sure. We'll see about that, she thought. The mage had sat on an extension of the wall that resembled a chair, or even a throne. He looked comfortable, even kingly.

But he's not Japhet Dhu, the acting king of this particular rat's nest. A rival? Good chance.

"And you may call me Wenlann," said Wenlann. "What do you plan to do with me?"

Nargach shook his head slowly. "You don't understand. It is *I* who will ask the questions. Or I will simply revive the paralysis spell . . . but you don't want me to do that, do you?"

"Of course not," she replied, sitting with her legs crossed.

Nargach leaned forward. "Now, little one. You have a mage in your company by the name of Odras. Tell me about him. Tell me everything you know." He sat back, awaiting her answer.

Odras? What *did* she know about him? Very little, that's what.

"Take your time," Nargach said casually. "We have plenty of time."

"Well," Wenlann began tentatively. *Where to begin*

when there is *no beginning?* "After the fall of Avalon, we had no mages, so we recruited . . ."

"Oh, come now," Nargach snorted irritably. "Every soul in Underhill knows Aedham is a mage."

" . . . we recruited," Wenlann continued, unperturbed, "volunteers to help us rebuild. They came from all over. Odras is a different sort of Seleighe."

"Oh, a different sort, to be *sure*," Nargach said, looking like he was about to laugh. "Please, go on. This is *most* amusing."

What is this mage getting at? "I believe he came from an Elfhame beyond Outremer. An obscure one." She didn't see the harm in letting this bit of information out to the enemy, since it was readily obtainable elsewhere. "I don't know the name of it."

"Yes, well, *that* I can believe. Is that all?"

"I'm afraid so." Out of the corner of her vision she saw the cave entrance a short distance away. She made a note of its location and returned her attention to Nargach.

"You may wonder why I'm interested in this mage," said Nargach, sounding tired, but not defeated. "It amazes me that you would trust a stranger so."

"And why shouldn't we?" she said heatedly, immediately regretting her bold question.

"Because, my dear child," Nargach said, ignoring her impertinence, "Odras is an *Unseleighe*."

Now *that* stopped her cold. Granted, this was the kind of tactic the Unseleighe would use to undermine the enemy, spreading rumors, breaking down credibility. But there was something about the way Nargach said it, combined with his line of questioning prior to the surprising announcement. She believed him. *Or he is incredibly adept at manipulation.*

"We are both old, Odras and I," Nargach continued. "Very old. We're from the original Unseleighe court, before it split up into its various factions. What is left of our clan resides at the opposite edge of Underhill, on a mountain we have come to call home. Odras and I studied together, mastered our avocation together, *killed Seleighe together."*

He paused, letting that last bit sink in. "Then he grew weak. Found our school of thought to his disliking. Did not have the courage to subdue the lesser creatures of Underhill, and sought a different path. A lesser, weaker path."

Wenlann listened in rapt attention. If it were a lie, it was a fascinating one.

"Our master didn't like the direction he was going, and called him to task. He refused what was asked of him. He would have been executed as a traitor had he not been so light of foot, and fled."

Now this was starting to reek of falsehood. No Unseleighe would be able to escape like that, and if one did where would they go? No Seleighe court would have them. They would be alone *and* isolated. Given the age Odras appeared to be, it would have had to be a miserable existence. *Alone . . . for centuries.*

A rustle at the mouth of the cave drew their attention. Nargach shot back immediately with a warning look. The gathering of figures at the cave entrance approached them; the one leading looked like Zeldan, with the pointed face, the black cape. Only when he was within speaking distance did she realize he was not Zeldan, but his son. But Japhet wasn't even looking at her as he stormed over to Nargach; it looked as if they would come to blows right then. The leader was furious about something.

This should be interesting, she thought, sitting back, restraining her amusement.

"My dear Lord Japhet, whatever is the problem?" Nargach said in a most oily and patronizing tone.

"You know *precisely* what's wrong," Japhet said.

"Perhaps I don't," Nargach said, suppressing a yawn. "Why don't you enlighten me?"

Japhet wasn't reaching for his sword, but his right hand twitched in that direction. "Your pet, Ha-Sowa. Seems she has a mind of her own. Seems she's attacked one of our prisoners, the human, Wolf, and spirited him away. Didn't I expressly prohibit such an action?"

Now this was no longer funny. A cloak of fear and anxiety settled over her, but she remained as still and silent as possible.

"Perhaps you did—"

"Perhaps *nothing!*" Japhet shouted. "What have you done with our human mage?"

Nargach regarded Japhet with a look of false patience. "Lord Japhet, I must remind you that you insisted on returning to Underhill. Ha-Sowa was a creature of the humans' world, and you knew she would not be accompanying us down here, because I *told* you she wouldn't. Certainly you can't expect me to control the demon from down *here*, can you?"

Japhet seethed, but it was starting to look like this was a stalemate.

Nargach continued, "At any rate, we have neither Wolf nor Ha-Sowa, so that puts us back to where we were, does it not?"

Wenlann saw what this really meant, though it remained unspoken: *Now we are even.* During this brief exchange she saw the weakness she could exploit to escape this charming band of elves.

Divide and conquer. It even looks like they're well on their way to doing just that, all by themselves.

Japhet turned his angular face toward Wenlann. "Secure the Seleighe wench," he said. "I don't want her to be any more trouble."

"With magic?" Nargach replied, sounding like this might be a problem.

"Yes, with magic! What else? Or is that beyond your abilities?"

Nargach ignored the insult, but held a hand to his forehead and closed his eyes. "I feel weak, my Lord. Too much magic will do that, you know. If you really need my abilities, perhaps I should conserve them for more important things. I feel a battle coming on."

Japhet threw his hands up in the air. "Then secure her with *that*," he said pointing a clawed finger at the roll of gray duct tape the other elf clutched.

Then Wenlann noticed the human boy, who had been behind Japhet, out of sight. Duct tape bound his arms behind him. He had a vacant, distant look as he stared at the ground. Nargach came over and pulled her arms roughly behind her.

"Feet too," Japhet said. "Both of them. I don't want to have to keep a constant watch. And I don't want them walking away." Japhet paused, as if considering an amusing thought. "Not that there's anywhere for them *to* go."

The motel room door had been left open. Odras entered behind Petrus, and growled deeply in frustration.

"She should have gone with us," the mage said, but Petrus wasn't listening. His foot had connected with something on the floor, and when he looked down he saw one of several pieces of the laptop. It had been smashed mercilessly, the two halves separated, the keys spread hither and yon like broken teeth. *Damn the Unseleighe and their hatred for technology!* He knew Japhet couldn't have known what the laptop was, other than a piece of human tech; and that had been the only reason they'd destroyed it. Among the broken pieces of laptop he saw the wolf-tooth necklace, intact. He absently picked it up and put it in his pocket.

Looks like we won't be contacting the King anytime

soon. But dammit, they have Wenlann, he thought in anguish. *And it's all my fault.*

"Her elvensteed will know what happened," Odras said, walking outside. Petrus moved to follow him, nearly walking directly into Wolf.

The human's look stopped him short; Wolf stared at him accusingly. *We left her alone. I'm at fault, and I know it,* he thought, then reminded himself, *we need his help.*

Wolf said quietly, "Were you supposed to be in charge of this operation?"

"Look, I really don't want to hear it," Petrus said. "We screwed up. *I* screwed up. I didn't know the Unseleighe had cased us out. But we need you. Do you have any idea where they've taken her?"

Wolf's expression softened, but his gaze remained intent. "I think I know exactly where they've taken her. The cabin."

Thorn came into the room, holding his leather helmet in his hand. "Excuse me, but I'm sensing the same energies that brought you here. It's coming from where they took Wolf."

"Another Gate," Petrus said.

Odras stood up from kneeling beside the elvensteed. "I had to remove a paralysis spell. They used one on Wenlann—"

"We know where she is," Petrus interrupted. "If we hurry, we might make the cabin before they Gate out of here."

And if we fail . . . he thought, but didn't finish the thought.

Wolf kicked the red bike back to life. "Let's get the hell out of here."

Having bound Wenlann and Lucas with tape, the Unseleighe left them to their own devices, limited as they were. The youngster was still a puzzle, and Wenlann considered ways she might put him at ease so they could understand each other a little better. They were lying more or less side by side, face down and looking at each other.

"Who are you?" the boy asked.

"I'm one of the good guys," she said, "And they are the bad guys. But I guess you already knew that."

His eyes widened. "Yeah, but what the hell *are* you? Martians?"

Wenlann sighed, considering the various half-truths the elvenfolk had offered the humans over the centuries. *At least he's over the first shock of seeing us.* Considering what he had likely already seen, and what he would probably see in the future, she decided that nothing short of the truth would do, no matter how bizarre it would sound.

"We are a race of beings, different from humans. But we are not from what you call outer space." The right side of her face was lying against the floor of the cave. In spite of the work some mage had put into making the cave, the surfaces were still Unformed-bland. Neither dirt nor rock, a sort of non-surface that, like everything else down here, had no real odor. "We come from another, well, *dimension.*"

"Like the one we're in now," he said. "I sensed something funny about the doorway we went through. I felt things change."

More sensitive than I thought. This might not be so difficult after all. "That's right, this is part of the dimension where we're from. We're *elves.*"

The left side his face was likewise resting on the surface, and despite his distorted face his smile was sincere. "No *shit,*" he said. "What I want to know is, where *is* this place? Am I going to go back home?"

Good question, she thought, *but one with an answer.*

"Yes, we are both going home. It's just going to take a bit of time to figure things out."

"I'm Lucas," the boy said. He struggled against the tape behind him, and succeeded only in turning himself around a revolution.

"And I'm Wenlann," she said. "And the rest of these guys, they belong to another clan. My clan is far away, and it doesn't look like they'll be much help. The leader, the one who brought you in, his name is Japhet Dhu. His clan and ours have been at war for some time—our king killed Japhet's father, Zeldan, after Zeldan had killed the king's father and destroyed our kingdom. We were in the middle of rebuilding when the son showed up."

Lucas rolled back over. "Looks like you're all a little outnumbered."

Wenlann turned loose a long sigh. *If this human child can see that, then why can't Petrus?* "The plan was not to take them on. We were to locate them, inform the King of their whereabouts, and lead the forces to them. But as you can see," she said, moving her taped arms, "This didn't go as planned."

"Okay, so they have you now," Lucas murmured. "What use are you tied up like this? Are they holding you for ransom?"

The question chilled her as surely as this cave would have if it were real, dank, and located north of the arctic circle. During the entire ordeal of capture the notion of ransom hadn't occurred to her. *That's just the sort of thing Japhet would contrive. But what would he ransom me for?*

"I supposed they might be," she said at length. "Actually, it's a very real possibility." Unwilling to take the situation lying down, as it were, she sent a tentative mental probe to see what node stores, if any, were nearby. Reaching for and using such energy was difficult for her, but not impossible, but she didn't want to alert anyone to her attempt. However even her subtle exploration of her environment met with a dark wall, similar to that of the paralysis spell, blocking her reach. *Oh well,* Wenlann thought, relaxing. *It was worth a try.*

Lucas too stopped straining against his bindings, and met her frustrated look with one of his own. "So if this is another dimension, then that light circle thing we came through must be the only way in . . . and out."

"Yeah, just about," she said, trying to think of something she could equate to Underhill that would be in his realm of understanding. "There are different areas, some more isolated than others. This one is, well, still under construction. Now it's possible," she said, as an encouraging thought came to mind, "there may be a permanent Gate somewhere around here. Did you see anything when they led you in? My sight was a bit restricted."

Lucas considered this briefly, then frowned. "I saw something weird. It looked like a big granite slab, with a bright oval or something over it. Not as bright as the one that brought me here."

So there is *one,* she thought, elated. "That has to be it. Was it guarded?"

"I don't remember," he said, looking pained. "Would it take me back home?"

"I'm afraid not. At least, it isn't likely. It would take us somewhere else in Underhill . . ."

"But if it took us away from these creeps, it would be an improvement," Lucas said, with a little smile. "There couldn't be anything *worse,* could there?"

Oh, yeah, there could, she thought, but held back the discouraging thoughts. "There may be as many as six different destinations, though it's not likely to have more than three. It's sort of like a junction on a highway, only the location of your destination was four dimensional instead of two." *Am I getting too deep for him?* Lucas was listening attentively, showing no signs of the blank gaze of the totally lost. *Evidently not.*

"And you have no way to tell where you're going?" he asked.

"Well, no. Not unless you are a mage, which I am not."

"Okay, then," Lucas said, turning over and showing his back to Wenlann. "If you're telling me all this it must mean you're on my side." He moved closer, and Wenlann heard something sloshing around in a container. "In my pants I have a bottle of something that might help."

Wenlann watched him wriggle a flat, metallic can out of the back of his jeans, which fell out on the cave's surface with a thunk. "Solvent," he said, fumbling with the can. "I swiped it back at the cabin. This stuff will eat right through this sticky tape."

"How can I help?"

"I think I can open it. But I need you to hold the can."

"Well, I can move around and hold it with my feet," she said, forgoing a lengthy explanation about elven allergies to iron. She slid around and reached the can with her feet. "Okay, I got it."

Lucas gripped the lid and strained. The can slipped from between her feet and fell over.

"Shit," Lucas said.

"No, I got it," she said again, working the can into an upright position. "I'll hold on to it harder this time."

Lucas twisted again, and this time the cap cracked open. "Now let's just hope this thing doesn't have a seal under the cap. I didn't think 'bout that." The cap clattered to the ground, and Lucas took the can in both hands, and rolled over. A good amount of solvent glug glug glugged out of the can, pouring over the tape covering his wrist and hands.

"Might take it a while to eat through . . . then, maybe not," he said, pulling his hands apart, the gray tape making a messy, gooey cat's cradle between them. "Easy. I'm loose."

Lucas pulled the rest of the tape off then freed his legs. A few well placed tears in the tape released Wenlann. Presently they were walking in the cave, Wenlann leading Lucas stealthily to its entrance.

"Shhh. Listen," she said, freezing in her tracks at the sound outside. It was a steady, familiar sound, of bronze scraping stone. *Someone's sharpening their swords. Good. Maybe it will be some time before they notice our absence.*

"It was around to the right," Lucas said, in a whisper. "I think."

"If they're close, we might not be going anywhere," she whispered back. "With these rock formations, I can't tell where that sound is coming from."

"What are they doing?"

The truth? Why not. "Sharpening swords. Big ones. Another reason we need to be out of here."

Lucas gulped audibly, but the new information seemed to stiffen his resolve. Wenlann listened, trying to get a focus. One moment it seemed to be coming from right in front of her, then from yards away. *I'd forgotten how weird the acoustics got in the Unformed. The only way to know where they are is to stick my head out and look.*

"Be ready to run like hell," she said, and peered around the corner. Indeed, the fools had posted no guards near the cave. She spied the two younger ones, sharpening their weapons with a stone some distance away. The Gate Lucas spotted was about as far away as the two Unseleighe were.

Suddenly, the sharpening ceased. Wenlann quickly pulled her head back in, then heard one of them say, "What was that?"

"Summon Nargach," the other said. "I'll investigate." For a moment Wenlann stopped breathing, locked in indecision. *If we stay here, they have us. The Gate is as close to us as they are, but only if we act now. . . .*

She whispered, *"Now."* Lucas dashed out of the cave and Wenlann ran after him. She became aware of another Unseleighe behind her, but she wasn't about to turn around to look.

"Run, Lucas! Don't stop!"

He leapt without hesitation; the Gate flared as Lucas vanished into it. *Go, you brave little . . .* Before completing the thought something poured over her like a net. She stumbled, then fell to her side. *Paralysis. Again. At least the boy got away.*

"It's a Gate," Odras said as they came around the bend on the dirt road. Already the circle of light was beginning to fade. Odras dismounted and stepped closer to examine it. "They left through there, and they took Wenlann with them. There is another vibration, a human." He squinted, looking at Wolf. "Do you know if they took other hostages?"

Wolf had to think about this a moment. "There was someone else there, but I never saw him. I was a bit . . . distracted."

"Perhaps we can find this other human too," Petrus said, trying to keep the anger out of his voice, a difficult feat since he didn't really know what he was angry at the most: himself or Japhet. *Or Wolf. Do we really need him for this?* "Odras, perhaps the time has come to test your new Gate-making ability?"

"Aie," Odras replied. This portal is too far gone to be of use anyway."

Petrus turned to Wolf. "You ever been to another dimension?"

"On occasion," the human replied. "I'm game."

"Should we notify the King first?" asked Odras.

"If we bother going back to Avalon, the trail will be too stale. And that's assuming they don't decide to Gate here first; we still don't know if Wenlann's message got to them, or if she even sent it. No, I move that we go after Wenlann now."

"Which in itself may be . . ." the mage said, his voice drifting off. Something Wolf was wearing caught his attention, and he walked over to him. "Wenlann's pendant," he observed. "A very strong relic. I can use this to focus on her location!"

They all rode back to a long, straight stretch of road.

Thorn pulled up next to Petrus. "It would be best if I went in with you. Otherwise I might have trouble finding you."

"You all must remain behind me," Odras said, "And gradually—*gradually*—increase your velocity to fifty-two miles per hour."

"We're ready," Petrus said. "Let's do it."

Odras started first, followed by Petrus and Wolf, riding side by side. After forty miles per hour Petrus saw the field forming, then Odras gunned it, as they were starting to run out of road already. An egg-shaped field of white light flashed in around them, pulling them into their destination.

Chapter Sixteen

The transition from the humans' world to Underhill was instantaneous, as blazing daylight turned to the ever-present dusk of Petrus' homeland. This, however, was neither Avalon nor any of the other carefully engineered elfhames. This was the fog-shrouded Unformed, and in this particular portion, the visibility was near zero.

The elvensteeds slowed to a crawl. Wolf had trouble slowing down, his front tire even brushing against Moonremere's rear tire.

"I think we should do this one on foot," Petrus said, though Wolf and Odras had already dismounted. "We're missing someone. Where's Thorn?"

They looked around, but saw him nowhere. "He may have ended up elsewhere in Underhill," Odras said. "He is, after all, spirit. The Gate I set up might not have deposited him in the same place."

They listened, but heard nothing in the gloom to indicate activity, or even life. Odras was probing the area gently, his eyes half closed in trance. If there was danger out there, he'd sense it.

"We are at the edge of a slightly developed pocket of the Unformed," he said. "There are primitive rock formations, and perhaps a cave or two, up ahead. I also sense a permanent Gate on the other side of it."

"What about Wenlann?"

The mage reached again, this time his head slightly bowed, as if praying to the gods for her well being. Then he looked up, with a slight twist of a smile. "She's here. Paralyzed by their spells, but she is here, and she is unhurt."

Wolf was clearly relieved. "Where?"

"Ahead," Odras said, pointing through the mist with a long, crooked finger. "Among the boulders. There is a cave. But I sense no other prisoners. The child is not here."

Petrus was not too far removed from being a child himself, and the human's sudden absence added more anxiety to an already troubled situation. *We must save Wenlann*, he knew. *Right now that looks like the only thing we can do*.

"There is a single Unseleighe, a short distance ahead. He doesn't know we're here, but he does suspect something amiss."

"A mage?" Petrus asked, in a whisper. Wolf had crouched reflexively at the mention of the other elf.

"No, but he thinks he felt the vibrations of a Gate," Odras said, reaching for his sword.

Well, he did, Petrus thought, drawing his sword slowly to make less noise. "Perhaps we should deal with him now, before he alerts the others."

"Aie," Odras said. "Quietly, now."

With combat imminent, Petrus screened everything from his awareness except his breathing, his sword, and his opponent.

Ahead he saw a lone figure, outlined in the mist; the Unseleighe turned around suddenly, his sword drawn. Petrus flew at him with everything he had, wanting this to be a swift kill as well as a silent one. But as their swords connected, clanking loudly in the mist, he knew this was not to be.

Petrus thrust, and the other stepped back, throwing him off balance; in that instant, he was quite vulnerable, and would lose the use of his right arm, if not the arm itself. An instant before the Unseleighe might have responded, he heard a *whizz, thunk,* and the Unseleighe froze. As his opponent fell over on his chest Petrus saw the large blade sticking out of his back, and beyond him, Wolf. The human came over and retrieved his blade.

"I don't know if he's dead or not," Wolf said, wiping his blade on the fallen elf.

"Oh, he's dead all right," Petrus replied. "That knife is steel, forged from cold iron. Death metal." Then he added, grudgingly, "I'm glad you have that."

Already there was motion ahead, amid the large boulders Odras had detected. From the mist two more sword-wielding figures charged, and Odras stepped forward with his weapon.

Petrus drove his attacker back, suffering a nick on his left arm for the trouble, but after the move he saw the rest of the clan. Japhet and the mage were carrying a still form between them. Petrus' blood turned to ice.

Wenlann.

Time for dirty swordsmanship. The Unseleighe parried an enthusiastic thrust, and stepped back; Petrus' sword came down on his opponent's booted foot, hard. The difficulty in pulling his sword out told him he had hit his mark, perhaps even cutting the foot in half.

The Unseleighe fell back, with a silent scream on his lips, and Petrus ran toward the leader and his mage at a dead run. Beyond them the Gate flared to new life.

They're not going to even try to fight me! he thought, maddened by the thought of them getting away with her. *The cowardly—*

His mental tirade ceased suddenly when he tripped over a large, substantial something in the mist. For an instant he was airborne, then his left shoulder connected with the ground. His sword clanked to a halt some distance away, invisible now in the layer of mist. When he tried to call out, he found the wind had been knocked out of him . . . while the others disappeared into the Gate.

NO! You're not getting away again . . . his mind screamed, as he watched Japhet and his mage do just that.

I'm going after them, even if I've a broken arm! He managed to get up on one knee, but that was as far as his body would cooperate.

The roar of the Indian motorcycle called out from the mist behind him. Petrus didn't know what Wolf could have in mind; the Unseleighe were gone. If he were trying to run them down with the beast of death metal, he was a bit late.

Wolf on the Indian roared past, going directly for the Gate.

He can't be . . .

He was. As the bike hit the Gate, going at least forty, the magics surrounding it wailed in protest of the cold iron, sending off a halo of red, yellow turning to white; Petrus shut his eyes against the sudden light. Once the brightness faded he looked again. Wolf and his Indian had vanished.

He lay back down, seething with the defeat; presently Odras came to his side. The mage was out of breath, but unhurt.

But wasn't there . . .

Odras said, "I finished off the one with the injured foot. Three Unseleighe down."

"And the ringleaders got away, with Wenlann," Petrus said.

"Without their elvensteeds," Odras commented.

"They just wanted to get away," Petrus said in anguish, wincing in pain as he moved his shoulder. "Did you see Wolf?"

"I tried to warn him about riding into that permanent Gate with that beast of steel," Odras said, examining Petrus' arm.

"I don't think it's broken," Petrus said, bending his arm experimentally. "Bruised, perhaps. We must go after them."

"I'm afraid we won't be going anywhere, for a while," Odras said, still probing the tendons of the elbow.

"There's nothing wrong with me!" Petrus objected, and moved to stand up.

"It is not your injury that has me concerned. It is our navigation." Odras stepped back, and regarded the Gate with a sour, frustrated look. "The pendant. Wolf had it, and it was the only thing we had to track Wenlann. Now that it's gone I'm not even certain how to get back to Avalon."

The Gate continued to glow, a solid yellow color, the hue of a well-made permanent Gate.

"We must follow them," Petrus said, but he knew this would be difficult, if not impossible. The mage walked through the gloom over to the glowing portal, and began probing it.

Petrus moved again to get up, and this time something jabbed him in the hip. *What the . . . ?* he thought as he reached for and pulled out the wolf's-tooth necklace Wenlann had given *him*.

"Uh, Odras?" Petrus said, getting up and hobbling over to him. "I think I have something that might help."

"What is it?" he said, holding the necklace up to the light.

"A possession of Wolf's," Petrus replied. "He gave it to Wenlann, and Wenlann gave it to me. Wolf has the heart pendant . . ."

The mage appeared to be well ahead of him. "Good thinking," Odras said, "And yes, this is a most powerful relic. This Gate will have to be our exit." Odras said. "I suppose I should release our elvensteeds from their present form." The casting made a bare glimmer of light, and parted the fog; Moonremere appeared first, followed by Odras' noble 'steed, both seeming rather spry and light of foot. The stones of amene, topolomite and diaspar remained as decoration in Odras's 'steed's bridle.

On their 'steeds they approached the Gate one final time, Odras holding the wolf's-tooth necklace to up the yellow light briefly before putting it on.

"I know where he went," Odras said after taking the reading. "There are six separate settings on this portal. And the trail is, again, a bit muddied. But I think I can reconstruct enough of the trail to put us in the correct realm. Stay as close to me as you can."

"Aie," Petrus said, and led Moonremere into the circle of light.

"Run, Lucas! Don't stop!" Wenlann called out as he plunged into the weird disc of light, feeling it close around him thickly as if he were entering a pool of water. On the other side was darkness and a soaring feeling of vertigo. His arms reached out automatically to brace his fall, connecting with another disc, which pulled him through.

From darkness and dizziness, to forest and light; Lucas lay stomach down on a thick layer of oak leaves, which had cushioned his short fall. He remained there, unmoving, waiting for something to happen. Only the wind, rustling the leaves around him, made sound. He looked back to the Gate, waiting for Wenlann. No one else came through.

No! he wanted to scream, but grief was seizing his voice. *She had to make it! They couldn't have gotten her. They . . .*

Lucas fought back a wave of tears, and when he wiped at them with a dirty hand, he got something in his eye.

The pain suddenly distracted him from his grief, and he spent several long moments blinking the debris out.

He sat amid a thick forest of oak and pine, with little sunlight penetrating the cathedral ceiling of green. A spot or two of light touched the ground around him. This was not New Mexico, but at least it was somewhere on Earth, or so he thought. *Hell, if I have to I'll fly Northwest home! If I can remember dad's Master Card number . . .*

Lucas got to his feet, discovering a few bruises and aches, but otherwise found himself intact. Beneath the Gate was a smaller slab of granite. Then he considered the creatures who were after him, and supposed they might yet follow him through this thing.

She said to run. To keep running, he thought, torn between waiting for her to make it through, and leaving the area in case she didn't, and something else made it through instead.

Out of here, he finally decided. *Getting caught by those things again would be no help to her. I still don't know where* here *is.*

He started walking away from the Gate, looking for a path or any sign of civilization, while suspecting the search would be futile in this pristine land. As his feet rustled among the fallen leaves, he felt as if he were the first person to ever walk here.

"You *idiot*. Not only did you leave our 'steeds behind, you've brought us back to *Avalon*," Japhet said, standing at the crest of a hill. Nargach, who had set the paralyzed Wenlann down on the ground, joined him to see for himself. From her skewed position, Wenlann saw beyond the hill the top of the new Castle, some distance away.

Hope soared. *They didn't mean to come here.* She prepared herself to send a message to the King.

As if reading her mind, Nargach promptly lay a broad

shield around them, increased its strength, then lay another one atop that.

"Dismiss this Gate," Japhet said, to the doorway they had just stepped from. "We don't want the others to follow."

From her limited perspective, Wenlann had determined that Petrus and Odras had indeed followed them to the Unformed, and had taken out the three Unseleighe warriors, leaving only Japhet and Nargach. This could be good, or bad: good, because the odds were even more against the Unseleighe. Bad, for the same reason, because Japhet would now be desperate. A desperate Japhet is an unpredictable Japhet. And they still had her firmly imprisoned.

"It's a permanent Gate," Nargach calmly replied. "I would need vast energies to rid ourselves of it, and if I so much as *looked* for these resources any mage in the castle would sense it." The mage approached the other, lowered his voice, and added, "Unlike our little band of outlaws, Avalon has more than one mage. Their *King* is a mage, and there are more. Do I really need to remind you of this?"

Wenlann had expected the usual angry retort from Japhet, but other things appeared to be occupying his mind, such as *how the hell do I get out of this jam?*

"We should return through the Gate," Nargach said, turning away from the hill. "Where we can retrieve our valuable elvensteeds."

Before he could say any more Japhet laughed sardonically, stopping him short. "I think not! No, this place will be fine, for now. Who would think to look for us in their own backyard? We should find somewhere to make camp. Somewhere away from this," Japhet said, gesturing toward the Gate. "Then we can concentrate on a plan."

Cautiously Wenlann tried probing Japhet. Nargach was

deep in thought on other matters, she surmised as her probe went unnoticed. She recoiled at the dark cesspool of paranoia and hate she found in Japhet's mind, then embraced his dark feelings as if they were clay, something she could mold into whatever shape she wished.

Here goes. . . .

In spite of the existing uncertainty swimming about in the Unseleighe's mind, it was not a simple task. She was, after all, doing this literally under the nose of an experienced mage. Her work was as subtle as she could make it, while keeping it strong enough to be effective.

Nargach is going to defeat you, Wenlann sent, gradually at first, then increasing the thought in strength, and repeating it. *What's to stop him? Why should he follow you? He is a great and mighty mage!*

Though she could not see Japhet, the two of them suddenly stopped walking.

"What is it?" Nargach said. "You wish to carry her for a time?"

"No, I don't. It's nothing . . ." he said, sounding annoyed. They resumed their walk. Wenlann restrained her elation, knowing she had accomplished her task.

Now, to work on him some more. My, this could get rather entertaining.

Wolf's red Indian dropped a half foot to a new land, new dimension, as Petrus had so dramatically put it. The bike's massive shocks took the impact with ease, as they were brand new. *Well*, Wolf thought, pulling up on the handlebars to keep it upright, *it kind of is*.

If this was where those other two Unsaylee had taken Wenlann, they were nowhere in sight. He stopped the bike on loose, sandy gravel, wondering briefly if he were back home in the desert. A quick glance at the horizon confirmed that he was nowhere near home, or perhaps not even on Earth. The forest that began a short distance away at first looked like stands of tall cactus. They were trees of some sort, maybe a succulent plant, but they were enormous. The branches were green and round, stuck out from the main trunks at right angles, with round, green shoots coming out from them, also at right angles. It reminded him of a picture of ancient conifers that were around at the time of the dinosaurs. With no leaves, the strange trees looked like dog's fur from a flea's point of view, the long stalks reaching for the sky like the spiky remnants of a forest fire.

The Gate he had just dropped out of hovered over a marble pedestal, carved in the ancient Greek style. On examining the ground around it, he found nothing besides his own tire tracks. His heart, and hopes sank, realizing the mistake he'd made.

Odras said they could go off into different areas, he thought. *This, obviously, is not where Wenlann went!*

The Avalon pendant hung heavily around his neck, reminding him of another blunder he'd made. *The only way they found her in the first place is that they used this to key in on her location! And now they don't even have this to use.*

His next move seemed simple: Ride back through the Gate and get back where he was. *I'm sure as hell not doing any good here.*

From the forest behind him came a loud chittering sound, from neither bird nor mammal, at least from any he recognized. He looked and saw nothing, absolutely nothing, that could have made the sound; unless the trees did. *Another reason to get out of here. This place is truly weird.*

He turned his back on the forest, and prepared to mount the Indian; the pedestal beneath the Gate would be difficult to negotiate, but he had ridden up steps on his old Harley that were taller than this. *Just as long as I have enough momentum, I can get up anything.*

Just as he was preparing to sling his right leg over the seat, he heard the sound of a sailing projectile, which was immediately followed by the projectile's landing square between his shoulder blades.

The impact threw him forward, then landed him on his face. The dirt tasted strange, as if it were laced with cinnamon. He couldn't have been down for long; he'd just been whacked hard by something small and heavy. No serious damage.

No big deal, right? he thought, rolling over.

There were at first glance twenty or thirty of them, but they were packed so tightly in a broad circle around him and the motorcycle that this was only a guess; the forest of legs that presented itself to him at ground level indicated many more. As he stirred the chittering started all over again, sweeping through the excited crowd like a gust of wind.

The reptilian creatures were not particularly tall, but given their vast numbers this was no consolation. Humanoid lizards with arms and legs circled around him in an excited huddle, large black macaw-like beaks snapping in agitation. Around half of them held slingshots in the form of long, leather thongs with rock-filled pockets; this explained what hit him in the back. And given the range and accuracy needed for such a hit, these guys must be really good with them. That, coupled with the massive parrot beaks that looked like they could crush a leg bone, added up to a rather iffy situation.

He might have made a dash for the Gate if the lizard folk hadn't blocked his way. The Indian stood unmolested, and the critters kept a healthy distance from it, for which he was grateful. *They must think it's alive.*

Wolf sat up, slowly, ignoring the pain in his back as much as possible. He took one long look at the assembled, and once he knew he had their undivided attention, cleared his throat.

"Say," he said, summoning instant silence. "Do one of you guys know how to Madison?"

He found a deeper, shaded area of forest, where the trees seemed to be twice their normal size. Lucas held up a Black Jack oak leaf, and spread his fingers against it, with leaf to spare. Both palms would fit within its borders.

The Gate had receded far behind him as he made his way through the woods, and the strange elven creatures who had been pursuing him, even if they'd passed through to this world, were now a distant threat. The journey yielded no clues as to who might live here, or to how he might return home. But the farther he advanced into the forest, the safer he felt. The suggestions of wildlife told him he might be able to stay here if necessary, and the prospect was more comforting than he would have guessed.

As he entertained these notions he came across a clearing, with a broad circle of rocks and a tiny log shelter with a thatched roof. With a start, he saw he was no longer alone.

She sat on a low bench, facing another low bench the size and shape of a coffee table; in the center of the circle was a fire pit with the charred remains of wood, but nothing presently burning. The young lady wore a long white robe, and an ocean of curly red hair cascaded down her shoulders and back. She turned to look at him; at first she seemed vaguely surprised, then charmed, by Lucas' standing there.

"Come closer, little one," she beckoned. Lucas frowned inwardly, feeling like he was being addressed like a little kid, but at this distance that's probably what he seemed to be. "You're safe, here."

He walked closer, hesitating at the circle, feeling like it was sacred and that walking across it would profane it. She seemed to sense his reason for hesitating, and smiled appreciatively.

"The circle is not cast," she said softly. "Until then, it is only a rock garden. Please, come over here," she said, patting the vacant spot on the bench beside her.

He stepped over the circle of rocks, but whether it was cast or not, he felt like he'd stepped into another world. The turmoil of Panic and the weird Damien, the imprisonment, the bloodied room, the skulls, and the escape from the elf critters he'd just pulled off was now far away, light years away. In the few days after his suicide attempt, he had intuited a world or path he knew was to be his, but it was a vague feeling, twisted apart by his own internal chaos. Without having the words to describe it, he felt the mystery he had been looking for was right here, in this circle, and this beautiful lady held the key.

He wanted to ask, *what is this place?* but a part of him knew the answer.

"I'm lost," Lucas finally said after a moment of awkward silence. He sat down beside her before what he now perceived to be an altar, with one large unlit candle on a pewter base, in the center. A single thin vase with a cut rose, petals, stem and thorns all black as ebony, to the right of it. On the left lay a pillow of black velvet, holding a crystal ball.

"And you have been found," she replied, turning to him. For the first time he saw the headpiece she wore, and nearly fled in terror. It was the pentagram, the symbol the Satanists used.

"What's wrong?" she asked, apparently sensing his alarm.

"That symbol. Are you a devil worshiper?"

Her look of astonishment turned to amusement, but it wasn't embarrassing, as such a look would normally be from an older girl. "This symbol," she said, indicating the headpiece, "is very old. Those who have used this symbol in the name of evil do not understand it. It is a symbol of peace, of harmony, of love for other beings, human or non. Plant or animal, or spirit. It's been perverted by others, in whatever position. One point up, for the Goddess. Two points up, for the God. But nothing can contaminate its true meaning."

This was all starting to fit, and unlike the Satanists he'd recently fled he was believing her, without being whacked out on drugs. He also knew, sitting beside her in this strange and beautiful forest, that spray-painting tombstones in the light of a full moon would be an alien, criminal act to her.

There are better things to do in the light of a full moon, he heard in his mind, knowing the words were hers. She reached over for the little black pillow with the crystal ball on it.

Much better things.

She held it forward, and he held his hands beneath hers, and when they connected a stream of images passed beyond the crystal, as if the black pillow were a movie screen and the ball was the lens of the camera; he saw the fire burning bright, with people dancing around it, wearing loincloths if they wore anything at all. Some jumped over the fire, some held drums to it, warming and tightening the heads, then returned to the outer circle where the drummers were, pounding a rhythm that was the heartbeat of the planet. Others danced in a spiral beyond the circle, then weaving back, toward the fire, to witness the rite. An old man wearing a headdress made from a wolf skin, fur coming down over his face as a mask. The wolf was the hunter, but this time he was also the sacrifice, as some of the younger braves danced after him, thrusting spears at him, mimicking the hunt. The wolf fell, but from the fallen wolf came the man, as if reborn. They were calling him *chakka . . . chakka . . . chakka . . .*

And among the dancers, standing out like a pearl on black sand, was the white, red-headed woman, the lady who sat before him now, whose hands he held in his own.

The vision shattered like broken glass, and he sat up, suddenly, and with a start, sucking in a deep breath; at some point during the vision he had forgotten to breathe.

"Now I know who you are," the woman said. "You're *Lucas*."

Lucas caught his breath, then looked up at the lady, who had a different look about her. "Who are *you*, then?" was all he could think to ask.

"My name is Margot Jameson," she said, "And I am a High Priestess of the Chaniwa tribe. At least, that's who I was before I passed on, to the other side." She paused, and for a moment her image became translucent, and Lucas knew then that she was a ghost, reviving his earlier guess that this land had not been walked upon by any human. *There's more to the universe than flesh and bone,* he was beginning to realize.

"Does 'Chaniwa' mean anything to you? Do you know Wolf, the Chakka?"

Lucas shook his head. She was making no sense at all.

"Dear me," she said, sounding resigned. "But your vision. It does explain why you are here, and how you got here. Fast Horse told the story to Wolf before they killed him. This is your journey, to find your path."

It sounded simple, but Lucas knew there had to be more to this than finding a trail in the woods.

"Well," Lucas said, peering into the forest. "Do you know where it is?" When she answered his question with a vaguely amused smile, he saw what she meant. And he could have kicked himself. *My path means my spiritual path, you dummy. It was something you felt the moment you came here!*

"I was looking for the path when I met the Satanists," he said finally, knowing it would do no good to leave anything out. "And for a while I thought I had found it. But everything I did, everything I agreed to, I did because I was stoned or high on whatever. I wanted to be a part of something too."

"These things you did, while you were 'stoned,' as you say. Are these things you would have done otherwise?" Margot asked softly.

"Of course not," Lucas replied, without hesitation. "They were stupid things. When I wanted to leave them they wouldn't let me do it. I think they were into killing people, and they were going to kill me before I got away. They weren't fooling around." He stared at his hands, remembering all the things he had done in their company, all of which he regretted now. "There wasn't anything to what they said, was there?"

"They may worship the god of their choosing, but they have no right to do harm. And they were doing a great deal of harm. To you, and to many others. I think you chose well to escape. And to think, you ended up *here* afterwards. Most interesting."

Lucas looked about him, noting again the altar, the circle, the simple dwelling "Where is *here?*"

"My home, where I choose to be, for now," Margot said as she stood up, letting the robe fall to her sides. "I may return to the living, if I choose. I will someday. I think I may have been waiting for this day before doing so."

With the altar to her right, standing with the sheathed knife in her belt, he suddenly knew. Lucas thought himself dense, going by some of the stereotypes, some of which Damien seemed to fit. But this was the real thing, and stereotypes didn't apply. "You're a white witch, aren't you?" he said quietly.

"Yes, I am a *witch*," she said, folding her hands in

front of her. "In the truest sense of the word. But there is no color to magic, as it can be used for both evil and good. Like fire, which can warm you at night, or burn your house down. It must be handled responsibly."

Lucas stood, and faced her squarely and triumphantly. "I know it has to be my choice, I have to ask. I want to be one too. Will you teach me?"

She sighed softly, a beautiful, intoxicating sound. "If I could, I would," she said sadly. "Perhaps someday I can. But for now you cannot stay here. You must return to your home, and find the teachers there. It may take a week, it may take a lifetime to find your teacher, but that is the way of things."

"But how do I find one . . . ?"

"Your heart will tell you. As will the wind, the flowing river, and the crackling fire, and the wild things in the forest. These five things will tell you, if you listen."

For the briefest moment, the pentagram on her headpiece flashed, as if sun had reflected from it. But night was already falling on this magical place.

"But first, this situation, with Wolf, the Chaniwa, the elvenblood. You are standing in the eye of a storm, a storm which is raging about you, its course determined centuries ago when the elvenblood first met the people of the new land. I was one of those people. But you don't yet see the storm, not yet. It will soon catch up with you."

"Can't you help me?" he pleaded, feeling like he was about to be left to deal with this completely alone . . . and he didn't even know the way home from here. Then he focused on the word *elvenblood*.

She must be talking about Wenlann!

"There are the good and the bad elves. I was held prisoner by the bad ones, along with a girl elf named Wenlann. She helped me get away, but I think they caught her before she could escape. Can you help me go after her?"

"I may be a witch," Margot said, her arms open in a gesture of apology. "But I have my limits. I may not be able to help you as promptly as you want, but I can summon someone who can. We serve the same master, so to speak. He will come if I call. In fact," she said, her head tilting to one side. "I think he's already embroiled in this divine mess."

Night never quite fell on Margot's home and circle, which remained illuminated in the dusk from an ambient light, source unknown. Lucas spent what seemed a lifetime, telling her what had been happening to him, how he felt, and where he wanted to go now. It felt good to heap this on her, this mysterious woman who seemed more than willing to listen to him; he had hoped she would have some kind of advice to offer, but the mere act of talking to someone who was *listening,* for a change, made the problems seem much less significant, and much more manageable.

Not knowing how long he had sat there talking to her, he was surprised to hear a motor, like a lawn mower or a chain saw, coming from the forest.

To his quizzical, if somewhat alarmed look she said, "That's my friend, the one who will be helping you back home. I told you he would come if I summoned him."

He glanced up to see a strange motorcycle, ridden by someone who looked like he flew planes for a living. The bike coasted to a stop, and Lucas became acutely aware the thing didn't have brakes, but it did have a sidecar. Then he saw the logo on the tank, *Harley-Davidson*, and stood up. *An antique Harley! This can't be happening. . . .*

The rider pulled up and got off the bike, then removed the leather helmet.

"This is Thorn," Margot said, and Lucas was stunned to see he was not much older than himself. "And Thorn, this is the surprise I mentioned."

"We almost met, before," Thorn said cryptically as they shook hands. "You and a friend, went riding on a Katana. I'm glad we didn't meet then."

"Why?" Lucas asked, uncertain he wanted to know.

"Thorn is a guardian angel, of sorts," Margot said, when Thorn didn't reply right away.

"If we'd met then," Thorn finally said. "It would have been because you had died."

"Oh," Lucas said, now wanting to change the subject.

"And you were looking at those bikes in the window, in Albuquerque," Thorn continued, in a friendly sort of way he found disarming. "Good thing you passed up that scooter. Parts are next to impossible to find, and it needed quite a few just to get it legal. This girl," Thorn said proudly, turning to the Harley, "is Valerie. The sidecar isn't exactly stock, but I needed to cobble one up to get us both where we're going."

And we speak the same language, too. "Can't we use the Gates?" he asked, but he was itching to climb into the sidecar.

"I can use them, but they're unpredictable for me. Sometimes they work and sometimes they don't. Just lost track of some friends because I forgot that I don't travel like the flesh and blood." He paused, glanced over to Lucas. "You knew I was a ghost, didn't you?"

"Oh, yeah," Lucas said casually, but his eyes were still on the Harley. "No big deal." Then he went over to Margot and attempted to give her a hug. Instead, he almost fell through her. "Oops," he said, regaining his balance. "Forgot. Thank you, for everything."

"You're most certainly welcome," she replied warmly, then she turned to Thorn. "Where will you two be going?"

Thorn started putting his helmet back on, and Lucas took this as a cue to climb into the sidecar.

"The Land of Shadows," he said, once the goggles

were in place. "It's a direct path to the land of the living, at least for me."

"You may find that your plans are changed, once you get there," Margot said. "This is not business as usual."

"Well, if they're changed, that's the way of it," he said, and signaled to Valerie to start herself up.

Odras led them through the Gate to yet another world which had the look and feel of an Underhill moor. The thick scent of burning wood and leaves filled the air, though its source was nowhere in sight. The grass that was visible through the fading mist was darker than usual, and in the distance rose a jagged and snow-capped mountain peak. If they were in Underhill, it was a place well beyond elfhame Joyeux Garde and even Outremer. Petrus recognized none of it.

"Ahead," Odras said, as his 'steed gaited briefly in place. He pointed toward a land of gently rolling, grassy hills, with a suggestion of forest beyond. "I sense two Unseleighe. No Wenlann, but she could well be concealed by other means."

At the mention of Wenlann, Petrus focused on their task; the moor had an eerie feel to it, as if he'd been here before. But no, it just resembled the one of Avalon, with a little less light and, he found as he took in a deep breath, a bit higher in altitude.

"This place," Odras said, halting his 'steed. "It reminds me of . . . but it can't be," he said, and pushed on. They came across the remains of a burned forest, the ground blackened by fire, the trees mere charred skeletons reaching for the dusky sky. Odras stopped again, this time clearly uncertain of where to go next. Then his eyes fell on the distant mountain, apparently for the first time since they arrived. His entire demeanor changed.

"I lost their trail," he said, uncertainly. "The two Unseleighe I sensed, I think they belonged to another clan." He looked directly at Petrus, and when their eyes locked, said, "I made a grave mistake by bringing us here."

"This isn't where Japhet ended up?" Petrus said, but already he knew something else was wrong, something Odras wasn't sharing.

"We should leave this place," he said, turning his 'steed around.

"And go where?"

"Anywhere," Odras said harshly. "We want to be anywhere but here. Trust me when I say this."

The old mage was more rattled than Petrus had ever seen him. *What would frighten Odras so? Something so powerful that he doesn't even say its name?*

Saying nothing more, Odras urged his 'steed back the way they came, between the hills they had just passed. Then, around the next bend, a party of four elves on elvensteeds blocked their way.

Unseleighe elves, Petrus saw right away, though he didn't recognize their clothing, or the banner. This was a different tribe, one he had never encountered, or even heard of. These Unseleighe wore bronze helmets, and their weapon of choice seemed to be the spear, not the sword. Their clothing was more animal skin than cloth, with crude fur breeches, moccasin boots and fur lined tunics. Tied to their 'steeds were more furs, either cloaks or bedrolls, or both. They seemed to be geared for living in the mountain that loomed in the distance.

"We must escape them at all costs . . ." Odras said, turning around once. But coming up behind them were six more of the same, with the unmistakable protrusion of bow staves and quivers behind their backs. Odras halted his 'steed. From the new group advanced their leader, his tunic and helmet more ornate than the rest. Behind him was a red banner, of a design Petrus didn't recognize.

"Put your sword away," Odras hissed. "These men are archers as well. We must talk our way out of this one, if we are to get out at all."

Petrus gradually returned his sword to its scabbard and tried to assume a neutral expression. "Odras, who are they? Unseleighe?" he whispered out of the corner of his mouth.

"Aie, Unseleighe. *Barbarians*. Of a clan I thought I would never see again." He gave Petrus an odd look. "Pretend I'm your leader. If we live, ask me later why."

Petrus felt no need to question this, and the mage didn't wait for a reply. The leader of the group had come to a halt some paces away, and Odras raised his hand, hailing.

The Unseleighe didn't respond; he seemed intent on sizing the two up, as if they were to be butchered for their meat. Odras dropped his hand, and both stood regarding each other for a time.

Petrus studied the Unseleighe, who under other circumstances might have passed for Outremer elves; they did not have the pointed face, the blunt, ugly features, the hideous grin that were characteristic of Japhet's clan. But other features, along with their demeanor, told him they were not friends, either. They were tall, with long matted hair. They would even resemble Odras, if they were cleaned up and groomed, and renounced their Unseleighe ways. . . .

The thought left Petrus feeling cold. The facial features, the height, Odras' resoundingly negative reaction to them, began to point to an unpalatable secret, one he didn't even want to consider.

Finally the leader spoke, in a dialect Petrus had difficulty understanding; what stood out clearly, however, was the betrayal the Unseleighe evidently felt.

"It has been a long, long time, my old friend Odraskonfor, son of Helias Dhu," the Unseleighe said, folding his arms across his chest and sneering at them both. "Why have you disgraced us with your presence?"

Odras bowed submissively, and spoke in his usual somber, humble tone. "I come bearing information for our clan leader, Tekran de Ahnn," he said quietly. "If I have intruded upon your lands . . ."

"You have intruded on no one's *land*," the leader said. "What you have intruded upon is our *honor*. De Ahnn is no longer our leader. He made the Great Way some years ago."

"Who then, is our new leader?"

A broad smile creased the Unseleighe's features, then he said, "Your father, Helias. He leads our clan. And if you hadn't shamed yourself you would be the prince!" He gave Petrus an acid look. "Not only do you associate with Seleighe, you babysit their children!" He shook his head sadly, expressively. "How the mighty have fallen, Odraskonfor. Tell me, did you ever pursue your mage craft? Don't tell me this fell by the wayside, along with your honor."

While the two were impolitely bantering back and forth, Petrus felt a subtle shifting in the energies around them. *Odras is up to something,* he thought, keeping his own demeanor as humble and neutral as the mage's.

Odras shrugged, a decidedly defeated gesture. "I fear so. Leaving our clan has been disastrous for me. I never pursued the teachings, and the few abilities I had, I've lost."

The leader stared at him a long time, as if gauging his answer. "How pathetic," he responded, at length. "You don't even have the courage to fabricate falsehood." He addressed his men, before and behind him. *"Kleasach! Hadderach! Pinat peturat . . ."*

The words of ancient Elvish sounded like a command, and like a well-oiled military unit the remaining nine drew and nocked their bows in one motion.

Amid the display of crisp military training, Petrus sensed something released from Odras' general area, and caught a glimpse of it as it passed over the soldiers' heads, distorting the horizon briefly before it.

"No, I never did become a mage," Odras lied casually, catching the leader's attention when it appeared he would return to the company of his men. "When Outremer, Avalon and Joyeux Garde decided to combine their armies in one large fighting force, their goal was to rid Underhill of these pockets of Unseleighe vermin, such as yourselves. And when the army advanced to *this* region, well, the obvious choice for a scout was someone who knew this land. That, old friend, is what I've been doing with myself."

The leader looked momentarily confused, then one of his men called out; alarm spread through the ranks. Petrus looked up, and fought hard to hide his amusement. From one end of the horizon to the other, a Seleighe army larger than any that ever existed had formed a solid line of mounted elves, foot soldiers, and wagons armed with enormous crossbows.

Odras, you clever mage, you. Did our army really have to be this *big?*

"I have come to send a message to . . . my father, as it turns out," Odras said. "We wish to discuss terms."

The leader looked uncertain, then after a few quick glances to the massive army beyond, he barked a few short orders, and the men lowered their arrows.

"You will die for this, Odraskonfor," the leader seethed, though he didn't seem willing to make true the prediction right then. "We will tell your father what his son has done," the Unseleighe said, then pulled his 'steed around and led his men away.

They had retreated a fair distance before Odras and Petrus exchanged looks.

"I will explain it all later," Odras said, looking away.

"I think I already understand. I admire you," Petrus said, hoping to meet his gaze. "I didn't know such bravery existed."

Odras seemed unwilling to bathe in the compliments. "Now we need to *get out of here immediately*."

Chapter Seventeen

"You may find that your plans are changed, once you get there," Margot's words echoed in Thorn's mind. *It's just like her not to mention the rest of it.*

Thorn instructed his new charge to keep his head as low as possible in the sidecar; he had never tried transporting a flesh and blood through the realms this way, and the transition from Margot's realm was tricky at best. A forest of oak shifted around him, and the Shadowland came into sharp focus. Valerie's front wheel touched down on the surface, like an airplane's landing gear kissing a runway.

"First stop," Thorn shouted over Valerie's roar. Lucas had obeyed his instructions to the letter; he was scrunched so far down in the sidecar it looked like he had fallen out.

If the Lord wants to give me further instructions, now is the time, he thought, feeling just bold enough to wonder what grand scheme the gods of the realms might have. Two other Guardians rode toward them through the trees, and pulled to a stop in a clearing.

"Greetings, Hans and Lawrence," Thorn said, getting off Valerie. "I take it the game's afoot."

"And you're probably wondering what the game is," Lawrence said, in his rich English accent. His shiny, nickel plated Brough Superior sparkled beneath him. Today he had chosen to wear a pinstriped suit of a style fashionable in Thorn's time. "Is your passenger with you or did he leap out during your journey?"

Lucas had crept down to the lower recesses of the sidecar, and gradually emerged, like a turtle from his shell. When his eyes cleared the edge of the car, Lawrence and Hans both laughed.

"Not the sort of ride you were expecting," Lawrence said, leaning over to look in the car.

But Lucas' eyes had fixed on Lawrence's motorbike. He sucked in his breath violently. "Holy *shit*," he said. "Is that an old Brough?" His initial shyness completely forgotten, Lucas practically flew out of the sidecar and was at the side of the motorbike in a flash.

"No," Lawrence replied stiffly. "It is a *new* Brough."

"That's a . . . that's an Alpine," Lucas stammered. "You know, Lawrence of Arabia died riding one of these. Got up to a hunnert 'n twenty."

Lawrence rolled his eyes, as if debating on how much to correct the young man. "Actually," the rider said, clearly suppressing a grin. "*Sir* Lawrence owned a number of them. This one has a top speed of one hundred *five* miles by the hour. Out here, of course," Lawrence said, regarding the Shadowland, "such measures don't really apply."

Lucas continued to salivate, like a puppy drooling over a slab of beef.

"I think he's one of us," Hans observed. "What do you ride, youngster?"

Lucas looked up, as if not fully understanding the question.

"He's a not-so-rare breed," Thorn supplied. "A rider without a bike. And he's a flesh and blood, don't forget that. He's not staying here."

Hans shook his head slowly, as if having trouble comprehending. "A rider without a bike?"

"How *horrible*," Lawrence said, and seemed ready to comment further when something in the forest moved, distracting him.

He wore a wreath of oak leaves around his waist; today he was the young Oak King, looking to be a year or two older than Lucas. The buds of two new horns on his forehead made him look devilish. He came over to them, tilting his head as he peered at Lucas with dark, brown eyes.

"Yes, this is indeed the one," the Lord said.

Lucas tore his attention away from the bike. "Who are you?"

"Today, you can call me Pan. As Margot told you, Lucas, a storm is about to descend upon you. Even I don't know the outcome." Pan stepped closer, his voice becoming serious. "Listen carefully, Lucas. Your task is to find your teacher. It may not be in the same tradition of magic as Margot, it may be something native to your home. The tradition doesn't matter as long as it feels right in your heart."

"A teacher? You mean, for . . ."

"You know what for," Pan said. "It's what you have been seeking. It's what you see in the forest, and hear in the wind. Margot told you as much." A mischievous grin graced his young, tanned features. "But don't take it too seriously! I am the Oak King, Lord of the forest and of wild things, but I am not somber."

"What about Wolf?" Thorn asked, but Pan gave him a warning look that was difficult to read. *Wolf's already involved. Does he understand what I'm asking?*

"Wolf can handle this situation," Pan said, at length "He *must* handle the situation, for its outcome to mear anything. You may now proceed to the land of the living," he said, then vanished.

"It is futile, absolutely *futile*!" Nargach roared as h came out of the trance. "The nodes are as protected a they were when we left. Do you have any more brilliant ideas that might give our location away?"

Japhet said nothing as he sat on the felled tree, apparently too deep in thought to notice his mage had still found no alternate energies to build a Gate. Wenlann watched all this from a short distance, considering more irritating messages to send him.

"We can't stay here," Japhet said, emerging from whatever thoughts that had been occupying him. "We must come up with a Gate. How did you build the first one we used to escape this place?"

Nargach looked weary, and short tempered; his curt reply confirmed this. "If you'll recall, it was a rather weak Gate, and required some recovery time between . . ."

"Yes, yes," Japhet said, "I recall now. And the power is no more?"

"Expended the first time around. Consider," Nargach said, his tone somewhat conciliatory. "Our only route out of here is the Gate from which we came. Presuming it is still there, we can use it to return to the Unformed and regain our elvensteeds. Or perhaps we could return to the humans' world again."

"Anywhere, but here," Japhet said. "This place makes me nauseous."

Well, I suppose it would, Wenlann thought sardonically. *When your army is reduced to two, there isn't much fight left, is there?*

Japhet looked over at Wenlann, as if she were a bug that had violated his personal space. "What of the Seleighe bitch?"

"It was your idea to take her," Nargach replied, and looked like he wanted to recall the words. "What I mean is, it *seemed* like a good idea at the time. I suggest we keep her close by, for protection, until we are ready to leave this place."

"I doubt she would be an effective hostage," Japhet

said, getting slowly to his feet. "The King is out for my blood, and I doubt she would stop him if he had the chance. Perhaps we should kill her now, and be done with it."

"Not so hasty," Nargach said, raising a hand. "You would be surprised to know what their females are worth to them."

Wenlann seized the moment to supply Japhet with a few opinions of her own. *The Seleighe bitch is far more valuable to you alive than dead. If you did away with her now, what would stop the Seleighe from taking you both out when they catch up with you?*

"She goes with us," Japhet said, rubbing his temples. "We'll decide later what to do with her."

Once at the Gate it was a simple matter to trace Wolf using the wolf's tooth necklace. Odras remarked that it was like Nargach to lure him to their old home using false vibrations, and other things that Petrus didn't pretend to understand. The mage rode into the other realm first, but that did nothing to dampen the rude surprise of finding a mob of agitated, sling-wielding gargoyles.

Petrus' first thought was, *Oh shit.* His second thought was, *where the hell did Wolf go? Is this the wrong place again?* But no, he spied the Indian bike, an incongruous piece of hardware in Underhill. And Wolf was on the ground.

The gargoyles noted their arrival with mild surprise and some of the crowd began moving back from Wolf. However the human had gotten into this nasty situation he was clearly in over his head. Petrus was about to ask Odras what his thoughts on the matter were, when the mage began barking out a long string of harsh but well formed grunts punctuated by a snapping of teeth.

Yet another esoteric talent Odras had that I didn

know about. He speaks Gargoyle. Petrus hoped it would be enough . . . whatever *it* was.

"What are you telling them?" Petrus asked, but Odras continued the short speech undisturbed. When he had finished a sound that must have been laughter rippled among the reptilian beasties. A moment later, more of the mob began to pull back.

Speaking Gargoyle required stresses and breath control that was nothing short of an aerobic workout. After catching his breath, Odras said, "Let's move now, while we can."

The Seleighe rode their 'steeds down to Wolf, who had struggled to his feet.

"Are you hurt?" Petrus asked, but Wolf already seemed to be shaking the injury off.

"Just a rock in the middle of my back," he said, glancing back at the mob. He looked at Odras, with a mixture of awe and disbelief. "What did you *say* to them, anyway?"

Odras replied, "That the human they had was an outlaw, and we had been sent to capture you. They find it . . . *amusing* when elves chase humans."

"Yeah, but for how long," Petrus said, already picking up signs of skepticism from the mob, which was still a stone's throw away. "Time is of the essence. Wolf, get on my 'steed. It's the quickest way out of here."

"I'm not leaving the bike," Wolf said, getting on the Indian.

"Well, that settles that," Odras commented, also looking at the mob. Already it looked like they were starting see through the ploy.

"Once I get a reading of where Wenlann went, I'll proceed first," Odras said. "Then you, Wolf. Can you ride?"

"I can ride fine," Wolf said, starting up the bike. Its sudden roar startled the gargoyles. Wolf twisted the throttle a few times, grinning as they jumped back from the loud, alien sound.

"Quit screwing around," Petrus said. "We gotta get out of here. Give Odras the pendant. *We need to find Wenlann.*"

Wolf became serious and handed the mage the necklace. "Then let's go," Wolf said, and Odras led them into the light. A moment later they were through; on the other side was a familiar forest.

They'd come back to Avalon? Petrus thought, astonished. The castle was visible through the trees.

"What could they have been thinking?" Odras asked aloud.

"Two of them, one carrying something heavy," Wolf said, pointing out fresh footprints on the ground. "They went off that way."

"Odras, contact the King," Petrus said, "And let him know what's going on." Odras closed his eyes and entered a trance. "We will follow these tracks. *We will find Wenlann.* And that motorbike, it makes too much noise. I really must insist it stay behind."

"No problem there," Wolf said. "I trust this place to be good to it."

"The King has been notified," Odras said, opening his eyes.

Petrus gave Wolf a hand up onto the saddle behind him. "Let's go get her."

"There," Niamh said, hovering over the crystal of elvenstone, as long and thick as his forearm. One of the Gate wards had gone off a candlemark earlier, and the mage was following it up. "The Black Forest. That's where they were the last time," Niamh said.

King Aedham stood opposite Niamh, pensive and preoccupied. Ever since they'd lost contact with their recon party he had been debating sending out another

Odras is with them, he reminded himself. *He may not be indestructible, but he is a powerful mage.*

Marbann, Aedham's trusted Ambassador to the outer elfhames, had recommended the mage for the task at hand: rebuilding Avalon. Yes, his birthplace, and initial training ground, was an Unseleighe Court. Odras had been a solitary mage, walking the land of Underhill for centuries, living among the poor, even the gargoyles for a time.

He is no more Unseleighe than you or I, the ambassador had said. *Give him a chance. I will stake everything I have on him.*

Strong words for a Seleighe. The King trusted Marbann, but found himself in a quandary—eventually his history would leak out. Skeletons seldom remained in the closet forever. How does one establish the trust of the court before that happened? Assign him to a mission to test his abilities and his loyalty. He had performed admirably during the first incursion by revealing Japhet's "army" for the mirage it was. Then came the recon of the renegade Unseleighe clan, which Aedham saw as the perfect opportunity. The whole thing might have established Odras once and for all as a trustworthy Mage of their court, whose loyalty would have been beyond questioning, if . . .

If what? Aedham thought, gnashing his teeth. *What has happened to them? Where are my people?*

Then this disturbing bit of news from Niamh:

The Unseleighe are back in the neighborhood.

"I believe they are using the intermittent Gate near the Black Forest," Niamh said. "Perhaps we should expend the energy to shut it down once and for all."

The King sighed at the news. "It's a little late for that, I'd say. We may need everything in the nodes to do battle, now."

The Gate in question was neither permanent or temporary, its classification falling somewhere in between. It only appeared, and opened in its location in Avalon when someone used another Gate to reach it. "I will investigate this personally," the King said. "Keep watch, if you will."

"Aie, King," Niamh said eagerly, his attention returning to the crystal.

As King Aedham turned to leave the workshop, the crystal flashed brightly, followed by an excited yelp from Niamh.

"Sire! It's Odras. He and Petrus have just arrived through the same Gate."

The King dashed back to the crystal. *"And?"*

The mage looked up, saddened. "Indeed, it was the Unseleighe. They have Wenlann. Taken prisoner. But the clan's numbers have fallen to two. Petrus took care of the other three already. They have a human among them, on a motorcycle."

"Thank you, Niamh," the King said. Unwilling to wait any longer he dashed out of the workshop and headed for the armory. *Time for battle,* he thought, savoring the prospect of striking Japhet Dhu down himself.

You don't want Nargach to get too tired carrying the wench, do you? Wenlann sent to the very edge of Japhet's awareness. *Time for a break.*

"Let's stop for a moment," Japhet said, and the ground beneath Wenlann, who was slung over the mage's shoulder, stopped moving. "Are you getting tired of carrying her?"

"At this point, yes I am," Nargach admitted.

It would probably be safe to remove the paralysis spell, she sent.

"Do you suppose we could trust her to walk on her own, then?" he asked.

"Perhaps," Nargach replied. "I suggest we keep her arms bound, though.

She can walk between you, with Nargach behind.

"Fair enough. Release her," Japhet said.

Inwardly, Wenlann sighed in relief. Being carried like a sack of potatoes was getting old, not to mention the soreness across her waist where she had been draped over the mage's shoulder. *Don't let Japhet get too far away,* she reminded herself. The paralysis spell lifted from her completely; in her compromised position she hadn't noticed how weak it had grown.

Saying nothing, she surreptitiously tested the magical bindings around her wrist. These, too, were weak. *I could pull my arms out of these if I wanted to,* she thought. *I just need to find a good time to do it. I can't get too far away if Nargach throws a levin bolt at my back.*

"Sit over there," Japhet ordered, indicating a large rock with a flattened surface. They were closer to the Gate than they suspected, but she wasn't about to tell *them* that. A line of familiar boulders were farther up the wooded hillside. *If I can just get them to fight each other, I would be home for real.*

"Japhet, you know there's really no way the mages could have missed us," Nargach said. They both stared at the castle, which was a little less visible now, but was still a formidable presence on the horizon. "Perhaps you could tell me how you intend to rebuild your forces."

Wenlann couldn't have picked a better line of thinking; it was just what she needed to bring this situation to a head.

Of course he wants to know, she sent. *So he can steal your ideas and use them for himself.*

This time Japhet didn't respond to Nargach. Instead, his head turned slowly toward her, and their eyes locked. Her blood turned to ice. Had he just figured out what she had been doing?

"I may appeal to some of the other Unseleighe Courts for recruits," he said, turning back to Nargach. "I am still considering a return to the humans' land."

Wenlann saw motion from the boulders, a vague blur that turned into a face, and ears: Petrus. Then Odras appeared, followed by a another familiar, human face.

Wolf? she thought. *What in the name of Avalon are you doing* here?

Japhet was staring at her; half a second later, he was following her eyes, to the boulders.

"*Seleighe vermin!*" Japhet shouted.

A tendril of power flashed from Nargach's fingertips, and danced around him in matrix. *He's creating a levin bolt! Out of what . . . ?*

The bindings gave way altogether; whatever power Nargach was gathering was coming from every available source, including her former fetters. Once she was free she saw Odras reaching for his own power, and his own levin bolt . . . and she was in the direct line of fire.

Quick like a rabbit she scrambled out of the way, in the direction they had just come. *I have no weapon, no nothing, unless I throw rocks! The best thing I can do now is get out of the way!*

Good, thought Petrus, clambering down from the boulders. *She got away. I only wish I had a sword to throw to her!*

If their plan had a fatal defect, it was that it didn't exist. This roundabout approach to the enemy's resting place had forced them to leave their elvensteeds behind. Odras stood with a most peculiar expression. *He's reaching for a node. A levin-bolt!*

"Let's go down and around," he said to Wolf. "Have your knife ready. Damn, I wish you had a sword!" Wolf shrugged and followed Petrus back around the rock formations.

"There," he said, then remembered the place, although now it seemed much smaller. *Gods, this is where Wenlann and I used to play "healer" when we were kids. I know exactly where we're going. Down, past this boulder, through these two.*

"The path," Wolf said, catching up to the spry elf.

"I see them, through there," Petrus said. "Hold on, I don't see Japhet anywhere." Their noisy passage across the forest floor stopped suddenly. Petrus turned an ear toward the two mages, but he was listening for Japhet, who must have run in the other direction. *The same direction Wenlann went. I don't like this.*

"Odraskonfor, miserable son of our leader Helias!" the Unseleighe mage shouted, partially obscured by the trees. "You are weak and foolish. Why taint yourself with the Seleighe court?"

Odras was a lone figure atop the huge boulder, and looked irritated at having to reply. "I no longer have a family, except for the one *I* choose! And this," he said, waving both arms expansively, "Is my family's land. I thought that we had made it clear you and your clan were not welcome here."

"Is that what that was?" Nargach replied, sounding amused. "That pathetic army that we escaped from with such ease? If such was the message, it wasn't made clear. What right do you have to this land, dear Odraskonfor?"

"We have every right to that which we have died for at Zeldan's hand," Odras replied. "As for the message . . . perhaps I should make myself more *clear*—"

Then the fireworks began.

Node power, a tingling, slightly uncomfortable feeling, something like electricity, trickled up Petrus' legs. Odras was building up to one hell of a bolt; he wondered if it were safe to be even *this* close.

Japhet is still down there . . . when this thing goes, it will probably take him out too. And anything else that's nearby.

Wenlann, you had better be far enough away . . .

It was the last thing he had time to think before the

bolt hit; the blinding flash, accompanied by a deafening concussion, threw them both backwards. Feeling nothing, hearing nothing, Petrus lay on the forest floor, contemplating branches of the oak trees towering over them, reaching for the sky.

After a time, Wolf appeared, leaning over him. His lips were moving, but he wasn't saying anything. The human extended a hand and helped him to his feet.

As Petrus' hearing began to return, Wolf said, "I was standing behind you when it hit. You took most of it. Are you okay?" The elf nodded numbly.

"I don't see Wenlann anywhere," Wolf said, having started off in the direction of the blast. Petrus followed. They found a blasted pit, blackened by recent fire.

This was where Nargach had stood, he thought, regarding the smoldering ground with awe. *Odras really outdid himself this time.*

A twig snapped from within some dense brush a few paces away. Petrus drew his sword, then immediately returned it to its scabbard. Wolf and Wenlann were kissing frantically, as if they were trying to devour each other's faces. Petrus' ears started to burn. Then they stopped, realizing they had an audience.

"Where's Odras?" Wenlann asked.

"I don't know, he's up here, somewhere," Petrus said. *Find the mage. See if he's okay. Leave these two alone.* "Odras! Where are you?" He returned to the blasted pit, got his bearings, and retraced his steps to the cluster of rocks.

He found Odras lying amid the boulders. The mage looked up feebly, then closed his eyes against an apparent wave of pain.

"Odras?" Petrus said, kneeling down beside him.

"Please, young one, don't speak so loudly," Odras said. "I have a headache that would rival the worst hangover I have ever had."

"Can you get up?" Petrus said softly.

"No, I cannot. I must lie here for a good long time first."

Wenlann and Wolf caught up. "Mage shock?"

Odras nodded, wincing. Even that amount of motion was visibly excruciating.

"Here," she said, kneeling beside the mage. "Let me try this. It's *shiatzu* for elves."

She leaned over and took the pointed tips of his ears between the forefinger and thumb of each hand, and applied gentle pressure.

"Does that help?" she asked hopefully. "If there's time I'll do a proper healing . . ."

"I'm afraid that what ails me is beyond acupressure," Odras said sadly. "And you don't have time for anything except going after Japhet."

"*He got away?*" Wenlann said, and clambered to her feet. Odras groaned at the sudden motion and sound. "I thought he was fried in the levin attack!"

"He was too far away," Odras said. "Go find him. Hunt him down. And kill him. We haven't won yet."

Chapter Eighteen

"Oh, bloody *hell*," Petrus groaned as they reached the top of a thinly wooded hill. "There he is!" Japhet Dhu was making short work of the distance between him and the Gate, his wounded pride oozing from every motion he made. The Indian was still parked on its stand, but the Unseleighe hardly looked at it as he passed it.

Wolf had pulled his knife, and looked ready to throw it, then shook his head. "Damn. Too far away. I couldn't hit a truck at this distance."

The Unseleighe turned and smiled triumphantly from ear to pointed ear before walking into the Gate. White light enveloped him, then he was gone.

"I'm going to kill him," Petrus said in frustration.

"But we have something else to contend with now. The King has arrived."

Great, just great. Just as soon as Japhet gets away—again—the King shows up. He'll probably reduce me by a rank, after this.

Why can't I get this warrior thing right?

Mounted on his 'steed, the King led Niamh, Fion and Scoriath through the narrow trail. Aedham took one long look at the Gate, then at Petrus and Wenlann. Wolf made himself discreet by attending his Indian.

Petrus stepped forward stiffly, feeling like he was going

before a firing squad. He forced himself to meet the King's eyes.

"Where's Odras?" The king asked solemnly.

"Recovering from mage shock," Petrus reported dutifully. "Back in the forest, a ways. He took out the Unseleighe mage with a levin-bolt."

"So *that's* what I heard. And Japhet, I take it he got away, through the Gate?"

Petrus had never felt more miserable. "Yes, Sire."

"Alone?"

"The rest of the clan died in battle. But Japhet, he's escaped, again. F-Forgive me," Petrus stammered. "I *failed.*"

King Aedham walked over to him, with a most surprising expression.

Aedham is . . . smiling?

"*Failed* me?" he said, shaking his head in disbelief. "Your mission was to locate the enemy, not take out the majority of their forces. And, I take it, with zero losses? Is anyone even *injured*?"

"Well, uh, no," Petrus said, feeling a bit giddy with relief. "Not really. Except Odras, and he'll be fine, after some rest." His arm was still sore from the sword fight, but that was hardly worth mentioning.

"I will overlook your enthusiastic interpretation of the word *reconnaissance*," the King said, extending a gauntleted hand, "and congratulate you on a job well done."

Wenlann chose this moment to step forward. "I second that," she said, giving Petrus a big hug.

Wolf, after spending a tactful length of time examining his motorcycle, came over.

"Sire, I would like you to meet someone," Wenlann said.

Good Gods, she's blushing, Petrus thought, nauseated. *It's like introducing a new boyfriend to her parents.* The quick understanding that this was pretty much what it was stung less than he'd expected.

"This is Wolf," she said and the human stepped forward, bowing slightly as he shook Aedham's offered hand. "He was—"

"He was a tremendous asset to the mission," Petrus interjected. "We would never have accomplished what we did without his help. I have him to thank for my right arm, and probably my life."

"Most noble," the King said, and his eyes met Wolf's; what took place then was the nonverbal communication between mages, one human, one elven. Mutual respect.

"As I have said," The King said, looking at the ground as he spoke. "I know this Japhet. He will not just go away. He will hold a grudge, he will hide somewhere, for a year or a decade, or even a century, building his forces from nothing, and strike Avalon again."

He looked up, now, with mage fire in *his* eyes.

"Therefore I *can't* just let him go. Once and for all, we must go after him. Fion and Scoriath. Prepare to Gate. Where's Niamh?"

"Here, Sire!" Niamh said, scrambling forward.

"Find out where that low life rat went," the King said, indicating the Gate. "We're going after him *now.*"

Japhet Dhu stumbled out of the Gate, onto the soft, hot sand. The drop was more than he'd expected, and his foot landed at an angle; the rest of him tumbled onto the desert. Face down, he tasted sand.

Ptoooey, he spat, clearing the grit out of his mouth. He rolled over and got to his feet, regarding the Gate warily; the Seleighe were right behind him, and would probably be coming through any moment.

There was little cover here. Desert, desert and more desert; is that all the humans had? A plateau rose from rust colored rocks, a thick slice of Earth thrusting through the horizon like a scab. Behind the Gate was a long ribbon of asphalt, and off in the distance was a triple strand of a barbed death metal fence. His hopes sank; he had anticipated some other place than this blasted wasteland.

Yet, I escaped, the Unseleighe reminded himself. *I escaped, and I made the Seleighe look like fools all over again.*

He set off walking, away from the Gate toward the highway, looking back at the Gate nervously for whoever might be following. *My entire clan is dead,* he thought morosely. *Not that they did me much good anyway.* Then his mood brightened: *Nargach's dead too. No more worrying about him.* The realization brought about a strong feeling of liberation; he was walking among humans now, alone, but with powers they could never match or even begin to understand.

I'm going to be a god, here, he thought eagerly. *My father set an excellent example. Perhaps I can get into the drug trade, like he did.*

His musings went on unimpeded for a time. The highway stretched out ahead of him, into the horizon, a road to nowhere. *Once I have my power base back, I will attack Avalon again!*

When his mood was really starting to lift, however, he sensed something dark and powerful behind him.

Oh, bother. Now what, he thought, turning around.

The black cat spirit, Ha-Sowa, was stalking him, and approaching at a good clip. Japhet stopped walking.

The cat came to a stop just before him, now seeming bigger and angrier than ever, and regarded him with red, piercing eyes. The circular claws, razor sharp and as long as Japhet's fingers, extended and retracted. The Unseleighe's throat began to itch; when he tried to speak, he found it had contracted to near uselessness.

"*Where is my master?*" the cat hissed. "*Where is Nargach?*"

Somehow, telling the spirit Nargach had been turned into a toasted cinder didn't seem like good strategy.

"*What of the human Wolf?*" Ha-Sowa continued. "*The Master promised me Wolf and another sacrifice.*"

Japhet's fear turned to inspiration; he relaxed, and considered how best to phrase the lie. "Your Master, Nargach, has told me to inform you that your sacrifices will be along presently," Japhet said. "Beyond, from yon Gate."

Ha-Sowa peered at the Gate, still visible in the distance.

"*This had better be so,*" replied the cat. "*Or you will be the sacrifice.*"

That I don't doubt, Japhet thought to himself, considering ways of enhancing the lie that would allow him to escape.

"Back, to the humans' world," Niamh said, after probing the Gate for its destination. "That is the path the Unseleighe took. But I caution against using this Gate . . ."

"Why?" the King asked, sounding impatient.

"A danger awaits. Spirit . . . a cat spirit?"

Wolf looked up, and away. "Ha-Sowa," he said in apparent aggravation. "That thing just doesn't want to give up."

"We could go in shooting," Wenlann said, "But it would still have the advantage."

"Japhet will know if something's about to come through," Petrus said. "And we have to assume they're working together."

The King scratched his head, and looked into the Gate again, as if it were an oracle. "What is Ha-Sowa?"

"A complication," Petrus said, turning to Wolf "Perhaps you should explain?"

"Ha-Sowa is a demon, which has been haunting my people for centuries. Our tribe was founded in part b your folk, the elven-folk, long ago. Nargach enslaved a demon to pursue my tribe. That's what's on the other side of the Gate."

The King stared at him, looking completely lost.

Then Wolf added, "Also, it wouldn't give me much time to turn into a Wolf."

Aedham rubbed his temples, wincing at an apparent headache, then started massaging the tips of his ears with forefinger and thumb. Relief came over him immediately.

"I see," the King said, although it was clear he really didn't. "You can fill me in on the details of your family tree later. Right now, I need a bottom line to work with. Is this demon a threat or not?"

"*Yes*," Petrus, Wenlann and Wolf said in unison.

"Now that we have *that* established," the King said, turning to Niamh. "We should avoid using *this* portal and Gate to the adjacent area using our own resources. Niamh, could you construct the appropriate passage for us?"

Niamh nodded eagerly. "Consider it done, Sire."

The contrast between Underhill and this vast, wide open space overwhelmed Petrus all over again; they found themselves at the mouth of a deep canyon, through which ran a shallow creek, lined on either side with the scrubby trees which never seemed to grow to maturity. A small brown lizard shot across the pebble-strewn ground.

Once Petrus and Wenlann had found their 'steeds, grazing lazily in the grove where they'd left them, preparations for the mission had gone smoothly. Wolf arrived safely with his motorbike, along with Fion and Scoriath, who carried not one but four different swords, of various sizes, on his 'steed. Seven total, with mounts.

"Glamories," the King said, once everyone was through Niamh's impromptu Gate. "I don't want to shut the Gate down yet, but I don't want it to be visible, either. And we can't be strolling around the desert in our standard attire."

"Aie," Niamh said, and in turn glanced over at the party that had just Gated to this dry, dusty destination. "Invisibility, or something else?"

"Invisibility would be the quickest solution," the King said, and Petrus agreed. Converting their original party to motorbikes had required great skill from Odras, who was currently recovering in the Castle. Niamh was an adequate mage, and shared many abilities with Odras; kenning bikes from Wolf's death metal beast was not among them. But these matters did not seem to concern the King as he moved ahead of the group a bit and took in the alien landscape. Petrus felt the glamorie ease into place, like a sheet of silk gracefully falling over them.

Presently the King turned to his party of six.

"Japhet is nearby," he announced. "The Gate is that way, through the canyon. I also feel negative magic of another sort, which seems to be tied to this land." The king dismounted.

"I can't follow you down there," Wolf said reluctantly. "This bike, it's for roads, not rocks."

"Perhaps you can aid us by riding around the flank then," Aedham suggested. "It wouldn't hurt to have an extra set of eyes back there."

"I may have my hands too full to be of much help," Wolf said, looking past them to the flat desert on either side of the canyon. "Ha-Sowa wants *me*. She's my problem."

"Take them both on together?" Petrus suggested.

"If possible, but I suspect we'll be in slightly different worlds before too long. Let's cross that bridge when we get there," he said, starting up the bike. With a brief longing glance at Wenlann, he rode off to the right of the canyon. He became a dust cloud on the horizon, the Indian's roar fading with him.

As they followed the creek through the canyon, Petrus heard the rumble of thunder. Behind them a thunderstorm was building, in a sky that had been clear when they arrived. *Weird weather the humans get to deal with,* he thought, shrugging the concern away. Fion and Scoriath glanced nervously back at it, then turned their attention forward. *No* storms in Underhill were this big.

The creek wound down into a steep-sided section of canyon. The group took a higher path over it which didn't quite reach the canyon's top. A cool, wet wind blew in behind them, followed by the false darkness of clouds blocking the sun. A flash of lightning, then thunder, much closer now.

The King had gone several horse lengths ahead when a sheet of lightning ripped from the sky, striking the ground to the right of him. Moonremere reared up with the rest of the 'steeds, screaming in protest; Aedham fell on the ground. He lay there without moving, and once Petrus and the others had safely calmed their 'steeds he rushed over to the King.

Wolf didn't dare look back at Wenlann, lest he lose his determination to fight this creature alone. Thunder rolled across the desert, an unfriendly, dangerous sound. With storms, which here were sudden and torrential, came the certainty of flash flooding, particularly in the rocky gorges where creeks turned to rivers in less than a minute.

Like the canyon they just went into, he thought, now concerned for the elves, for other reasons. A flood could wash them right into the enemy, if it didn't drown them first. *They won't know about floods,* he realized, as even humans who were not native to the area seldom understood the ferocity of floodwaters resulting from even the mildest of storms. And the storm looming over his shoulder looked like a double whammy.

I've got to warn them. Slowing the bike, he made a wide U-turn. But once he negotiated it he became aware of a strange feeling, unusual but not unknown; he'd felt this way when he had been handcuffed on the floor of the adobe. On his arms and hands, hair started to grow wildly.

Wolf resigned himself to the change, offered a silent prayer to the gods for his companions and pulled the bike to a stop, flipping the kickstand out. Not a moment too soon, either. Nose and mouth became a snout, and his clothes started to tighten in areas where they definitely shouldn't. Before too much happened, he stripped his pants and everything else off.

"Oufff . . ." he muttered, his insides shifting again as he fell over.

Light rain began to splatter, not on skin, but fur. Wolf got up on all fours, and anger and hunting hatred welling up from his soul and spilling into his wolf body, growing from the base of his tail and spreading to the very tips of his pointed canine teeth. Saliva pooled under his tongue and hung from his jowls in long, sticky strands.

I'm hungry for cat, his wolf-self said.

As if in answer to a spell, Ha-Sowa came into view at the top of the nearest hill, regarding the wolf with a snarl.

Then, in the back of his mind, came Fast Horse's voice: *You are both spirit and body, you are both equal. You exist on the same plane. That is why you change into a wolf, to defend yourself, to defend the Chaniwa. Today will be different. Today you will* destroy *Ha-Sowa, not just chase her away.* This was not merely his voice, but Grampa's soul speaking as well; he was still with him, hadn't made the great journey yet. *He's waiting for me to succeed or fail, before going on,* he thought. *Why is this all falling on me?*

Grampa answered him, *Because you* are *the last Chaniwa. There is no one else to do this. No time for this talk! Ha-Sowa approaches.*

Man-self went away, wolf-self came back, hungrier than ever. Ha-Sowa stalked down the hillside toward Wolf, slowly, as if knowing its intended prey was not going to run. Wolf's hackles rose. More change surged through him, and he felt matter swarming into his wolf-body as the gods imported it from elsewhere. Wolf grew, until his head was looking upon the ground as if from its human perspective.

Ha-Sowa had grown too, he noted as the cat paused several paces away. At first glance they seemed to be of the same size, evenly matched; but the other had claws, their tips just showing through the toe's fur-folds. A display, and a challenge. Wolf had blunted claws, but powerful jaws. Equal match? Since the first clash ended in a stalemate, such was entirely possible, though Wolf didn't feel equal. *Is it going to leap? No. It is waiting. For what, for me to attack?*

Then the cat approached, and they began circling, head to tail, tail to head. The circle closed, by narrow increments. Their eyes locked as they paced, and the wolf was ready to lunge at the slightest muscle twitch.

Ha-Sowa froze in mid-stalk, turned.

Then leaped . . .

All was blood red, as cat and wolf tumbled in the dust, teeth ripping real, solid flesh; The storm raged beyond and raged within the circle they had marked out by their walk. As he snapped and bit and fought in the dust, he became aware of the boundary they had marked out by their pacing, the division between worlds. Within they were spirit as well as beast, matter and ether. They separated, and Ha-Sowa was bleeding, their blood mixing on the ground between them. Wolf was injured, but he cared nothing about it, being only vaguely aware of the bites and the long bleeding gash down his back.

Spirit and matter, matter and spirit. To get past those claws, wolf-self thought, not in words, but abstract images emphasized by the damage those claws had already done. *To get past them . . .*

Spirit and matter. Use both, he considered. *We are spirit too.*

Wolf made an image of his spirit, an outline of the wolf he had become, and he made the outline solid, and real. Spirit-self and wolf-self became separate, and the image lunged.

Ha-Sowa spun about, exposing her neck. Wolf attacked, jaws clamped down on the throat, stifling the cat scream that rose in protest. Tumble, tumble and roll; cat blood flowed over the wolf's tongue, rejuvenating him, giving him fresh power despite the loss of his own blood. Cat's jaws worked open, pressing against the wolf's, snapped shut on nothing. Cat claws dug into wolf's back, stayed there. The pain made him hold on even tighter, as he knew that to release now meant certain death.

Wolf held on, held on with everything.

"Aedham," Petrus whispered urgently, but the King was not responding. Wenlann and Scoriath joined him, as Fion held the 'steeds' reins.

Wenlann felt his pulse, checked his eyes. "He's in shock. But he's breathing. Damn, that lightning was close," she said, looking anxiously at the black sky. "We need to get him out of this open space."

Petrus didn't argue. With Scoriath's help he carried the King to an overhang of rock beneath a sheer cliff; meager shelter, but the best they could do at a moment's notice.

Aedham opened his eyes, looking stunned. "Don't stop now," the King whispered. "Go after Japhet. Destroy him. Bring me his *head.*"

"But Sire, you—"

"But nothing. I will recover. But this storm is the perfect cover for him to escape. That lightning bolt was brought on by something greater than the Unseleighe, but they know we're here."

"I'll stay with him," Wenlann said, not looking altogether convinced that the King would be fine. "Niamh, what healing can you bring?"

Niamh closed his eyes and concentrated on the appropriate powers. The King looked up, met Petrus' eyes. "Fion is commander now," he said. "Do as he says, Petrus. No hero shit, now."

"Aie, Sire," Petrus said, and obediently turned toward Fion, who was returning to the 'steeds. The rain had started to fall a little heavier now as he followed the captain down to the edge of the gorge. It felt good to be following, for a change. He didn't feel particularly capable of being in charge of this situation.

Fion had taken the reins of his elvensteed and was looking down at the depths of the gorge. Petrus rode Moonremere over to him. There they both saw a swiftly flowing river that was once the creek.

"It's rising, but I don't think it will be a problem," the captain said at length, then with Scoriath climbed onto their mounts. "Let's go find Japhet and get this over with."

I'm all for that, Petrus thought.

Fion led them down closer to the river, picking through the rain with a little more caution now that their visibility was reduced to practically nothing. With his own limited mage sight Petrus sent a tentative probe forward, to see if he could sense their enemy anywhere nearby. As the high ground receded behind them, Petrus began to feel a little vulnerable, as the river water had risen noticeably; once the water was covering their 'steeds' hoofs, Fion was starting to look uneasy.

"This may have been a mistake!" Scoriath shouted

over the rain and the roar of the river. Petrus barely made out his words, and rode closer to hear what he wanted to do next. The downpour concealed whatever was ahead of them.

"Go back!" Fion shouted. "The water's rising too fast!"

They turned their 'steeds around and began a more spirited ride back, the water now flowing swiftly over the vast, flat area that they had just crossed over.

We're in trouble, Petrus realized, urging his 'steed forward, faster now, but Moonremere was not negotiating the uneven terrain, now that it was obscured by the swollen river. Fion shouted something; Petrus looked back, just in time to see the leader's elvensteed stumble. Fion held on, but it appeared to be a losing struggle. Moonremere had stopped and when Petrus turned back around, he saw why. A surge of water, just about even with his shoulder, was raging toward them, cutting off any passage to the safety of high ground. The wall struck them sideways, and Petrus fell into the raging current.

He was not wearing a full set of armor, but Fion and Scoriath were; the current carried him downstream swiftly, the rock face of the gorge spinning past, offering no chance to grab onto it. Then something struck him, hard, in his stomach. His breath, forced out, stayed out. A big rock, which his body took the full force of, flowed past as water closed over him. Despite the pain that wracked his body the sudden cold flooding over his head gave him new life, or at least a semblance of it.

I'm going to sink like a rock if I don't get rid of this sword, he thought, but the warrior part of him screamed in protest at the idea. There was still a battle to be fought, and to walk into it without his sword was ridiculous.

But how the hell am I going to fight a battle if I drown? he thought, moments before the cold turned to numbness. He felt himself floating, from the water, from his body.

Numbness became darkness, with a coldness that carried the pain away.

Once Wolf's teeth found the artery, he nearly choked on the resulting flow of warm, pulsating blood. Ha-Sowa ceased to struggle and relaxed her claws, which seemed to take forever to withdraw from the flesh of his back. Breath, which bubbled up through her crushed throat, stopped completely after a final gasp. He backed away from the dying cat, aware now that his own wounds were as bad. Blood soaked the sand, making a morbid, sticky mud.

Rain began falling a little more heavily now, but Wolf hardly noticed it as he fell over, painfully, on his side. He watched the lifeless cat form take on a yellow, glowing aura that stood out like a headlight; it brightened, faded, then vanished, taking Ha-Sowa with it.

Ha-Sowa is no more, he thought, feeling less then jubilant. With the spirit gone, his body began its change back to human form, despite the injuries. At one point he passed out from the pain, then came to, cognizant of arms, legs, and a torso. He lay on his left side, his right side bleeding from open wounds; much of the damage was absorbed in the transformation, but not all. Laying naked in the rain, bleeding from his wounds, Wolf knew he was far from being safe.

Panoei, ananatta Okoshi? he heard from somewhere behind him. *Now do you doubt what old man Fast Horse says?*

Grampa was still here, lurking just beyond his sight. Pain blinded him. But Grampa was still here, still . . .

He thought the wolf that walked past him then was from this time and this land, here to investigate the scent of blood. But the wolf was transparent, the rain falling through and beyond its image. He watched the animal walk away, aware now that it was part of himself that was leaving. The wolf Okoshi had found dead nine hundred years before would finally go on to its destiny, after serving the Chaniwa so well for so long.

Po-kwa-taea, kakuna ka wana, Wolf tried to whisper, but made do with the thoughts instead. *Farewell, dear friend.*

The rain subsided, and Wolf lay naked and shivering on the ground, praying for the return of the hot desert sun. A moment later the gods answered his prayer, spilling warm sunlight over the desert, burning the clouds and rain away as quickly as it had arrived.

Distant thunder turned into the sound of a motorbike, an unusual sounding bike but one he remembered. Thorn on his old Harley rode into view, but attached to it was a sidecar, with a passenger. Only then did he think he might live to tell the story of this unusual afternoon.

But do I know anyone who would believe it?

Thorn pulled up beside him, as transparent as the wolf-spirit who had just departed. But the boy who climbed out of the sidecar was solid, a flesh-and-blood. He was a kid, fifteen at the most. But his eyes looked like they belonged to an old man.

"I'm going for help," Thorn said, and sped away.

"You're bleeding," the boy said, taking off his t-shirt. With his teeth he started a tear in the cotton knit, and started shredding it up into bandages. Wolf hadn't noticed the wound in his wrist, bleeding profusely; he couldn't have done a better job if he'd cut them himself. The boy wrapped a strip of cotton cloth around it, tied it just tight enough to stop the blood. Wolf would have sworn he was a paramedic.

"Who are you?" Wolf managed to whisper.

"Lucas," replied the boy, applying pressure to the gash in his side. In shock, Wolf didn't feel anything. "Don't talk. You're really messed up."

No shit, Wolf thought, before he passed out again.

Chapter Nineteen

"I think we should cut our losses and get the hell out of Dodge," King Aedham said morosely, leaning on Wenlann for support. "*After* we find Petrus." He didn't sound hopeful that they would, but Wenlann knew they would take whatever time was required to find their comrade, alive or not.

The King is right, she thought. *It was not our fate to succeed in this land. Japhet may get away yet.*

Fion and Scoriath had returned, half drowned and minus their armor. Their 'steeds had survived, and after a short search they turned up Moonremere, grazing on a juniper bush. But there was no sign of Petrus.

"If you can help me onto my 'steed I will be fine," the King said, and Wenlann obliged by giving him a leg up. "Let's go find Petrus before Japhet does."

Until now, that had been the unspoken fear. Now that the King had voiced the concern, a new urgency revived them. Niamh had tried to scan the area for any elven presence, but the electrical storm made it too difficult for him, and the King's mage-sight was still on the fritz from the lightning hit. All that was left to do now was to search for Petrus using non-magical means.

Niamh was intently looking at something else, and everyone seemed to notice this at the same time; all turned their gaze to the desert, where a motorcycle was approaching.

Thorn pulled up, looking rattled. "Begging your pardon, Sire," he said, nodding slightly toward Aedham. "I need your help. Wolf survived his confrontation, but at great cost. He's bleeding to death as I speak."

Oh dear Gods no, Wenlann thought, terrified. *I can't . . . I don't want to lose him!*

"Aedham, please, let me . . ." she began.

The King said simply, "Go to him, Wenlann. You can work a healing?"

She nodded quickly, but her thoughts were elsewhere. Without another word she hopped on her 'steed and followed Thorn back to the location. In less than a minute she saw the Indian with a pile of clothes beside it, and beyond it two figures, one naked and lying down, the other at his side.

Look at all the blood, she thought in anguish. *I should have gone with him!*

Too late for that, of course; she leaned over him and took in the damage, only slightly aware of the other person.

"He had a cut on his wrist, and I got it to stop bleeding," a young, male voice said. "I've been putting pressure on this big one. That's the main problem."

She looked up, noticing the other person for the first time.

"*Lucas?*" she said, momentarily baffled. *I'll ask later how he happened to be here, of all places.* "You did the right thing. But he's still . . . in trouble." She turned his head, and looked into his eyes, which were dilated and glazed over. *At least he's still breathing.*

Wenlann calmed herself and concentrated on her hands, stilling them, preparing them to receive the native energy. *I just hope it's enough. This isn't all his blood, is it?*

Her rudimentary knowledge of elven healing did not include training in Earth magic, so she had to improvise.

Now I know it's enough, she thought uneasily, regarding the work ahead of her. *I hope it isn't too much!*

Once the link between her hands and the power was established, she held her palms over the deep gash in Wolf's side. His entire torso was caked in blood, but the wound in question, the long rip under his arm, exposing four ribs, could not have been caused by anything but a claw, and a big, nasty one, at that. The heat left her arm, and went directly into the injury. Wolf's eyes shot open, and he started to moan.

"Hold him. Hold him *still*," she said, and Lucas held his shoulder. He was still writhing, if not as violently. *This probably hurts like hell,* she thought, wishing she could speed the process up. But this was as fast as she dared take it, and with this much blood loss she didn't think a sleep spell would be a good idea.

Beneath her hands the wound stopped bleeding, and the blood that had caked around it began to fleck off from the heat, revealing other, though smaller cuts. *I'll come back for those later,* she thought, concentrating on stopping the bleeding. After the first pass the wound had a thin layer of transparent skin, and she looked him over for any more leaks. There were none; Lucas' quick action had saved him. After the second pass the wound was covered by a bright pink scar, and she had started on some of the others when the fatigue caught up.

I have to stop now or I'm going to burn myself out. Then I'll be the one who needs a healer, she thought, then looked at Wolf's face. He was awake now, and gazing at her lovingly.

Petrus rolled over on the river's shore, feeling the water trying to pull him by his legs back into the current. He dragged himself onto the relatively dry land, on what at first appeared to be an isolated island in the middle of the river. But no, there was a shallow part, bridging the island to the main shore. In the island's center were more massive rocks, which he would have likely smashed into if the river were any higher. All told, a good place to wash ashore.

He sat trembling on the rocks, amazed to find his sword in its scabbard still at his side. After coughing up some water he struggled to his feet and inventoried his injuries. Chest and stomach would become one big bruise; perhaps the cold water would keep the swelling down, perhaps not. He stood up, testing his legs, and looked around in vain for Moonremere. No one was in the river, or on the shore.

Over the roar of water, he heard a footfall on the loose rocks behind him. Pulling his sword, he turned around to confront the source. By the time his eyes met Japhet Dhu's he was in a full fighting stance.

"Oh, it's *you*," Japhet said, looking disgusted. He'd already drawn his sword, a long, dark bronze piece with jewels in the hilt. "I was hoping for a challenge. Instead, it's only a *child*."

Now that the danger was clearly defined, his senses sharpened, filtering everything out including the pain wracking him from head to toe. Petrus lunged immediately, the blade glancing off Japhet's hilt; the Unseleighe jumped back in surprise, and Petrus thrust again. Swords met in a blur of bronze. Petrus drove Japhet back, against the large rocks, where he ducked and rolled out from under the young elf's attack.

Now the tables were turned, Petrus had his back against the rock. Victory graced Japhet's features with a hideous snarl. Petrus knew he had fallen for the trick, looked for ways out. He hopped backwards onto one of the smaller boulders, Japhet's blade striking the stone where Petrus' midsection had been a moment before.

Over there, he thought, seeing a possible way out through the rocks. *If I can get him over there.*

Already the fight was taking its toll; he could ignore pain, but summoning energy when one was already exhausted was another matter altogether. Indeed, Japhet followed him, stumbling in the process; he recovered from it before Petrus could take advantage. Japhet seemed to be exhausted, too; he'd been running nonstop, while they had been chasing, non-stop.

No time to assume, Petrus said, finding an energy reserve.

"You *would* have to get up there," Japhet sneered, and swung at his legs. Sword tip sliced through the laces, and the boot started to loosen. He couldn't believe the hit had been anything but luck; this was dirty street tactics.

Return kind with kind, Petrus thought, their blades clashing madly now. Standing on the rocks had its advantages, but the boot was getting looser, and would soon eliminate any mobility on the uneven, rocky surface.

"Hard to dance around with one boot, is it?" Japhet laughed.

The Unseleighe struck again, this time a vertical slice that barely cleared the end of his nose. But with a resounding *thunk*, the blade landed in the fork, and stayed there. Japhet pulled, but it was not coming out.

Petrus saw his only chance for a clean kill, and took it. He tumbled from the rocks, and landed face to face with Japhet's severed head.

The King insisted they stay together, even if they would cover more ground in separate teams; he didn't want to risk losing any more of his people than he had to, and there were other dangers out here besides Unseleighe ones. The search party returned after searching one side of the river, in a hilly area that anyone could get lost in. The paths to the creek were limited, but they explored every possible way, looking for signs of either Petrus or Japhet. They came back to the cliff, which had become their informal headquarters, empty handed and depressed.

When an elvensteed came around the bend, the King raised an eyebrow and grinned; Wenlann had returned, with not one but two scantily clad young men, riding in front and behind her. Evidently her healing skills were sufficient to revive Wolf, although even from here he saw the pink welts that were a sure giveaway of quickly healed skin. As for the other youngster, he was not much younger than Petrus, but didn't seem the slightest bit astounded at the sight of all these elvenfolk.

She rode the 'steed up to the cliff's shade, helped the boy off first, then herself, then Wolf, who was moving very slowly.

"Petrus?" she asked hopefully.

"We still have the other side of the river to search," the King said. "I'm not giving up yet."

"I think he just got washed downstream," Scoriath said. "As for Japhet . . ."

The rest remained unsaid. Wenlann came forward with the young man, who was younger than he had first thought.

"This is Lucas," she said, "And this is King Aedham, our beloved leader."

"A king?" the boy said, astounded.

Not to mention an elf! Aedham thought, *I need to talk to Wenlann about this. I'm not so sure it's a good idea for him to be aware of us. . . .*

"My pleasure," Aedham said, shaking Lucas' hand. He felt weak, and took a seat on a large, vaguely throne-shaped rock. "Wolf, did you succeed in your conquest?"

The human didn't look much healthier than he felt; in the shade he looked even paler than he had before, a sure sign he'd lost blood. "Yes, I did. The cat spirit, Ha-Sowa, is no more."

"I'm grateful that part of our expedition was a success, anyway," Aedham said, trying to fight the unhappiness away. *If Petrus died because of all this I'll never forgive myself.*

Aedham was about to suggest checking the other side of the river when Niamh, who had taken a moment to explore an interesting strata of stone, came running back to camp.

"Petrus is coming," he said, winded. The King clambered to his feet, and instantly regretted the quick move; he sat back down, willing the dizziness away.

"Is he injured?" the King asked.

"He's walking on his own, that's all I can say for sure," Niamh said.

As Petrus came closer, it became evident that he'd had a rough day, too. But he was triumphant; when the gathering parted to let him through to the King, Aedham saw why.

Without a comment, he walked up to the King, deposited Japhet Dhu's head at his feet, and folded his arms proudly. For an insane moment Aedham thought of a cat, bringing home a dead rodent. The King regarded the head for a long time. Wenlann turned away politely, but in the background Aedham heard her laughing hysterically. Lucas seemed fascinated if anything, but Wolf looked paler than ever.

"Good work, Petrus," Aedham finally said. "Whatever happened, however it happened, this is indeed a job well done! Are you hurt?"

"Not enough to matter," Petrus said.

"Now," the King said, to Wenlann. "What are *your* plans?"

She had obviously thought this out already, as she took no time to reply. "With your leave, I would like to stay here with Wolf for a time. He still needs someone to take care of him. And I need to go fetch my 'steed: she's still at the motel isn't she?"

"Should be," Petrus replied. "Our week's about up there anyway."

Wenlann continued, "But right now I think I should make sure Lucas gets back home. His parents are probably worried sick about him."

"She's right," Lucas said. "I have been gone a while. I don't even know what day it is, do you?"

The King shook his head, "No, not in this world, I'm afraid. Wenlann, I trust you to use your good judgment in this matter. We are not unknown to humans, but those we do confide in are those we can trust."

"Of course, Sire," Wenlann said. "We can trust these two."

Aedham nodded, satisfied. "That's all I needed to hear."

"I would like to stay, too," Petrus blurted out. "I mean, to help out. Make sure everyone gets home okay."

Aedham cast a wary look to Wenlann, who returned it with a hesitant, affirming nod. *Yes, they do indeed have some things to work out.*

"Not a bad idea, Petrus," the King responded. "Once we are back in Underhill we have a few Gates to shut down. By the way, Wolf, where did your motorbike go?"

"It's where it was," Wolf replied. "I'm in no shape to ride, not today. It's hidden. We'll get it later." He looked back at the 'steeds, which still wore the elaborate tack of Avalon, and Petrus and Wenlann, who were dressed in their usual Underhill attire. "What about the way y'all look?"

"Easily tended to," Aedham said. He had already begun removing the glamorie on the Gate; the shining, shimmering disc was closer than he had thought. "Now, for you," he said. When he was done the two 'steeds wore typical western tack, and Petrus and Wenlann wore boots, jeans, western shirts and cowboy hats. "After we return Underhill I will instruct Niamh, or Odras, if he is well, to leave this Gate open until your return. Concealed, of course."

"Aie," said Petrus.

"I understand," Wenlann replied. Yet the King already knew, from the look in her eyes, that she would be staying here. *That is her right, to live among humans if she chooses. My sister did the same, and it wouldn't hurt to have one of us in the area.* He regarded the two, Wolf and Wenlann, who had moved closer to one another. They looked so right together it made his heart ache for his own loves, Ethlinn and young Traig.

"I'm ready to go home," the King announced.

Using the Sandia Mountains far to the North as a reference point, Wolf determined they were on Puerco Creek. From there, they would go to Wolf's shed, and rest. Lucas had finally got up the nerve to say he really didn't want to face his parents, at least not yet, and Wolf had graciously offered his home as a sanctuary.

I know I have to go home eventually, Lucas said to himself. *I just need a place to get my head together.*

He rode behind Petrus on his 'steed, while Wolf and Wenlann rode the mount Scoriath loaned. It didn't take long for him to pick up on what was going on, and wondered if it was such a good idea for Petrus to come along; the jealousy vibes from Petrus were thick, and Lucas read them with ease. If Wenlann noticed, she gave no indication. She seemed to be perfectly content riding with Wolf's arms around her, oblivious to everything else.

Meanwhile he became aware of a pressure in his groin, and realized he had to relieve himself, in a bad way. But there were no private places anywhere in sight. He decided to hold it until one happened along.

The rocky, hilly terrain leveled out somewhat, but they were still far from the highway. Wolf noted a passenger jet high overhead but it was going away from where he thought Albuquerque would be. And yes, it was descending. . . . He scratched his head, clearly puzzled.

"I'm not so sure we're going the right way," he said, after sizing up the mountains in the distance. "At least I thought those were the Sandia Mountains."

"Could be the Manzano," Lucas said, squinting into the vista. "I live in the city so I don't know the mountains very well. The Sandia Mountains are right on top of the city, though. I don't see anything that looks like a city."

They rode a bit longer, picking through the rocky ground with care, until they spied a house way off in the distance.

"Let's ask them," Wolf said. "We'll just tell them we're lost."

The gravel road they took toward the dwelling was more rutted dirt than anything, and didn't look like it had been used much lately. Low hills, however, flanked the road on either side. And Lucas' bladder was reaching critical mass.

"The house is just around the corner," Petrus said, pointing to the corner of the adobe building, visible ahead.

"Look, guys," Lucas said. "I've got to, you know, take a leak. It can't wait. I'll catch up with you in a minute."

Lucas hopped off the 'steed and walked toward one of the rises, each footstep pure agony. Petrus shrugged and the others followed him down the road.

Once his business had been taken care of, he went back to the road, saw the 'steeds up ahead, in front of the adobe.

Then, parked beyond them, was a black van.

He halted as he recognized it, remembered who it belonged to.

Damien.

And the adobe house. It looked different in the daylight, and when Japhet had marched him out of there he hadn't been taking notes. Still, it was the same one.

He remembered the rotting meat and paint thinner, dirty mattress, and skulls. *This is where they were keeping us.*

Petrus had already dismounted, followed by Wenlann, and both of them went to the front door.

I've got to warn them. He forced himself to move, taking it one step at a time. Petrus and Wenlann were standing right in front of the adobe, but something was wrong. They had frozen in place, completely motionless, just outside the front door.

Someone was shouting, but he couldn't make out what was said, who it was. Wolf slowly dismounted, and alarmingly, raised his hands in the air, then clasped them over his head.

What's going on? Lucas stopped again. Now that Wolf was off the 'steed, he saw Damien holding the rifle, standing beside the van.

Must be some kind of elf devil spell shit, Lucas thought frantically, remembering Japhet Dhu and his involvement in this place. *If they could move, they would.*

So far, Damien hadn't seen him, and to keep it that way, he backed off, and looked for a roundabout way *behind* the van. There were several small hills of gray gravel; this place had once been a mining operation of some kind, but whatever they were digging up was long gone. The hills, each about the size and height of a long school bus, provided excellent cover as he crept around behind the adobe, and the van. He avoided a heap of scrap metal, which looked like it would clank if you even looked at it. Off to the side, separate from the scrap, was a half-buried piece of galvanized pipe. When he dug it out and knocked all the gray mud off, it was a little longer than his forearm.

Before he had time to talk himself out of it he climbed to the top of one of the hills. With any luck at all the guy with the gun would be facing the other way.

"I told you Satan would overcome!" a familiar voice shouted, much closer now. Lucas stopped to listen. "He sent me to claim you, and I promised him I would succeed! And now I am following through on that promise. Here," Damien shouted, then came a rattle, and a clink. *Handcuffs.* "Put those on. *Now!*"

Wolf mumbled something, unintelligible. Then the sickening ratcheting of the cuffs.

Lucas peered over the top of the hill. On the other side was a sheer face, against which the van had been backed up. Below him Damien was standing next to the passenger's door, holding the rifle relaxed at waist level. The van's back doors were open, and on the ground just behind it lay a blood-covered body. It was Satanic Panic, his lifeless eyes staring straight up, as if gazing at something a million miles away. In his limp right hand was a bloody straight razor. The source of the blood, his throat, had been cut not once but several times.

Lucas crawled back, out of sight, fighting the sickness that tried to rise from his stomach. Stars, wild with vertigo; he thought he was going to fall over. . . .

Then the symbol, the star in the circle, flashed in his mind as if branded by a red-hot iron.

Those who have used this symbol in the name of evil do not understand it, came Margot's words, from somewhere deep in his memory. *It is a symbol of peace, of harmony, of love for other beings. Plant or animal, or spirit. It's been perverted by others.*

He opened his eyes, and saw Damien, pointing the weapon at Wolf, his new friend.

It's been perverted by others. . . . he thought, and remembered the conversation all over again, with the witch in the glade. *You must return to your home, and find your teacher. It may take a week, it may take a lifetime, but that is the way of things.*

Lucas curled up as tightly as he could around the pipe,

the weakness coming over him like the sudden onset of flu. Sweat broke out on his forehead, but he was too weak to even reach up to it, to brush the salty water out of his eyes.

Then the drumbeat, the darkness, the fire.

Flames burning bright. The people dancing in loincloths if they wore anything at all. They leaped over it, clearing the flames or passed briefly through them. Some held drums to it, warming and tightening the heads, then returned to the circle pounding a rhythm that was the heartbeat of the planet.

"I can't let him . . ." Lucas whispered, shaking himself from the dream, vision, whatever the hell it was. The sickness was gone, and he felt rejuvenated.

Margot's voice returned, urgently and as clearly as if she stood right behind him.

"Your heart will tell you. As will the wind, the flowing river, and the crackling fire, and the wild things in the forest. These five things will tell you, if you listen."

"Today my heart has told me plenty," he said softly, clutching the pipe closer. Wolf stood with his hands cuffed in front of him. He didn't move his head, but Lucas saw his eyes, and his eyes saw him.

Wolf is my teacher, he knew. *If anything in the last day tells me this, it's what is happening right now . . .*

The cue was obvious, but unexpected. Wolf groaned loudly and fell over, squirming on the ground as if he had been shot by something. Yet the rifle hadn't discharged. Hesitating, as if vaguely puzzled by Wolf's actions, Damien lowered the rifle until the barrel was touching the ground.

Now is the only time . . . Lucas knew, and with the pipe gripped in his right hand, jumped over the steep hillside.

In mid flight, he raised the pipe . . . the ground rushed at him as the pipe struck Damien, hard. Lucas dropped and rolled, came to a rest against the front wheel of the van.

Damien was on the ground, out cold. The rifle lay across him, and already Wolf was running toward them, his false malady now magically cured. Lucas reached the rifle before Wolf did, just in time to yank it from Damien, who was starting to wake up. He held it up by the barrel as if it were tainted with poison. It was a big assault rifle, with a clip sticking out of the stock. *Shit! This is an AR-15!*

"Where's the key to these?" Wolf demanded, holding up the handcuffs. When Damien didn't answer right away, he landed a kick in the side of his ribs, hard. *"Where's the key!"*

"It's . . . in here," Damien said groggily, reaching into a leather bag he wore on a strap.

It's not a key, Lucas thought, not liking the look Damien had as he reached for it. It was a look of victory. Lucas brought the rifle around and aimed it awkwardly at him, put his finger around the trigger.

At the first glimpse of the wooden grip and blue gun metal coming out of the bag, Lucas squeezed the trigger, and kept it squeezed.

The gun in the bag went off, once, into the ground between them. Damien's carcass bounced around on the ground as if it were having a seizure. Wolf ran like hell for cover. Once the rifle was emptied of its ordnance, Lucas could only think about how little recoil the thing had. Parts of the rifle were pretty hot now, so he dropped it on the ground.

Without really thinking he picked up the leather bag and looked into it. There was a key ring, with a small silver key hanging off it. The handcuff keys were in there after all, along with a snub nose revolver.

"Here," Lucas said, tossing Wolf the keys. He looked down at Damien, who wasn't moving very much. "Is he dead?"

Wolf undid the cuffs and tossed them on the ground beside Damien. "That's a silly question," he replied, looking down at the perforated corpse.

Lucas turned away from what he had done, feeling nauseous. He stumbled as far away as he could before throwing up.

You did the right thing, Lucas told himself, wiping his mouth, but still having a hard time believing it. *The others . . .*

Wolf was with Petrus and Wenlann, who were still frozen in place. Their lack of motion was absolute; they looked like a photo still.

"There's some kind of field, thrown up around here," Wolf said. "If we can get them back, away from this place, we might be able to shake them out of it."

"Why isn't it freezing you?"

Wolf shrugged. "Guess it only freezes elves." He reached for and grabbed Petrus' arm, and pulled. The elf tipped over like a concrete statue, and with Lucas' help dragged him away from the house. Lucas felt him relax into their arms when they had covered a certain distance, and immediately he was on his feet.

"Was that gunshots?" he said, looking around wildly.

"Yep," Wolf said. "It's okay. The bad guys are gone. More or less." He was already going over to Wenlann; he had no trouble carrying her out of the field, and when she relaxed out of the paralysis, he continued to hold her in his arms.

"You know, we've got to stop meeting like this," Wolf said, giving her a kiss. Petrus was over near the van, surveying the damage.

"You knew there was another dead kid over here didn't you?" he said.

"It's one of his people," Lucas said. "He's the one who got me into this thing in the first place."

Petrus looked up from beside the van. "What thing?"

"Satan worship," he said, having to spit the words out like something bitter.

Wenlann got to her feet with Wolf's help, then he entered the adobe cautiously. She held her hand up, as if feeling the field that had paralyzed them. "It starts about here. Dammit, this is Unseleighe work."

"It will fade with time. Their stuff always does," Petrus said. The elvensteeds had wandered a short distance away. "I'll go get our mounts."

Wolf came out of the adobe, looking pale. He was carrying a pair of boots and clothes that looked like they belonged to him, and Lucas remembered Wolf had been kept here too—for the brief time before Ha-Sowa showed up. "No one else is in there. Looks like they were doing human sacrifices."

"Hmmmm," Petrus said thoughtfully, holding their 'steed's reins. "No wonder the Unseleighe liked them."

Wenlann rubbed her arms, as if from a chill. "This place gives me the creeps."

After a moment's reflection, Wolf said, "Come on, let's go. I've had enough of *this* happy horse shit."

Not a bad idea, Lucas thought, as they all mounted and started back down the gravel road. They didn't get very far when another man on horseback appeared, riding toward them. Petrus pulled Moonremere to a halt.

Right away, Lucas saw there was something unnatural yet familiar about the way the light reflected off him, as if he were only a clip from a film, superimposed over the landscape. Petrus also looked suspicious, but the glance he shared with Wenlann indicated he didn't know for sure what this was, either.

The rider came closer, rolled an unlit, hand rolled cigarette in his mouth, and regarded them with a wary, watchful eye.

John Wayne?

"That's right, it's the Duke," John said, taking the

cigarette from his mouth, and pointing it at them. "You think you're clever, you Seleighe folk, just because you won this round. Well, maybe you are. And maybe you aren't," he drawled, and the cigarette lit itself. The Duke's image faded, and morphed into someone else . . . now Clint Eastwood, in a dusty red shirt and vest, and a brown cowboy hat with a bullet hole in it, was looking down the double barrel of a shotgun. "Or is it just luck?" Clint said, dropping the barrel. *Do you feel lucky today, punks?*"

Wenlann leaned over and said to Petrus, with a frown. "He's getting his movies mixed up," she said.

Who? Lucas wanted to ask, but also knew he would have to wait for an explanation.

Petrus nodded, his look of confusion now a look of resigned annoyance.

Clint Eastwood morphed again . . . now the image was clearly taken directly from an old black and white. The cowboy, in a white hat, a gray suit, kerchief and a black mask. "Well, you should," the Lone Ranger said. "Because you ain't seeing me anymore!"

"Is that a promise?" Petrus asked, not sounding very hopeful.

The Lone Ranger changed just a little bit, looking something like a black gargoyle with bony, knobby knees and elbows.

"Now, would old Mort lie to you?" the creature said, then the horse reared up. "Hi ho Silver, away!"

And the horse and rider vanished in a plume of acrid, purple smoke.

They stood there, saying nothing, for some time. "I'd forgotten Mort was still running around," Petrus said. "Must have teamed up with Japhet when Zeldan went down."

"Who the hell's Mort?" Lucas wanted to know.

"A weak demon," Petrus said. "Underling of the

Unseleighe. Only, there's no more Unseleighe here for him to serve."

"That was no weak demon," Wenlann said. "He's gained some power to be able to pull off all those changes. And I'll bet we *do* see him again. Mort lies like a rug."

Chapter Twenty

Running Duck rose from his bedroll and peered out
of the teepee's door, having heard something moving
outside. A deer grazed in the half light of dawn; he
grabbed his bow and arrow. Hunting had not been good
lately, and the elders had decided the tribe would move
further north, away from the wagon trains that were
bringing the white settlers in from the East. The rest
of the tribe was still sleeping, and he hoped they would
stay that way. If anyone rose and made noise, the deer
would run away; a fresh kill before the long trip would
be good for the tribe.

The deer moved further away, but was not aware of
Running Duck. The brave crept up closer, nocking his
arrow, aimed; the arrow flew, struck home. The brave
ran up to the fallen deer, pulled his knife, and cut the
animal's neck, while offering a prayer to the Great Spirit
for the animal's soul.

This will sustain us for at least a few days, he thought,
ecstatic over his fortune.

Running Duck was preparing to carry the deer back
to the camp on his back when he heard something strange
and alien pulling up behind him.

A big, green pickup truck with a red and blue lightbar
in its roof screeched to a stop. The driver's door opened,

with a big gold star and the words "Game Warden" on it. Out stepped a man in a deep green uniform and Smoky the Bear hat.

"You're in a whole heap o' trouble, boy," the Warden said. Over his shirt pocket was a gold plate that read "Sgt. Mort." The Warden looked like a lizard in Ray Bans. "Do you have a tag for that deer?"

Huh? A what . . .

The truck's headlights came on, twin beams of blinding light.

Petrus woke with the sun shining directly in his eyes, and rolled over, pulling the blanket around him. The dream's strangeness jabbed at him, making a return to sleep impossible. Besides, he caught the aroma of something really good cooking, complemented by the sound of sizzling bacon.

Weird dream, he thought, closing his eyes against the sun. *Weird, weird, weird!*

He sat up, stiff and feeling like hell, reminding him why they'd stopped here at Wolf's place. Everyone was too tired to move on, and graciously accepted the human's offer to stop and rest here, however meager the accommodations. Wolf had offered floor space in his shed, but he'd turned it down in favor of a bedroll outside, under the stars. He knew they wanted to be alone, and would have felt uncomfortable being in the way. Lucas slept outside too, but his bedroll was empty now.

He counted three elvensteeds now, one of them in beemer 'steed mode, the one they'd left at the motel. *They must have already gone into town and fetched it. What time of day is it, anyway?* He looked at the sun, which was immediately overhead. *Early afternoon. Time to get up,* he thought, with a mental groan.

"Rise and shine," Wenlann said. She stood over an electric skillet on a makeshift table. "Hungry?"

"Starving," Petrus replied, noting the plastic spatula, paper plates, plastic utensils.

Wolf was pouring a cup of coffee, and looked up. The aura between the two was absolutely glowing; now he was glad he had made himself scarce the night before. "I'd offer you some, but Wenlann said elves can't have caffeine."

"Yeah, it does pretty bad things to us," Petrus replied, sitting down on a cinder block. "Where's Lucas?"

"Meditating," Wolf replied, pointing to a lone figure, shirtless, sitting cross-legged a good distance from them in the desert, facing the rising sun. "His first lesson. I'm taking him on as an apprentice," he said, taking a sip of brew. "I'm not a full Chaniwa medicine man until I pass the knowledge on to others. And I figured, hell, I owe him twice for my life. Not to mention the prophecy . . ."

Wenlann brought Petrus a plate of bacon and scrambled eggs. It smelled so good he thought he was going to pass out.

"What prophecy?" Petrus asked, before thinking. Perhaps he shouldn't ask. This might be a private matter.

If it was, Wolf didn't seem bothered by the question. "Before my grandfather died, we had a long talk about our tribe," he began, sitting down next to Wenlann and putting his arm around her. "The medicine men would pass down prophecies involving the future of the tribe, and the most important one had to do with the death, and rebirth of the Chaniwa. A new cycle, every nine hundred years."

Petrus listened intently, forcing himself to eat slowly, a difficult feat in his ravenous state.

"Grampa told me that when there was one Chaniwa left, there will be a new cycle. Well, I was the last one, after those cult assholes murdered him. Then there was the final showdown, between me and Ha-Sowa. Then he said something that I didn't get at first. But I do, now." He squeezed Wenlann's had. "He said, 'The *chi-en* will rise from their underworld, the good and the bad. Nargach will return to seek his vengeance, as will others who are his enemy.' Odras took care of him, for us. Then he said, 'there will be a white brave, but he will not know his true path until he goes on a great journey to the underworld.'"

Petrus looked out, toward Lucas, sitting among the rocks. His head had bowed the slightest bit.

"Well, this is the rebirth of the Chaniwa," Wolf said. "We're starting over."

Petrus looked up slowly, and met Wenlann's eyes. "You're staying here," he said, not particularly happy about the way his voice cracked. His throat closed up, and the unwelcomed tears came.

Dammit, I hate this, Petrus said. Wenlann was next to him, her arm around his shoulder, hugging him. Wolf politely excused himself.

"I had no idea you were in love with me," Wenlann said softly. "Forgive me for being so blind."

"It's okay," Petrus said, knowing that eventually it really would be. "I think I need to grow up first. If I've learned anything these past few days, it's that I'm still a child."

"A child wouldn't have slain an Unseleighe leader single handedly," Wenlann pointed out. "And deposited the head at the King's feet. That took some balls, no matter what you think."

"That's not the same thing," Petrus said. "Anyone can swing a sword. Dealing with others, on an intimate level . . . that's what takes skill. And maturity. Which I don't have yet." Petrus hugged her back. "I'll tell the King. What of your 'steed?"

"She should return to Avalon," Wenlann said firmly. "It would not be fair to her to keep her in a world where there were no other elvensteeds. I'll ride her back to the Gate. She can go in by herself."

Petrus nodded agreement when a car driving up the gravel road to the shed caught his attention.

"Oh, hell," he said, wiping away the rest of the tears. "It's a cop."

"*What?*" she said, looking up. "Wolf, we got trouble. Maybe."

"It's all right," Wolf said, emerging from the shed. "At least I think it is. I know him."

The car pulled up and stopped some distance away. On the side was a shield and the words "Socorro County Sheriff."

The deputy who got out was light skinned and a bit overweight, "What happened to your trailer?" he asked, taking in the burned-out dwelling.

"Grampa would have wanted me to do it," Wolf said solemnly. "It's an Indian thing. Gets rid of all the bad spirits."

"I see," the deputy said, handing Wolf a paper bag of something. Apparently that was as far as he wanted to get into the matter. "It's coffee," the deputy said, glancing at Petrus and Wenlann behind him. Their glamories were still in place, so what the human saw was two people in western clothes, in dire need of a bath.

"Thanks," Wolf said. "Meet my friends," he said, and the elves got to their feet. "This is Wendy and Pete. Guys, this is Deputy Clarke. Any news on Grandfather's murderers?"

The Deputy eyed Wolf for a moment, an unnerving expression. "Well," Clarke began, hesitating. He looked uncertain. "I think we've solved it, if that's what you mean. There was a suicide-murder at the old Hull gravel pit. Looks like a kid shot this guy, then did himself with a razor."

Wolf waited for him to go on. "The guy was named Damien Szandor. We searched his house, found all kinds of devil worship shit. Most interesting were the black candles. They had the same wick, a type found only in California, that we found here at this scene. So we're pretty sure it's the same people. You don't know anything about it, do you?"

"Well, no," Wolf said, careful to meet the Deputy's eyes when he said so. "Last I heard the pit was closed down. Never been out there myself."

"I had to ask," the deputy said. "Shit, there weren't any witnesses. Sheriff wants to close that case as soon as we can, and I think that will happen today. We're not really wanting the Satanic aspect to get out to the press. Turns out the kid is the nephew of an Albuquerque councilman. Sheriff wants to forget the whole damned thing." He said, spitting on the ground. "But I'm not forgetting it. Not after what I saw in that building. There's more of them out there, if not in the same cult, then elsewhere."

He started back toward his car and paused at the driver's door before getting in, moving slowly, as if what he'd seen at the gravel pit was still bothering him. "Next month I'm going to a Satanic Crime seminar in Long Beach. Seems that's where this Damien Szandor came from." He shook his head. "There's more to this than meets the eye. And we ain't seen the last of it. In fact, I'm afraid this is only the beginning."

After breakfast, Lucas fell back on the mattress in the shed and fell sound asleep. Petrus envied him; he wished he could do the same. But first he had to get back home, and to do that, they had to return to the Gate near the cliff. *Then* he could crash—after telling the King of Wenlann's decision, of course. Wolf still had to recover his motorbike, and now that he'd rested he felt strong enough to ride it back.

The bike was right where they'd left it. In silence they rode over to the cliff, Wolf and Wenlann on the bike,

Petrus riding Moonremere and pulling the other behind by the reins.

In the bright sunny day there was no trace of the darkness that had fallen only a day before.

"You're sure about this?" Petrus asked, once they'd parked and dismounted.

"As sure as I can ever be, about something like this," she said, defensively. Then her face softened. *Yes, I understand. this hurts,* her expression seemed to say. "Is the King's sister, Samantha, still working in Dallas?"

"Last I heard," he said. "Stay in touch. Get a computer. Log onto the net. I need to see if Niamh has any extra laptops back at the castle."

The talk was small, and he knew it, and it was making him uncomfortable. His thoughts turned to the victory the day before, hoping it would revive the same sense of triumph he'd felt when he dropped Japhet's head at the King's feet. But the most it did was remind him how he got to feeling the way he did now; sore, and utterly exhausted. *I need rest. I need rest in a big way. Please, let's get this over with.*

"Don't worry about me," Wenlann said, as she gave him another, departing hug. "Help make Avalon strong."

Again the tears came, but he had better luck choking them back this time. He led the three 'steeds into the Gate, leaving the desert behind him.

For information on sound track for *Spiritride* composed by Mark Shepherd contact:
Firebird Music
P.O. Box 30268
Portland, OR 97294-3268
1-800-752-0494

MERCEDES LACKEY

The Hottest Fantasy Writer Today!

URBAN FANTASY

Knight of Ghosts and Shadows with Ellen Guon
Elves in L.A.? It would explain a lot, wouldn't it? Eric Banyon really needed a good cause to get his life in gear—now he's got one. With an elven prince he must raise an army to fight against the evil elf lord who seeks to conquer all of California.

Summoned to Tourney with Ellen Guon
Elves in San Francisco? Where else would an elf go when L.A. got too hot? All is well there with our elf-lord, his human companion and the mage who brought them all together—until it turns out that San Francisco is doomed to fall off the face of the continent.

Born to Run with Larry Dixon
There are elves out there. And more are coming. But even elves need money to survive in the "real" world. The good elves in South Carolina, intrigued by the thrills of stock car racing, are manufacturing new, light-weight engines (with, incidentally, very little "cold" iron); the bad elves run a kiddie-porn and snuff-film ring, with occasional forays into drugs. *Children in Peril—Elves to the Rescue*. (Book I of the SERRAted Edge series.)

Wheels of Fire with Mark Shepherd
Book II of the SERRAted Edge series.

When the Bough Breaks with Holly Lisle
Book III of the SERRAted Edge series.

HIGH FANTASY

Bardic Voices: The Lark & The Wren

Rune could be one of the greatest bards of her world, but the daughter of a tavern wench can't get much in the way of formal training. So one night she goes up to play for the Ghost of Skull Hill. She'll either fiddle till dawn to prove her skill as a bard—or die trying. . . .

The Robin and the Kestrel: Bardic Voices II

After the affairs recounted in *The Lark and The Wren*, Robin, a gypsy lass and bard, and Kestrel, semi-fugitive heir to a throne he does not want, have married their fortunes together and travel the open road, seeking their happiness where they may find it. This is their story. It is also the story of the Ghost of Skull Hill. Together, the Robin, the Kestrel, and the Ghost will foil a plot to drive all music forever from the land. . . .

Bardic Choices: A Cast of Corbies with Josepha Sherman

If I Pay Thee Not in Gold with Piers Anthony

A new hardcover quest fantasy, co-written by the creator of the "Xanth" series. A marvelous adult fantasy that examines the war between the sexes and the ethics of desire! Watch out for bad puns!

BARD'S TALE

Based on the bestselling computer game, *The Bard's Tale.*®

Castle of Deception with Josepha Sherman

Fortress of Frost and Fire with Ru Emerson

Prison of Souls with Mark Shepherd

Also by Mercedes Lackey:

Reap the Whirlwind with C.J. Cherryh

Part of the Sword of Knowledge series.

The Ship Who Searched with Anne McCaffrey

The Ship Who Sang is not alone!

Wing Commander: Freedom Flight with Ellen Guon
Based on the bestselling computer game, *Wing Commander.*℗

Join the Mercedes Lackey national fan club! For information send an SASE (business-size) to Queen's Own, P.O. Box 43143, Upper Montclair, NJ 07043.